TAMISAN

TAMISAN BOOK 1

SUSAN McKENZIE

Cover art © Lauren Dawes of Sly Fox Cover Designs

Ream Stories:
https://reamstories.com/susanmckenzie
Amazon author page:
amazon.com/author/susancarter
Visit Sue's website:
http://susanmckenzieauthor.com
Follow Sue on Facebook:
https://www.facebook.com/SueMcKenzieAuthor

YOUR FREE BOOK IS WAITING

The novelette
THE ALIEN

is free for a limited time. You just need to tell me where to send it

When Lilliana crash-lands her spaceship on a Primitive planet, she'll have to rely on help from an attractive local to survive.

Use the QR Code to follow the link, then enter your name and email address to get your free book delivered to your inbox

Or type this link into your browser: https://www.subscribepage.com/thealien

WHAT READERS LIKE YOU ARE SAYING...

"This book is stock full of adventure. The depth of the characters and their feelings is awesome. This book should be made into a movie. I would definitely go to see it."
  – Kimberly Rose (Amazon review)

"Wow, was this book packed with Action! It was Intense. The world building was off the charts good. The description of the various people and Talents were in depth and done really well."
  – WindRider (Goodreads review)

"If you are into high action interesting sci-fi-novel then this one won't let you down right from the start there's action that just keeps on going right throughout the book. Great plot and characters and now I will have to read book 2."
  – Kazza (Amazon review)

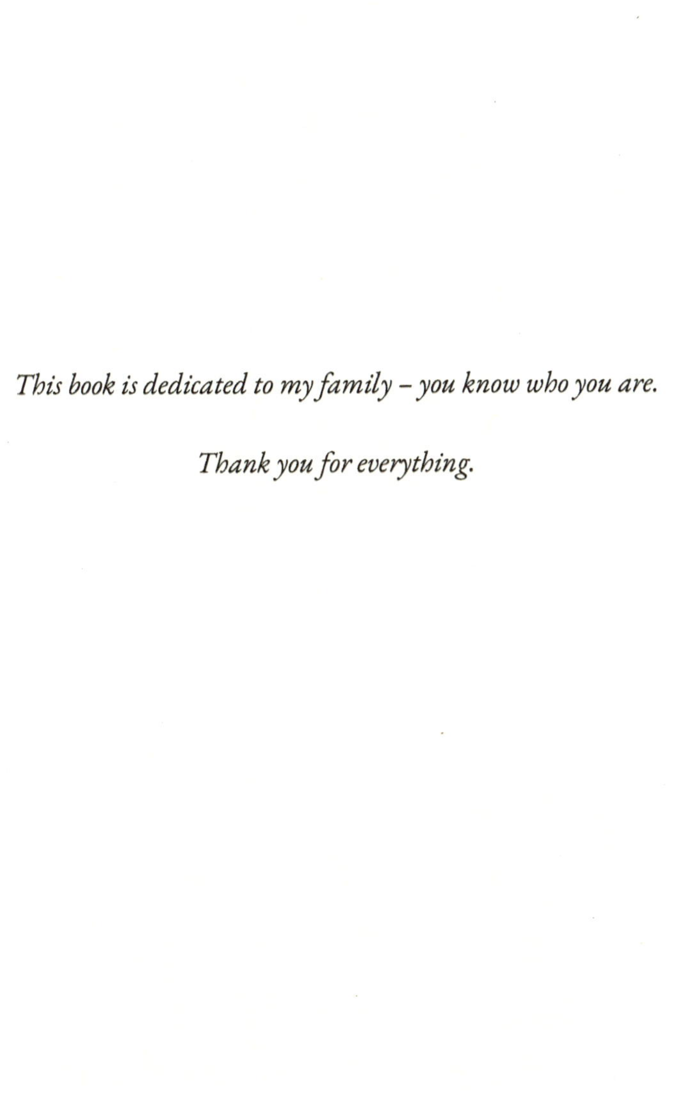

This book is dedicated to my family – you know who you are.

Thank you for everything.

CHAPTER 1:
I Have a Bad Feeling

I felt a strange apprehension when I stepped out of the shuttle into the sunlight and it sent a shiver down my spine, but the feeling quickly subsided as I looked around me. This place was magnificent! It was a tropical jungle paradise.

Tall trees surrounded us on all sides. The only break in the canopy big enough to let in the sunlight properly was the clearing where our small shuttle, the Outrider, had landed for emergency repairs.

It was so wild and free and different to the world I knew. I'd grown up in a city on Earth, which was so ordered and sterile and 'civilised.'

Craning my neck, I turned in a circle. All around us were huge tree trunks with vines that intertwined around them and through the branches of smaller trees and shrubs, slowly choking them to death while reaching ever upward to the sun. There were ferns that spread their fronds several metres in all directions and fungi in various shades of orange, red and yellow. The scents and smells of a hundred different flowers, plants and animals were concentrated in the thick, humid air.

The other five passengers around me were awed by Althar 3's beauty too, and they stood open-mouthed in the clearing. I stifled a laugh. We looked ridiculous.

We'd travelled across the universe to start work with the Voyager Division to study and observe the natives on this super-primitive planet, but the shuttle taking us from the main ship to the surface had developed engine trouble, forcing us to land in the middle of the dense jungle.

This wasn't part of the plan, but it was a great diversion. We had been headed to Station Jannali, a hidden underground base somewhere in this jungle, and now we were getting an up-close-and-personal look at the local scenery.

I could see that the shuttle pilot had already started working on the engine.

As soon as Station Jannali had heard we had to land, they'd located a suitable spot and given us orders to collect some plant and soil samples so we could make ourselves useful. They gave us a list of the kinds of plants they wanted, so we took some sampling equipment and a PocketPC that contained the pictures they'd sent of what was required. We spread out, wandering amongst the vines and blooms at the edge of the clearing.

I didn't start work straight away. My mind was trying to process everything I was seeing. It was so surreal. We'd been briefed on the flora and fauna on Althar and what to expect, including the kind of wildlife that lurked in the jungle, and it was actually full of very large and very dangerous creatures that basically belonged in the Jurassic or Cretaceous Period of Earth's distant past. They were so similar it was kind of unnerving.

Another shiver travelled the length of my spine at the thought. What if one of those dinosaur look-alikes was nearby right now? Why did Jannali give permission for us to wander around out here without any training or weapons for protection? What kind of company had I signed up with?

I started to think that maybe I'd made a huge mistake. I was a new graduate from the Academy. I was qualified to deal with *computer*-related problems. I had so many options open to me, but I chose to go to the edge of the Known Universe. *I must be crazy.*

What was I doing here? Why did I apply for a job way out here? Was my life at the Academy *that* boring that I jumped at the first opportunity to go off-planet?

My mind answered immediately. *Yes.*

That realization had my mind reeling. I'd been prepared to leave everything and everyone I'd ever known. That was kind of scary.

Part of our work would involve studying the family units, which would be weird — and also very intriguing — for some members of our group because we didn't have families. The people from Earth were cloned and raised in groups according to age and gender.

I'd learned about the family units that still existed in some of the older cultures on Earth and on other planets. And there were some people on Earth who were against cloning.

A sound like something flapping around in the breeze, followed by an ear-splitting screech, pulled me from my thoughts and I turned to see a large leather-winged reptile flapping its wings madly as it made its way across the clearing, bringing screams from the other female crew members, Larissa and Bazeelia. Even Janssen and Lanu gave a shout as the creature flew past.

Bazeelia was a tall Ziflarian with long, black curly hair that she kept tied up in a high ponytail. She scowled at Janssen and Lanu for laughing at her. "Don't be laughin' at me. That thing was a monster! And it scared *you* too!"

Janssen turned to her, his long white-blonde hair almost blindingly bright in the sunshine. "Hey. Take it easy. We're just messin' with ya."

Lanu got up awkwardly from the spot where he was kneeling in the dirt and stalked over to them. "You've got to admit it was amazing though."

Bazeelia stared at him open-mouthed. "*Amazing?* No. It wasn't. It was *terrifying*!"

Lanu smiled, a look of awe on his face. "But that thing is so similar to the Pteranodon from Earth's past and it flew within a few *metres* of us. It's like going back to the Cretaceous Period and getting a first-hand look."

"Well, you can go look at it and admire its beauty if you want. Pat it. Study it. Although I'm not sure being a Sociologist will help when it comes to dinosaurs. Me? I'm glad I'll be working indoors once we get to Jannali." She flipped her long hair over her shoulder and went back to work.

"Miss Rhodarma?" I jumped. Once I realized who had called me, I cringed inwardly. Kami Olion, the other Sociologist in the group, was standing at the hatch of the shuttle. He was nothing like Lanu. He was a prickly, annoying person. "I heard screams. What has happened?"

If you hadn't refused to come out here, you'd already know.

He'd said the engine trouble was a bad omen. I'd ignored him. I didn't believe in superstitions and had jumped at the chance to see the jungle first-hand.

And what was with the 'Miss Rhodarma'? Did he have to be so formal?

"Please call me Zhenna," I said.

He inclined his head. "Very well."

I gave him a small smile, feeling awkward. "Everything's okay. It was just a flying reptile. It flew through the clearing and gave us a fright."

He shook his head. "Going outside was a bad idea. I said it was a bad idea. But would anyone listen? No, they didn't. Will you come inside, please, where it's safe? The others won't listen. And I have a *bad* feeling." He drew out the word "bad," like that would make me believe him.

I frowned. Why was he only asking me? "Umm, I can't. Jannali wants the samples. It's going to give a bad impression if we refuse."

His eyebrows drew together and his mouth turned down at the corners. He turned on his heel and went back inside.

I sighed, relieved he was gone. He'd been a pain in everyone's butt on the journey out here. He must have been really good at his job because I was sure he didn't get hired for his personality.

"Don't worry about him," Larissa said as she walked up to me, her long white-blonde hair as blinding as Janssen's. "He's just a superstitious old grump."

I laughed, then cringed. I hoped he couldn't hear her.

She noticed my reaction. "I don't care if he hears me."

I giggled.

We'd met on the trip out here to The Fringe, as some called it, and became friends right away. It had taken us two weeks at Warp Delta and there wasn't a lot to do aboard the Acronis. We both had an interest in art and liked similar types of music and had spent a lot of time together.

I turned my attention away from the spot where Kami had stood. I needed to actually do the job I was sent out here to do. We headed a bit further into the jungle. I was looking for an orange flower and Larissa was after a type of fungi, which should've been easier for her since she was a Botanist.

As we searched, I saw Larissa stealing glances at Janssen. This wasn't the first time I'd seen her watching him. I was sure she had a crush. She'd shown an interest during the trip out here, but she always insisted that she didn't like him all that much. I smiled.

The next time she looked at me I said, "I saw you looking at him."

CHAPTER 2:

Don't Damage Them

"No, I wasn't."

I cocked an eyebrow at her.

"Okay. I was."

I watched him ducking under a low-hanging vine and his long hair fell over his shoulder. "You like him."

Her cheeks turned pink. "I... Uh... maybe. I don't know."

"Well, you'll have plenty of time to find out since you'll be working together." Janssen had also majored in Botany.

Her eyes never left him as he bent down to look at a lavender flower. "Is he unattached, do you know?"

"It has taken you two weeks to even ask that?" I asked. Her cheeks flushed even more. "I heard him telling Mosuti he doesn't have a girl. Or boy," I added.

She looked relieved. I chuckled, thinking they'd make a great couple. They had a shared interest in botany and they even came from the same planet: Shakira.

I looked at her long hair again and wished mine was longer. I came to the conclusion that even if mine was as long, it wouldn't look the same because it was a light brown colour.

Mosuti, our telepathic crew member, wandered over to where we were. "Hey, girls."

"Hey," we both said together.

"Found your specimens yet?"

We both said "no" at the same time and laughed.

From the corner of my eye, I saw movement. It was Kami again, staring at us with a furrowed brow and his mouth set in a thin line.

"Mosuti. Kami doesn't like you, does he?" I whispered.

"I'm afraid not, Zhenna. Says he doesn't like my 'kind.'"

I narrowed my eyes as I kept watching Kami. "Don't let it worry you. He's a douchebag."

"He doesn't worry me."

Kami called me again. "Zhenna, dear, why are you talking to *him*?"

"Uh, because he's my *friend*."

"His kind can't be trusted. He's probably reading our minds right now."

Mosuti stood up straighter. "I would *never* do that. It is against the Talents' Code of Conduct to read a being's mind without consent."

The Code had been created years ago to protect people's privacy and to protect Talents all over the Known Universe.

Larissa took a step forward. "You're a jerk! What would you know about Talents? You're so narrow-minded!"

He waved his hand in the air dismissively. "They are nothing but freaks. Mutated beings that taint our genetics."

I clenched my fists, trying to keep my temper in check. "What do you suggest we do with these 'mutants'?" I asked him.

"We need to keep them under control. They shouldn't be allowed to wander free where they can manipulate our minds and wreak havoc across the universe."

"So, we should enslave them?"

"I... wouldn't use that exact term... but what else can we do? They're freaks of nature and they are a danger to us all."

My fingernails were digging into my palms and my face felt like it was on fire. I couldn't believe what I was hearing.

I heard Mosuti's voice in my mind. *"It's okay. I'm not worried about him. Don't let him get to you. Don't cause yourself unnecessary worry."*

It always gave me a thrill to hear his voice in my head. We'd messed around with it a couple of times on the trip out here. All I had to do was think my answer and Mosuti could read it. And, of course, he had my *permission*.

I know, I replied. *But he's such an ignoramus!*

I turned back to Kami. "I'm glad I won't be working with you when we get to Jannali. You're such an arrogant, narrow-minded, backwards hick!"

Before he could answer, there was a loud zapping noise like an electrical current arcing. I looked around. "What was that?"

Instead of answering, Mosuti grabbed Larissa and I by the arm and practically threw us to the ground. "Stay down!" he ordered.

I heard more zapping sounds and people screaming. I looked at Mosuti's rugged face and wide eyes from my position in the leaf litter and he whispered, "Laser fire."

I froze and could feel the warmth drain from my face. *Laser fire? In the middle of a prehistoric jungle? How?... Who?*

I heard another scream and looked up to see Bazeelia fall screaming to the ground with her hair on fire. I quickly put my head back down on the soft earth, trying to somehow block out the sound. There was nothing I could do to help her. We were all unarmed.

From where I lay on the ground, I heard more laser fire as it struck targets all around us. I was too afraid to move and it took all my willpower to keep from screaming. I knew that no race native to this planet possessed laser weapons, so my brain tried to figure out who could be attacking us.

The only answer I could think of was that the attackers were the Varekai. They were basically space pirates and had a reputation for being totally brutal. My heart constricted in my chest. Were we all about to die?

Our shuttle must have been followed somehow. But why would they bother? It's not like we had anything valuable on the ship.

In the chaos, I noticed that the soil and leaves around me seemed to be moving. There were ants and a half a dozen other crawling insects moving about on the forest floor, some of which were starting to crawl up over my hands and arms. Again I had to resist the urge to cry out. I had to let them crawl. If I made any sudden move, the lasers might target me.

I could see the fear churning in Mosuti's eyes as we lay on the ground side-by-side. Larissa was on his other side, but I couldn't lift my head to see if she was okay. There was a weird beetle crawling on Mosuti's arm, but he didn't move.

The laser fire and the screaming stopped, and I froze where I lay. I heard footsteps all around me. I closed my eyes. I couldn't bring myself to look, but I knew they were there, looking down at me. The left side of my face lay in the soft earth and I hoped that the position I was in made it appear as though I'd fallen that way and was either unconscious or dead. If they thought I was dead, they might leave me and return to their ship.

I knew I wouldn't be so lucky.

I could feel their presence, making the hairs on the back of my neck stand up. Fear was creeping up my spine, eating into my flesh.

I tried to keep my breathing as shallow as possible, hoping they wouldn't see my ribs expand and contract. They were right behind me. I imagined their piercing eyes, staring down from above. My lungs desperately needed more air, but I didn't dare suck in enough to satisfy their hunger.

Someone said, "These ones are good..."

Something was crawling on my neck. Another 'something' was climbing along the length of my right leg. But I had to stay there. Had to let them crawl.

"Don't damage them," said another. What were they talking about?

I couldn't just lie there. I desperately wanted to turn around and face my foes, to see who they were, but I couldn't do it. Something was starting to bite my leg, but before I could give myself away by swatting at it, I felt burning pain surge through my whole body. Every muscle convulsed and the darkness closed in quickly around me.

CHAPTER 3:

Not a Good First Impression

I opened my eyes to darkness and all the jumbled thoughts in my head seemed to ease up a little. Almost as if they were afraid of what my waking mind might do to them. I tried to hold on to some of the images in my brain to try to make sense of them as they tumbled over each other.

They seemed to be memories. I could make out the faces of my friends, Oliana and Kaliya, as we shared some laughs in the cafeteria at the Academy. Yes. That made sense. It wasn't just a flash of jumbled up stuff.

There were lots of other faces, too. My mother and fa ther... My father's face was clear... he was the Zheav... our leader... I could see my brothers, Axiak and Jadidi, running and diving off the rocks and into the ocean at The Dive... There was a sea of faces I recognized as my classmates at the Academy... I frowned up at the ceiling in the darkness. Something was definitely wrong with this picture. I didn't *have* any brothers. *Or* parents... I was a clone... What the...?

A flash of something... Oliana's smiling face... "Travelling to the edge of the Explored Universe," she said, "studying new races and exotic planets — *and* being paid for it — how could a New Graduate with an adventurous spirit refuse?"

My friend faded away and was replaced by the image of an old woman with wrinkles so deep that they looked painful. Tasha, the Old One. Tasha took one look at me and scoffed. "So I ask for a pupil I can help to hone their Mind Skills, and this is what they send me? Ha!"

Tasha floated away into the depths of the ocean and then there was the beautiful sight of so many colourful fish, swimming in and out of the coral and the rocky outcrops on the ocean floor. Once the fish dissolved away, there was a large computer screen on a wall in a small classroom. The room was filled with students sitting with their heads bent as they worked on their exam papers.

Then my mother stood before me. "You are the daughter of the Zheav. You know there are certain things expected of you. You cannot abandon your duties and run off to play with Jarleth and your brothers."

"But Mama, we weren't gone long..." Before I could finish pleading with my mother, that image faded to nothing. It left me confused. How could she be my mother? I didn't *have* a mother...

Panic crept into my chest and I squeezed my eyes shut. What was happening? Who *were* these people? I knew them all, but I didn't know them. My head was filled with memories of two distinctly separate worlds and two different lives; the civilised and technologically advanced Earth and the wild jungle planet... Sovoli, my memory supplied. None of it made sense. My heartbeat picked up so fast it felt like it was fluttering inside my ribcage. I needed to calm down. I needed to think rationally. These memories could not all be mine...

More images flooded in... swimming under the sea... studying computer programming at the Academy... Jarleth, a warrior of the Waikari people and my Betrothed... running and laughing on the beach... Oliana sitting in front of her computer monitor studying for her classes...

My name was Sifayah... *NO*, I was Zhenna! It was too confusing. Too much... I put both hands up to my head and squeezed, hoping it would help and knowing that it wouldn't.

I could see my father's face, but I knew I was a clone and didn't have a father in the proper sense of the word. I was made in a lab and genetically altered so I didn't look identical to the original human I'd been cloned from. We all were. But the image of him was there in my mind all the same, looking down on me with a proud expression... then Kaliya was there — the close friend I affectionately called "Mum"... then my father again... Impossible! I was a clone! Clones do not have *parents!*

I didn't know who I was... I felt lost. They *seemed* like my memories — like I'd actually lived them — *all* of them — but the chances of that were as slim as me flying through the air like a Hovercar.

How could this happen? Something must have happened to me before I woke up here... wherever here was. There must be something I was forgetting...

My train of thought was derailed by the memories of what had happened in the jungle. We'd boarded the shuttle from the main ship, the Acronis, and headed to the surface of the planet. Then there was the problem with the shuttle... landing to do repairs... the beautiful sights of the amazing plant life and the colourful birds... a prehistoric-looking flying thing swooping into the clearing and nearly scaring us half to death... the stupid argument with Kami... the attack... laser fire and screams echoing through the trees...

I pulled my thoughts away from those terrifying moments and opened my eyes to the darkness again. I realized I was trembling all over and took some deep breaths to try to calm myself, heart pounding again.

I could make out a ceiling above me with a small light fitting to my right. I also sensed that I was lying on a bed. Hearing the soft hum of a Bio-scan as it passed down the length of my body was very reassuring as it confirmed that I must be in a Medical Facility. I closed my eyes briefly and relaxed a little. The knowledge that I was back in civilised hands was very comforting. Jannali must have sent out a team to rescue us from the Varekai. At least, I *thought* we'd been attacked by the Varekai. Who else would do such a thing?

Wait — did that mean those memories were *real?* Was there a place called Jannali? Station Jannali... I couldn't be sure.

Were we really attacked in the jungle by pirates? Was that the reason I was in a Medical Facility? I had so many questions. Like why would they be out here, in the middle of nowhere-in-particular, waiting to ambush a shuttle full of scientists, botanists, a linguist and a computer programmer? What would they gain from that? We'd had nothing of any real value on board.

My heart rate wasn't slowing down. I felt like I might be on the verge of a panic attack and tried to slow my breathing down. Maybe that would slow my heart down a bit, too. *Breathe in... then out... in... out...*

I needed to think rationally. Needed to sort out this mess. Those other memories of the ocean and the primitive Waikari tribe didn't tie in with anything like this; Bio-scanners, electricity and Medical Facilities. There was nothing like that in the ocean or cove where I lived — or where whoever it was lived. Maybe those memories were only dreams... or something...

Hmmm... There was something — something I remembered in the back of my mind. Memories... There was a company I'd heard about that could implant memories into your mind so you could have the experiences of going to a new country or new planet, without leaving home. It was like going on a holiday, without really going anywhere. It was a bizarre concept, but it could be that I'd paid to have one of those 'holidays' implanted and had forgotten the part where I'd gone in to the company and had the procedure done.

Maybe that was where I was. Maybe that was why I was in a bed with a busy Bio-scan checking my vital signs. If so, I was going to tell them there was something wrong. The memories were all over the place. A jumbled mess. Not pleasant at all. And it didn't seem like a holiday. Memories of someone's life. It made for a pretty dull holiday. And it didn't make any sense.

I want a refund.

But I didn't remember paying any credits to anyone or visiting a Memory Centre. *What have they done to my brain?*

I stared up at the ceiling again. Once my eyes had adjusted to the darkness, the room seemed to brighten and I could see quite well. Or did the lights brighten a little as I watched?

My mind wandered. Would I pay credits for a holiday like that? Was my life *that* boring and empty? Once I thought about it, I realized my life was pretty sterile and ordered. My whole life revolved around my education and the betterment of the human race. Sure I had my two best friends, but there was something missing in my life... Wait a minute. I'd already had this conversation in my head... right before we were attacked.

That was weird.

Then my mind kept on the same track and I kind of couldn't stop myself.

I'd read about how the other people lived and it seemed to be so much better than the empty life I'd had growing up.

What had gone wrong with society? Why had humans decided to live like this - cloning themselves and living such regimented lives? I was raised this way and taught not to question it, but I couldn't help it. I felt it was wrong. Unnatural. The memories that were now in my head proved that family relationships were vital to the human spirit.

So maybe I *had* paid for some memories to be implanted in my mind as a way to escape.

I lifted my head and looked around. I was in a small white room, with discreet light fittings on the walls and a full-length mirror on the far wall. It looked like I was in a Medical Facility, with everything all white and sterile-looking. The lights didn't look like they were turned on, but I could see everything around me clearly now. To my right there was a small plain bedside table with nothing on it — no hint of any sort of decoration or even a clock. There was a door on my left that was barely visible as it blended so well with the wall itself. I slowly raised myself to a sitting position and sat staring at it for a moment, wondering where I was and what was on the other side.

Suddenly the lights in the room came on at full brightness and the door slid open, making me jump. A man appeared in the doorway and strode into the room as my heart did a weird dance inside my chest. He was a tall, slim-built man with hair the colour of sand and eyes that were a bright, almost sky blue. I guessed he was in his early forties. He wasn't what I would have called attractive, but he wasn't unpleasant to look at either.

His facial expression was cold steel, but once he turned his eyes to me, it quickly moulded itself into a smile that didn't quite reach his eyes.

I immediately went on alert. I'd seen that look before. I clearly remembered seeing it on the face of one of my professors at the Academy one day after I'd walked in on him blasting one of my classmates for no real reason. The fake face he turned to me as he tried to pretend everything was fine. He'd even patted Jus on the shoulder for added effect.

I looked at the man in front of me now. *Not a good first impression,* I thought, and tried not to cringe. Was this man as fake as my old professor?

He greeted me with the same weird smile, "Good afternoon, Miss Rhodarma, how are you feeling?"

Rhodarma... that name was familiar... Yes, I was *Zhenna* Rhodarma. My heart rate picked up. Maybe I would get some answers now about everything.

CHAPTER 4:

Where Are the Others?

When I tried to speak, my voice broke. I cleared my throat and tried again. "I'm fine, but I'm confused. What happened? Where am I?" My voice sounded strange to me, different somehow...

"You are presently at Station Maztec — Althar 3's newest research base," he said proudly as he gave me a slightly warmer smile. "This is actually where you were destined to do most of your research and case studies. You were only to be stationed at Jannali for a few weeks."

Yes, I could remember Jannali, but not Maztec. I couldn't recall anyone mentioning a second base on the planet. So the memories relating to me being a clone from Earth, sent to Althar 3 to study new alien races, had to be real. From this new information, I guessed we *did* get attacked in the jungle and I *was* in a Medical Facility.

The theory of the memory implant was looking very unlikely, but where did all those memories come from? I had no answer.

I must have been injured and taken to a Medical Facility, but I couldn't feel pain anywhere. I felt fine. And who was this man before me? My doctor?

I frowned. "Who are you?" I blurted out before I could stop myself. I cleared my throat again. Why did my voice sound so strange? It sounded higher pitched or something. Was my throat affected somehow from the attack?

I forced myself to think about what I could remember. I was face-down on the floor of the jungle with bugs and crawly things wriggling all over me, trying not to freak out or scream. The painful surge I felt before everything went black could have been a stunner. Maybe stunners contract your muscles enough to give your voice a higher pitch temporarily.

The man apologized and introduced himself as Dr Leonard Starrick. "I am in charge here at Maztec."

So he *was* a doctor. I started to worry again and my heartbeat picked up speed. How bad was I hurt?

"I hope you will forgive me," he continued, "I become so involved with my work that I forget my manners *and* my head, so I apologize for my rude behaviour." I realized I was sitting there staring at him and looked away toward the mirror. "I'm pleased you are feeling well and that you are finally conscious. You gave us quite a scare when you first arrived from the jungle."

I looked back up at him. *You're kidding, right? I gave you a scare? I could have been killed!*

His expression changed to that of deep concern and I wondered if he'd practiced it in a mirror. "Now, I need to ask you some questions to see how you are going. Are you feeling light-headed, disoriented or nauseous?"

"No." I coughed to try to clear my throat. Maybe that would help. Maybe a drink of water would help.

"How do your muscles feel?" he went on. "Do you have a headache at all?"

"Well... my muscles do feel a bit stiff, but otherwise I feel fine," I replied. My voice was wrong. Could it just be from a stunner? Or was it more than that?

"Do you have a sore throat?" he asked.

"I, ah — no," I replied. "What... What happened? I have all this stuff spinning around in my head..." I pressed my fingers on my temples. I needed to make sense of it all. And get my heartbeat to kick it back a notch or two. It was still all over the place.

My brain wouldn't slow down either... So, if I was Zhenna, who was Sifayah? And also, I *felt* different somehow. Not just my voice. Something else. I couldn't put my finger on it. Maybe it *was* only the stiff muscles...

My thoughts returned to what had happened in the jungle... After the flying dinosaur thing had spooked us all, we'd all breathed a sigh of relief. Then we weren't paying any attention to anything around us while we were telling Kami what we thought of him and his pathetic ideas about Talents.

The attack came from out of nowhere and I was glad Mosuti had pulled me down to the ground.

I remembered Bazeelia getting hit by laser fire. My stomach dropped. "Where are the others? Are they okay? There was laser fire and — Bazeelia — is she alright? I saw her fall..."

"Well, er... let me explain what happened..." he said, his voice taking on a sombre tone and he shifted his weight uneasily. He told me they had been monitoring the shuttle's progress as we entered Althar 3's atmosphere and landed in the jungle. Another ship carrying the Varekai had followed us undetected, apparently using a very sophisticated cloaking device. So I'd been right about who was responsible.

The pirates had beamed down to the surface and attacked the group, but by the time Dr Starrick's men had discovered them and sent troops to intercept, it was too late. They didn't have a

Transporter at the base, so they couldn't beam there in time to help us.

"You were in a bad way when you arrived here at the base," Dr Starrick continued and my stomach sank. "You actually died a short time after your arrival at the base. Your major organs had completely shut down."

CHAPTER 5:

We Had No Other Choice

"No!" I blurted out. Dr Starrick stared at me. I didn't feel bad about my outburst. "No. I don't believe you! I couldn't have died. You're lying!"

"I can assure you, there is no deception—"

"No. I'm here, right here, right now. So don't even try to tell me that..." I took a huge breath. "Everyone else *can't* be dead. It's not possible. I was only talking to Mosuti and Larissa right before the... the... oh..." I trailed off, feeling nauseous.

"It's okay. This reaction is to be expected." Dr Starrick placed a warm hand on my arm in an effort to calm me. It didn't work. "There's more," he added.

My eyes widened as I looked back up at him. *More?* Then it clicked... *Well, of course there's more to it. I'm alive, aren't I?*

"Try to slow down your breathing. In through the nose and out through the mouth."

I felt like telling him I was well aware of what to do, but I decided to do as he suggested. I concentrated on the mirror on the far wall, trying desperately not to think of what had happened in the jungle.

Once I'd calmed down enough, he told me they discovered that my brain still showed signs of activity, so they kept the life support going. The only way to save me and the very essence of who I was was to find a suitable body and attempt a procedure he had mastered many years before — the Eibhlin Process.

My chest tightened and I felt a zing of adrenalin rush through me. I'd heard of this procedure before. The technique was originally developed to help patients with severe brain damage. Scientists discovered that they could map out the damaged areas of the brain and replace the thought patterns with new ones from another person's brain. In most cases, it worked well. It was a revolutionary procedure that enabled many people to again live a normal, happy life.

Then a group of scientists found they could modify the process so they could transfer *all* of someone's thought patterns and memories to another person's brain, replacing all of the original patterns. It was like a brain transplant without the dangerous operation and related risks. Their full consciousness was moved across into the other person's mind.

The modified procedure — later called the Eibhlin Process — opened up so many possibilities. The option would be open for people to escape a body with failing health, or opt for a younger and/or more attractive body — so it, in effect, made the dream of *eternal youth* a reality. When a person's body grew too old, they could simply have their mind transferred into a younger person's body — and live longer.

In theory, it seemed like a wonderful idea. However, as the consciousness that was transferred to the second person's brain replaced the original person's consciousness *completely*, that person's mind — and their personality, memories and identity — were *wiped* from existence. It was basically murder.

This of course meant there were no willing donors and there was almost no *legal* way of obtaining them. So when there was a dramatic increase in the number of abductions and missing persons, the authorities were forced to put a stop to it. The procedure became outlawed throughout the Known Galaxies.

There were other dilemmas too — moral and spiritual dilemmas — such as the question of what happens to the souls of the two people involved.

It was mind boggling to think about. It was dangerous, morally and ethically wrong, and it caused more problems than it solved. The original procedure was still practiced, of course, as it was still a fantastic medical breakthrough.

I was horrified, "You mean to tell me you did that brain transferral thing on *me?*" I almost shouted the words.

"Yes, but we had no other choice," he insisted. "We either attempted the transferral — or we let you die. It was as simple as that." My chest felt like there was a band around it that was getting tighter by the second. "We had to make a decision fast. We weighed up the risks, and the decision was made. Enough lives were lost already."

I opened my mouth to protest, but nothing came out. What could I say? I thought about it for a moment. Dr Starrick was right. I wouldn't be alive if they didn't act quickly, and I was glad they'd saved my life. But it meant they had basically *killed* the other person. It went against everything inside of me.

But what could I do? It was too late now — it was done. I was alive, and all I could think was that the cost was too great.

And it meant that I was now a different person. That band pulled tighter and it was getting hard to breathe. I would look completely different. But who was the other person? Who was the donor? The answer hit me like a punch to the gut: Sifayah.

Was Sifayah the body donor? Was *I* now Sifayah? In *her* body? Of course I was. It was the only explanation for where all the strange memories came from. They weren't implanted

— they were already there. They were supposed to be totally replaced, but had somehow remained.

Something must have gone wrong. So much for him 'mastering' the technique! He had failed miserably in wiping out all the donor's memories.

I wondered if he could fix it — then I wouldn't have all those confusing memories scrambled up with my own. But maybe that wouldn't be a good idea. He could make things worse. I didn't want him to go messing around with my brain some more. I would have to learn to live with the weird memories. It shouldn't be too hard to tell them apart from my own, once I'd had a chance to sort things out in my head.

My chest tightened even more and I didn't think that was possible. All the things he'd told me were starting to sink in. I was now another person. But not just any person — I was an alien! Sifayah was an alien from a barbaric and primitive planet. A jungle planet. Just like this planet.

I wouldn't be able to go home and carry on with my life as if nothing had happened if I wasn't even human. I could not even hope to live life as Zhenna Rhodarma, nor could I pass myself off as Sifayah. Not that I wanted to live among the Waikari people for the rest of whatever.

What kind of life would I have now? What was I going to do? I would have to start my life again somewhere else — as *someone* else. I wondered why people would want to do this to themselves. Why people paid top credits for it. Maybe they *wanted* to get away and start again. If that were the case, it would have been their choice, but I didn't *choose* this.

A thought struck me. This was the reason my voice sounded different. It was *Sifayah's* voice!

This was too incredible to believe. I realized I was trembling. I felt my face with my hands and caught a glimpse of something black out of the corner of my eye. I turned to see long black hair cascading down my back. I quickly brought a handful of hair around to the front so I could see it more clearly, and it was so long that it reached the blanket that was covering my legs.

I was reminded of how much I had admired Larissa's long white waterfall of hair on the trip here. I couldn't help staring at it and wishing my own hair was longer. Now *mine* was like that — flowing like a river over my shoulder. Just jet black instead of white. It was so dark it appeared bluish where the light touched it.

This could not be happening, I thought desperately as my heartbeat picked up again. *It must be a trick or a practical joke.*

Tears welled up in my eyes, but I blinked them back so they wouldn't fall. My next thought was to get to the mirror. I wanted to see myself — my mind was refusing to believe this could be real. Holding my hands up in front of me, I was shocked to find a pair of slender, well-tanned hands instead of my own fair-skinned ones. (But in Sifayah's memory, these *were* her hands.) It was hard to see them clearly through the tears, but I could see enough.

It seemed so unreal, but it *was* real. I was really in someone else's body!

I looked up at Dr Starrick and tried to keep a rein on my thoughts and emotions. My mind was racing, trying to take in what was happening. My heart beat faster and it still felt like it was beating kind of erratically. Maybe my new heart had a problem... I frowned... Maybe this body was old... Maybe it had major health problems...

Dr Starrick gestured toward the mirror, "Go on. Go and see what you look like. I think you'll like what you see."

But I already know, I thought wildly as I looked across to the mirror in anticipation. But still, I just *had* to see.

CHAPTER 6:

What Had They Done?

I flung the blanket aside. Carefully swinging my tanned legs over the edge of the bed and sliding off onto the floor, I sensed the muscles in my new body were firm and taut, though they were a bit stiff, probably from lying in bed too long. For a moment or two, it was difficult to stand and I shifted my weight from one foot to the other in an attempt to work out the stiffness.

Wiping my eyes with the backs of my hands so I could see properly, I looked up at Dr Starrick again. "How long have I been unconscious?"

He paused as if calculating the time took a lot of effort, "It has been three days since you were attacked in the jungle and we had you Transferred within the first two hours." He seemed very proud of that fact. Then he added, "I think the reason you were out for so long was because of the trauma you suffered from the events in the jungle. And so your muscles wouldn't deteriorate while you were inactive, we have been administering a rigorous physiotherapy program..."

He kept rambling on, but I tuned him out as I made my way to the mirror and stood in front of the opaque glass for a moment. I drew in my breath and let it out slowly before waving my hand in front of the sensor to activate the mirror. It flashed to life and the vision of a strange woman wearing a white robe appeared before me.

I caught my breath and goose bumps spread across my skin. The woman before me was fairly short, slim and well-tanned with very long black hair. It flowed over her shoulder - *my* shoulder - from when I'd pulled it forward and it came down to my hips. I thought again of how it looked like a waterfall. A black velvet waterfall.

It's beautiful! And it's so long!

Then I remembered to breathe.

What attracted my attention next were my dark brown eyes, bordered with thick black lashes. Beautiful dark eyes. I kept staring into those eyes. They were now *my* eyes. I had to get a grip on that. This was what I would see in the mirror from now on. I sighed again - out loud this time. Would I ever get used to this?

The rest of my face was also very attractive; it was just the right shape. My lips were full and I had a neat little nose. When I turned my head from side to side, the strange woman did the same, and I had the sense that it *was* all a trick, that there was a person standing on the other side of a sheet of plain glass, mimicking my every move.

I kept staring at the stranger. This new body was, I admitted to myself, so much prettier than my own. I'd had short, wavy, light brown hair (regulation shoulder length), bluish-grey eyes and a fairly pale complexion and I'd always believed that I looked a bit too plump. Well, maybe not plump, but I didn't consider myself slender or dainty. And I was just plain. And I'd never thought of myself as really attractive (although Oliana and Kaliya had always insisted I was).

I kept moving and watching my reflection move. I couldn't help it. It really seemed like someone was trying to fool me. I resisted the urge to move suddenly to try to catch the woman out and prove it was all fake. Doing that would make me seem childish or maybe even a little crazy.

I looked down at myself and didn't find myself. Not my *real* self. Not the one I grew up knowing. It was all so strange. Too strange. My heart was still thumping in my chest and it still felt wrong. The more I thought about the fact that something wasn't right with it, the more it thudded away against my ribcage. I had to fight the panic until I could calm myself down.

I looked back at my reflection. In the past, I'd envy other women sometimes who were more attractive than me, but I wasn't a vain person and had never sought to change my appearance. Besides, I was too busy with my studies to worry about things like that. I'd never had much time for socialising either, and so my friends were few. But the few I had were very good friends, and that's all that mattered to me.

That thought made me stop and think. I looked at the face in the mirror. They wouldn't recognise me now. I'd lost them. Lost my life. The pain of it struck suddenly like a knife deep in my chest. Tears filled my eyes once again. What had they done?

The image of my friend, Oliana, popped into my head, smiling as she sat on her computer chair, spinning a little. "Travelling to the edge of the Explored Universe, studying new races and exotic planets — *and* being paid for it — how could a New Graduate with an adventurous spirit refuse?"

I'd frowned at her as I sat on the edge of my bed in my college quarters. She'd made it sound so adventurous. So exciting. My heartbeat had quickened at the thought — at the adventure.

Kaliya had come into the room and joined Oliana in convincing me to go. It sounded like something I'd been waiting for — something to get me out of my sterile, empty life — and I loved the thought of travelling to the stars and seeing some of the newly discovered planets, but my heart ached at the thought of leaving my friends.

Oliana still pushed for it, "We would only be like, a Vid call away, albeit a scratchy one. We could still visit each other like during holidays and the Festive Season and stuff, and maybe I could eventually get assigned to the same planet — you know, once I've finished all this..." She motioned toward the messy desk where her computer stood in amongst all her clothes, ornaments and Note Tablets. "Then we could have some *real* fun together."

They kept it up till I agreed. It was hard to say goodbye to them, but I didn't think at the time that it would be a *permanent* thing...

Dr Starrick couldn't stay silent a moment longer. "What do you think? She is a real beauty, isn't she—" and he gave a chuckle. "I mean, aren't you?"

"Oh, yes..." I breathed, then blushed when I realized I was talking about myself. Blinking my tears away, I asked, "Who was she?" — though I already knew.

"Her name was Sifayah," he began, but hesitated. "Well, actually, I don't want to tell you too much about her yet. There's already a lot that you have to take in at the moment..." he trailed off.

So I was right. Sifayah *was* the body donor. An unwilling donor, I was sure. She'd been wiped from existence so I could continue to live. And Sifayah's memories were all that remained of her life...

"She isn't human, is she?" I ventured, knowing full well what the answer would be, but wanting to hear what he would say about it — how much he was willing to tell me.

He seemed reluctant to answer. "Well... no..." he said slowly, "she is — ah — was — a native of Althar 3, but she was the only suitable donor we could find — especially on such short notice. She had been brought to our lab recently for study, so we decided to use her body to save your life."

He was just so matter-of-fact about it all. Didn't he realise what he'd done? And did he even care about Sifayah? Of course he didn't.

"Information on her species has not been released yet as we have discovered so little about them," he continued. "We *do* know that their biological structure and genetic makeup is very similar to ours, and their brain patterns are almost a mirror image on the screen. The only physical differences, as you will find out, are only an improvement on our own species."

What? What differences?

CHAPTER 7:

Have You Ever Tried to Talk Underwater?

My heartbeat quickened. I was frowning at him, which seemed to make him uncomfortable, but he continued. "These natives have actually adapted to be able to breathe underwater. They have lungs *and* gills — like amphibians. The gills are not visible from a distance, though. If you look closely or feel with your fingers, you will notice that there are slits below your ribcage. These are the gill openings. We observed that they seemed to remain fully closed while Sifayah was out of the water."

I gasped. I was now an *amphibian*? Even though this news was quite a shock, I couldn't help thinking that this was even more incredible than the fact that my new body was so beautiful. I found myself feeling just under my ribs through my robe, without even realising I was doing it. There was something there, but it was too hard to feel it properly. And I wasn't about to have a look with him standing there. I could feel that I was wearing nothing at all underneath the robe, and that on top of everything else creeped me out.

My attention was drawn back to my erratic heartbeat again. What was wrong? Should I say something? It was starting to really worry me.

I tried to focus on the conversation and recalled some of the things that had been spinning around in my head before I fully regained consciousness. There were memories of living on the shore *and* of swimming under the sea. Swimming for great periods of time without surfacing... The pieces were coming together now — it was starting to make sense to me.

"There aren't many visible differences," he continued, "So you *do look* human. No one will have to know — we can give you a new identity. But the important thing is that you will be able to help us study these aliens much more closely than we ever thought possible!"

What? Is that all he cares about? I thought to myself, glaring at him. *Studying the natives of this primitive planet? What about Sifayah? What about me? What — what if I don't want to do it? You can't make me!*

Then for a second I thought I caught something...

Just cut the hair, reduce the tan, do a few touch-ups here and there and she'll blend right in.

I stared at Dr Starrick open mouthed as my stomach tightened — his lips didn't move, but I'd *heard* what he'd said! It was impossible! His mouth was closed and I hadn't taken my eyes off his face!

No — *not* impossible. I must've heard what he'd just *thought!* Had I actually *read* his mind? No. Surely it was my imagination. But in my mind I found the answer. Sifayah's people communicated through telepathy — what they called Mind-touch. This was the way they communicated underwater.

Well naturally! I thought. *Have you ever tried to talk underwater?*

Somehow I must have gained the ability — the Talent — along with Sifayah's memories! *Whoah! This is amazing!*

Dr Starrick would have assumed that my blank expression was from the shock of hearing about all the things that had happened to me and that I was now an alien — and I *was* shocked — but I was so astounded that I'd just read his mind that I almost forgot everything else.

For me to read someone's mind was incredible — but how? How was I able to do it too? When I thought about it, it made perfect sense. Normally, humans only used ten percent of their brain capacity, but in the case of the Talented, they used the other areas of the brain that are usually dormant. These areas would not have been mapped, transferred or overwritten by the Eibhlin Process, so it would only make sense that they would still be intact afterwards. But for me to be able to access it successfully? That was amazing.

Dr Starrick tried to reassure me, but the impact of what had happened was starting to sink in. I felt overwhelmed. It was too much. My excitement and awe melted away and through my despair came a heat I couldn't push down. I clenched my fists and glared at him.

Did he realise what he'd done? Did he care? I wasn't Zhenna Rhodarma anymore — I was an alien, a guinea pig in a lab, and I would never see Mosuti or Larissa or the others again. Never be able to go home again. Not to *my* life, anyway.

I turned to face him. My breathing was shallow and I found it hard to breathe. The heat spread all over my body.

Without realising what I was doing, I turned on him. "You *know* that what you've done is illegal, don't you? When Starfleet Federation or The Six Star Alliance finds out about this, you *do* know the consequences, and they are *not* pleasant!"

My head suddenly felt cold and my heart continued to beat erratically. I reached for the bed to steady myself.

There's something wrong with my heart! I thought frantically. *I must be having a heart attack or something!*

Dr Starrick sighed heavily. "Yes, I know the laws concerning this type of procedure, but there was no other way to save your life—"

"What about the life of the woman you used for this brain swapping? You've *killed* her!" I snapped. I was getting colder. And why couldn't I breathe properly? I put a hand to my chest. My heart pounded.

"Well, that could not be avoided, unfortunately, but she was only a specimen we were studying in the Lab—"

"Only a specimen? *Only* a specimen?" I almost screamed the words. "She was still a person!"

CHAPTER 8:

I Can't Go Back

"There may be some hope, however," he interrupted me. "There may be something of her mind left. You see, we've developed a new technique, which we hope enabled us to preserve part of Sifayah's mind, the part that deals with memory. If we were successful, we should be able to find out more about her people."

So that explained why I'd retained Sifayah's memories. It hadn't all gone wrong. He'd kept them deliberately. "Now, can you tell me if there are any strange things," he continued, "Memories or thoughts in your mind that are not your own?"

Seriously? You're asking me now? "No. Nothing unusual," I lied. I was not about to trust him after what he'd done to me — even if it *was* to save my life. There was something not right about him. Not right about the whole thing...

I tried to take slower, deeper breaths. It was extremely hard to try to calm down, especially when my mind was racing a million miles an hour and when I thought I might be having a heart attack. Or something...

"Oh," he sighed. His face clearly showing his disappointment. "I was hoping... It doesn't matter... It may be too soon yet..."

You're disappointed? I thought. *Ha!*

I looked him in the eye. "You think Sifayah's life was meaningless because she's not 'civilised' like us? And what difference would keeping her memories make? Her whole consciousness and everything that made her who she was is gone!"

I felt cold all over now and breathing was close to impossible. I knew I was getting myself too worked up, but couldn't stop myself. "How could you do this to me? How could you change me — my whole life — without telling me — asking me? I can never be the same. I can't go back. I can't be with my friends. I can't keep this job... How are you going to explain where I came from? With a new identity?"

He ignored my questions and continued, "We were having trouble communicating with her, and the linguist — Talent Mosuti aboard your shuttle — was sent here to help us. But now he is dead and we haven't been able to get another one appointed on such short notice..."

DEAD.

It was so final. I hadn't had time to really think about what had happened to the other passengers and the pilot of the shuttle until now. Not properly. I had only known them for a few weeks, and now I would never see them again. The thought of their burned bodies in the jungle made me feel ill. They'd been cut down by laser rifles and burned and murdered and I'd somehow survived to be thrown into the body of an alien. I felt like I was drowning and couldn't come up for air... They were dead. They were gone. I'd never see them again...

I knew the reason I felt cold was because the colour had drained from my cheeks. My head started to tingle and I felt cold and clammy all over. My stomach went queasy like I was going to be sick. I knew this feeling; it was how I felt when I was going to faint.

I needed to lie down. I needed to get back on the bed before I fell to the floor. "I ... I need to l-lie down..." I stammered. Then I started to tingle all over; my heart beating out a radical tune...

Blackness was crowding in at the edges of my vision, clouding it and trying to take over. My hearing was strange too. Everything sounded kind of hollow and far away. I tried to get to the bed. I needed to get there fast.

"My heart is... I'm going to..." I couldn't even finish a sentence.

Dr Starrick immediately reached into his coat pocket and pulled out a small Injectorgun. "I had this sedative prepared, just in case," he told me, and pushed it against the side of my neck.

I could sort of feel the weird cold sensation as the contents transferred into my vein. My hands and feet were numb. Everything was fading away. His voice was far-off, like he was moving away from me.

One of my last thoughts was that he was an idiot. I didn't *need* a sedative when I was on the verge of fainting. I didn't need to be helped into unconsciousness.

Before I could say another word, my legs started to give way. It caused me to twist around as I fell and I could make out a very clouded vision of myself briefly in the mirror — sinking toward the floor. The darkness closed in around me before Dr Starrick could get me back to the bed.

◦

When I woke up, it was like waking from a strange dream. I was bombarded with flashes of memories again and the confusion that came with it. As I was struggling to clear my mind and work out where I was and what had happened, I heard voices and opened my eyes to find a man standing over me. I blinked a few times in an attempt to focus on his face. Then I recognized him as Dr Starrick, which brought the memories flooding back of the attack in the jungle and of how they'd changed me, turned me into an alien. That cleared out the cobwebs. My mind was now crystal clear. My heartbeat picked up. I looked up at him. I needed to get away from him. He did this to me. I tried to sit up, but Dr Starrick put his hands on my upper arms and guided me back down.

"Now then, Miss Rhodarma, just lie back down," he told me. "You need to take it easy. That sedative was a strong one. You need to rest for a bit longer."

I did as I was told, then lifted a hand up in front of my face to check that it wasn't a dream. It took a while for my eyes to focus on it properly. It wasn't my own hand, but that of the strange Althari woman. But wait — I spread my fingers a little wider — the fingers were webbed! I hadn't noticed before through the tears. But, of course — I needed them for swimming!

Whoah! This is cool! Weird, but cool! What else didn't I know about this body? What about my feet? Were they webbed, too? I could bet credits on it. I'd have to check them later. I was sure Dr Starrick wouldn't let me do it now.

I realized Dr Starrick was speaking to me. I slowly looked up at him. "I'm sorry, what did you say?"

"I simply asked how you were feeling," he snapped, but composed himself quickly and gave me an almost-warm smile. His voice changed to a calmer tone as he continued without waiting for my answer. "I can't say I blame you for reacting the way you did. It's not easy to accept such a drastic change in one's life —

especially when it wasn't planned or expected. You must've had quite a shock."

"Yes, it was a shock," I agreed. I'd play along with all of this for now, even though I felt like yelling at him again. Even though he'd practically yelled at me right then. I forced a smile onto my face. "But I'm feeling a lot better now, thanks."

I suppressed a frown. His outburst wasn't called for. He didn't need to snap at me like that. I had the impression that he was a very different person under the facade.

I took a deep breath and I asked the question that had been playing on my mind. "What about my friends back on Earth? Oliana Kyeema and Kaliya Jumanah. They were listed as my 'next of kin.' Have they been told? I mean, have you sent a message back to Earth?"

Dr Starrick shifted his weight as if he was very uncomfortable with my questions. "Well, under the circumstances, we were reluctant to send anything at first," he began. "It is a sensitive issue. I have sent a preliminary report stating that you are in fact missing after an accident, and I wanted to discuss things further with you so that we can decide what to do. You know, get your input on the matter."

Missing after an accident? Was that the best he could do? Well, I guessed he had to say something neutral like that while they worked things out. And what — *now* he wants to get my input? It was a bit late for that.

I felt strange. I wasn't sure what to say. What could we tell Oliana and Kaliya? What could I possibly say to them? *"Hey girls, it's me, Zhenna! Yes, I know I don't look like Zhenna — but it's me. You have to believe me. They gave me a new body... ille gally... and now I'm an alien..."* Yeah, that will work, I thought bitterly.

Also, it wasn't like Dr Starrick was going to tell people he'd broken Intergalactic Law to save me. We would have to come up with some kind of story. Something believable. *Like what?*

"I — umm, I don't know. I would have to think about it," I stumbled. *Whatever we think of, it would be a huge lie...*

"Mmm, yes," he said. "We will talk about it soon. We will think about it and gather some ideas together and come up with a suitable solution."

He sounded like he was simply working through another scientific equation. I guessed that that was all it was to him.

There was a long pause, and my thoughts kept returning to Sifayah. The young Waikari, daughter of the leader that had unwillingly and unknowingly given her life to save mine. I had the images of her and her life right there in my mind, but I wanted to ask him more questions.

"What about Sifayah?" I ventured, "Is there anything more you can tell me about her?"

There probably wasn't too much he could tell me that I didn't already know, but I wanted to know more about what *he* knew. Also, I had to pretend I knew nothing about Sifayah if I wanted to keep the truth from him.

"Not a great deal, unfortunately," he told me. "She was captured while walking alone on one of the beaches southwest of this base. We think her people are called the Waikari. They live in a small cove a little north of where she was found. They are a new discovery and there is little more I can tell you about her people and their culture.

"We only really know the physical and anatomical differences between our species as she wasn't very cooperative with us. We were unable to communicate without the help of a Talent, and she seemed determined not to help us in any way. It was quite strange really. We usually find that any new species are curious and will try hard to communicate in any way they can."

I felt a strange feeling in the pit of my stomach, like I knew why Sifayah had refused to communicate with them. Something just out of reach...

"We also calculate that she is about sixteen Earth years old," he continued, "So you've gained another four years onto your life."

So what! I thought. *That's not going to give me my life back! An extra four years without all the people I know, the people I love! Without Oliana. Without Kaliya. My life is ruined! How do I start over without them?*

Tears stung my eyes. There was a short silence, then Dr Starrick decided this was a good time to blurt out that I also had two hearts.

CHAPTER 9:
Who am I Now?

My chest tightened and I gasped. *Two hearts?* I stared at him open-mouthed.

Well, that explains why my heartbeat is so erratic! I thought to myself. *There's nothing wrong — It's because I'm feeling two heartbeats!*

I put a hand on the left side of my chest, then put my other hand on the right. Sure enough, there were two heartbeats. Both pounding out a rhythm inside my ribcage. That would take a bit of getting used to, but at least I could stop worrying about what was wrong with me. I'd been thinking that I might only inhabit my new body for a short time and then die from a heart attack or something.

I drew in my breath and let it out slowly. It was such a relief. Knowledge was such a beautiful thing.

"That is another improvement on our own physiology," Dr Starrick continued, "To have two hearts keeping the blood pumping is a definite plus when it comes to a lot of physical activity like swimming..."

He seemed to have run out of things to say. There was another long silence, and I lay there on the bed thinking as Dr Starrick checked the stats on the little electronic chart next to my bed. So much for him not knowing a 'great deal' about Sifayah. He only knew just about everything about her physiology that there was to know.

I heard the friendly hum of the Bio-scan, but didn't bother to look as it hovered past. I knew that once it scanned my entire body, it would return to its bay at the head of my bed. Then it would send the updated data to the electronic chart for Dr Starrick to see.

My mind was too busy to worry about such trivial things. I was trying to think and make sense of everything. As I thought long and hard about it, I began to actually *like* the idea of being someone else. Well, sort of. Especially if that someone else could *breathe* underwater and communicate *telepathically*. It still seemed so surreal.

Well, maybe I could get used to it after all, I thought... I knew I *had* to. I really didn't have a choice. There was no reversal for what they'd done. No body to transfer back to. No way possible that I could be Zhenna Rhodarma again. I was now someone else. But what did that actually mean? What did it mean to me? How was I going to deal with it? How was it going to change me?

I sat up slowly, swung my legs down and slid off the bed, then padded bare-foot across the bland white room to the mirror once again. Dr Starrick didn't try to stop me this time. He simply watched me go. With a wave of my hand, the image of the alien woman was staring back at me again. I sucked in a breath. It was still too hard to believe that it was me.

I studied the features carefully, deep in thought, forgetting Dr Starrick was even in the room. In the name of science, I'd been given a new face and a new body, which were far more attractive than my own. Maybe fate had had a hand in this somehow.

Another thought came to me. I'd always loved swimming in the pool at the Academy and I'd been so intrigued by the marine life I'd encountered while scuba diving on the few trips that I'd been on with the other students. Now that I had the ability to swim under the water unaided by breathing apparatus and unrestricted as to how long I could stay down there, I could roam freely in a beautiful underwater paradise, swimming around amongst the fishes and other marine life. There would be so much to see and learn. And, of course, I'd be helping Dr Starrick and his associates study them *and* the Waikari people. Maybe I could make this situation work for me. Maybe I could do this.

Dr Starrick's voice interrupted my thoughts and made me jump. "Well, then. Your stats say you're in perfect health. And now you're awake, we should be able to get started with some preliminary tests." I looked over at him. "We'll start on them at noon tomorrow," he announced, "if that is okay with you? It'll give you some time to rest and familiarise yourself with your new... appearance."

I turned back to the mirror slowly. "Yes, that will be fine," I answered absent-mindedly, transfixed on the beautiful alien woman's face.

And with that settled, he said, "I'll see you at noon, then," and when I nodded, he turned and disappeared out the door. I watched the reflection of him leave the room and heard the door swish shut, then looked back at the reflection of the new me again and smiled. The stranger in the mirror smiled back.

I breathed a huge sigh of relief. Now I finally had the chance to be alone and think. I needed to clear my head. I needed to process all of this.

If this was to be my body now, I needed to *familiarise* myself with it, as Dr Starrick put it. And that included my mind. I would need to somehow learn how to use my newly acquired Talent properly if it was to be of any use to me. Maybe I could do some training, like they do at the TTC (Talent Training Centres) back home.

But first, my new body. What did it really look like?

The garment I was wearing was a loose-fitting robe with long sleeves and a belt, which was tied in a knot at my left hip. The length of the robe extended a little past my knees. I glanced over my shoulder instinctively to make sure I was alone — even though I knew I was — then carefully untied the belt and pulled the sides of the robe apart to reveal flawless brown skin, a flat stomach and full breasts. My breath caught. There were no scars anywhere and my muscles were taut and firm from a lifetime of swimming.

Sifayah's memories had provided the image of what I now looked like, but the mirror showed a clearer picture and a lot more detail than a reflection in still water. I looked closely and could see the slits running along the bottom of my rib cage, just as Dr Starrick had said. I ran my fingers along them again, to confirm that they were real. It was still hard to believe they were there. They were sealed shut, and I knew better than to try to pry them open for a better look. Although, it was hard for me to resist the temptation to poke at them.

Pulling the robe back from my shoulders and letting it drop to the floor, I turned around slowly to see myself from every angle. I still half expected to catch the woman on the other side of the glass out as she failed to keep up with my movements.

I couldn't find fault with my new appearance — only that it was all too obvious that I was *not* human. The larger breasts, the gill slits under my ribs, the colour of my skin, the webbed hands and — I looked down — webbed feet and that black, black hair. All those things set me apart from every human I knew.

It wasn't that I thought I might be disliked or persecuted because I wasn't human — that wasn't what was bothering me. It was just that I was *not* Zhenna anymore. It kept coming back to that fact. Nothing could or would be the same. Then I thought, *So who am I now? What do I do?*

CHAPTER 10:
Something Broken

Could I travel back home and try to convince Oliana and Kaliya that it was really me inside this body? Would they believe me? Would *I* believe it if a stranger walked up to me and said that she was really Oliana? No, probably not. And even if they believed me and everyone else believed me, it still wouldn't be the same. Maybe letting them think I was dead was the kindest, sanest way of dealing with this. I would have to let go of my past and move on with my life. Somehow. Put all my efforts into work for now and try not to think about it too much. Or something...

It suddenly occurred to me that my little room was probably an observation cubicle, which meant this mirror was more than likely fitted with a camera so Dr Starrick could keep a watchful eye on his latest experiment. I quickly stooped down and snatched up the robe. Turning my back to the mirror as I dressed myself, my face flushed hot. He probably would have seen my naked body already — considering what I was wearing and the fact that he knew everything about my physical features and anatomy — but not while I was conscious and aware of him watching. It was unnerving and more than a bit creepy.

I walked back and sat on the side of the bed, looking across at the mirror. I watched as it automatically switched itself off after it no longer detected my presence in front of it. My human body wasn't all I'd lost; I'd also lost the right to my privacy.

They'll be watching my every move, I thought with a sudden surge of despair, *I've lost my body, my privacy, and my life, and there's nothing I can do about it.*

Why did this happen to me? Why can't I wake up and be back at home? I want to get out of here! Away from the testing and all the questions that will be endless. Will all the testing and prodding and poking ever stop? Will they ever leave me alone?

A tear rolled down my cheek.

I'd have to *demand* that they stop when they'd learnt all they could about Sifayah and the Waikari — or rather, when I decided not to tell them any more. I would take it up with Starfleet Federation if Starrick wouldn't listen to me.

⸺◆⸺

I was supposed to rest, but that was impossible. I'd spent the rest of the day and half the night thinking about it all and searching through the memories in my mind.

I'd been lying in bed trying to sleep, but I was too wide awake, too restless. The thoughts in my head were no longer tumbling over each other, and now that they were coherent, I could focus on them.

There were so many memories there that belonged to Sifayah, and when I wondered how Sifayah was captured by Starrick in the first place, the memory drifted into my mind and it was like it was happening to me.

I was on the sand, walking back toward the village, when I sensed danger. I'd just left Jarleth and my brothers at The Dive.

51

We'd been playing there most of the afternoon, seeing who could do the most interesting dive off the rocks and into the surf. I wondered how they could stay there and play all day. I'd had enough. It was time I made my way to Tasha's cave to attend my Mind Training.

I'd looked back as I waved goodbye, just in time to see Jarleth push Axiak under the waves, then Jadidi joined in and pushed Jarleth under. I walked along a bit further, and by the time I looked back again, they were all up on the rocks, ready for another turn to show off their skills.

I wanted to get my training finished and get back home before the sun set, and was enjoying the cool sea breeze on my wet skin when the dark feeling came. I wasn't sure what the danger was. The feeling was like nothing I'd felt before. I looked around; at the sea, the rocks on the beach and the trees beyond — even back at The Dive where I could still make out the shapes of the boys — but found nothing of any threat.

I reached out further with my mind and sensed that the danger was coming from above.

When I looked up, there was a large shiny creature hovering high above my head. It made a humming sound and didn't appear to have any wings. I wondered how it could stay up there without wings of any kind. It was so big and heavy that it should have fallen out of the sky.

The object was a silvery colour and seemed to be made of some sort of metal. How could a living thing be made of metal? I cringed as it came closer — both hearts racing. The only weapon I carried was a dagger, which I knew would do little damage against this huge wingless monster, but drew it anyway. A blinding light like the brightest sun struck me and I instinctively ducked down into a crouching position and put my arm up to cover my eyes, then the light seemed to swallow me up...

I opened my eyes. I was shaking all over — feeling all the terror Sifayah had felt as she was beamed aboard the shuttle. I took a few slow deep breaths and the panic subsided. I was amazed — the memories were so real. It was as if I'd been there myself. Part of me had been.

Someone could go crazy thinking about this stuff, I thought to myself.

It was really strange. Like there were two people inhabiting my mind. Only, Sifayah didn't have a conscious mind. No will of her own anymore. Just traces of her life left behind... It was sad...

I continued to read Sifayah's memories long into the night. I knew Sifayah was the Zheav's daughter and that she had two brothers; Axiak and Jadidi. I discovered she was the oldest child who also had three sisters; Shanae, Melina and Channia. Her mother, Tamari, was a proud woman and was well respected within the tribe. Her father, Silurian, was a wise and strong leader, and the Waikari people stood by him and respected his judgement.

Sifayah was born under the waters of Akilina Cove and had lived in the cove all her life. She'd learned the ways of her people and had grown to be a beautiful young woman. Their cove was surrounded by cliffs that rose about twenty metres on all three sides. The cliffs were almost impossible to pass, so they seldom had contact with the other races on their world. They called the people from the land, the *Jungle People*.

The Waikari had never really ventured across the land any great distance either. There was no real need to, but mostly it was a case of fearing the unknown. And the few outsiders they *had* come into contact with were not very friendly toward outsiders, especially when they discovered they could breathe underwater and were telepathic. It seemed to disturb them or scare them, which puzzled the Waikari. To them it was a natural part of life.

So the Waikari decided to guard their cove from outsiders to avoid any trouble.

Despite all this, Sifayah believed one day the Jungle People would be ready to become friends, but this view wasn't shared by many of her clan. When faced with such opposition to her ideas, Sifayah simply decided to keep many of her beliefs and opinions to herself.

The cliff face was interspersed with lots of different sized caves, which served as homes for the Waikari. They lived on the land, rather than beneath the sea, as it was safer up in the caves than under the water. Some generations before, when they still lived under the ocean, it was not uncommon for a villager to be taken by a Water Dragon during the night.

The Waikari knew a lot about the ocean, but little about the land. They called their world Sovoli, meaning Sovereign World, though they didn't realise how much their world stretched out across the land.

I read the memories as Sifayah matured into a young woman, promised to a young warrior named Jarleth. They were to be Joined in the Garsha Ceremony during the third moon of the Cool Season. And that had been taken from her when she was captured. I could see Jarleth's face clearly in my mind and knew Sifayah had loved him. He'd matured into a brave warrior and had passed all the traditional Initiation Tasks set before him. He would make a fine mate for the daughter of the Zheav.

Sifayah had been proud to be betrothed to such a brave and handsome young man. He had long black hair — as black as hers, but it only came down to elbow length — and a beautiful boyish face. His tanned, scarless, well-muscled body made Sifayah the envy of her all friends.

All of the Waikari people could communicate telepathically, but Sifayah was different. Her kinetic abilities were not only rare, they were much greater than that of any of the Gifted Ones in her clan. This was discovered when she was young and she'd been sent to Tasha, The Old One, to be trained in the use of her Gift.

As strange as it seemed to me, telepathy wasn't considered a Gift amongst the Waikari. Everyone possessed the ability. It was hard to fathom — a whole race of people that were Talented, but it was natural and just a part of their daily life. I'd never heard of such a thing. It was only other Gifts — or Talent — such as Telekinesis and the other abilities like Empathy and Seer that were thought of as anything special.

She also seemed to have a very good memory, and this was a very useful tool where her Talent was concerned. Back on Earth, I'd seen how Talents could teleport an object into their hands from a great distance simply by remembering it — what it looked like and what it felt like. The more you could remember about something, the easier it was to teleport.

My thoughts returned to Jarleth. Through Sifayah's memories, I saw him standing there before her, sea spray showering down over them both. They were at The Dive, alone. Her brothers had gone home and she and Jarleth had lingered for a while so they could spend some time together. They'd known each other since childhood, and they knew each other so well. Sometimes they needed no words to communicate, so they would stand on the outcrop and look into each other's eyes — not even using Mind-touch. They could feel what the other was feeling.

He held out his arms to her and she melted into them. It was a place she'd always felt comfortable and safe. They stayed there a long time, letting the sea throw whatever it could at them…

I'd drifted off to sleep thinking about that. When I finally woke up, it was nearly nine in the morning. Three hours to go. I still had the memory of the two of them on the rocks fresh in my mind, and I felt a warmth, but also a strange sadness inside.

There was a door to a little bathroom next to the mirror. I hadn't noticed it at first as it blended into the wall even better than the main door, but I'd discovered it the previous day as its sensor was right next to the mirror. As I entered, I grabbed the pile of clothes I'd found on a small shelf the day before. The pile contained some undergarments and a one-piece day suit. All white, of course. And some white shoes. Why did everything have to be so white and stark and boring? It was worse than being back at home. Even a small hint of colour would have been nice. Anything at all would have been better than this.

I used the bathroom, dressed myself and sat back on my bed. I spoke to the computerised food dispenser while I brushed my long, long hair and ordered something nutritious for break- fast. It was in a panel in the wall to the left of my bed head. I kept brushing while I waited for my meal. It would take a while to get used to the extra length, but I didn't care.

There was something bothering me. Something I couldn't stop from popping into my head. When they transferred my brain waves and somehow my whole consciousness and memo- ries across to this body, what happened to my soul? Did it follow me? Or was I a soulless being that was no longer human and no longer capable of love and joy or be able to care about another person? My emotions were all over the place, but I didn't seem to feel joy or love. And I definitely didn't care about anyone in this place. Was there something wrong with me?

Maybe the Eibhlin Process had created an army of soulless creatures that would one day do something terrible because they were no longer quite human...

Those dark thoughts were tearing at my insides, making me feel like there was something wrong. Like I was something broken. I had to push those thoughts back. They felt like they were crushing me. What did it mean to have no soul anyway? What was the purpose of a soul? Can someone live without one?

I tried again to push the thoughts away and out of my head. It wasn't easy. I had to concentrate on the positives. I had to think about my new abilities and my new body and the fact that I could breathe underwater. I tried to feel the excitement that those facts should bring out, but it fell flat. I needed to get out of here and away from my thoughts.

After eating alone in silence, I decided to see if I could leave my room and take a look around the base. I pressed my thumb against the Thumb-lock beside the door and the light flashed red. Locked. So I was a prisoner. Why wouldn't they let me out? Surely I could stretch my legs and look around to stop the boredom from driving me mad.

Well, they don't let lab rats out of their cages...

But I wasn't a rat. I couldn't see why they wouldn't let me out. There was nowhere to go — we were underground. Maybe they didn't want me snooping around. Did they have something to hide?

Unless I wasn't well enough to be allowed out. Maybe there was something Dr Starrick wasn't telling me about...

Oh, stop it! I told myself, *You've been through hell and they are keeping you under observation!*

CHAPTER 11:

I Needed to Get Out for a While

I found that I was pacing up and down. I still wanted to get out. I'd been there less than a day — well, I'd been conscious less than a day — and already I was getting restless. Although I'd spent many hours studying in front of my computer console back home, I always made sure I took regular breaks and did enough exercise. I couldn't stay in the one place too long. I'd been in this poky little room too long.

Okay, how to get out? What can I use?

I started looking around the room. Maybe if I could create a build-up of static electricity, I could short circuit the lock long enough for it to open once. I'd seen it done before.

Pity there's no carpet on the floor, I thought.

I spotted some rubber gloves in a little compartment at the foot of my bed and there was a small mat on the bathroom floor. Grabbing two of the gloves and the mat, I raced over to the doorway. I put the mat down on the floor and started shuffling my feet on it. The slippers I wore had rubber soles, so that would increase the static charge. I rubbed the gloves on my hair.

I continued the rubbing and shuffling for a few minutes — feeling silly — then pressed my thumb against the lock again. It emitted a strange series of beeps and the door swished open. I peered outside. The corridor was empty. Good. I could hear that the corridor to the left was buzzing with movement somewhere out of sight, so I decided to go to the right. I didn't want to run into anyone. I only wanted to satisfy some of my curiosity and look around. I needed to get out for a while.

I ditched the gloves and stepped out into the corridor before the door swished shut again. I walked silently through the corridor and turned down another, then another, keeping track of the turns. I discovered that I liked the way my long hair swished from side to side when I walked at a quick pace. I thought about my identity. It seemed to have been taken from me without permission, without warning. Who was I now? I wasn't sure anymore. Would I get a new name? Would I get a new ID?

Finally, I came to a door at a bend in one of the corridors. The symbol below the Thumb-lock was one I recognized as being for a laboratory, which also meant restricted access, and my curiosity rose considerably. I pressed my thumb to the lock. As I suspected, it didn't let me enter. I knew whatever was inside the Lab would prove to be very interesting, as I'd already seen some of the exotic flora and fauna this planet had to offer. I pressed my thumb to the lock again. Nothing.

Like it was gonna work the second time! I scoffed.

I could hear footsteps heading my way and managed to duck around a corner before the approaching procession entered the corridor. I held my breath as I listened. They stopped, and I realized the sign on the wall opposite me was inside a glass cabinet, and the glass allowed me to see the reflection of the people fairly clearly from my position. Realising that I was holding my breath, I let it out slowly and let myself breathe again.

There were three men standing together. One of them wore a loose-fitting robe like the one I was wearing when I'd woken up, and his hands seemed to be bound in front of him. The other two wore some kind of uniform, and I thought that maybe they were transporting a prisoner. Otherwise, why would his hands be bound?

I concentrated hard on the reflection, and somehow it seemed to become quite clear. I thought my new abilities were somehow helping me to see them more clearly. I didn't know how my mind could do the things it could do — I only knew that the Talent was there, and it seemed to just come freely sometimes.

The uniformed men were poking at the prisoner, taunting him and laughing. He tried to pull away, tried to say something, but the words came out garbled. This made them laugh even more. I tried to figure out what could be wrong with him. The more he tried to speak, the more he would mess it up. I looked back at the guards. One of them was laughing so much he was hugging his ribs.

I tried to concentrate on the prisoner's mind. What could be wrong that muddled up his speech so much? As I focused, I found I could see into his mind. This surprised me, but I steadied myself. Sifayah had done this countless times. There were thoughts scattered everywhere, like someone had stuck a hand mixer in his brain and turned it on. As he became more agitated, I could see thoughts and memories in his head that reminded me of when I was still unconscious — right before I woke to find that I was no longer human.

Some of the jumbled thoughts were of the jungle and some were familiar. I could see some of the things that Mosuti had told me about when we were aboard the Acronis, on our way here. Then I saw memories of our times together.

I had a sinking feeling in the pit of my stomach. Could it be...? The guards provided me with the answer.

"What's his problem, anyway?" one was saying.

"The Eebalin thingy didn't go too well on this guy," the other answered. "He's s'posed ta have that Mosuti guy in his head."

I sucked in my breath and held it. I could hardly believe what I was hearing. They did it to other people? To Mosuti? Dr Starrick had told me that all the others were dead, but Mosuti would have to have been alive for them to do the procedure and transfer his consciousness into this man's head!

CHAPTER 12:
ACCESS DENIED

I could feel the tears in my eyes. What if he was still alive right now? He might still be okay. The procedure was supposed to leave him unharmed.

"Yeah, well, it ain't the first failure he's had," the second guard said. "So many of 'em have been stuffed up. The only one it's worked on so far is that Zeena girl. I tell ya, he's losin' 'is touch or somethin'."

"Better watch whatcha say, Marik, or maybe *you'll* be the next 'body donor,'" the other warned him.

I realized I was holding my breath again and willed myself to breathe normally.

"Starrick wouldn' do that!" Marik said in a half whisper.

"Don' you bet on it! Who do ya think this guy used ta be?"

"No..." he said incredulously as he looked closer.

"Yeah. Kaylan. He used ta clean the kitchens. Now I guess we need a new mop-and-sponge boy."

They grabbed him by the arms and led him into the room in front of them — no longer amused by the state of the poor guy. After a short while, they emerged and Marik used his thumbprint as identification to lock the door behind them.

I waited until the sound of their footsteps and voices faded away, then headed back down the corridors toward my horrid little room, deep in thought.

If Mosuti was alive, could I find him?

On the way back, I found an open door not far from my room. It must have been closed when I'd come past before. I didn't remember seeing it along the way. I peered in and saw that the room was filled with tables and chairs, with a Vid phone on the far wall. My hearts leapt — maybe I could contact someone! Alert the authorities and they could come and get me out of here and arrest Starrick and all the others that were involved!

I hurried over to it, feeling shaky and on-edge, pressed the button that turned down the sound, put my thumb on the scanner, waiting and wondering if my ID would work, or if I even *had* one.

"GOOD MORNING RAJENDRA SHEA," appeared on the screen, along with a small blinking red light.

Rajendra Shea? That was my new name? Assigned to me by Dr Starrick? I didn't like it. I stood there frowning at the machine. Rajendra. No. It was awful.

I want to pick my own name! That's only fair after what they've done to me! ... Or they could at least find something decent.

Yeah, I know that sounded childish, but I couldn't help it. I looked at the screen. It wanted my attention.

"WOULD YOU LIKE TO MAKE A VIDEO CALL OR VOICE ONLY?"

Voice would be quicker to connect, but I chose to make a video call so they could see my new face as evidence. I punched in the code for Interplanetary Communication, but was presented with an "ACCESS DENIED" message that flashed red on the screen.

"YOU ARE NOT AUTHORISED TO USE OUTSIDE LINES, RAJENDRA SHEA."

I pressed the button to see if I could access a line within the base, but received a similar message.

Then why ask me if I would like to make a call?

I shouldn't have been surprised, and I guess I really wasn't, but I couldn't help the heat rising up to my face. I turned from the machine and hurried back to my room.

"Shoulda known," I mumbled to myself as I walked, my hair tickling my arms when it moved. *As if they were going to let me call Earth and tell them what they did to me. Of course they're not going to let that happen!*

I wiped away tears. Tears of anger. It was stupid of me to think I could get the word out so easily. This was a serious situation when you consider that the Eibhlin Process was highly illegal and Starrick was set up here and running experiments without his employers having any knowledge of or giving any authorisation for it. Well, at least, I was fairly sure they didn't know. He would be prosecuted and sent to prison for this. They might even throw away the key.

I made it back to my *cell* without being seen and pressed my thumb on the lock. Nothing. What if I was locked out? How would I explain what I was doing outside the room to Dr Starrick? Before I could panic, the door swished open. It must have still had a problem after I shorted it out. Or maybe it wasn't locked from the outside. Either way, I was glad I'd made it. I raced in and sat down on the bed to think — still shocked about Kaylan and what they'd done to him. And as silly as it sounds, the new name I'd been given still bugged me.

I *knew* I couldn't be Zhenna Rhodarma anymore — I'd already come to that conclusion — but I really felt I should've had a say in the choice of my new identity — or at least been told about it. I wondered if I didn't like it because I thought it was a horrible name, or because someone else had chosen it for me. I was sure it was because *they* had chosen it. Was I just being selfish? Was I being silly? I hadn't had a say in my *birth* name. But then, I was now an adult, and quite capable of choosing a name for myself. It wasn't like me to be this upset. What was wrong with me? There was a whisper in my mind about me having no soul. Was that why I was feeling so angry? Maybe it had nothing to do with the name at all. I pushed it from my mind. I had other problems to worry about. I was stuck here. Trapped and at the mercy of people who obviously didn't care about me or any of the other victims of their experiments. And I had no contact with the outside world.

What was I going to do? How could I get away? How was I going to sit through the tests like everything was fine and pretend nothing had happened? Pretend I didn't see the guy with scattered brains. Pretend that I didn't know Mosuti could still be alive... I had to bide my time somehow, and I *had* to get out.

Dr Starrick wouldn't want anyone knowing what he was doing here at Maztec, so I had to be careful. I was determined to contact someone and tell them everything I knew. Someone had to put a stop to the horrible experiments that were being performed here. I hoped I could do something before someone else got hurt. But how?

I sat, thinking hard. Not moving. Hardly blinking. I didn't know how long I sat there. The things the guards had said were eating at my thoughts. I wasn't the only lab rat. Mosuti had also been through it, but his mind hadn't been successfully transferred. He didn't make it through in one piece. I wondered if any other crew members were still alive after the attack. If Mosuti was alive, it was quite possible there were more.

Dr Starrick had taken advantage of a disaster and used it to further his sick research. He must have saved the lives of any passengers he could, but told Jannali and the company back on Earth that we'd all died.

How many? How many made it?

It was driving me crazy. I had to resign myself to the fact that I might never find out. He wouldn't tell me, I was sure. He'd deny everything. I was locked in my room — sort of — kept away from everyone and told a bunch of lies.

The guards had also said I was the only successful experiment. I shuddered to think how many things must have gone wrong with the others. Would any of them be alive after he'd finished with them? And what else did he have planned for me? He could do anything he wanted really. What could I do about it? How could I stop him?

Oh, crap. I have to get out of here!

CHAPTER 13:

Let's Begin

My best chance of contacting someone would be the other station here on Althar 3 — Station Jannali. If I could at least find out where it was...

I was still deep in thought when Dr Starrick arrived to start the tests, and I gave a start when the door slid open and he strode into the room. "Well, then, ready for the first tests, my dear?" he asked with great enthusiasm, apparently not noticing my reaction.

I frowned up at him. *Haven't you ever heard of knocking? I could have been naked.*

It was hard for me to be enthusiastic when my mind was still filled with thoughts of his experimentation on innocent humans — and innocent natives — but I forced a smile that probably looked more like a grimace and nodded my agreement. I would have to play along until I could figure something out. I wondered how long he could keep me here before the authorities caught up with him. *Too long...*

But then what would happen to me after that? Maybe I would become someone *else's* lab rat. I shuddered.

"Let's begin then, shall we?" He hadn't noticed the shudder either. He was probably too excited about the tests and too self-absorbed to notice anything around him. I stood reluctant-ly and followed him from the room.

The first tests were to determine the strength of my muscles, the quality and range of my hearing and vision, and general reflexes. Starrick informed me that they couldn't perform these tests accurately on Sifayah because of the language barrier, and, as hard as they tried, they couldn't obtain the necessary co-operation from her. I searched Sifayah's mind and knew why. Sifayah had *read* Starrick's mind and could plainly see what he was really like, and so she refused to cooperate at all. A smirk crept across my lips. *Clever girl.*

I decided I'd do the same, sort of. I wouldn't give him any more information than I had to. Wouldn't tell him anything important. Just give him basic answers to his general questions and some I don't knows and nos when he asked about the Waikari or about memories that weren't mine.

Dr Starrick informed me that it was also necessary to do the tests to find out if any of my basic functions were still normal and unharmed by the procedure. I wondered how they could possibly know what was *normal* for Sifayah.

The tests revealed that I now had — as I'd first observed — a very strong and fit body. My vision and hearing were enhanced — I could actually see quite well in the dark and I could hear a range of sounds above and below the normal human hearing range. My reflexes were also pretty good. I didn't tell Starrick anything about being able to read his thoughts or that I could remember almost everything from Sifayah's life.

When I thought about it, the enhanced hearing, vision and reflexes were needed for life under the ocean. It could get very dark in places deep down in the ocean or in muddy rivers. And even back on Earth, the sea creatures emitted several sounds that were inaudible to the human ear. Quick reflexes were a tool of survival, and all that swimming would keep the body strong and fit.

Dr Starrick asked me more than once during the tests if I could remember anything or if there were thoughts or images in my mind that were not mine. I lied outright, determined not to give him anything. He seemed to be getting annoyed and frustrated about it, but I didn't care.

There was an instant during the testing where I thought I'd heard what Starrick was thinking again, but I wasn't sure. I tried harder, like I did with Kaylan, and I heard everything that was in the forefront of his mind.

His mind was on the task at hand, running through the data they'd gathered. I was surprised at how easy it was to see into someone's mind. It was second nature to Sifayah, but this was something new to me. It was amazing. But then I had to turn my attention away to answer a question one of the other doctors was asking me. That broke my concentration.

⚬

That night I probed Sifayah's memories again, and spent a long time 'remembering' the good times and bad times of a person who no longer existed. It was sad to think that a life had been taken to save my own. Sifayah was young, intelligent, Talented, and had everything to live for. She was such a vibrant person and so full of life. So unlike me. My life before I came to Althar 3 was boring and monotonous. There was no adventure and no one like Jarleth to give my life some kind of meaning. There was a part of me that really missed him, and another part that was jealous of Sifayah. That was messed up.

I decided to push all that aside and move on with other aspects of her life. I learned more about Sifayah's Talent. Her Talent enabled her to move larger objects than most and she could communicate telepathically over a greater distance. She was a powerful Talent, even amongst people who used telepathy in their everyday lives.

It was expected that she would lead one day, although there had never been a female Zheav before. Sifayah had no real wish to lead her people, but knew it was expected and had accepted it as her future. Aside from that, all she hoped for was a future with Jarleth and a happy, carefree life. And of course, that was now impossible...

I found myself wondering if I'd gained any telekinetic abilities as well. That would be awesome. I couldn't see any reason why I wouldn't have the ability. The part of the brain that used any psychic capabilities would have been left untouched if my theory was correct.

It was some time in the early hours of the morning that I finally drifted off to sleep, but even my dreams were filled with visions of swimming in the oceans of Althar 3 with my friends all around me, mingled with visions of life on Earth and then death and violence in the jungle.

<hr>

After a few days of testing, it was getting repetitive and boring. The next tests they had lined up for me were in water, and I'd been looking forward to them all morning. But still, I sat staring into the tank, thinking about how my life had completely changed, and a tear rolled down my cheek. Was this to be my life now? Being poked at and watched and tested until they were satisfied that they could gain no more from me?

Then they would probably pass me on to the next team of scientists to play with when they were done with me. I was a lab rat. Nothing more. The moment the Eibhlin Process had commenced, my life was forfeit. I was Dr Starrick's property, like a piece of lab equipment. And so were the other people they'd subjected to it.

I refused to join the hustle and bustle going on around me. I wanted to stay there in the safety of my mind.

Although my old two-piece swimsuit didn't fit me as well as it used to, I'd still wanted to wear it. The top was adjustable, thankfully. Starrick's people had recovered some of my belongings from the shuttle and it turned out the swimmers were almost the only things that would fit me now. I hoped that if I wore them, I might somehow feel a bit like my old self. But it didn't work. I hadn't really felt that way since I woke up here at Maztec and found out what they'd done to me. And I certainly didn't feel that way right now. How could I when I was about to dive in and breathe underwater while they watched?

The thing was, they could only find about half of my belongings. That didn't make any sense. My bags were all in the cargo hold with everyone else's and I had one small carry bag with me. And the only thing I really wanted, the thing that was missing and couldn't be replaced, was my locket. Kaliya had given it to me for my birthday three years ago. I usually wore it everywhere, but I'd taken it off when we'd headed out of the shuttle and into the jungle because I didn't want to lose it. I'd put it in my carry bag before we went outside. Before we were attacked. They didn't find the carry bag at all.

I looked down at the small tabs that were stuck to various parts of my chest and arms. They were sensors that were waterproof and could send a signal remotely so the doctors could monitor my vital signs while I was in the tank. I could feel them all over my head too. And I looked ridiculous.

The doctors were nearly ready for me. I looked at the tank. It was deep and large enough for me to swim around freely, with a viewing window on one side for Starrick and the other quacks to observe my movements, but I did *not* want to be on show.

From the corner of my eye, I saw Starrick walking over to where I sat, and felt a strange sensation as I became part of the rest of the world again. I was no longer in a private place within my mind. I looked up at him with distaste, but forced myself to smile.

"Okay, let's begin," he announced, and I read his thoughts and emotions as plainly as if he had thrown them at me. Annoyance, boredom, an eagerness to get started, and an interest in what I could do, but he wanted to get it over with.

I was shocked and disgusted at what I'd felt from him. So much so that I nearly fell into the water. I was amazed that my Talent was so strong, and shocked that he was definitely not what he seemed.

"Come on, Zhenna, we don't have all day!" he squawked.

CHAPTER 14:

My Only Chance

Yep. That's more like the real you.

I glared at him. It took him a moment to regain his composure. Then he smiled awkwardly and said, "I'm sorry, I have a bad headache today. It was rude of me to take it out on you."

I could see his real thoughts, even as he spoke the words, and of course they didn't match. I simply nodded.

This man was going to be impossible to work with. Most of the tests so far had been handled by other doctors and scientists, with Dr Starrick overseeing, but from now on he was the one I would be dealing with. And things were off to a bad start with him giving me a small peek into what he was really like.

How am I going to put up with this? I asked myself. *He's like a spoilt child. Snapping at me for no reason. And he doesn't even have a headache!*

I'd just have to 'grin and bear it,' as the saying goes. What else could I do? I'd have to do as I was told for now — until I could figure out what to do.

I hoped that maybe now I could grab his attention long enough to talk about what story we were going to tell everyone back on Earth about what had happened to me. So far he hadn't had time to sit down and discuss it properly. Or so he said.

I wanted to give my friends some news, one way or the other. They would be worried, thinking I was missing somewhere on a strange planet on the far side of the universe. But it would have to wait. I needed to focus now on being good and behaving like a good little rat. Or fish...

Let's get this over with then...

He finally gave the signal for us to start. As I stepped into the tank, the water felt very refreshing on my skin. I continued down the ladder into the cool liquid until it swirled about my neck, bringing my hair with it. This was so cool. My skin seemed to drink in the moisture. Simply having a shower was not enough to give my new skin the hydration it needed.

I hesitated. I knew from Sifayah's memories that I could breathe once I was under the water, but my instincts were telling me it was not possible.

I took a deep breath and plunged into the water. I waited, and then expelled the air slowly, blowing bubbles everywhere. Now I had to breathe in. I felt panic grip me as I sucked in water through my mouth, expecting at any moment to choke on the water and be forced to push my face up and out, coughing and gagging. But instead the movement was smooth and natural, with the water being expelled through my gill openings. It felt strange as they opened and the water tickled as it passed over my stomach.

As I took in more 'breaths,' the panic quickly subsided. And as I started to swim toward the bottom of the tank, I thought, *This is fantastic!*

I found my webbed fingers made swimming easier and when I stopped swimming and my hair swirled ahead of me, I looked down at my webbed feet and noticed that on the outside edge of each foot, a flap of skin extended outwards to make the foot much like a flipper. These were well hidden when I didn't need them.

As I started to swim again, my movements through the water were smooth and graceful. I swam by using my arms in a breaststroke action to propel myself and kicked my legs. I was surprised at how fast I could swim. I stopped kicking my legs and let myself glide forward. My long hair swirled about me in the water again as the momentum kept it going. I marvelled at its length and how it moved in the water. I'd never let my hair grow really long before, and I liked it — the way it looked, the way it felt as it brushed across my arms and back, and how the colour of it was so very intense in and out of the water.

I turned around and as I began to swim this time, the movements were instinctive and natural to Sifayah, but very strange to me. I was moving both legs together in unison to propel my body and my hands by my sides, fingers spread, were used to manoeuvre my slim body through the water, much like a fish uses its pectoral fins. This increased my speed dramatically, though the tank was too small for me to swim like this for more than a few swishes of my legs.

As I stopped at the other end of the tank, my hair swirled about me again, covering my exultant expression. It was incredible. I thought of how much swimming Sifayah would do in one day and could see how effortlessly I moved through the water. This was definitely why my body was so fit. I turned around and rocketed back to the other end. Swimming around in this tank would eliminate the stiffness in my muscles, though I knew I needed a decent swim to work it out completely. At least a kilometre.

I could feel how powerful my muscles were, especially in my legs. And the extra flap of skin on my feet — that was unexpected. I'd been wondering why the outer edges of my feet felt strange. The weird thing was that Sifayah's memories hadn't provided me with an answer. I seemed to be able to call up anything most other times, so that was kind of weird.

I enjoyed swimming around with such freedom, but I knew all too well that this was to be the first of many long and tedious tests.

⎯⎯⎯◦⎯⎯⎯

By the end of the fourth day of water tests, I'd formulated a rough plan and decided to put it into action. As I stepped out of the tank after the last test for the day, I asked Dr Starrick if we could conduct some tests out in the open ocean amongst the marine life and have me fitted with a camera to record all that I saw. That way they could study me in my — or rather, Sifayah's — natural environment and study other life forms at the same time.

He paused for a long moment, frowning and rubbing his brow.

"I will need to think about it," he informed me. "There's a lot of preparation involved. A lot of equipment to take with us..."

Okay, not the answer I was hoping for, but at least he was considering it. He wandered away, deep in thought.

I headed back to my room — my prison cell — accompanied by two guards. I had to keep my face neutral when I recognized one of them as Marik.

About two hours later, Starrick strolled into the room without knocking. I was sick of him bursting in. How *dare* he? Why didn't he think that maybe it was wrong to just barge in? Why didn't I have any privacy? Any life? I opened my mouth to tell him what was on my mind when he told me he was organising everything for the tests to be done in the ocean.

I closed my mouth. Then I bit my lip to stop myself from ruining everything by saying something stupid. As angry as I was about him barging in without knocking, I couldn't jeopardise my chances of getting out into the open ocean. I *had* to get out of here, and the ocean was my only chance. I couldn't see myself being able to locate the entrance to the underground base and walking out of here.

———— ◆ ————

That night after eating dinner alone again, I tried to watch a documentary on HoloMovie, but couldn't concentrate on it — I was too excited and too nervous about what I was planning to do.

I'd requested a HoloMovie player and some discs so I could watch some HoloMovies to pass the time and to learn about Althar 3, among other things. One of them was all about the psychic and paranormal. I wanted to learn even more about my newly acquired Talent and abilities.

I'd told them I had an interest in Talent because I'd become good friends with Mosuti during the trip through space and he'd told me some wonderful stories about his life and what he'd done with his telepathic ability. It wasn't a lie. I really was fascinated, and now that I had those abilities...

The only problem was — I couldn't tell anyone.

The disc showed footage of Talents *lifting* objects with their minds and performing various tasks in industrial and many other occupations. The other Talents that could *find* objects or people were also in great demand in both Planetary and Galactic Police Forces for their ability to help solve difficult crimes.

I desperately wanted to try *lifting* something myself, just to see if I could, but I knew Starrick would be watching. I looked across to the small table and chair they'd put on the other side of the room for me. The cup that stood next to my dinner plate would've been a perfect object to try. But no. If he wasn't watching right now, there would be some other moron sitting there watching my every move. They could even be recording everything. I abandoned the idea.

The show I was watching had a report on the ability to read and feel someone's emotions — Empathy. Mosuti had told me he had Empathic ability, but I didn't know much about it.

The report was quite interesting. It even showed how they could project their emotions to another person as well. I guessed that I must also have an Empathic ability because I could *feel* Dr Starrick's emotions.

There were many other situations where the Talented could utilise their abilities, but my mind wandered. I started to wonder if my makeshift plan would work. There was no great detail, I only knew that when they took me out of the station and into the ocean, I would somehow escape and dump the camera so they couldn't track me. Then from there, I would swim ashore and find Station Jannali.

I would have to be good on the first trip out there so they would trust me. After that, with their guard down, I could maybe overpower the people that would be swimming with me, watching me. I would only have to remove a mask or two to slow them down as I swam away. It's hard to chase someone through the water when you can't breathe. When you have to find your mouthpiece or die.

One of the HoloMovies gave me some valuable information I thought I could use. It showed how some Talents could *persuade* someone to do something by painting a picture within the person's mind of a whole scene or idea, *suggesting* different concepts and *motivating* them until they believed it was a good idea.

Only the most powerful Talents could do it. An example they used was when a woman convinced a man that he was laying on a beach on the other side of the country. He lay back in his chair and enjoyed the sun — even started looking for where he'd put the sunscreen and towel.

I thought maybe I could use this technique to somehow escape from my watchers once we were in the ocean. I could maybe make them think I was still with them while I swam away... or something... I hoped...

I had to try.

Another HoloMovie showed maps of Althar 3, so I utilised my almost-photographic memory to memorise the local area so that when I escaped I would actually have some idea of where to find Jannali. I was so desperate to let them know exactly what Starrick was up to.

I didn't want to arouse suspicion, so I'd asked for maps of the whole planet, and to see HoloMovies on other subjects as well. I hoped it would maybe fool them for a while — like until I was gone.

With a bit more of a plan formed in my mind, I decided to take a shower. The water was very warm and refreshing on my skin. I'd noticed that my skin needed more moisture now. I guessed that the Waikari had to hydrate their skin regularly to keep it from drying out. Sifayah's memories confirmed this. I pressed the button that activated the soap jets and closed my eyes while being sprayed with suds. The jets were located at various points in the cubicle so I didn't have to move at all to receive the full benefit of the spray. I rubbed the soap over my skin and hair and tried to relax as best I could, then pressed the next button and the water ran clear to rinse the suds away. When I was finished, warm air dried my body until I stepped out of the cubicle and dressed myself for bed. It took much longer for my hair to dry because of its length, but I didn't care — there was *no way* I would let them cut it. I didn't care that it would make me look more human. I didn't *want* to look more human — as weird as that sounded. I liked the way I looked and would *not* let them change me... again.

I sat on the edge of the bed. Life in the little white room was dull. When I wasn't doing the continuous tests with Starrick and the other doctors, the physiotherapy and the exercises, I was sitting alone staring at the walls and thinking or watching the HoloMovies.

I wasn't allowed out without an authorised person to escort me. They'd told me the day after my little walk around the corridors that I'd been seen on camera and my attempt at calling someone on the Vid had been recorded. Starrick had a few words to say to me about that. And now there was a guard outside my door night and day, in case I decided to go for another walk.

I desperately wanted to scream at him. Wanted him to let me out. Wanted to be free. But, of course, they would never allow that. And now there was no way I wanted to do anything to jeopardise my plans for freedom. Not when I was so close. I consoled myself by thinking about when I would be free.

I couldn't help wondering what I was going to do once I was free. After reporting everything I knew about Starrick and feeling a sense of justice that he got what he deserved, then what? I wondered what was in store for me, and how I was going to cope with life as a different person. More importantly, life as an Altharian. I'd been through what it all meant in my mind so many times. The tests, the questions, the analysing and reporting — I wanted nothing to do with any of it. I came here to do a job, and so far hadn't had the chance to do it. Instead, my world had been turned upside down...

The tests over the last few days had become increasingly difficult to withstand. I wanted to run, to be free of it all. But I sat and tolerated it. And Starrick was beginning to really grate on my nerves. He was a very insincere, selfish, and malicious person. And it wasn't just me that had to put up with it. He seemed to always be snapping at someone about something that wasn't perfect.

I felt I just *had* to get away, and if he asked me one more time about memories that weren't my own, I'd slap him upside the head.

CHAPTER 15:

Focus

But I was going to do something about it, and soon I would be free!

I had to wait a little bit longer...

Another thing had been bothering me. Some of the first tests they'd performed involved using an electroencephalograph to analyse my brain waves, and they had stopped once they'd started the water tests. But for the last two days, they'd taken me back after the water tests and hooked me up to the EEG again. It may have only been routine, or maybe Starrick had realized I was lying to him.

Or maybe it was because I read his mind while hooked up to the EEG the previous day. I didn't really mean to do it — it was starting to come more naturally now — but I was worried that they may have recorded it. I tried to tell myself not to worry. There was nothing I could do about it now anyway. It was done. Besides, I was leaving. After that, I didn't really care what they knew about me.

I still had some niggling doubts — doubts about the sheer simplicity of the plan, and was sure it was doomed to fail, but I told myself that once the first move had been made, there was no turning back. I had to go through with it. I tossed and turned in my bed, dozed for a while, then tossed and turned some more.

When I couldn't stand it anymore, I sat up and decided to watch another HoloMovie on telepathy.

I knew the reason Mosuti was assigned to Althar 3 as a Linguist was because he was a Talent. It was very clear to me now how telepathy could be used for something like that, using thoughts and assimilations within someone's mind of different objects and even behaviour. I could easily interpret Sifayah's language and understood every word. No, it was more than that because I was remembering what the words meant through her memories. It messed up my mind just thinking about it.

Maybe Starrick tried to put Mosuti's brain waves across into Kaylan's mind so they could still use his Talent to break the language barrier with the Waikari. But that had all gone wrong.

I thought about that. They wouldn't need to do that if Mosuti was still alive, but they needed him alive to do the transfer. So why do it? Because they could?

I wondered if I could communicate with Mosuti somehow, but I wasn't sure how to do it. And I knew I couldn't communicate with Kaylan with his scrambled mind. I forced it all from my mind and finally dozed.

⋅◆⋅

The mini-sub was positioned beside a reef of beautifully coloured coral south of the little island we'd landed on in a small cloaked ship, and I was waiting in the airlock with two fully suited divers: Rori and Shandar.

The water rushed in around us in swirls until the chamber was fully flooded. I was wearing a wetsuit with knee-length leggings and had the camera strapped to my shoulder. Because

I had no mask and therefore no microphone, they'd given me a small writing tablet and pen so I could still communicate with the sub. All I had to do was write on the tablet and they could read it on a screen on the sub's communication console. To answer, they'd simply type their messages back to the tablet.

It was a weird feeling, being the only one without air tanks, but once the outer hatch opened, I felt a strange sense of freedom that was exhilarating. I'd never experienced anything like it before. After being underground, the open ocean looked so incredible, and I swam out of the sub with a quick burst of speed, then stopped to watch my hair swirl around and cover my face. It was beautiful out here. I could see that once I'd moved my hair out the way. I turned and swam back to the divers so they wouldn't think I was going to rush off on them. Well, not yet anyway. I would have to stick to my plan.

There was so much more to do and see out in the open ocean than in the poky little tank at Maztec. It had been fun at first because breathing underwater was new and fantastic, but after a few laps around the tank, there wasn't much else to keep me interested.

All morning my stomach had felt uneasy, but I'd made up my mind to go through with it. I would not let anything ruin my plan. I would bide my time for now, and on my next visit, I would wait for an opportunity to make a dash for the open ocean.

I still felt a sense of euphoria as I looked around, but also a sense of dread. My heartbeats picked up. What if something went wrong? What if I couldn't escape? I couldn't bear the thought of being stuck at Maztec for the rest of whatever. In fact, the thought of going back to my prison cell was too much. I couldn't stand it any longer.

I should just go now, I told myself. *Why wait till next time? What if there isn't a next time? He could change his mind, or say that they've gathered enough information for now. I might not get another chance at this...*

I swam amongst some fish that were feeding in and around the coral, looking at all the strange shapes and colours and didn't have to pretend to be interested in them — they were very unusual and fascinating. They were new to my mind, but Sifayah knew them well. As I looked at each one, I reported the names the Waikari had for them back to the team of doctors aboard the sub by writing them on the tablet. I had to guess the spelling. The Waikari had a form of writing, but I could hardly write that on the tablet.

My hands were shaking as I was so nervous, but I forced myself to be calm, or at least to appear calm. I needed to keep my mind on the job at hand. The words I was writing on the tablet were wobbly. I'd never written such messy letters in all my adult life.

My hearts were racing and I tried to calm myself and slow my breathing down. Maybe they would just think I was excited, rather than nervous about escaping. My stomach was churning, reflecting my inner turmoil.

I looked at the two divers. How was I going to do this? And why did there have to be two of them? I'd never done this before and now I had to try it on two people at the same time. My mind was speeding a million miles an hour.

Calm, I whispered into my mind. *Calm. Be calm. Relax. You can do this... Think... Focus...*

I closed my eyes for a few seconds, then opened them to look directly at the men. I could feel their minds. I could see into them, but not as clearly as I could when I was concentrating on Dr Starrick's mind. I wondered why.

Probably because you're looking at two at a time...

I concentrated hard. I tried to paint a nice picture in their heads. I was floating near the big rock... floating near the big rock...

They both turned their heads around to where I was really floating and looked at me with strange expressions on their dopey faces.

My hearts sank. It didn't work. They still knew exactly where I was. They weren't falling for it.

I almost cried. I really thought I'd be able to do it. I'd seen the people on the HoloMovie doing it. Sifayah had done something similar before and she was an exceptionally gifted Talent. So why didn't it work for me? What more could I do?

My stupid plan was a big failure. I might as well head back to the sub now.

And tell them what? That I felt down about not being able to escape? Yeah, that would be great. Tell them all about it.

So now what? Should I try again tomorrow? Should I even bother? I'll be Starrick's guinea pig forever! There's no escape!

Then I scolded myself for being so negative. That wasn't going to help me at all.

What else could I do to get away? I tried to think of an alternative. I *did not* want to go back! Not when I was this close to freedom. It was right there. I could taste it...

CHAPTER 16:

Bye

Get back to what you're supposed to be doing, I told myself.

I turned only part of my attention back to the task at hand. Looking at sea life and plants.

As I was inspecting a strange orange and black sea anemone that the Waikari called Kitu, I saw movement from the corner of my eye. It was the two divers. I hadn't been paying them any attention while I berated myself, and now they were signing to each other - even though they could hear each other over their mics. Rori was telling Shandar there was a problem with his mask — there wasn't enough air coming through. He was heading back to the sub. I assumed he would want to get back quickly before it failed altogether.

Yes! This was my chance! I couldn't believe my luck! My heartbeats quickened. This was it — I would have to move now before Rori came back or before Starrick called us all back to the sub.

I felt the adrenalin flooding my veins. I watched Rori swim away while pretending to admire a purple and fluorescent-blue starfish with eight points on it. I told myself this was what I'd been waiting for.

Now. It had to be now. My nerves were so shot that I was sure if I was standing up at that moment, I would have collapsed in a heap on the floor.

When Rori entered the sub's airlock, I started concentrating on Shandar's mind. I could feel the effects of the adrenalin pumping through my body. His thoughts were of Rori's safety and he was wondering how long this woman was going to keep him out here floating around like an idiot.

Yes! I read his mind easily. One mind was definitely easier to work with than two. Looking at both of their minds that were full of thoughts that changed every second was very confusing.

Okay, focus...

My hearts were racing even faster now, echoing through my brain, but I gave the outward appearance of complete calm. At least I thought I did.

I exerted a little pressure on his mind, suggesting everything was fine. I chose a different location this time — not the big rock. That could make him suspicious or too confused. I suggested to him that I was still over where I'd been looking at the Kitu. He kept looking over there, watching what he thought was me doing my job and being a good little lab rat.

Slowly at first, I started to wander further and further away from Shandar. Gradually, I increased my speed until I could just make out the outline of the diver. I could barely see, but I was sure he had turned my way. Maybe he'd heard them telling him what was going on through the Com. I dropped my hold on his mind and sped off into the deep blue. I'd done it!

Once I'd let go of his mind, he definitely would have heard all the people in the sub calling out to him to tell him I was getting away. He would be in so much trouble, but I didn't care. I tried to envision the faces of the doctors when they found out the most important specimen in their lab had outsmarted them and escaped right under their noses. Starrick would turn a slight shade of grey. This was *his* project and he'd no doubt told them it was *his* idea to let me go out into the ocean. How was he going to explain this? I let out a giggle and blew small bubbles in the water. That was funny. My lungs had retained a small amount of air while I was underwater.

After a while, I slowed down considerably to save my strength and my heartbeats had slowed to match. They were no longer pounding in my ears.

Suddenly remembering the camera strapped to my shoulder, I quickly unfastened the straps and let it fall to the ocean floor.

Damn! Should have dumped it sooner, I thought. It would definitely be fitted with a homing device.

I scribbled the word 'bye' on the tablet and let it fall to the bottom too. They would find it when they tracked down the camera.

A smile crept back across my lips as I kicked off and swam away at an amazing speed. I kept heading out to sea until I could no longer see the camera, then turned so I was travelling along the coastline, not wanting to put too much distance between myself and the shore so I could find Station Jannali and let them know what Starrick was up to. I was fascinated with Althar's undersea world and desperately wanted to be able to take the time to explore, but Starrick was under the water right now, so that's where I *didn't* want to be.

Sifayah's memories let me know that I was moving away from Akilina Cove, Sifayah's home. I was glad I didn't have to go near the cove in case I was seen by the Waikari. I was no longer Sifayah — and they would know it instantly. They would see it in my mind. I followed the coast for about twenty minutes and was amazed at how long I could swim without even feeling tired. That twenty minutes beat any physio or exercise routines Starrick could dream up for me. My muscles were alive, no longer stiff and kind of sore.

While my body thrived on the physical exertion, my mind was all over the place. I kept looking around, expecting to be found at any moment. My brain was on overload. I'd escaped so easily. Maybe a little too easily. That made me shudder.

I wondered what would happen once I reached the shore. I had to hike through the dense jungle, but I was sure Sifayah's body — I mean, *my* body — could take it. I should have studied up on what kind of animals lived in the jungle. I had a vague idea from what they'd told us before we got here, but I should've had a better plan...

There was no point in thinking about that. I'd made the move, and there was no going back.

According to what Sifayah knew from the underwater landmarks in the area, if I turned shoreward now, I would reach a place that her people called Lamani Cove. There were never any people about on the beach as it was too rocky, which would make it easy for me to walk up onto the sand and into the jungle without being seen by anyone.

I headed toward the cove for a while, then I surfaced and peered out of the water to check my bearings. I recognized the cove ahead, so I slipped back under and headed for shore.

According to the maps I'd memorised, this cove would be a good place to go ashore as it would lead me to the river I needed to follow to get to Jannali. The actual mouth of the river was further along the shore to the east, but if I went in from Lamani Cove — where there were no people — straight through the jungle, I would meet up with the river and be able to follow it right up until I was very close to where Jannali lay hidden. It would be a perfect shortcut.

I marvelled at the beautifully coloured coral along the shelf as I passed it. Shoals of multi-coloured fish swam across my path and darted in and out of the coral. When the coral was replaced by sand and the water became shallow enough to stand, I surfaced, but only my eyes and the top of my head could be seen by anyone who may happen to be on the shore. It was a small deserted beach with rocky outcrops on either side. There were also some rocks I'd have to climb to get to the jungle beyond. I waded in slowly; keeping my attention focused on the shore. I didn't want to bump into any natives. That would only complicate things. I just wanted to get to Jannali.

The waves splashed against me as I walked up to the beach. Once I was on the sand, I felt heavy after the weightlessness of the water — especially my hair. The water poured from it, running down the backs of my legs.

I made it up the sand and to the rocks undiscovered and started to climb. My heartbeats quickened. The chances of running into someone were very slim, but I was still anxious.

The place I chose to climb up was the lowest part of the rock wall and was easy enough, but I still managed to graze my left knee on a sharp rock. The salt water made it sting, but I ignored it.

I hurried to the shelter of the nearest trees, which were about thirty metres from the rocks. I kept a fast pace for fear of being seen amongst the smaller trees — Dr Starrick had probably ordered an air search by now and the cloaked ship we'd travelled in was close by on that small island — so I'd have to be careful.

The jungle wasn't as dense here as it was where the Outrider had landed what seemed like years ago — *Mustn't think about that,* I told myself. *Mosuti's brain is scrambled and the others are most likely dead.*

DEAD.

CHAPTER 17:

I'd Lost Everything

It hit me full force. At that instant all the horror flooded back into my mind... seeing my friends being shot at by laser weapons in the jungle... Bazeelia's hair on fire... surviving it all, only to find I was now an alien... the way I'd been treated by Starrick and the other doctors... Kaylan and the guards... being subjected to all the continuous testing and being locked up with no way of contacting anyone... no hope of getting back home... never seeing my friends again...

I can't believe it. It's like my dreams all went up in smoke and I have to try to get back to where I was, where I was normal and not an alien and I know that it's impossible.

I stumbled along through the underbrush.

It's too late now. I am what I am. Why did I listen to Oliana and Kaliya? Why didn't I stay home? Why did I ever volunteer to study alien life forms on-location instead of back home where it was safe?

I looked down at myself in dismay and wished I could wake up from this nightmare to see Kaliya and Oliana again and be home and safe. Kaliya would know what to do and what to say to make everything alright. She always did. And I really *needed* her right now.

I remembered the time I was having trouble with a program I was writing and thought I'd fail one of my finals, but Kaliya was there to help me and get me through. She knew nothing about programming, but it was her unwavering support that enabled me to take a fresh look at it and find the solution.

That was what true friends did for each other. I knew I would've done the same for either of my friends. But now that part of my life was over. Those friendships were gone. Gone forever.

Why did they do this to me? I screamed in my mind. *Why me? What were the Varekai doing out here? Why did they attack? Now I can never go back home. Can never live like a normal person. Even if they give me a new identity and a 'touch up' to make me look more human, I would miss everybody. Even now I miss them so much...*

As I walked, I cried for the life I'd lost and the life Sifayah had lost. *She was going to marry Jarleth. Now she's dead and he won't know what happened to her and her family won't know and they'd be searching for her and wondering how and why she disappeared.*

I looked around me at the dense jungle. There were trees and vines and flowers and fungi dotted here and there on the trunks of trees. It got thicker as I walked and it got harder to keep going at a reasonable pace. There were more rocks and tree roots to step over and more shrubs to duck around and low-hanging branches to duck under. Then there were all the rustling noises as insects and small animals scurried out of my way. *What was I thinking? What am I doing here alone in the middle of this prehistoric world with nothing to guide me but the memories of an alien whose body I've involuntarily stolen and a piece of a map I've memorised? And I don't even know whether it's accurate!*

It was no use. There were no answers to my questions. I felt like I was drowning within my own mind, struggling to stay on the surface and failing miserably. All my bottled up emotions came pouring out of me like a dam that had broken under the weight of the water.

I covered my face with my hands, then sank to the ground sobbing, letting myself sink in the floodwaters in my mind. I'd been keeping my emotions under control, blocking everything out as much as I could so I could keep going — keep on enduring all the tests and the endless questions — telling myself it wasn't so bad, but I couldn't keep it at bay any longer. I let it all out. The sobs racked my body, and I felt completely helpless.

I would miss everyone and everything I'd ever known. I would miss being Zhenna Rhodarma.

I didn't even have an identity now. Sure they'd given me a stupid name that I didn't like, but I didn't know who I was anymore. I wasn't human. I didn't know if I even had a soul... Maybe I didn't have a soul to start with. Maybe the cloned humans on Earth didn't have souls after all the cloning and conditioning and genetic manipulation they'd put us all through. Maybe that was why I was the only successful lab rat. I could transfer to another body seamlessly because there was no soul being left behind... I didn't know what to do. I didn't know anything anymore... I felt like I'd lost everything...

⸺◈⸺

It was some time before I lifted my head again. My sobs had slowed, and finally stopped, and I had lain on the soft earth, almost asleep — feeling so exhausted after all that swimming, walking, and then from crying so much. There'd been the occasional creepy crawly making its way along my arm or leg, and I'd freaked out and flicked them off quickly without even looking at them. I didn't want to know what they were. I shuddered just thinking about them.

I felt the tickle of something crawling on my hand and quickly looked down. A large, furry spider was making its way across the back of my hand. I lifted my hand and shook it off like a crazy woman as my hearts felt like they were going to jump out of my chest. I leapt to my feet and moved away from the place I'd been laying. I didn't know where the spider had landed. I shuddered again.

It took me a few moments to recover. Looking around me through sore and puffy eyes, I guessed by the position of the shadows that it was about midday. I instinctively looked at my wrist to confirm the time, but found myself looking down at a bare arm. They couldn't even let me wear the smallest little thing like a watch. I'd asked for one, but was refused. Did they think I was going to somehow use it to escape? I almost laughed at the thought.

I would have to rely on the sun, like everyone else that lived in the jungle. Thinking about the path the sun would take across the sky reminded me that Althar's day was about six hours longer than Earth's, so a time piece of any sort would've been useless anyway unless it was programmed with the extra hours.

I started walking again, brushing off dirt and leaves as I went. I looked around. My surroundings looked different somehow, brighter — or maybe it was just that I was looking at them in a different light. Things didn't seem so grim now that I'd released all the tension inside me. The leaves on the trees even looked greener somchow. The flowers and the fungi that were spread out amongst the greenery seemed to cheer me up and brighten the day.

I thought more clearly now about my situation. I thought long and hard as I trudged through the increasingly dense underbrush. I felt I was no longer Zhenna Rhodarma, just as my body no longer belonged to Sifayah, but I was a mixture of the two — almost like conjoined twins. I was two people forced into the one body. I remembered reading somewhere that some identical twins were so close that their minds seemed to be linked. One would start a sentence and the other would finish it. Like one mind in two bodies.

Yes, I supposed I was kind of like that, but in reverse. There were two minds in the one body. Now that Sifayah and I were merged together as one, neither one of us was the same anymore. I needed a new identity, and a new name. It seemed a logical way to get things straight in my head and to be able to move forward with this situation I'd been struggling to deal with.

Starrick had given me a new identity, but at the time, in my head I was still Zhenna. Everything was different now. I wasn't the same person that had left Earth a few weeks ago, excited about a new job on the other side of the universe. The one dying for an adventure that would fill the hole in her chest from living such a mundane, sterile, boring existence.

I ducked under some low hanging vines, some as thick as my calf. The undergrowth was getting even thicker.

I'd wanted adventure, but I didn't want this. This wasn't thrilling and exciting. This was disturbing, and being in the jungle was dangerous. *Not* my idea of fun.

My mind went back to the idea of finding a new identity. I ran through names and their meanings in many different languages and said them out loud to myself as I went. None of them seemed to really appeal to me. There had to be something that sounded nice, but also had some sort of meaning that suited me. Finally, as I stepped over yet another fallen tree, one name jumped out at me — *Tamisan*. It meant *twin* in some ancient dialect I couldn't quite remember the name of, so I thought it fit me perfectly. It was close to a Hebrew name, *Tamasin*, which also meant *twin*, but I liked Tamisan better.

I repeated the name in my head, then out loud over and over as I edged my way around the roots of a humongous tree. I liked the sound of it and searched Sifayah's memory to see if it would be a word that would not seem too strange to the Waikari. It seemed to work just fine. I stopped walking.

Okay, it fits me perfectly. I'll have it! I nodded my head to no one, and started off again with a silly smile plastered on my face.

With that settled, my mind seemed clearer and my thoughts unclouded. It seemed that a heavy load had been lifted from my chest and I stood a little taller as I continued to walk. There was no way I would've believed that giving myself a new name would change so much inside of me, but somehow it had been something I'd needed. It helped a lot toward me working out who I was. It wasn't a miracle cure or anything, but I felt different. More comfortable with my new self.

Okay. Back to the task at hand. I tried to get my bearings. If I had my facts right, I needed to make my way to the river, follow it to the east, veer right at the first fork, left at the second and third fork and head northeast toward the start of the river. Once there, I only had a bit more jungle to tackle before I reached Station Jannali. Then I would have to find the hidden entrance. That would be the hardest bit. I was sure it would be well camouflaged.

I stopped again and looked around me. Looked up into the canopy high above. It was beautiful here. And the sounds — insects buzzing about and birds singing cheerfully.

No more taking orders. No more experiments or being locked up against my will. Now I'm free!

Now that I was away from the ever-watchful eyes that were trained on my every move at Maztec, there was something I'd been dying to do since I'd watched those HoloMovies; *lift* something with my mind.

I was determined to try it now. *Right now.* I didn't want to wait a moment longer.

I looked around me for something small to *move* and found a stone lying amongst the leaf litter, about ten centimetres in diameter.

"This will do nicely," I said with more confidence than I felt.

What if it didn't work? What if that part of Sifayah's Talent had not been preserved? There was only one way to find out.

I picked it up and placed it on the gnarled root of a huge tree. Standing back a few steps from it, I concentrated all my thoughts on it. Nothing. I took a huge breath. I needed to focus and concentrate harder. I looked at the stone. I needed to move it. I needed to visualise it moving in my mind. Still nothing.

I took another deep breath and let it out slowly. I needed to calm my mind. I imagined it moving up off the root and hovering in the air. Just as I was starting to lose my concentration because I thought it wasn't working, it moved! It almost fell off the root. *Whoa! That was amazing!*

I concentrated again. It lifted off the root slowly and I was so excited I dropped it on the ground. I tried again and this time, I made it float over to my open hand.

"I did it!" I exclaimed to no one. "I can do it! This is great!"

CHAPTER 18:

Something Quite Romantic About a Race of Mermaid-Like People

I opened my hand and *lifted* the rock up again. I made it go up and down, from side to side, and around in a big circle. Then I *threw* it away into the jungle. I started walking again and picked up other objects as I went. Sticks, stones, leaves and small branches that had fallen from the trees above. I even made a leaf follow me through the forest, as if it were a pet bird.

As I wandered along, I noticed I was feeling tired. Not just tired from all the walking through the dense foliage, but mentally tired.

What about heavy things? I wondered, after dropping the leaf. I searched for a suitable 'heavy' thing. Part of a fallen tree. That should be heavy enough. It was about five metres long and about one metre wide and had lost all of its branches. It would be very heavy, even if it was hollow inside.

I found a large rock that didn't seem to have anything crawling on it and sat down. I felt I couldn't do it while I was standing up, I was too exhausted.

"Piece of cake!" I shouted out telepathically, after lifting it up and putting it back down. I didn't realise I'd projected my thoughts outward.

In a sudden rush, I felt light-headed, but my body felt really heavy. *What?*

I almost fell off the rock. I steadied myself and took some deep breaths. What was wrong? Why was I feeling like this? The answer came to me. I'd been sapping all my strength by using my Talent so much, then, to top it off, I'd lifted the log. I made a mental note to be more careful — not use my Talent just because I could. I gave myself a mental rap over the knuckles. Here in the jungle, I may need to use my Talent to defend myself against some wild animal, but if I didn't have any strength left... I didn't want to think about what could happen.

After a short rest, I set off again. I still felt exhausted, but could not afford to rest for too long. I still had a long way to travel. It was a lot further on foot than it had seemed on the maps. Even though they were 3D, they could never give you an accurate idea of real distances. I was determined to press on.

I will *make it,* I told myself.

As I weaved my way through the jungle, I was amazed by the plants and animals I saw. The problems that had seemed so overwhelming and devastating were now forgotten. The plants were similar to the ones I saw when we first touched down in the jungle, but the animals and birds that were now everywhere to be seen, were quite unusual. There was such a wide variety of different forms. I pushed thoughts of our landing out of my mind. They were *not* helpful.

The neighbouring planets, whose people had been conducting experiments on different life forms here on Althar, had probably changed some of the creatures I was now admiring. I wondered which ones had been tampered with. Some of the mammals appeared to be similar to those found on various planets in the Zoltrix System, but the reptiles looked positively

Prehistoric Earth in origin — especially the type of flying reptile that had flown over our campsite... I pushed those thoughts away.

Of course, there was always the chance that these creatures naturally evolved on Althar, but because it was extremely rare to find amphibious creatures that were so human-like, I thought the Waikari were most likely engineered by scientists, although I hoped I was wrong. There seemed to be something quite romantic about a race of mermaid-like people. And the thought that they'd possibly evolved naturally made it even more so.

Of the many colourful birds I saw, some were similar to Terran parrots, but others were very unusual, with long flowing tail feathers and long, thin beaks. There were other small flying creatures that were definitely reptilian rather than avian that swooped down from the tallest trees to grasp their prey with sharp talons. It made me shudder to watch as they flew off with the poor little mammal struggling to get free, even as the talons dug deeper into its flesh.

I stepped on a sharp stick and started to wish I'd included shoes in my plan. The jungle floor had already been very rough on my bare feet, and now I had a small cut on my foot to make things worse. Looking down at my bleeding foot, I noticed there was less leaf litter and sticks where I stood. Once I looked ahead, I could make out a sort of path through the trees. If I followed the path, walking would be easier and I would be able to travel faster. I checked the position of the sun. The path was heading in the right direction, right to the river, so I picked up the pace.

I'll be there in no time! I thought.

As I walked, I remembered reading that animals would travel the same routes through the forests and jungles on Earth, so it stood to reason that this path had been made by animals. I started wondering what kind of creatures had worn a path as wide as this one through the jungle. They would have to be big, and would probably use it regularly to get to the river to drink.

What if I run into one of them now? I thought.

I didn't have to wonder about it for long. I heard a cracking noise up ahead. Ducking behind a tree saved me from being the next meal of a large two-legged reptile that stalked its way noisily along the track. After it passed, I dared to peek through the branches of the tree to get a better look. Its scaly hide was an earthy green that faded to a greenish-yellow on its underbelly. Its appearance resembled the Allosaurus from Earth's distant past. I marvelled at this wondrous, though dangerous creature and was awestruck at being so close. It must have been at least two-and-a-half metres tall. Similar reptiles had been extinct on Earth for millions of years and here I was watching one strolling past less than a few metres from me!

CHAPTER 19:

Should I Eat It?

I realized I'd been holding my breath and let it out slowly. I hoped I wasn't upwind from it, although there was never much of a breeze in the jungle. I waited until I could no longer hear its footsteps before I dared to move through the jungle again. I made sure I moved away from the path as quickly as I could. I wanted to put as much distance between me and the giant flesh-eating lizard as possible.

Judging by the amount of noise it was making, I figured it wasn't hunting for food, but still, alerting it to my presence would've been a very bad idea. I also figured that keeping off any paths, no matter how much easier they were to walk on, would be a wise move.

After my close call with the Allosaurus look-alike, I travelled for nearly an hour through the tangled undergrowth and fallen trees before I could hear flowing water amongst the other jungle sounds. I breathed a huge sigh of relief. It was just as the map had shown. I'd have to check how far I was from the fork in the river once I was in the water, but I was sure it would only be a little further downstream from here. All I needed to do was follow the flow of the water until I reached the fork, then swim upstream to the right from there.

I followed the noise, exhausted now, pushing my way through the dense scrub toward the sound. The undergrowth became thicker as I neared the river.

My body was screaming at me to stop and rest, but I pushed on. I had to get to the river. It wasn't until I'd heard the rushing water that I realized how thirsty I was. My hunger began to make its presence felt too. I'd been concentrating on walking — determined to reach the river by nightfall — and hadn't noticed that my mouth was very dry and my stomach was very empty.

My skin needed some real moisture too, although it was coping fairly well with the high humidity. I was thankful for the humid climate, though I knew full well how awful, sweaty and sticky I'd felt a few weeks before after I'd been in the jungle only a short time. I'd ended up lying in the dirt that time too. I was beginning to make a habit of it.

Thinking about the last time I was in the jungle made me shudder. But I'd told myself I wasn't going to think about that now. I couldn't break down again. I had a job to do. I needed to keep going.

I could feel the dirt all over my body and it was working its way under my wetsuit in various places, which was becoming very gritty and itchy, so I was looking forward to diving right into the cool, refreshing water to wash it off.

The ground was starting to slope downhill toward the river's edge. I could almost taste the water. As I stumbled along over some thick vines and shrubs and over a fallen branch, I looked up to see a small tree that had pear-shaped fruit and large pink flowers on it. I stopped, breathing hard from all the walking, ducking and climbing. Were they edible? Searching Sifayah's memory was useless; she'd never travelled into the jungle any great distance before and had never seen this type of fruit.

My stomach grumbled some more, which made me seriously consider eating the strange fruit that could possibly be poisonous — something I would never have even dreamed of doing in the past, but I hadn't eaten since breakfast and had been expending a huge amount of energy for the last few hours. Using my Talent had drained my energy a lot more than any physical activity. I had to consider that I might not make it to Jannali if I didn't eat something.

Now I had to decide whether to eat the fruit or try to somehow find something that Sifayah knew was edible. I doubted that I would be able to find anything this far from the sea. My hunger pains made it unbearable to contemplate leaving the fruit uneaten and finding another source of food, so I reached for one of the nearest pieces. The plant gave up its produce easily and I hoped that that, and the fact it was soft to the touch meant that it was ripe. It smelled a lot like an apricot. Should I eat it? Should I risk being sick or even dying? My mouth watered.

What was I doing? What was I thinking? This was stupid! I should just go without — get to the river to drink. The water should be fresh this far from the ocean. My new body could tolerate drinking seawater anyway, I just 'remembered.'

Yes, go and get a drink.

My stomach growled.

I knew it wouldn't be enough. Maybe I could have one small bite and wait to see what happened. My stomach seemed to tie itself into a huge knot. The smell was driving me crazy. I *had* to try it.

Putting it to my lips, I chanced a small bite. It tasted like a nectarine. It was so sweet! The juice ran down my chin. Maybe it tasted so sweet because I was so hungry, but I was sure that wasn't the reason.

Now wait! I ordered myself.

I waited — *very* impatiently — for a few minutes to see if there were any ill effects before taking a second bite. My mouth watered the whole time as I paced up and down. My poor stomach and taste buds cried out for more while I waited. It was really hard to resist the temptation to scoff the whole thing as quickly as possible.

Okay, so no pain. No nausea. I should try to eat the rest of the fruit.

I managed to eat three of the fruits slowly without any problems and decided to continue my way to the river for a much-needed drink. To do this I had to edge my way between the tree and the overgrown shrub next to it, as the sound of running water was coming from somewhere beyond it. Grabbing four more of the delicious fruits for later, I stepped sideways to move between all the intertwined branches from both plants and came across a large flower on one of the branches that hung down level with my face. It was a beautiful shade of pink and the bulb from which the petals emerged was about the size of my fist.

The flower exuded a sweet fragrance similar to the flavour of the fruit and as I leaned closer to inhale the scent, the bulb popped, making a loud noise and spraying particles of pollen straight in my face and into my eyes.

CHAPTER 20:

Make it Stop!

I quickly turned away; exhaling and closing my eyes tightly until they began to water. Then I started to blink rapidly to try to wash the pollen out. My eyes started to burn. I didn't have anything to wipe my face with, so I had to somehow get to the river to wash it off completely.

I could feel some of it in my mouth and in the back of my throat and I coughed to try to clear it out.

This must have been the plant's defence mechanism against hungry herbivores, and it turned out to be much more effective than I first thought. It didn't just hurt my eyes, I started to feel disoriented. I turned frantically toward the sound of the water and started to walk slowly in that direction, with my hands stretched out in front of me. I was still blinking and found it increasingly difficult to keep my eyes open.

Branches scratched my arm and I staggered, not knowing if I was headed in the right direction or even if I still held the fruit I'd picked. I realized I was kind of numb all over. The trees around me swam before my eyes and I found it extremely difficult to stay on my feet. The realization that I was in real trouble hit me. I *needed* to get to the water.

My surroundings became unreal and the ground began to sprout large green vines that swirled up toward my face. I moved my head back out of the way as they grew past me and reached up to the canopy.

I kept watching as they grew out of sight, trying to reach the sun, but the action of putting my head back caused my head to start spinning wildly.

The whole world seemed to spin and I lost control. I couldn't feel any part of my body at all. There was no way for me to tell if I was still standing or if I'd fallen to the ground. I looked down at my hands and poked my left hand with the fingers of my right hand. I felt nothing. That was weird. Then my fingers started to grow and turned into long vines that intertwined around each other. I screamed. What was happening to me?

I heard a roar. I looked up. The jungle was distorted... A huge reptile burst through... It looked like the one I'd seen on the track... the track... why was I on the track? I couldn't think... It came at me and snapped its jaws at me... I screamed... tried to get away...

Nooooo!

I squeezed my eyes shut, but there was nothing. Did it bite me? I couldn't feel anything. I opened my eyes. It was gone... but when I looked again, there was a spider... a really *big* spider... bigger than my hand... crawling down a branch... toward my face... I cringed... I couldn't move away... It came closer and closer and I looked down... more of them... more spiders... all over me... *I can't... I can't move... can't escape...* couldn't flick them off... could only stare in horror... The big one reached my face... it was on my face... I screamed as it sank its fangs into my cheek...

The pain was so intense, my flesh was burning... then it faded... I opened my eyes... the spiders were gone... I felt something on my leg... weird because my legs were numb... I looked dow n... a snake slithered across my right leg... I screamed and it... it slithered all over me and up to my face... opened its mouth... big fangs... really big fangs... came at me... at my face... I opened my mouth and nothing came out... All I could do was squeeze my eyes shut...

Then nothing. Again. Just like with the reptile.

My head felt a little bit clearer. The pain from the spider bite was gone. The spiders and the snake were gone. That must have meant they weren't real. I hoped they weren't. My mind screamed at me that it wasn't real. It couldn't be... *Make it stop! Make it stop!*

But then I seemed to slip away... my brain was fuzzy and I couldn't focus...

When it focused, I could see Dr Starrick... He was holding long, shiny, sharp-looking instruments... dressed in scrubs... I was lying down... strapped down... No... It wasn't real... He came closer... I struggled... couldn't move... I needed to get away... run away... I screamed... I yelled at him... Closer... the straps too tight... closer...

"Nooo!"

He didn't stop... kept coming... A pair of shimmering scissors appeared in his hand... He reached down and cut off a large chunk of my hair... He held it in his hand and laughed hyste rically...

"No!" I had broadcasted that thought — not even aware I'd done it.

I imagined what my hair would look like after he'd hacked it off... How bad it would look... It was hard to look at the hair in his hands and not be upset... I tried to get away, but my body wouldn't obey me... Oh... I was strapped down anyway... Next, I saw a scalpel coming closer... I opened my mouth to scream again... no sound came out... As he started cutting into my chest, his form melted away and disappeared... The pain of him cutting me was searing through my body, spreading like ink being poured into water. It was unbearable. I was spinning... falling...

I couldn't stop myself... I screamed out again and again... The pain was all I could feel, all I could think about... I didn't know how long I just lay there like that, trying to breathe and cope with the agony...

Then it faded away to nothing...

I opened my eyes to see Kaliya... I was home... Oliana? Where was she? I was home... I looked around... could see my class mates... they were smiling... I tried to smile... I needed to find Oliana... I looked... I found her... she turned around to look at me, but didn't smile... She was... scared of me... Why would she...? I looked down at myself... only, it wasn't me... it was some hideous, scaly creature with fins and claws...

No! I'm home! I'm... I'm free!

They laughed... all of them... Their words crushed me.. . "You'll never fit in... You're not Zhenna Rhodarma anymore!"

They dissolved away into nothingness... but then... I looke d... I tried to focus... I couldn't see anything... there was the ju ngle... all the green leaves all over... then a hideous face looming over me... more than one hideous face...

They looked like some kind of half-men, half-ape hybrid... and they were ugly... I'd never seen a race of aliens like them... they kept looking at me and I could see teeth... sharp teeth... close... too close... There were three... or maybe four... all look ing... staring and... laughing. They were laughing... at me...

When they spoke, I couldn't understand, but I was sure somehow that they were laughing because I was stupid enough to go too close to that flower... I didn't know how I knew that, but I did...

They were starting to blur in front of my eyes... I waited for them to disappear... They didn't... I focused again and they were further away... like they were standing up and I was lying on the ground... I looked up at them... so far above me...

They were amused. One of them reached down and grabbed me by the arms, dragging me forcefully to my feet... It should have hurt... I felt nothing... They couldn't be real... If it was real, my arms would be sore... He held me in place, his grip tight... He was the only thing keeping me from falling to the ground... They weren't real...

What did he want from me?

CHAPTER 21:
Battling Hard for Control

I tried to turn my head to look at them... My head was still kind of spinning... everything was one big blur... everything around me was swaying... If only it would stop swaying so I could get my balance...

They looked me up and down, and turned me around, supporting me because I couldn't stand on my own... My head kept spinning long after my body had stopped turning... Why wouldn't everything just stop moving?

"Sabah emalla," the one that had picked me up muttered under his breath.

"Sabah emalla?" another bellowed, "Ma lakka en dana fort Turak!"

I tried to look into his mind to work out what they were saying, but couldn't focus... 'Turak' was all I got. It popped into my mind, but I couldn't read anything. An image of a person. I was sure that Turak was a person... He looked human, unlike these Beast People. But something about him was wild and barbaric.

"Ta aymar pa rattar," was the reply and I got the impression he agreed with the other.

I tried to focus on his mind again... Nothing. They kept talking to each other, but still I got nothing. The rest of what was said was a blur — a mess of incoherent babble to my ears. My brain was too fuzzy. I'd only had a flash when they'd said the word Turak.

This hallucination was different... It didn't fit. All the others had involved someone I knew or something I'd seen. My imagination was really running away with me now... Maybe I saw this stuff in a HoloMovie once. I couldn't remember anything like those Beast-men though.

I decided to wait till it faded away. Maybe it was in my head longer because the pollen was starting to wear off... hopefully... Maybe as the poison wore off, the visions slowed down.

I was led stumbling to a group of people swirling amongst the green of the bushes in which they were sitting. At least I *thought* they were sitting down. As I was pushed to the ground, the trees and faces before me spun out of control until they were replaced by blackness.

———◦———

Regaining consciousness didn't bring me any relief. I opened my eyes to find the leaves above me were growing longer and as I watched, they transformed into slithering green snakes that reached down toward my face... I screamed and tried to roll out of their path, with no success, and heard laughter to my left. I managed to look in that direction and saw the ugly men that I'd seen before. I wondered if they were real. I couldn't be sure. They were still there...

No... Nothing was real.

To my right I could make out the shapes of people. I tried to look at them properly, but could only move my eyes in their general direction. Maybe it was the group of people I saw before I'd passed out, but I really didn't have any idea.

My mind was reeling, trying to gain some sort of control. My hearts were pounding and my breathing shallow. I had to try to calm down, but my mind was waiting for the next horror to jump at my face or crawl all over me.

I looked back to the ugly Beast-men again. It was easier to see them. Maybe because my head was tilted to the left a little. I wasn't sure what position I was lying in. I was still numb all over. I could see the Beast-men more clearly now. They had long canines protruding from their mouths and they were very hairy — almost furry. They didn't stand erect like men either, they hunched forward — it reminded me of HoloMovies that I'd seen on Prehistoric Man. Maybe that was where I'd conjured them up from. The spotted hides they wore completed the picture, along with the primitive weapons — daggers and swords that hung somehow at their waists. I couldn't make out how they were attached.

I tried, but couldn't reach their minds. My Talent kept failing me. And because these visions were lasting so much longer than the others, I was starting to think that maybe I wouldn't be able to see reality again. Shouldn't the poison have worn off after I passed out? Wouldn't I simply sleep it off or something? I guessed not. Maybe the poison was so strong that the victim never recovered. I worried that maybe I'd hallucinate till I died from the effects of it. Or until a hungry predator found me...

My mind was really battling hard for control, and it seemed that I was losing. I thought I was still lying on the ground, but nothing felt right. Nothing seemed real. I couldn't feel any sensations in any part of my body at all. It was still fuzzy. And all

I could really see besides the ugly Beast-men was a blur of green from the surrounding trees and plants.

After more visions of impossible things flashed in front of my eyes and after lying there for a while longer, I realized I was facing the other direction, looking at the people that were sitting huddled together, with no recollection of how I'd rolled over. I'd been there for quite some time, I was sure, but I didn't know how long. It could have been hours. If these Beast-men were really here — and I was starting to think that they were — they also seemed to be holding the other people here against their will. That much I could make out in the haze of my semi-conscious state. I couldn't really see it, I just knew it.

I strained to see my fellow captives more clearly — if that's what they were — but couldn't focus my eyes well enough to calculate how many figures sat in the little group before me.

Suddenly, more strange creatures appeared in front of my eyes. It was so unexpected. I'd been concentrating on counting the people and trying to focus to see them clearly. Now everything was way out of control again. It was kind of like a roller coaster. It seemed to fade in and out. One minute I was in a haze, but everything was calm, the next, all hell broke loose and my mind could focus on nothing else. All I could do was endure it again until things calmed down once more and I was able to think more clearly.

The only problem was, when things were calm, I kept seeing the Beast-men and the group of people near me. So, logic would suggest they were real. I felt a sinking feeling in the pit of my stomach. If they were real, then I was in trouble. If the other people were really captives, then so was I.

CHAPTER 22:
That Huge Knife

I wondered what sort of people would capture *people*. Then of course, I had to remind myself that these creatures were not people. Still, what did they want with me? There were all sorts of terrible possibilities floating around in my mind. Slavery was one of the main ones. Was I now a slave? I shuddered and pushed the thought out of my mind. Not because I was dismissing it as a possibility, but because it *was* a possibility and I didn't even want to think about it right now.

＊◦＊

After a long while, in one of my saner moments when I could look over to where my captors sat, I could make out that they were sitting on the root of a large tree eating some kind of meat. How had I rolled over again? I must've been thrashing around when I was hallucinating. That would explain how I'd been rolling over and not knowing that I was doing it.

I noticed that my body wasn't as numb as it had been. I hoped the poison was wearing off. I didn't know how much longer I could take the horrors that had been running through my mind.

As I stared, one of the beasts stood suddenly and strode out of my line of sight. The other two simply returned to their meal. Time was very hard for me to judge, but I was sure the first Beast-man hadn't been gone for very long before the other Beast-men got to their feet and approached me. Maybe the poison *was* wearing off. The image of their hideous bodies was only slightly distorted now. I cringed at how ugly they really were.

I saw the insolent smirks on their grotesque faces, but they were still hazy. They were snickering and talking in low whispers and to my horror, one of them drew his dagger.

I stared at it, unable to move. There was a sinking feeling in my chest, but not much else. The poison was still smothering my senses. I assumed the adrenalin was pumping through my veins, but I couldn't feel its effects.

He waved the dagger in front of me and I guessed the blade was about twenty centimetres long, but I couldn't really focus on it. This amused them. One of them stooped over to look down at me and the other one with the dagger knelt by my side and pushed me over onto my back. I tried to move away, but my body wouldn't obey me. I felt like screaming at my useless limbs, but knew it was hopeless. The only movement I could manage was to flail my arms weakly. More laughter. Panic wrapped its hands around my throat and I found it hard to breathe. My jaw worked helplessly, but no sound came out. Both hearts pounded in my ears.

The one with the knife seemed interested in my clothing; obviously it was something he'd never seen before. They both leaned forward to take a closer look. I was reminded of when the Varekai had found me at the Outrider's campsite, which filled my mind with renewed terror. There were no laser rifles here, but just the thought of it... and the thought of what they might do to me... and that huge knife...

I wondered if they were going to kill me. They seemed to be just drooling over me instead. Maybe they had other plans. I kept thinking about what those plans might be and tried to drag my thoughts away each time.

Don't think about that! I screamed to myself. *Think about walking on the beach... Oliana when she fell off her chair... or when she coloured her hair and it had gone wrong and turned it purple...*

It wasn't working. It was impossible to keep calm. There was nothing I could tell myself that would distract me from this. There were only a million questions. What did they want? Why? What were they going to do with me? Where were they going to take me? What work would they make me do as a slave? What *other things* would they make me do? The possibilities made me cringe inside and filled me with a terrible dread. I *had* to escape — but couldn't even *move!*

The beast with the dagger moved closer to my face and held the blade to my throat. I couldn't feel if it was touching my skin, and with the state I was in, he could have been cutting my throat from ear to ear and I wouldn't have known it.

Is this it? Am I going to die here? Right now? Did he cut me? Am I bleeding to death right now? There would be nothing I could do about it. I would fade away as the blood drained from my body...

I noticed something was definitely wrong with the left side of his face. When I concentrated, I saw he had a large scar that went from his brow to halfway down his cheek, going right across his eye. The eye itself was missing, and the socket was left distorted and ugly.

You sure are ugly... so ugly... I wish I was hallucinating. I wish you'd go away. Go away and leave me alone... I... uh... I... I...

My mind started to float away and I had to force myself to concentrate hard so I could focus on what he was doing. Now was *not* a good time to drift off into Nightmare Land again. I needed my wits about me. But was that even possible?

Yes... Focus... I willed myself to do it.

He put a gnarled finger to his ape-like lips as if to tell me to be quiet, knowing full well I wasn't in control of my body, and then laughed loudly. With fingers that looked like old leather, he gave my body such a vulgar caress it made me feel sick to my stomach.

How could I feel that? I'd been numb for so long, and I thought I was still mostly numb. Then suddenly, when someone touched me, I could feel it. I wished I was still numb. It would have been better if I *didn't* feel that.

I watched the dagger move slowly down to my chest and he pulled the front of my wetsuit out and away from my skin with his free hand. He hacked into the top at the collar and started sawing the material, cutting the wetsuit down the middle, next to the zipper. He sliced through the tough material carefully until he'd reached my belt. If only he'd known how much easier it would've been if he'd unzipped it.

He started to attack the belt and panic sliced through me. I kept thinking that at any moment he could slip and cut me. What could I do but lay there and watch and hope he only cut the material? In my mind I was screaming to get away. Every part of me wanted to run, but although I was starting to feel parts of my body again, and could feel nausea rising in my stomach, I still couldn't move.

No amount of effort from him would sever my belt, so he by-passed it and continued down to my crotch. I held my breath. I felt as if each heart would beat a hole through my chest. It was like they were trying to get out and run.

No no no no no!!! my mind was screaming.

CHAPTER 23:

Are You a Kinetic?

At that point, I no longer wanted to move. I didn't want that blade to touch my skin. As I was wondering what he was going to do next, he changed the angle of the blade and cut down the length of the left leg of my wetsuit.

No! Stop! No! You can't do this! Somebody help me! I wanted to scream and kick and punch and scream some more. But I couldn't. And as he cut the last of the material, the knife nicked my thigh.

I sucked in a lungful of air as I winced at the pain, glad that it was dulled by the poison in my body. I held my breath for maybe twenty seconds, and then I remembered to breathe again. The other Beast-man yelled at him, and he protested loudly, but then he turned back to me, grinning broadly. I managed to scream — if you could call it that — a pathetic little sound, but this only served as further amusement and they laughed even louder than before.

No!!!

This couldn't be a hallucination. This had to be real. The pain was real. *They* were real. I tried to scream again and nothing came out. Panic gripped me even tighter and adrenalin raced through me. I looked at that enormous knife, dripping with blood — *my* blood — and without really thinking about it or realising what I was doing, I squeezed my eyes shut tightly and let out a mental scream, as loud as I could...

"Whoah! What was — Who is that?"

My eyes flew open. I couldn't believe it — somebody *heard* me! And they answered me!

"What?... Wh-where are... you?" I stumbled. It was hard to form any coherent thoughts.

"I am in Sector 7 on Althar 3. Where are you? You practically deafened me — and every other Talent here!" The Mind-touch I felt was definitely male.

"I — I don't... know... know... on Althar... jungle..." I stumbled again. I took a deep breath and pushed the thoughts out slowly. *"Can... you... help... me?"*

The Beast-man with the scar was still there, with a puzzled look on his face. It was as if he'd heard me too. Was that even possible?

I was shocked that anyone had heard me at all. I wasn't expecting to reach anyone — it was just an instinctive reaction to scream out somehow when I couldn't manage to do it verbally.

"Yes, of course. I can try. What is wrong?" he asked.

I had to make a conscious effort to get every word out as the poison was clouding my thoughts and making it very difficult to send them to him. It was like trying to run in a dream — the more you try, the harder it is to get to where you're going.

"Some flower... bulb... pop-popped in my..." I took a breath to give my brain a chance to get the rest of the words out, then continued, *"In my... face... I... I can't... think..."* Another long pause. *"Lots of-of... weird... stuff... seeing... weird... stuff... and I ... I... I c-can't... s-top them..."*

His voice sounded alarmed at this. *"You* what? *Cannot stop them from what? Who are* they?"

"The... ugly... men... beasts... ugly... caught m-m-me... and I think... they... are r... re... real. N-now... they... cut... my... wet... wet... suit... and... and..." I couldn't finish.

"Oh, by the— What are— you need to—" He stopped to gather his thoughts. *"Are you a Kinetic?"*

"A what?"

"A Kinetic — can you move things telepathically?"

"Uh. Yes... I— yes... I did... it... and got... tired... tired..." I answered slowly, and then muttered some incoherent babble. My mind was struggling to keep focused so I could hold at least an understandable conversation and it seemed that it was starting to lose the battle again. The floating sensation was creeping in again. My eyes were still open, but I was looking inward and saw nothing. And I could no longer hear the Beast-men.

There was a period of time where I kind of floated. They were somewhere above me, and I didn't know if they were still touching my body or if they were cutting me again...

No! Can't... gotta focus...

Terror started pushing its way into my mind. That brought me back to reality. What if they *were* cutting me? Then I realized the man's voice was calling me over and over, panic in his tone.

"Huh?" was all I could manage.

"Are you okay?" he asked, *"You were not answering and you had me worried."*

"Yeah... I... think... so. I don't know... what they are... doing... don't... know... if they're... cutting... me... again..."

"They cut *you? How badly? Are you okay? Try to see them. You need to see them. Try to focus,"* he urged.

CHAPTER 24:
Now, Run!

I had the feeling of stepping off a moving walkway onto solid ground. Something made me more alert. I looked around. The Beast-man had dropped the knife only inches from my head! Right next to my right ear. It was sticking out of the ground and if it fell, it would hit my right shoulder, slicing into my wetsuit. Maybe slicing through it into my flesh. I resisted the urge to roll away from it because I knew I didn't have any real control, so I'd probably end up with the knife cutting my throat or something instead.

The beasts themselves were standing at my feet, yelling at each other.

"Yes," I struggled to say. *"They are yelling."*

I'd managed a sentence without pausing between words. A *three-word* sentence, but that was a good start.

"At each other." I added.

"Okay. While they are busy, we can do this together," he continued. *"Now you have to trust me. I am going to try a Mind-link."*

"What?"

"A Mind-link."

"Huh?" Things were getting crazy again and I was really struggling now to even understand what the guy was saying. I

started to panic again. Just when I thought I was maybe over the worst of it...

"Are you okay? Can you hear me?" he asked. I could sense his concern for me, even through the haze, with a mixture of frustration thrown in. *"Stay with me now. Take a few deep breaths."*

I tried... It wasn't working... More panic...

He sent warm feelings to me and it seemed to have a calming effect. It seemed to steady me, like an anchor in the deepest ocean in the middle of a storm. I desperately needed it as my mind was drifting away, threatening to sweep into more hallucinations. Then I'd be lost...

"Focus," he urged. *"Focus on my voice... You need to concentrate. Do not give up... That is good! I can sense your thoughts clearing... Can you speak?"*

"Yes," I managed.

He spoke slowly. *"Good. Now listen carefully. I want to try a Mind-link. Open your mind to me so we can link our minds and merge our Talent. Together we will be stronger. Then I can help you rid yourself of the poison. We can speed up the body's natural process of fighting the hallucinogen."*

A Mind-link? How could I link my mind with his? I didn't even *know* him and I was going to link minds? I knew how close he would be in my mind... how personal a Mind-link was. What if he could take control? What if he was lying? What if he wasn't going to help me at all?

"It is okay," he reassured me. *"I will not harm you. I want to help. It is the only way for you to get the poison out quickly. Then you might be able to defend yourself. You need to trust me."*

How could I trust him? How could I not? What choice did I have, really? It was either a Mind-link with this man I didn't know, or stay dazed and chance whatever the beasts had in mind for me. That made my decision for me.

"Okay," I told him.

"Good." And I could hear the relief in his voice. *"Let us begin."*

I closed my eyes and opened my mind the way Sifayah had been taught and felt his mind link with mine. The feeling of being surrounded by a safe, warm blanket engulfed me. I was safe. I felt like I was going to cry with relief.

Sifayah had done this many times before with Tasha, but this was new to me and it felt strange allowing someone so close, intruding on my thoughts. But this man was here to help me, not to invade my privacy, so I pushed those thoughts from my mind. I felt myself relax a little bit, although I still felt so exposed and vulnerable.

The Beast-men were still arguing somewhere above me, but their voices faded and I became oblivious to it all. I hoped that that wasn't a huge mistake.

"Now, what you need to do is start with your head, then your arms and legs and pull the toxin from them and in toward your body — avoiding your heart," he urged gently. *"Good. You need to pull it so that it gathers into your stomach."*

With his help, I could sense the poison within my body. I could feel the poison moving, could feel his presence there, pushing and guiding me. Slowly, the floating feeling started to recede. I felt panicked thinking about the poison flowing to my stomach. *What will it do to me? Will it make me feel sick? What do I do with it once it's there?*

He answered my thoughts without hesitation. *"You will feel sick once it is in your stomach. You will need to push all of the poison there, and then expel it from your body."*

My stomach roiled at the thought, and I could already feel the vile toxin gathering and causing the nausea, but I had to do this. I kept pushing, with his help, until all of the poison had reached my stomach and I was feeling really sick. I couldn't hold it in any longer. Oh... I hated being sick...

"Okay," he told me, *"make sure you bring it all up."*

I rolled to my left, away from the blade, and hurled the poison onto the jungle floor. I kept vomiting until I could feel that there was nothing left in my stomach.

My head felt clearer and I suddenly had control of myself again. The numbness in my body and the cloudiness in my mind dispersed. Now that it was completely gone, my sanity returned and I felt alive again!

I felt relief flooding over me, but not all of it was mine. Some of it came from my rescuer. Then for one fleeting moment, I looked deep into his mind and read his innermost thoughts. I *knew* him, knew his name. I felt so much emotion overwhelming me, then he dropped the Mind-link and I felt strange, kind of empty, like a child that had been robbed of a sweet lolly.

I sat up slowly and wiped my mouth with the back of my hand. The Beast-men were standing above me, probably wondering why I was throwing up everywhere. I looked up at them. They were no longer arguing. One of them reached down and grabbed my arms and I could feel that my left breast was completely uncovered. My adrenalin spiked and my face flushed, but the voice in my head told me to focus. The stranger's Mind-touch was still with me, and he told me to push with all the Talent I could muster — push them away from me so I could escape.

I sat forward as I pushed, my arms coming up in front of me, and saw the Beast-men stumble backwards suddenly. One of them even fell over.

Did I really do that? I wondered. Then I heard someone yelling behind them — it was the third Beast-man back again, and he was angry. The one that had fallen quickly got to his feet.

I dragged myself up to a standing position, hearts pounding and stomach still feeling queasy. I needed to do something. Now.

"Yes, you did!" My rescuer sounded excited and proud. I was still trying to process everything. *"Now, run!"*

CHAPTER 25:

Darion

The third Beast-man took one look at me with my ruined wetsuit and the cut on my thigh. He stalked over to where the others were standing and proceeded to beat them both about the head with his fist as he continued his bellowing. They cringed and raised their arms in an attempt to ward off his attack.

I was dazed for a moment, but then I held my left arm across the front of my clothing and, looking about me wildly, I saw the other captives as they huddled together in the underbrush. I was seeing them clearly for the first time, and was surprised to find that they were in chains. There were four males and two females in the group.

Of course they're in chains! They wouldn't stay here with these beasts if they could get away.

I turned from them and decided to make a dash for the river. I could hear it clearly now.

As I started to walk, I stumbled a few times. I hadn't quite recovered fully yet. Going without food and water for a long time wouldn't have helped any either. I made my way past the captives and tried to pick up some speed. My leg muscles were jelly and made it hard to step over the tree roots and rocks on the jungle floor.

"Keep going!" my rescuer urged, but with my next step, my foot caught on a gnarled tree root and I fell. I just had enough sense to put my hands out in front of me and avoided face-planting the leaf litter. As I was about to push myself up from the ground, a large, hairy spider, bigger than my hand, ran toward my right arm with its front legs up in the air. As I jumped in fright, a knife landed right in the middle of the spider's thorax and killed it instantly. I quickly regained my senses and turned to see the scar-faced Beast-man standing over me.

I pushed myself away from the spider and up to a standing position, only to be grabbed firmly by the arm. My hearts leapt into my throat as I turned to look at him. Now that my vision was clear, he looked like something out of a nightmare with the scar and the missing eye. He took a step forward and retrieved his knife, wiping the tip on a tree root to dislodge the spider. I shuddered.

He'd saved me from being bitten, but stopped me from getting away. I winced at his firm grip and instinctively tried to pull away. It hurt even more and his nails — which were more like claws — dug into my flesh. He brought the knife up to my throat again as one of the others grabbed my other arm. He growled a warning to me and I didn't have to know the language to understand what would happen if I tried to fight against him. My hearts thundered in my chest. Caught again.

It was strange. Although my hearts sank at the thought of not being able to escape, I'd still been freed — freed from the horrific hallucinations, and so much of the panic I'd felt subsided. I could breathe easier. All my senses were alive, and I could hear the sounds of the jungle again. But I could also feel his nails digging into my arm and a throbbing pain in my thigh.

Then I remembered the Talent who'd helped me. I reached out with my mind and could still feel his presence.

"Do not worry. I am still here. You did a great job," he exclaimed with delight. *"The poison is gone."*

I was so relieved that he was still there; my emotions must have poured out to him like a river. Tears welled up in my eyes and flowed down my cheeks. Then a name suddenly popped into my head. *"Darion!"* I exclaimed. *"You're Darion!"*

"Yes," he answered with a smile in his voice. *"Darion Andiyar from the planet Moftar. But you had a peek and probably know that already. I am currently stationed on Althar 3 studying its people."*

My 'peek' didn't let me know where he was from. It had gone much deeper. I could see what kind of person he was, but not which planet he'd come from. It was strange. Like what I saw was selective.

I felt more relief thinking he was from the 'civilised' world. Maybe even Jannali. No — that would be too much to hope for. *"Which station?"* I asked eagerly.

"Station Jannali," he replied. So it *wasn't* too much to hope for. I relaxed a little more, even though I was still their prisoner.

Jannali. I was so relieved. I didn't want to speak to anyone from Maztec for fear of being handed over to Starrick. I couldn't bear the thought of being rescued by someone I thought was a kind stranger, but then I find out he's Starrick's second-in-command or something, who then took me back to Maztec. I pushed the thought from my mind.

Jannali was also the station I was headed for when everything had gone wrong and I'd gotten myself caught by these beasts.

I thought about the seemingly innocent flower. I'd never experienced hallucinations before, and I hoped never to do it again. They'd been so horrifying and felt so real that it was impossible not to react or feel the pain and all of the emotions they evoked.

I looked around me. Things were looking a little brighter, even though my captors still had me. The knife had been sheathed and they were walking me slowly back to the other captives. I was too busy talking to Darion to try to resist them — plus, the knife was still within their reach should I decide to be uncooperative.

"I'm Tamisan," I began, thankful that I would at last be able to speak in full coherent sentences. *"My name was Zhenna Rhodarma...but they changed me... transferred my mind... um m... it's kinda hard to explain..."* So much for coherent sentences...

"Maybe if you show *me what has happened to you. Do you know how to do that?"* he asked.

I wasn't sure what he meant at first, but Sifayah had been taught this before. I let him read my thoughts by recalling the key events leading up to the instant I'd cried out for help. Things were a lot clearer in my mind now, and as I showed him what had happened, I could feel his anger rising.

I was so focused on communicating with Darion that I was hardly aware of the Beast-men or what they were doing. I jumped when I realized they were in the process of putting shackles on my wrists, but there was nothing I could do to stop them anyway. I paid them a lot more attention when one of the shackles dug into my wrist, making me gasp in pain. I quickly focused my attention back to Darion. I didn't want to lose the connection we had. I wasn't sure if I could get it back.

I could tell using my Talent like this was making me feel exhausted. And my legs were still made of jelly. I desperately needed to sit down. But I didn't want to stop talking to Darion. I couldn't lose him. Not now. There was a long silence as Darion absorbed the information, and I experienced a tinge of panic, thinking that he'd left me.

CHAPTER 26:
As You Can See, They Lied

"I am still here," he said hastily, sensing my fears. *"I cannot believe they would do such a thing. This Dr Starrick has a lot to answer for. Station Maztec is a new installation, but he does not have any authorisation to perform such procedures — even if what he did to you was to save your life."* I caught a thought he'd failed to hide — the thought that he was glad they *had* saved me.

I could feel that Darion always had a mental shield up, the way the Waikari always did — the way Sifayah had been taught from an early age. He was probably well trained and I sensed that he had a lot of control over his mind, so I thought maybe he'd *meant* for me to see that. The more I thought about it, the more I was sure of it.

"Are you feeling okay?" he asked, and I could feel his genuine concern.

"Yes," I replied, *"I am* now. *I feel really tired, but I'm a lot better. I can't thank you enough!"* And I conveyed the feelings of gratitude and relief that were overwhelming me.

"Well, you are not out of the woods yet," he warned. *"They still have you, and until you are free and out of the jungle, you are not safe. And now that I know you are there, I will do everything in my power to find you. And I am not going to let anything happen to you, okay? You will be alright."*

His words were wrapped with feelings of reassurance and affection, which had an unexpected effect on me — like I felt an overwhelming love for him. I tried to hide my reaction, telling myself not to read things into his intentions. He was only trying to reassure me after what had happened. I hoped I'd been quick enough to cover what I'd felt. I wasn't very good at keeping a mental shield up yet. Sifayah was an expert, of course, but she was no longer in control. I would have to practice some more.

"We had received the report about the attack in the jungle," Darion told me. *"I will have to see if I can find out more about it, but we were told there were no survivors."*

I felt a pang in my chest. No survivors. I knew Starrick would've reported that we were all dead, but it was still hard to hear it. *"Yes, well, as you can see, they lied..."*

I felt bitter inside. How dare they? Friends and relatives of all of the passengers and the pilot would have been notified of our deaths and some of us were actually still alive. I was in a different body, but I was alive. And I hoped with everything in me that Mosuti was still alive after the procedure. And Larissa... And the others... I didn't know, but could only hope...

The pain in my left thigh started to really throb as if it was trying to get my attention. I looked down to see that the knife wound was oozing blood. I'd been so preoccupied talking to Darion that I'd forgotten about it. The blood had flowed round to the back of my leg when I was on the ground, and while I'd been standing, it had run right down the front and over my foot. I needed to do something to stop the bleeding and I wasn't strong when it came to the sight of blood — especially my own blood. I started to feel queasy just thinking about it.

I took some deep breaths through my nose. I didn't feel so good. Now if it was a little cut, I was fine. But there was so much blood. It was also on my other leg and on the ground where I'd been lying. My stomach churned. I closed my eyes and tried not to think about it. *Breathe...*

I tried to exert some pressure on the wound with my left hand, but it needed some sort of bandaging. The pain increased with each second. How deep was it? I needed to *not* think about that right now. The light-headedness was creeping up the back of my skull.

"Do not think about it so much," Darion told me. *"You are* not *going to faint! Keep looking away and keep both your hands there."* The chains made it hard to put both hands on the wound, and my wrists hurt, but I did as I was told. *"Now, take deep, slow breaths... In through the nose and out through the mouth..."*

I did as I was told. I felt very tired. Leaning forward while I felt like fainting was probably not the best idea, but I had no choice. There was a moment when I thought I would fall over. I swayed a little, but managed to stay upright.

Darion taught me how to exert mental pressure on the wound to stop the blood. He told me to imagine the sides of the wound knitting themselves back together. I told him Sifayah wasn't a healer, but he insisted that I didn't need to be. I just needed to put pressure there for a while. I tried it. I imagined the cut sealing itself closed and held it there for a few minutes. When I removed my hands, the bleeding had stopped. I was surprised and wished it was that easy to get rid of the pain. I thanked him again for his help.

I was led over to where the other captives sat and one of the two women offered me a strip of hide to wrap around my leg, unaware that the bleeding had already stopped. She looked to be about ten years older than me, with deep blue eyes and fiery red hair that cascaded over her shoulders. Her body was lithe and pale and although she was sitting, I guessed the native was probably taller than me.

I thanked her in Sifayah's native tongue as I took the hide from her, but it was obvious the woman wasn't familiar with the language. She could guess what I'd meant by my gesture and smile, and she smiled in return. At least there was *someone* native to this barbaric planet that was kind enough to help!

I sat down and looked away. I wasn't sure what I should do or if I should try to talk to the woman. It would be pointless with the language barrier so I decided to put what was left of my energy into talking to Darion. The Beast-men added a link to my chain and attached it to the chain that held the other captives and I was left to sit with them. It was so good to sit down. I tried to relax as I pressed the hide onto my leg. I couldn't see how I could tie it around my leg with my wrists in chains. After a while, the throbbing in my leg started to fade a little.

"I feel so exhausted — so drained," I sighed. The light-headed feeling had passed, but I felt cold in the face, like I did when my face was really white.

"Yes. You need plenty of rest now," Darion suggested. *"Take advantage of the time you have now and recover. You have used a lot of energy, both physical and mental, and a good rest will do you good."*

Even though I didn't really have to, I wanted to try to wrap the hide around my leg so I could keep the dirt out and keep the sides together. Besides, I didn't want them to know I'd stopped the bleeding by using kinetic energy. I draped one end over my thigh and tucked the other end under my leg. I shimmied around until I could pull it out from under the other side of my leg, pulled it up and tied it to the other end. It wasn't neat, but it would have to do.

I suddenly realized how thirsty I was. I was hungry too, but my mouth was so dry. I licked my lips and tried to find some saliva within my mouth to help to at least dampen it, without much luck. The worst thing was that the water was so close... I could hear it and smell it...

There was a long silence between Darion and I as I tried to relax and rest, but the Beast-men had other ideas. They gathered up the chains and pulled on them to make us get to our feet.

"Oh, no! They're making us get up!" I moaned. *"But I'm still so tired!"*

Chapter 27:
I Will Find You!

"Come on," Darion urged. *"You can do it. You* have *to."*

I forced myself to stand and we were pushed and shoved until we started walking in the direction our captors wanted us to go. My leg started to throb again and I groaned.

If I thought travelling through the jungle was hard before, it was ten times harder when chained to a group of six people. I couldn't help stumbling, and I kept bumping into the male captive in front of me.

He was quite handsome; tall and well-muscled with long brown hair and blue eyes. He turned to look down at me a few times, and I apologized as my face flushed with embarrassment and I tried to hold my wetsuit in place. He wouldn't have understood me, but I hoped the tone I used would be enough.

As we walked, I looked down at what was left of my wetsuit. The belt kind of kept it together at the waist, but there wasn't a great deal I could do to keep my left breast covered properly. I pulled the side of the wetsuit around me again. It was coming apart along my thigh, so I tried to pull it back again. I felt so humiliated by what the Beast-men had done and shuddered to think of what they could have done if Darion hadn't come to my rescue.

Darion interrupted sharply, *"Do not think about that now! It did not happen, and now that you have your wits about you, you will be better equipped to defend yourself against them. And I will be here to help you too."*

I felt a lot of comfort in that thought, and clung to it as I stumbled along. There was a short period of silence, then Darion called me.

"Tamisan, we need to conserve our strength. We have been communicating for a long time. I am exhausted too, but I also have to get back to work — they are asking me what I am doing and they are waiting for me to move some computers and equipment around. Will you be alright for a while by yourself?"

"I—" I felt panic rising — I didn't want him to leave me alone in the jungle with the Beast-men, but I knew we needed to stop. *"How long?"*

Technically, I *was* alone in the jungle with the Beast-men, but I didn't feel alone with Darion there in my mind. I was desperate to keep him there with me, and I had to fight the urge to beg him to stay. He was right. We needed to stop before I collapsed or something.

"My shift ends in about three hours. I will be able to talk to you then, okay? Talking like this is sapping our strength, so we should really stop now so that we both can recover. I will sort something out and I will find you!"

"Yes, okay. You're right," I reluctantly agreed. I had to force myself to remain calm. *"Goodbye... And thank you again!"*

No no no! I thought privately to myself as I put my mental shield up, *Don't go!* I *so* hated goodbyes.

"Do not mention it. I wish I could have done more. Be strong until I call you again. I will talk to you soon. Goodbye, Tamisan." And with that, he was gone.

No! I don't want to be alone. I don't want you to leave me here... I took a deep breath. *I need to pull myself together and do this. I can do this until he comes back. I can just walk and do what they say and... I'm so thirsty!*

I felt like I'd been abandoned.

I nearly tripped over a small rock that was jutting out of the earth and the jolt to my leg made the wound hurt. I had to get a grip. Darion's absence seemed to make me feel off-balance somehow. Maybe it was because he'd been so close in my mind, or maybe it was that he'd helped me regain my sanity when I needed it so desperately. My feelings toward this stranger were all over the place, but they were strong. Was there something more to it?

Don't be ridiculous! I scoffed.

What was I thinking? I hadn't even met him. Didn't know anything about him. (But I had seen into his mind!) How could I expect that he would feel anything but friendship toward me — if that? And yet I'd looked deep inside his soul for that brief moment and had known him — that he was a caring and honest man. He had instantly dropped whatever he was doing to come to the aid of a stranger, and I would always be thankful.

The group wove their way through the twisting branches and hanging vines of the jungle, and suddenly the ground wasn't as rough and there were fewer vines and branches in the way. It took a few seconds for me to realise why — we were on a path. My first reaction was a mixture of relief and panic. It would be an easier walk, as I'd discovered when I walked along the path I'd found before, but I did *not* want to run into an Allosaurus look-alike while chained to six people. Of course, I didn't want to run into it *at all*.

The two Beast-men at the front of the group stopped using their spears as walking sticks and held them at the ready. I looked behind me and saw the other one do the same. That made me feel a little better, but what were they planning to do if Allosaurus *did* show up? Could they successfully fight it off? I had to remind myself that they lived here and dealt with these nightmarish creatures on a daily basis, so I had to trust that they would protect us.

As we walked, I couldn't help thinking about what had happened to me since I escaped from Starrick. It was a case of jumping 'out of the frying pan and into the fire' for me. I shuddered when I thought about all the terrifying things that had come out of my imagination while I had the poison in my system. I didn't know my mind could conjure up such horrible things. Thinking about them made me start to shake, so I pulled my thoughts away from it all, only to start thinking about what had happened next.

The Beast-man with the knife.

The look in his eyes while he touched me and while he hacked into the wetsuit. The anticipation. *Ugh!* It made me sick. The things he planned to do to me... and the other one? Was he going to watch, or was he going to join in? I stumbled and nearly fell over just thinking about it. And there was nothing on the ground to trip on.

My stomach turned over and I had a feeling like I was dirty and needed to wash myself all over. I was physically dirty from lying on the floor of the jungle, but this feeling was more than that. I think it was all in my head. And I didn't think washing myself in the nearby river would get rid of the feeling. Was this normal? Is that how rape victims felt? I'd heard something about it once, I was sure. If that had actually happened to me, this feeling would be ten times worse. I felt bad enough now. And it wasn't just that he was super ugly. That was only part of it. It was the thought of what he wanted to do and that he didn't care that I didn't want him to touch me. He was going to do it anyway. What I wanted didn't matter. I was a captive. An object, not a person. I shuddered.

I needed to concentrate on something else to try to make the feeling go away. I tried to look around at the trees and flowers and passing birds. It didn't help much. I thought about swimming in the open ocean and that only helped a little bit.

We trudged along the trail for a while until we reached the bank of the river again. We were led over to the water's edge and I looked down at the clean, clear water. I'd been so dry for so long. I needed this.

I knew it would be pollution-free here on Althar 3 — the crews at Jannali had tested it — so I joined the others in drinking my fill.

It was such a huge relief! I felt alive again. My skin needed some moisture and a wash, so I tried to splash some over my arms and face, only to find an angry face either side of me, dripping with water.

Oops! I apologized and drank some more. It made me feel better, but I was still so weary.

The fact that I was so thirsty may have been an after-effect of the poison, but it was more likely to be that I hadn't had a drink since I'd walked up on the beach. How long had it been since I'd arrived in the jungle? How long had I been hallucinating? How long had Starrick been looking for me? I had no idea.

Was it a day? Or was I lying on the forest floor all night? I tried to recall whether it was dark at any point when I was partially sane. I couldn't remember.

The Beast-men gave us all some pieces of fruit to eat and I realized they were the same kind of fruit that I'd eaten earlier. It was a relief to know they were safe to eat. I sat down with the group and ate them quickly.

I thought about what happened to me. Everyone else obviously knew to avoid the flowers when they picked the fruit.

They kept saying the word Chumana, and I got the impression that that was the name of the fruit.

Once I'd finished eating, I still felt hungry. I looked to where the Beast-men were sitting. They weren't making any moves to hand out any more food. My hearts sank. *At this rate, I'll starve to death before Darion gets here,* I thought.

CHAPTER 28:

I Can See Every Tree Out There

Althar's sun was sitting low on the horizon. I hoped that this meant that we would stop here for the night. I felt like I couldn't take another step.

To my immense relief, they started to set up camp. They built a fire in the centre of the clearing we were sitting in and one of the Beast-men positioned himself so he could keep watch.

I couldn't help wondering why they would light a fire. It wasn't cold. Maybe it was to keep the wildlife away. It made sense. Judging by some of the sounds I'd heard since I'd regained my senses, I was thinking that the fire was a good idea.

As the darkness set in, I was reminded of something that I'd forgotten — I could see in the dark. So it didn't bother me that the fire they'd made was only bright enough to light up the immediate area. I could see beyond it and well into the dark jungle.

This is so weird — I can see every tree out there, I thought. *It's almost like daytime.* After a while, I thought, *Will I ever get used to this?*

I didn't really have a choice — I'd have to learn to live with all the changes, and hide the fact that I was an amphibian from these barbaric people. Things were bad enough as it was without them knowing that I was 'different.'

Don't complain about being different, I told myself, because the one thing I had 'acquired' from Sifayah that transcended all else, was the incredible things I could do with my mind. It would be worth all the trouble that I'd been through just to be able to communicate telepathically and move objects through telekinesis.

Now all I needed to do was get out of this nightmare alive!

We were given large leaves and the other captives started placing them on the ground to sleep on. At least we weren't going to lay directly on the leaf litter, sticks, rocks, vines, and tree roots. I found a spot to put my leaf and sat down on it.

I thought back to the times when Kaliya and Oliana had suggested that I be tested for Talent. They suspected I might have been gifted somehow because there were times when I seemed to know what they were thinking. But I'd put it down to coincidence and didn't bother about it, saying that I didn't have time for that nonsense — I was too busy with my studies (though I didn't really think it was nonsense; I just didn't believe I had any Talent).

But now, as I thought about it, I realized that if I'd *had* Talent back then, it would have helped tremendously in my career. I would've had a wider range of choices. How stupid I'd been! If I'd had this ability all along, it would've changed my life.

But there was no use wishing, and now with my mind combined with Sifayah's, I possessed more Talent than I could've ever been capable of as my old self, I was sure. And I didn't have to do any training in the use of my Talent — I just had to call on Sifayah's memories.

We were all told to lie down to sleep, so I obeyed and tried to find the smoothest spot to lie. The leaves were soft, but there were too many lumps and bumps underneath. I finally settled in one spot and tried to relax.

There was something out there lurking in the jungle. I could hear it. Something stalking through the tangled underbrush. It did not come near the dancing flames in the clearing and I was glad.

My eyelids grew heavy but sleep didn't come.

Go to sleep, I told myself. That wasn't going to be easy.

I heard more noises and tried not to think about it — whatever *it* was — and told myself that the fire and the Beast-men with the spears would keep us safe. I turned my thoughts toward my new abilities instead. Anything to get my mind off imagining what kind of horror it was out there.

To actually communicate telepathically was so incredible — especially with someone like Darion. I felt so close to him, as if I'd known him all my life — but I didn't know him at all. How was that possible? Why did I feel that way? I had no answers.

A loud roar erupted in the distance, making me jump and making my hearts pump so fast I thought I'd have a heart attack. I could tell it had scared all of the captives too, and when I looked up to the Beast-man on guard, he was standing up and scanning the tree line.

I tried to relax and breathe through it, but it was so hard. I couldn't imagine the three of them being able to protect us from whatever had made that noise.

Just as I was getting my heartbeats to slow, another loud roar split the night. This time, though, it was a lot further away. Even with my brain telling my body this fact, it was still ready to jump up and run.

CHAPTER 29:

Dead at Scene

My thoughts were all over the place, but they landed back on the Beast-man with the knife. I kept reliving the moments, ending with him cutting me and me screaming out inside my mind. How did I call out like that? I didn't even know I was doing it. It didn't matter. The end result mattered. Darion had heard me and I was saved from whatever they'd planned to do with me. I shuddered.

I pushed my thoughts forward to my conversation with Darion. We hadn't really had the chance to talk about too much, but I guess I covered a lot with him when I showed him all the things that had happened to me. I was glad that I knew how to do that, because trying to explain it all was too much. How do you tell someone that your mind has been dumped into another body?

I couldn't wait to talk to him again. I hoped I could actually reach his mind to talk to him again. I didn't even know how I'd done it in the first place. Did I have to call him or do something to initiate the connection? If so, I didn't think I could do it again.

What if I couldn't find his mind again? What if I was stuck here and he couldn't find me? The thought made me panic. I couldn't stay here. I had no idea what they were going to do to me. If what had already happened was any indication, I was in big trouble. The only thing that gave me the slightest bit of ease was that the third Beast-man didn't seem to want the others to touch me. He'd been very angry when he came back and saw what the scarred one had done to my wetsuit. He'd hit both of them pretty hard. Or maybe he'd been angry that they'd cut me. Damaged the merchandise. I shuddered again. What would've happened if he hadn't cut me? Would they have all taken turns? I cringed inside and my heartbeats soared. Nausea rose in my stomach and I took some deep breaths.

I needed to get away from them, but I had no clue — I didn't know anything about how to survive in the jungle. I thought I was doing okay, but I was no match for the Chumana tree. At least I had the safety of the fire and their weapons while I was with them. As crazy as it sounded, I was safer with these beasts that kept me in chains.

A wave of exhaustion hit me. I needed to try to relax more, so I could sleep. I had to shut my brain off. Easier said than done.

I started to do the exercises I'd been taught at the Academy by my Mental Processes teacher. I had to try it. I had to get some rest. I had no idea when they would make us start walking again.

At some point while I was trying to relax, I finally drifted off to sleep.

— ◦ —

"Tamisan?"

The voice in my mind roused me from a deep sleep.

What? Who? My mind started to work slowly. Oh, yeah. That was me. That was my name now.

"Tamisan? Are you there?" I was only half conscious and wondered if I was dreaming. Who was calling me? *"It is me, Darion."*

That woke me up, once I'd realized it was *Darion* calling me and not a dream. It all came rushing back to me. All the things that had happened. And he'd kept his word.

"Darion? Yes, I'm here." I managed to send back. My worries about not being able to connect with him again had all been for nothing. Thankfully.

It was still night and there was no moon — but that didn't bother me. I could see all the sleepers lying around on the ground by the dying embers of the fire — even the Beast-man on watch. He was asleep too. That made me feel nervous. The fire was there to keep the predators away, wasn't it? I wished I could do something to wake the ugly lump and get him to feed the flames.

My stomach felt unsettled. It was probably protesting about the unusual fruit it was forced to digest after such a long period of time without any food at all. And I was hungry again, too.

Darion apologized for waking me, and for the delay, as it was more than three hours since we last spoke. *"My shift ended later than I expected due to an equipment breakdown and I could not wait until morning to speak to you."*

I felt a spark of delight to think that he couldn't wait a few more hours to talk to me again, then I quickly tried to hide my reaction. If Darion sensed what was going on inside my head, he didn't show it.

"I have made a few enquiries about Dr Starrick," he informed me. *"It seems that he was actually one of the scientists who developed the procedure. Not the original procedure, just the Eibhlin Process. He was heavily involved with the Eibhlin Process and*

*similar operations up until they were outlawed and had quickly
packed up his clinic and shipped out to a remote planet in the Eira
Galaxy called Gamma Alpha 89.*

*"While he was there he managed to keep out of trouble, but
there were rumours he was still experimenting in that field. The
problem was — there was no proof. And apparently he jumped
at the opportunity to work as head of Station Maztec. Of course,
now we have evidence that he is running illegal experiments again
right here on Althar."*

I shuddered. How many people had he done this to?

"Also, as I said earlier," he continued, *"as far as the official
records show, you are officially deceased. The report states 'dead
at scene' along with the rest of the Outrider's passengers and pilot,
and there are no records of what they did to you. He has tried to
cover his tracks."*

My eyes stung and I felt really strange. Zhenna Rhodarma
no longer existed in the civilised world. All my friends would
have been notified that I was dead and would be grieving for
me. Oliana would most likely blame herself because it was her
idea that I should take the job in the first place. Kaliya would
be heartbroken. And there was no way for me to tell them I was
still alive. Even if I could, would they believe it was me? Probably
not.

I would miss them. My eyes welled with tears. I was a
mixed-up mess. Again.

"Are you okay?"

I nodded, then realized he couldn't see me. *"Yeah. Thanks."*

After a while Darion added, *"Earth would have been notified
by now. All friends and relatives would think that they have lost
you all. I am very sorry..."*

CHAPTER 30:
Grieving for Nothing

"That's so horrible! Oliana and Kaliya are grieving for nothing! Some of the others probably are too! I'm sure I'm not the only one to have survived. That guy had Mosuti's scrambled thoughts in his head. Mosuti would have to be alive for them to do the procedure. If there is anyone left, they need to be rescued before Starrick messes up their heads!"

"Yes," he told me, *"my superiors are organising something for tomorrow morning. They are going to conduct a raid and catch them by surprise."*

"Good!" There was a period of silence and I thought about my old self, now dead, and my new identity. *"I'm not Zhenna anymore and I'm definitely not Sifayah. My life will never be the same again. And all the people I knew back on Earth think I'm dead now. So much for Starrick's little story about reporting me missing! No wonder he didn't want to talk about what we were going to tell everyone back home about me! It was already too late!"* After a pause, I said, *"I picked Tamisan because it means 'twin,' and that's how I feel, like two people."*

I shifted around on my leaf bed. It was so hard to find a comfortable position. I couldn't believe I'd actually fallen asleep on it. I must have been really tired to do that.

I looked over to the dying fire again. It was starting to really worry me that the fire was almost gone and the Beast-man was still snoring.

"Well, I must admit, it was rather strange, finding someone else's memories in your head when we did the Mind-link, but I did not have a chance to ask about it at the time. I was too busy trying to help you. I guess it must have been a bit unnerving for you, finding Sifayah's memories when you regained consciousness. What did they hope to gain by leaving all her memories behind?"

Ouch! Something pointy had dug into my leg from under the big leaf. I had to move again. *"Sorry. Something stuck into me. They had a great deal of trouble trying to communicate with Sifayah and didn't have a linguist,"* I told him, *"so they wanted to use me to study her people — probably by going back to their village and pretending to be Sifayah. But what they didn't know is that the Waikari are all telepathic — and they could look into my mind and know instantly that I wasn't Sifayah."*

"Yes, they would."

I sighed. *"You know, something told me straight off that there was something not right with Starrick. I couldn't quite put my finger on it. It wasn't just him being cold and arrogant, you know? Then I saw that man whose mind had been jumbled up by Starrick's experimentation — he was seriously messed up. I actually read Starrick's mind a few times and realized he wasn't telling me everything, and half the time he was lying anyway. His attitude was all wrong — and I had no access to any outside Vid lines to call for help. I was a prisoner."* I sighed heavily. *"I decided to tell him nothing about the Waikari being telepathic — and I didn't tell any of them about the Talent I'd inherited from Sifayah or about her memories, either."*

"Good move," Darion replied. *"I would say they want you back bad enough as it is, judging by the amount of air and sea activity coming from the base."*

I managed a laugh at that thought, but then realized I'd have to be careful not to be seen from the air. That would be easy with all the cover from the trees — I would have to be careful where there were breaks in the canopy. Like here by the river.

"Won't they be in breach of their contract with Voyager Division if they make too many unscheduled flights?" I asked. *"We're supposed to observe these people unnoticed."*

"Yes. They have been warned once already and failed to give a reasonable explanation for all the extra activity," he informed me. *"Also, they have not released any reports about the Waikari at all. They are keeping it all under wraps. I presume they do not wish to be caught for all the illegal experiments they are conducting on these poor people. And on you."* I cringed at that. *"And when the incident happened in the jungle, Maztec told us they would take care of all matters like informing the families and arranging transport of the bodies back to their respective home worlds. We did not think anything sinister was happening at the time, but we now know why they wanted to take care of it all."*

I thought about it and wondered what they were sending back. Were there any bodies besides mine in the sealed containers that would have been sent home? My stomach lurched at the thought of them sending my *body* back home. I had to force myself not to think about it any longer.

For the others, I guessed they could send the bodies back as they were, but then would have to explain how they were shot by lasers on a primitive planet. Or would they send a pile of ashes and say that was all that was left of them or something? How would they fake a death?

That was a really terrible thing to do. And so sad for all the people involved. What would happen if there were other survivors? They would have to tell their relatives there had been a mistake — that they weren't dead after all — that would be so traumatic for them. I tried to imagine being told that Oliana had died. We would hold a funeral and grieve for her, only to be told a few weeks later she was still alive and well. It almost brought tears to my eyes.

Only in my situation, I wasn't the same person. And they would have buried my body for real. I couldn't go home and say they made a mistake. How could I ever tell them I was Zhenna?

Darion sent feelings of encouragement to me. *"Tamisan, we will think about what to do later and work something out. Right now, we need to make a plan. I have told my superiors about you, and they agree we need to find you, and quickly. I cannot teleport you to Jannali because I do not know where you are. I cannot teleport to you for the same reason — it does not work like that. I need an exact location. And if you have the ability to teleport, you cannot port yourself here because you do not know the exact location of Station Jannali. Teleporting blindly is very dangerous. There is no telling where you might end up. You could materialise inside a wall or a tree."*

I cringed. *"Um, I can teleport. Sifayah knew how to, anyway."*

"That is good to know, but if you have not done it yourself, it would be dangerous, even if you knew where you were going. Now, I may need to organise the search party myself," he continued, *"and that would mean I would have to lead the team to you."*

Another spark — he was coming to get me! *But do I dare to hope that he will find me?*

CHAPTER 31:
You Will Find Out When We Meet

"Okay. Do it," I said. *"I can't stay here. I've got to get away. There must be a reason why they have captured people and put them in chains. The only reasonable explanation is that we are some sort of slaves. I want to get away from them* before *I find out. And — and I need some decent clothes too."*

I instinctively brought my arms up to try to cover myself, although no one else was awake. Thinking about that reminded me of the dying fire. *We need the fire! Wake up you moron!*

"Slavery would be the most likely explanation. This is something we did not know about the natives on Althar..." He paused. *"I will speak with Dr Aimery about this new information... Do not worry Tamisan, I will find you — and I will bring you some clothing to wear."* And it was clear he meant every word. *"Try your best to get some sleep and I will see what I can arrange, okay? I had better go and get some sleep, too. It will be a big day tomorrow. I will contact you tomorrow morning. See you later."*

"Bye," I reluctantly replied, *"and thank you for everything!"*

I felt him leave my mind and tried to squash the lost feeling that welled up inside me.

Get some *sleep?* How could I sleep? There was too much to think about — too much buzzing around in my head. I was too excited, knowing Darion would soon come to rescue me and take me away from the horrible Beast-men and this prehistoric, nightmarish jungle. It was like something out of a horrific HoloMovie, but I knew it was no movie. It was my reality.

I knew I had to get some rest before the start of the day — they would probably keep us walking all day. That thought made me wonder where they were taking us and what they planned to do once we got there. A lot of horrible things whirled around in my mind, bringing the sting of tears, but I had to push those thoughts out before they made it so I couldn't sleep at all.

I ordered myself to relax and breathe normally. They would probably get up early and I needed to sleep right now. I suspected that we'd only stayed in the one place for a long time because they were waiting for me to be able to walk again.

I shifted my position again in a vain attempt to get comfortable. My stomach had settled a bit, but it still didn't feel right. And the hunger pains were starting to really get to me.

A loud cracking noise made me jump and I looked up to see the Beast-man throwing some more wood on the fire. I breathed a sigh of relief. At least I could stop worrying about what might come strolling into the campsite while we were sleeping.

Then I closed my eyes, calmed my thoughts, slowed my breathing, and practiced some more exercises to put myself to sleep, and it eventually worked.

⚬

The group had been walking along one of the animal paths for half the morning when Darion called me again. It had rained just after dawn, which made me wake with a start. I'd struggled to rub my legs with my bound hands in an effort to try to wash the blood and dirt off before it stopped raining. As it turned out, I needn't have hurried. There was more than enough water in that downpour to wash myself twice.

I'd removed the crude hide bandage from my leg and inspected the wound. It was knitting back together surprisingly quickly, so I left the bandage off. I didn't really want to put it back on once it was wet as I was worried that it would increase the chance of the wound getting infected. That was the last thing I needed.

And the shackles were doing their best to scrape my skin off.

It had felt good to get the dirt and blood off — though I desperately wished for some decent clothing. *Anything* would be better than what I was wearing. The fact that my wetsuit was cut down the middle, exposing my left breast if I didn't hold it in place, didn't seem to concern the other captives or the Beast-men in the slightest, but I was finding it hard to deal with. The younger of the two women wasn't wearing anything that covered her breasts at all, so I guessed it was fairly commonplace for them to be at least half-naked.

I knew it was the culture in which I was raised that made me feel uncomfortable having certain parts of my body uncovered, but I couldn't help the way I felt. And I wasn't going to expose my breast just because *they* didn't have a problem with it.

We'd eaten fruit again for breakfast, along with some sort of mushrooms that tasted kind of like a sweet meat. I was grateful for the pleasant taste as I really didn't like the mushrooms from Earth. I hoped the mushrooms wouldn't affect my stomach more than the fruit had.

After drinking from the river, which I desperately wanted to dive into, we were made to start walking again. I tried to take in my surroundings as we walked. I noticed the spider webs were a lot easier to see after the rain. The sunlight made them look like they were strung with jewels, with a large spider in the middle with its legs splayed outwards completing the picture. Everywhere I looked, the leaves and flowers were covered in beads of water.

We were travelling up-river toward the mountains, which meant we were moving away from Jannali, but there was nothing I could do about that.

Darion brought me some good news — his superiors had organised a search party, and they were letting him lead the expedition. Well, not really. There was a military leader for the team. They needed Darion to locate me by using his Talent, so he would be leading them in the direction they would be going through the jungle.

I could feel my heartbeats quicken just thinking about it. I wished they could arrive right now and take me away from this place.

"We leave in an hour," he informed me.

The sooner the better.

I wondered if the image of him I'd seen in his mind before was what he really looked like — I knew some people saw themselves differently to the way others see them. And different to reality...

"Oh, you will find out when we meet, sweetie — but not before!" and he sent a laugh with that thought. I realized I wasn't shielding any of my thoughts. Then he added, *"Can you describe, or better still,* show *me your surroundings so I can try to pinpoint your location on a map?"*

"Okay, I'll try," I replied, and sent him mental pictures of what I could see around me, as well as where I'd been — especially where I'd come ashore. He asked me to wait while he was consulting a map and a Geologist, and I wondered how it

was that I'd mastered my Talent so well in such a short time. The power I possessed was incredible. It seemed that there was almost nothing I couldn't do.

After a while, Darion let me know that the information had been very helpful. He left me so he could continue getting ready.

The path had taken us back round to the river's edge and my captors stopped again by the bank and gestured for us to drink. After walking for so long in the humid jungle, I welcomed the cool, refreshing water. I was dehydrated. Again. And my stomach had become uneasy. Again.

I kept an eye on the water, making sure there wasn't anything lurking beneath the surface, but again I had an overwhelming urge to dive in and give my skin a much-needed drink. If I wasn't chained to six people, it would also be the perfect escape. I tried to see if I could slowly pull one of the shackles off over my narrow hand. Trying to push all my fingers together to make it thinner didn't help. All I succeeded in doing was scraping more skin off and causing myself more pain.

Damn!

When I finished drinking, I looked over to the Beast-men to try to gauge what their intentions were. I didn't want to keep walking and was dreading the signal to get moving, but they did nothing. It seemed like they were waiting for something. I hoped it was more food. I needed something more filling. Something that would stop me feeling hungry for a few hours. That would help a lot.

After everyone had finished drinking, they gestured for us all to sit down, and still they waited. And waited. I was in no hurry to start walking again, but it puzzled me that they'd stopped for so long after everyone had finished. They'd been pushing us and seemed to be in a hurry to get wherever they were going, so this was weird. Judging by the behaviour of the other captives, this wasn't the usual procedure after stopping for a drink. They seemed confused and anxious.

I sat on the outer edge of the group, resting my legs and trying to keep my hands in the best position to avoid pain from the shackles. I noticed the others were doing the same with their shackles. The woman that had helped me — the redhead — smiled at me. So did the young man I'd bumped into so many times. A half smile was all I could manage in return.

The beasts didn't offer us any food. They sat and talked in low tones while watching the jungle. What were they doing? What were they waiting for?

CHAPTER 32:

Buyers

Don't complain, I told myself, *If it means we're not walking, then it's good.*

Two hours passed. That's how long it seemed to me anyway. I was uncomfortable and restless and hungry, but it was better than walking. In that time, Darion had returned to tell me they were leaving. We'd talked for a while, then he was gone again.

I'd just flicked a creepy bug with three long horns on its head off my leg and was watching it crawl away into the leaf litter when five men appeared from out of the dense underbrush and greeted the Beast-men. They had been so quiet in their approach that I didn't realise they were there until they emerged from the jungle. My heartbeats picked up.

These men weren't beasts. They looked human — possibly the same race as the other captives. They wasted no time in walking right over to us and started looking at each of us carefully as the Beast-men motioned for us to stand up. I had a sinking feeling in the pit of my stomach. They were *buyers!*

Oh no! I've gotta get out of here!

As the men inspected the captives, I took more notice of what the other captives looked like. Up until then, I'd tried not to look at them. I tried to keep my head down and keep out of their way.

I didn't want any trouble. The redhead and the guy I'd bumped into were the only ones I'd interacted with.

Besides him, there was a younger male that was shorter than him with long black braided hair and brown eyes. He was fairly slim and his skin was slightly darker than the others, and he was always staring at me anytime I glanced at him.

Some of the men — the buyers — were looking at them keenly, while the others were interested in the other two males that were older than the others and seemed to dress and wear their hair the same. I guessed they were from the same tribe — maybe even brothers. One was slightly taller than the other and they both had brown hair, partly braided and tied back behind them. One had blue eyes, the other green. Two of the buyers were looking at both of them and kept saying the word *Chara*. Was that their tribe or something? Maybe.

I guessed they thought they would be good, strong workers. Is that what they wanted them for? I had no idea.

There was one buyer that had taken a keen interest in the women. He was a young man, probably only a few years older than me. He was tall and slim. He had long, sandy brown hair and green eyes. He was boyishly handsome, though he looked a bit rugged in his spotted hide loincloth.

He'd looked at the other two women when he approached the group, but now he walked straight up to me. He looked me right in the eye, then averted his gaze. He looked me up and down. He hesitated, and he seemed unsure. Nervous. None of the other buyers looked nervous. They all seemed very confident in what they were doing. He called out to the Beast-men. "Charan?"

"Naya," one of them called back.

He looked puzzled. "Chavez?"

"Naya. Una perra sinno tee."

He stepped away from me and went back to the other women. The redhead looked him in the eye, as if daring him to do something. The younger woman had long dark hair and seemed to be quite timid. She always stayed in the middle of the group. She stepped back when he came close to her.

All the captives were pushed and shoved until we were standing in a line as the men walked up and down, poking here and there, even looking at the teeth of some of the males. I heard the word Charan mentioned again. Maybe they were tribe names. They all sounded similar. Chara, Charan and Chavez. That would make sense. He must have been asking which tribe I was from and the Beast-men didn't know.

One of the males was singled out. He was the young male I'd kept bumping into and I could feel his anguish. I guessed he looked like a strong worker.

The buyer who had looked at me closely turned from the other women and came back to me. My insides froze. I wanted to run, but even if I wasn't chained to the others, I doubted I would get far through the dense undergrowth before they caught up with me again.

I forced myself to stand still while he looked me up and down again, feeling the tone of the muscles on my upper arm and thigh, and he even looked at my teeth. He seemed a bit unsure of what to do, and had only felt my muscles and inspected my teeth after watching the other buyers doing it.

It was degrading, being treated like an animal, an object, but I gritted my teeth and stayed where I was.

How could they do this? How could anyone *sell* another human being? How could anyone *buy* another human being? I was disgusted. What sort of person was he to be wanting a human to be his slave, to do anything and everything he commanded?

He returned to the Beast-men. They negotiated for a long time, and I was seething the whole time, then they approached me. My chains were released from the others and handed over to the man. He in return gave the Beast-men a pouch made of a reddish-brown hide. I couldn't guess what was inside and didn't think to probe their minds to find out. They also gave him a crude black metal key that he placed in a small pocket of sorts at the hip in the loincloth he wore. I assumed the key was for my shackles.

He stood staring at me for a few moments, and all I could do was glare back up at him. His mouth tilted up slightly on one side, like he wasn't sure if he should smile, but couldn't help it. My hearts sank. I didn't smile back. I kept glaring at him. I wanted to run. I'd been *sold!*

CHAPTER 33:

But Then He Turned Back to Me

Sold.

Like an animal at a livestock auction. I'd seen it in Holo-Movies I'd watched on Earth's history. I'd even seen footage of humans actually being sold as slaves as well. I shuddered.

Livestock were usually being sold to be slaughtered, except the horses, of course. So what did they want with *people?* What did he want with *me?* I shuddered again. What else would a male be buying a female for?

How could they treat me like a piece of meat? Like a cow? I felt a surge of anger building up inside me. How *dare* they? I looked across at the Beast-men with renewed hatred and my face flushed with heat.

"Tamisan!"

I jumped. It sounded like it wasn't the first time Darion had called me. *"Oh — uh... yeah?"*

"What happened? You were not answering me." He sounded worried.

"Nothing," I lied, and pushed my mental shield up. I didn't want to tell him what was going on. I wanted to stay angry. I wanted to seethe with the heat coursing through my veins. They were animals. Barbarians.

Darion could sense something was wrong, but for some reason, he didn't push for an answer. *"We have narrowed it down to a smaller area,"* he said, and he sounded more confident now that they would find me. *"Our guess is that you are in Sector 6 near the Amali River, which is close to the only cove that matches your description of Lamani Cove. That bend in the river ahead should sweep around to meet the foothills of the mountains. According to this map, which is the latest one available, there are a number of caves there."*

Amali River. The map I'd memorised was fairly new and the river hadn't been named yet, so it could be the one.

"Okay. I'll look out for them if we keep going in this direction and let you know," I managed to reply. I was still glaring at the Beast-men. I could feel the man with the other end of my chain in his hand staring at me. I turned back and gave him a look of pure disgust. He looked surprised.

What was I doing? Why didn't I tell Darion what was going on? I needed to tell him. Why was I being so stupid?

Tell him, I told myself, *Tell him! ... No! He is right in the middle of planning my rescue,* I argued back. *He doesn't need a distraction.*

I bit my lip. *Just tell him, you idiot!*

"Alright. Keep a low profile and do as they say until I can track you down," he continued. *"At least if you stay with them you will get food that you know is safe to eat and some kind of protection against the elements and any predators. And call me if you need any help, okay? I will go now and get organised and I will contact you when we are setting out. See ya!"*

No! Don't go! I felt my eyes welling with tears. I kept my shield up. He needed to concentrate on what he was doing. *"Okay bye,"* I managed to say, *"and thanks!"*

I squeezed my eyes shut to try to stop the tears and took a deep breath. *I should have told him...*

I felt his mind leave mine, but this time I didn't feel so alone, which was weird. And although I was now the property of some wild man in the middle of a dangerous jungle, at least I knew I was one step closer to getting out of this horrible place. I was filled with hope — he was coming to rescue me like a knight in shining armour in a medieval fairytale!

The pain from the shackles on my wrists brought my thoughts back to reality. I'd been trying to hold the chain's links up to help reduce the constant rubbing against my wrists while I'd been walking, but it didn't help much. My feet had begun to hurt too — even standing still they were hurting me — and I shifted my weight from one foot to the other. The jungle floor didn't have too many jagged rocks or sharp sticks — mainly leaves or leaf mulch, moss, logs and tree roots covered with moss or fungi. Still, it was rough on my feet. Even though the Waikari never wore shoes, walking barefoot for so long was getting painful. The Waikari were accustomed to walking on smooth, water-worn rocks and sand, or swimming.

As I looked down at my sore feet, a crawly thing that looked like a giant centipede walked toward my right foot and I quickly shifted out of its path. I felt a shudder go through me.

I hate bugs!

I was glad I'd looked down when I did. It could've crawled up my leg. I shuddered again and pushed that thought away.

I should have told Darion! I scolded myself again. *But what could he have done about it? Nothing. So there was no point telling him, was there?*

I knew arguing with myself wouldn't help, but I did it anyway. I had to wait until he got here. *Darion will come and take me away from all this. Away from the dirt, the creepy crawlies, the wild beasts, the dinosaurs and the barbarians that trade in humans.* I looked over to the other captives and sighed. *I still should have told him...*

Another buyer was negotiating for the sale of the young male captive. The one I'd bumped into. Then there were the two men wanting to buy both of the brothers. No one else seemed interested in buying and they stood in a group talking. No one attempted to talk to the Beast-men outside the negotiations for slaves. That didn't surprise me — they weren't a very friendly or sociable lot.

A man approached us and started up a conversation with my, uh, master. They didn't seem to know each other. I dared to probe their minds. It seemed like they were asking each other where they were from. The man holding my chain said the word Chandra and the other mentioned Chakotay.

I looked at the other people around me. I could make out parts of conversations by the repeated words and images in their minds. The two buyers had bought the two slaves and I could make out that the slaves *were* brothers and they were from a tribe called the Chara. The buyers were from a tribe called Chakotay, like the man standing with us, and the other slaves were from the Charan. The Beast-men were called the Bahadori. I didn't try to read any of the Bahadori's minds. I was afraid of what I might find there, especially when they looked directly at me. And then there was the one with the scar... I had a creepy feeling running slowly up my back and had to try to focus on what was going on around me instead.

What is this man going to do with me? I wondered again. What if he was like the Bahadori? What if he wanted the same thing? How could I stop him? How could I get away from him?

At least I wasn't hallucinating anymore. That should help. And I could use my Talent to push him away from me if he wouldn't take no for an answer.

I wondered why he was still hanging around and talking to the other man. Did he want to buy another slave?

I heard the rustle of leaves at the edge of the clearing and turned to see a man pushing his way through the foliage. He strode toward the gathering. The Bahadori greeted him as he passed, and he grunted his reply. He was a tall, well-built man with wild eyes and long dark brown hair. He didn't have any animal hide across his chest and over one shoulder like a lot of the others. He had a loin cloth thing around his hips, with his bare chest showing off every ripped muscle. There was an air of arrogance about him. He walked straight over to the captives, ignoring the males as he passed. He looked the other female captives up and down, but then went straight up to me. My mind kind of stumbled and the adrenalin started pumping. What was he doing?

He looked down at me for a few seconds with his dark, piercing eyes, then turned his head back toward the other female captives, as if he was comparing them to me. They cringed as he looked at them, as if his eyes had singed their skin. But then he turned back to me, his smile turning to a sneer.

CHAPTER 34:

Turak

I cringed too, but tried not to let it show — I didn't want to give him the satisfaction of knowing the effect he had on me. My heartbeats quickened. My anger washed away, replaced by an icy feeling that spread out from my chest. Something about this man was really intimidating. It seemed to affect everyone around him.

He looked at me intensely for a few more moments, then began to feel my upper arms as the other man had done. I held my hands tighter against my chest to help ease the pain in my wrists and to keep myself covered at the front. What did he think he was doing? The other man was holding my chain and the Beast-man — Bahadori — next to him was holding the payment. It was obvious I'd already been sold to someone else.

He started to feel my thighs as well, but he was not doing it to check the hardness of my muscles. My stomach churned. He was caressing the inside of my right thigh with one hand, gradually getting higher until he reached my crotch, which made me instinctively take a step back and I lowered my hands to try to push his hand away. My hearts raced faster. I was shaking all over.

I pulled back further away from him, but he stepped forward and followed my movements and he grasped my right arm fiercely to keep me from pulling away again. I winced at the pain.

I opened my mouth to tell him to let me go, but nothing came out.

I was vaguely aware that the slave traders had come over to where the stranger and I were standing and my new 'master' was pulling on the stranger's arm and protesting loudly, but he ignored them all. He was still staring into my eyes with that awful grin on his face. He was so tall that my eyes were directly in line with the middle of his bare chest. He was built, rugged, and he was kind of handsome in a rough sort of way, but I was repulsed by him. I got the feeling that because of his size, he was used to getting his way.

The Bahadori were yelling at him now, and he reached up behind my head and grabbed my hair firmly with his huge hand, forcing my head back. It was painful, and I knew struggling would make it worse, so I had to stand there looking up at his angular face. They were pulling on his arms and clothing as he leaned down and kissed me, open mouthed, pushing hard against my lips. Revulsion rolled through me.

I'd never been kissed by a man before. I'd only ever been kissed on the cheek by my friends. It shocked me that he was kissing me so savagely, so hungrily. I shrank back away from him, but his grip was too tight for me to get away. He kept on kissing me, filling me with terror, and I felt like screaming and yelling and kicking. The icy feeling spread to every part of me.

How dare force himself on me? He was worse than all of them put together! I couldn't move. I couldn't stop him. My mind reeled and I felt like I was losing all control.

How could he do this to me? Why wouldn't he stop?

No one intervened. How could I break free and escape him and the horror I was feeling? It was impossible. I squirmed under the force of his death grip on me.

I had my eyes squeezed shut while he was kissing me, but it didn't help much. I tried again to get away from him and pushed against him with my bound hands — all Talent forgotten — but his grip was too strong. My wrists felt so raw under the unforgiving metal. Maybe if my hands were still at my chest I could've pushed harder. I wriggled and twisted to get free, but it was no use. He was too strong, and his grip on my hair was too painful.

Just as I felt like I would explode, he pulled away and let me go. Stunned at the sudden movement, I opened my eyes to see what was going on. He stood tall, smirking down at me, and he started laughing loudly. Mockingly.

I stepped back and turned away from him. I was shaking uncontrollably and could barely stand. My legs had turned to jelly and my head felt like I was going to faint. I decided not to fight it and I sank down onto my knees, then sat back on my heels. That made him laugh louder, but I didn't care anymore.

A stabbing pain made me lurch forward, holding my stomach. The mushrooms were probably to blame.

When I turned to look up at him, I saw that the Bahadori had drawn their daggers and spears and were threatening the stranger with them while waving them wildly. I hadn't even heard their protests, their yelling — I was too caught up in what he was doing to me and how terrified it had made me feel.

It reminded me of when the Bahadori had cut my wetsuit in half. And that vulgar caress... But the caress had nothing on what the stranger had done. My mouth felt dirty and my lips felt bruised and swollen. And he'd been touching my crotch. I shuddered. I felt dirty all over. My fists clenched and I gritted my teeth.

The stranger finally turned his attention to the others and to the knives, and spoke to them until eventually all had calmed down. I picked up a word I recognized — Turak. They were calling him Turak. That was the name I'd seen in the Bahadori's minds before. I realized the image I'd seen was him. So they were planning to sell me to Turak in the first place, and he was beaten by someone else because he was late. That would've only added fuel to the fire in this confrontation.

After staring defiantly at my master, he tossed his long hair in the air and followed the slave traders over to the other two female captives and proceeded to bargain loudly for one of them — the redhead. I cringed inside. I felt sorry for her. I looked away as he started to feel her legs.

It disturbed me, but at the same time I was glad I'd already been sold to someone else — but *only* because it meant I wouldn't be sold to *him!*

CHAPTER 35:

Not Him!

I needed to think about that. *Was* this 'master' any better than *him*? Surely he was — he didn't humiliate me and touch me the way *he* did — but still, he had just *bought* another human being. I was still at a loss as to what kind of person would do such a thing.

Maybe he was waiting till he got me alone before he did anything. Maybe then I would find out what he really wanted me for. I cringed. I would have to be ready for anything that might happen.

What was I going to do now? He owned me — or rather, he *thought* he did. No one can truly own another sentient being. I still felt so helpless and dreaded what might happen next. I was still shaking. I was glad he hadn't told me to get up and start moving yet. My legs probably wouldn't have supported me anyway.

What am I going to do? I have to contact Darion and tell him. I should have told him before. But there was no point in berating myself about that now.

I knew his mind well enough now that I should've been able to find it anywhere, but this was something only Sifayah had done. I tried my best to calm myself, remembering what Sifayah had been taught. Wiping the tears that had started to well up in my eyes and casting my mind outwards, my only thoughts were of Darion.

"*Darion?*" I called. My hearts were still racing and even my arms were like jelly.

"*Tamisan? Is that you?*" he asked, though he knew it was me. "*What is wrong?*"

"*I had to call you,*" I told him. "*They've just sold me!*"

"*They what?*"

"*A bunch of guys came out of the jungle to buy slaves and he — one of them bought me.*"

"*We have to get you out of there!*" It was like he shouted the words in my head.

I could feel Darion's anger through our connection. Mine had disappeared. I was in shock after what Turak had done. Tears ran down my cheeks.

"*What kind of barbaric planet is this?*" he almost roared. "*Listen, I am in the shuttle now. We are going to be dropped off somewhere near your Lamani Cove. We chose that place because it is a positive point that you have identified on the map and it is usually deserted. We do not want anyone to see us.*"

"*No. That wouldn't be good. Okay then.*"

Then he added, "*Oh I wish we had a Transporter...*"

"*Me too.*"

My new master gestured for me to get up, and I was too scared to disobey. I hated that word, but what was I supposed to call him in my mind?

My muscles were still jelly, but I managed to get to my feet. He led me away from the slave traders and into the jungle and the metal cut into my wrists. I opened my mind to Darion a little so he could *see* where the man was taking me.

"That is a good idea, Tamisan. It could make it easier to find you."

My cheeks heated a little at his praise.

I stumbled and nearly fell over a rock on the edge of the clearing and I felt a familiar exhaustion sweep over me. I knew now that it was from using my Talent. It didn't help that I was already worn out before I'd started.

"We are lifting off, so it will not be long now. Lie low and do as you are told. I can feel that you are tired. Do not try to communicate with me for the time being. Otherwise you will wear yourself out. I will check in from time to time to see how you are, okay?"

"Yes, okay," I replied, and he left again. I'd kept my mental shield up as best I could and didn't tell him about what had happened with Turak. I didn't really know how to tell him. I needed to process it all, it had happened so fast. Tears were slowly making their way down my cheeks.

We'd been trudging uphill through the jungle and away from the river while I'd been communicating with Darion and as we entered a small clearing, I saw a huge animal. My first instinct was to run the other way, and I pulled back, causing pain to my wrists — but my master urged me forward. He said some words I couldn't understand, and I pulled back again. When I didn't respond to what he'd said, he frowned and repeated the words. There was a sinking sensation in my stomach. He'd realized I couldn't understand what he was saying. That didn't help the situation at all.

I looked back at the animal. It looked like a kind of prehistoric reptile similar to ones that I'd studied back on Earth, like the Apatosaurus or Anatosaurus. It was about four metres long and about two metres tall, with four thick legs that looked similar to

that of an elephant, but with longer toes. It had a long neck —
but not too long — and a relatively small head compared to its
body, but didn't have any bony protrusions or horns. I guessed
it was a herbivore like the Apatosaurus and other similar species.

My master looked at me for a few moments, then said something that sounded like a question. I frowned.

"I don't understand," I told him. I didn't bother with answering him in Waikari as he wouldn't have understood that
either.

Now it was his turn to frown. He repeated the question a
few times, then uttered a loud high-pitched yelp, which made
me jump. I guessed he was testing to see if I was deaf. I dared to
send a quick probe into his mind and could see he was surprised
that I didn't understand him. He'd obviously assumed that even
though the Bahadori didn't know which tribe I was from, I
would still speak the same language as the rest of them.

Frustration and anger were foremost in his mind, and I could
guess why. It would be very difficult to make a slave obey you if
they couldn't understand a word you said.

I told him I didn't understand, using Sifayah's native tongue
this time, but that only served to anger him more.

He urged me toward the beast again. It wore a sort of harness
and had skins draped over its back, fashioned into a rudimentary
saddle, so it was obviously domesticated. They probably used it
as transport.

I winced at the pain in my wrists and he stepped forward to
look at them. They were red raw and bleeding and the skin had
been scraped off in places. I hoped he would take them off, but
instead he reached into a pouch in the skins on the beast's back
and took out some large leaves. He unrolled them and pushed
them under the shackles to stop them from coming into contact

with my skin. He used some tough grass to tie them there. The soft texture of the leaves brought me a lot of relief. I knew he wouldn't remove the shackles — that would be too much to hope for — so I'd have to be content with the relief he'd given me.

I wondered again what his plan was. Why did he purchase a slave? I shuddered at where my thoughts led me — the experience with Turak and even the Bahadori still fresh in my mind.

I realized he was speaking to me and tried to grasp any words that might sound familiar to Sifayah, but nothing he said had any meaning. He was really getting agitated now, and started repeating the same phrase over and over.

I could understand his frustration, but what could I do? I couldn't even hope to pretend that I knew what he was saying. I shook my head and said a few words to him in Waikari again, hoping that maybe he'd heard that language before. The Waikari didn't associate with the Jungle People at all, so I knew I was grasping at straws. He rolled his eyes upward and raised both fists in the air, shaking them angrily and muttering something aloud. Suddenly, he turned and started back toward the campsite of the slave traders. I felt panic grip me — he was going to complain. He was going to take me back there and confront them...

No!!!

I reluctantly followed. What choice did I have? I felt a strong urge to call Darion again, but decided to save my energy and to wait to see what happened first. I did *not* want to go back to the campsite — Turak could still be there — and if I was returned to the Slave Traders, I was sure he would buy me and I did *not* want to be sold to him!

We trudged back through the jungle to find that all the other buyers had left, *except* Turak!

No no no!! Not him! Take me back!

CHAPTER 36:
If Looks Could Kill

My hearts sank. I wanted to pull against my shackles, but I knew I would only cause myself a lot more pain and would still have to follow him anyway.

My master gave me a strange look before marching right up to the three Bahadori and yelling, pointing at me and waving his fist at them. They responded by yelling back and waving their fists around too. I could sense their anger. It was so strong that I had to block it out. I could guess what they were saying by their gestures and the tone of their voices.

All the moving about was jolting the chain and causing pain to my wrists, despite the soothing leaves. I grimaced as I stepped forward and pulled a bit more of the chain into my hands to reduce the pain.

Turak stepped forward and raised his money pouch, even though he was now holding the redhead's chain.

No! Not him! Don't sell me to him!

I realized he was staring straight at me and I quickly looked away. The smile on his face suggested that he had plans for me.

I thought of yanking my chain out of his hand and running if they sold me to him. But who was I kidding? That would be impossible. There was no way I was strong enough to make him let go of anything.

The argument was getting louder. I looked back to see Turak approaching them, holding up the chain for the red-head. It seemed like he wanted to swap slaves. I cringed inside. What if they agreed? What could I do? My master looked like he was starting to like the idea. I wanted to run as fast as I could through the jungle and away. Away from all of them. Away from *him*.

It looked as though the Bahadori didn't like the idea. Then something changed the whole tone of the conversation. My master shook his head firmly and repeated the word "Naya" over and over. I got the impression that it meant no. I didn't know what had happened to change his mind, but didn't really care either, as long as it meant I would *not* belong to Turak. Turak looked angry, but finally gave up. He backed off, but stood there staring at me with those horrible dark eyes that seemed to look right through me.

Whatever made my owner change his mind about the swap also seemed to make him give up on the negotiations with the Bahadori altogether. I sighed heavily. I was so relieved that I had avoided being Turak's *property*. My owner turned from the Bahadori without so much as a wave and I followed behind him, feeling like a pet on a leash. Turak called after us and as we walked away, I could hear him laughing again. I shuddered. I couldn't help it.

Before long, we were back in the small clearing where my master had left his beast. I realized it was tied to a low hanging tree branch. He turned and glared at me and all I could think was, "If looks could kill..."

Was he going to take his frustrations out on me? I cringed at the thought and prepared to thrust my arms up in front of me if I needed to.

Instead, he clasped both his hands together and hunched himself over at the side of the beast, holding his hands out low in front of him. I stared at him for a few moments before finally realising he was offering to help me up onto the creature's back. I stepped forward reluctantly and put one foot on his hands and swung my other leg up and over the beast's back as he lifted. I found it surprisingly comfortable sitting astride the large reptile. The fur saddle was very soft.

I soon found that sitting in the saddle made the leg of the wetsuit start to come away, and I had to try to pull it around to the front. I pulled the wetsuit across my stomach and breast as well, hoping the belt would help to keep it there, but couldn't get the material to meet up or stay where I'd put it. It was impossible. I cursed the tough elastic that was preventing me from closing the gap.

My thoughts returned to what had happened and questions burned in my mind. Why didn't I use my Talent to break free from Turak? He'd forced himself on me and I felt violated. Humiliated. I'd forgotten to use my Talent because I'd forgotten *everything* in those terrifying moments.

It took little effort for him to mount the beast using what looked like some kind of stirrup made of fur and he moved up behind me to take the reins. It was unnerving having him sitting so close behind me with his legs touching mine and his arms around me on either side to reach the reins, but there was little I could do about it. Then he leaned forward suddenly and I gasped. He grabbed my chain and gathered it up enough so it wasn't hanging down near the beast's legs, then put it in my hands, expecting me to hold it there. Once he could see that I wasn't going to let it drop, he signalled the beast with a clicking noise and it lurched into motion.

I had to fight the compulsion to try to slide down off the beast's back and run. Besides the fact that I wouldn't get far once he grabbed my chain, I could fall underneath the beast and be trampled. And even if I made it to freedom, I'd be back where I started. I didn't know how to survive in the jungle and would have the added problem of having my hands shackled together. That alone would probably be the death of me. I knew I had to stay with this man for now and bide my time.

I wondered how Darion was planning on getting me away from him. We were supposed to be observing these people, not interacting with them. I quickly came to the conclusion that I didn't care how he did it or if he broke any rules to do it. I just wanted to get out of here.

It was difficult for the beast to manoeuvre its way through some of the trees and bushes in the jungle, and at times both of us had to duck under low branches or move a leg out of the way to avoid injury. When we both hunched forward, he had to lean right over onto my back, and I was very uncomfortable having his half-bare chest touching me and feeling his breath on my skin. It sent shivers down my spine. But there wasn't a whole lot I could do about it. And holding onto all the links of the chain was starting to hurt my hands.

We soon found a path for the beast to walk on and that made it easier. I began to feel nervous, knowing what it meant for us to be on a path, but my master didn't seem to be worried. That didn't make me feel any better. He had a dagger in a sheath at his waist and there was a spear sticking up out of a large sheath in the fur saddle, so I guess he felt confident that he would be able to protect us from attack.

For a moment or two my head started spinning and my sur-roundings became surreal and I thought maybe I still had some of the poison left in my system, but my vision cleared and I felt normal again. I decided it was more likely to be from the mushrooms, as I still felt queasy and the stabbing pain in my stomach had turned into a dull ache.

As the beast ambled along, we were startled by some small furry mammals scurrying through the underbrush, and I nearly dropped the chain. I was relieved that I'd managed to hold onto the links as I was sure it would have been very painful for the beast if it had slipped. The weight of the chain as it fell would have caused me a lot of pain too.

After a while, we came to a place where the remains of a large reptile lay across the roots of two large trees. I could see some bushes sticking out from underneath its prone body that had been crushed when it fell. It must have been over six metres long, and the smell...

There were several emu-sized reptiles feasting on what was left of the flesh and they weren't pleased to have their meal interrupted. They shrieked their protests and strode toward us, bloodied mouths gaping open. Adrenalin shot through my veins and I couldn't help cringing.

CHAPTER 37:
What if He Was Worse?

My master drew his spear and didn't have to tell his mount to move — it wheeled around so abruptly that it nearly lost both its riders and ran through the jungle with about half the meat-eaters on its tail. My hearts were in my throat as one of the lizards lunged forward, almost landing on the beast's rump. It missed its target and plunged headlong into a tree, falling helplessly to the ground.

It was hard for me to see around my master's body to see what was coming up behind us, which made my chest tighten even more. It was terrifying knowing that at any second we could be attacked by a reptile that looked like a smaller version of a Velociraptor.

I held my breath, waiting for one of them to jump onto the beast's back, anticipating the pain of claws and teeth digging into my flesh, but nothing happened. Our mount kept on running, and after about twenty more metres, the rest gave up the chase to return to their meal.

The beast kept up the pace for a while longer, then slowed down to its usual pace. My master put his spear away and I tried to slow my breathing and relax. It took some time for my heart rates to return to normal. Meanwhile, we were plodding along through the trees and twisted vines.

Finally, my master pulled on the reins for the beast to stop, then dismounted. He gestured for me to dismount, but did not offer any assistance. I didn't need it — I held onto the front of the saddle, swung my leg over and slid down. The ground was a bit further down than I thought and I stumbled when I landed. An expression that looked like concern crossed his features, but I wasn't sure if that's what it was. I wasn't sure if a person that owned another person was capable of such an emotion. I resisted the urge to glare at him. I didn't think that making him angry was a good idea at this point. The fact that we were alone in the jungle and I didn't know what he wanted from me made me feel very uneasy.

He grabbed my chain from out of my hands. I realized too late that I'd had a chance to run, but I knew I wouldn't have gotten very far anyway.

We'd stopped in a small clearing with a couple of logs across the middle of it in a sort of V shape.

He pulled a length of rope from out of another pouch in the beast's skins and attached it to the end of my chain. He tied the other end of it to one of the logs. I assumed we were going to stop here for a while. He then went to the other side of the beast and pulled out some pieces of fruit, a large fur bag, and something that looked and smelled like some kind of dried meat. He gave half of the food to me and sat down on one of the logs to eat.

I thanked him in Waikari, sat on the other log opposite him and we ate in silence. I kept my left arm up against my body as much as the shackles would allow, trying to keep my breast covered, which made eating more difficult. All the while he stared at me, which made me feel very uncomfortable. It wasn't the same way Turak had stared, but I didn't like it. My hearts pounded and I felt kind of hot in the face. I tried to think about something else. Maybe that would bring my heart rates down. I focused on the food he'd given me.

There were two different types of fruit that were long — one was green and the other was red. And there was a third piece, a Chumana. Was I ever going to be able to look at one of them without cringing? The long fruits were very juicy and the juice ran down my fingers as I ate. They were delicious too, better than the Chumana. The meat tasted good, but I tried not to think about what kind of animal it may have come from. I pretended it was lamb so I could get through eating it without freaking out or feeling queasy. I kept telling myself that if it tasted good and was keeping me from starving, then it didn't matter where it was from.

If he'd offered me more mushrooms, I would have declined — politely — as I was almost positive they were the cause of much of my discomfort and pain — and the dizziness too.

When we'd finished, he offered me the large fur bag, which, to my surprise, contained water, and I drank deeply. Although I was really thirsty, I wasn't sure how much water he had, so I only drank about a quarter of the bag's contents before returning it to him. Because we'd been travelling away from the river, I presumed the supply of water could be limited. I thanked him again, with no response. He just stared.

I really needed more liquids to help flush out my stomach and lessen the effects of the mushrooms, but I'd have to be content with what I'd already drank from the bag.

"Anjou," he said suddenly, and put his fist on his chest. Then he put his open hand out to me.

I blinked. I didn't need Mind-touch to figure this one out.

"Tamisan," I answered, pulling my fists up to my chest. The chains clinked and I grimaced as the shackles hurt my wrists. I was so thankful for the leaves protecting them from the harsh metal.

He seemed shocked — maybe he didn't expect me to catch on so quickly, but then a smile crept across his lips. "Ta-mi-sun," he said.

I gave a heavy sigh of relief, even though he'd pronounced it wrong. Maybe he wouldn't be so angry if he realized we would be able to communicate after all — with a bit of effort. I tried again. "Tamisan."

He repeated my name and got it right this time. Maybe this could work out. I really needed to learn this language.

"Anjou," he said again, with a fist to the chest. I repeated his name and he smiled.

He returned the water bag to me and pulled out another for himself. I drank some more, but didn't drink all of it.

As the light faded from the sky, I was surprised that it was so late in the day. We must have been riding for much longer than I'd thought. I watched as Anjou built a fire in the middle of the clearing between the logs. He used the top layer of leaf litter and some dry-looking air ferns he'd gathered from the branches of a nearby tree for kindling, and topped it with some pieces of one of the dead trees. The two stones he'd pulled out of his saddle bag and struck together gave off a bigger spark than flint, and soon we had a roaring fire.

Anjou set about gathering the large leaves of a nearby plant and it looked like he was putting them down for bedding, which made me very uneasy, thinking about what his plans were for the sleeping arrangements. My hands started to tremble. The memory of Turak filled my mind. I couldn't imagine Anjou being that disgusting… but, I didn't really know anything about him. What if he *was* that bad? What if he was *worse?*

He was putting the leaf beds right next to each other and my stomach pitched and I felt dizzy.

CHAPTER 38:

The Lure of the Stars

"Tamisan?" I nearly jumped out of my skin at the sudden voice in my head.

I'd felt Darion's Mind-touch from time to time since our last conversation when I'd told him what had happened with the failed attempt at a 'goods return,' and I answered him immediately.

"We have made some progress today — some of the land-scape looks familiar to me from what you sent me before — but we are calling it a night and are setting up camp. What is happening with you?"

"Well... We're setting up camp, too," I began. *"Umm... I found out his name is Anjou. He still isn't impressed that we speak different languages, but he's treated me okay so far. He put some soft leaves under my shackles to ease the pain to my wrists, and he gave me nicer food than the Beast-men."*

"That is good!" Darion answered. *"I was worried about you."* After a pause, he added, *"What is he doing now?"*

"He's putting some leaves down for bedding..." I remembered to read Anjou's mind instead of guessing his intentions. *"Looks like he's setting out separate beds."*

"That is such a relief!"

I could feel his relief like a warm flood washing over me. I must've had a smile on my face as Anjou was frowning at me. He was gesturing for me to lie down on one of the beds, so I reluctantly sat down on it, facing the fire. He continued to frown, but I wasn't ready to lie down yet.

I sucked in a large breath and let it out slowly, trying to calm my racing hearts. Trying to relax. I closed my eyes, but it didn't help. I opened them slowly and saw Anjou staring at me. It was unnerving.

Was it just an 'I've got a new toy' look in his eyes, or was it more like 'I've got a new sex slave'? I shuddered. I couldn't tell what he was thinking and didn't try to find out. I didn't think I could take it if I did.

Anjou stopped his staring and set about putting some extra wood on the fire.

After a while, I shifted around so I could lie down on my back. I tried to put my arms up in front of me in an attempt to cover my breasts, but it only made the shackles hurt my wrists. I finally found a position that wasn't too awkward or painful.

"The Beast-men are called the Bahadori," I told Darion. I needed something to say to fill the silence.

"That will be good to know. I'm not sure if their race has been discovered and recorded yet," he said. *"We can tell my superiors once we get you out of there."*

Hope flared up in my chest. I tried to push it down. I didn't want it to be burning brightly, just in case something went wrong and they couldn't get to me. That would be too hard to take.

Anjou grabbed the end of the rope and tied it securely around his waist, then he checked that the other end of the rope was secured to the chain. I noticed he'd put his spear within easy reach, leaning on the log. His dagger was still sheathed at his hip. Were they for me or protection from wild animals? Probably both.

He made himself comfortable in his own leaf bed — which was way too close to mine — facing me so he could keep a watchful eye on me. He made sure to hang on to the place where the rope was tied to the chain with one hand and put the other hand over the knot at his waist. I turned my face up to the canopy of trees again, not wanting to look at him. The light from the fire danced on the leaves and branches high above me.

I needed a distraction from him and all his staring. And from my thoughts. Thinking about everything was getting to me. Thinking about Turak was driving me mad. The silence stretched out and I couldn't stand it any longer.

"Darion?"

"Yes?"

"Talk to me."

"What do you mean? Am I not talking to you already?"

"Yes, but, I mean, talk about something that will keep my mind off things."

"Oh. Yes. Okay. What would you like to talk about?"

Am I not talking to you already? Who talks like that? "Do you always talk like that?" I blurted out without thinking.

"Like what?"

"Always so formal?"

"Yes. Why?"

Oops... "Sorry. It just seems so... I don't know... umm... formal. Like you can't relax or something." *Did I really just say that?*

"You do not like the way I speak?"

I cringed. *"Oh, umm, yes. I mean, no, that's not what I meant. I don't want to offend you or anything. I... I guess I'm not used to it."* I paused. *"I'm sorry. That was rude. Forget I said anything."*

"No. It is okay. I am not offended."

Why did I have to put my foot in my mouth? I needed to learn to control my mouth when I was tired or anxious. In this case, I was both. And the irony that I hadn't even used my mouth wasn't lost on me. Time to change the subject. *"Uh, so, what is it like to live on Moftar? Where did you grow up?"*

"Uh, on a farm in the country. My parents run it and we breed Taurens. They are like cows."

"That's cool. Do they look like cows?"

"They are very similar. They are quadrupeds and herbivores. They give milk and even have two horns like a cow."

I tried to imagine a cow that wasn't a cow. *"Wow. That would be so awesome. I've never seen a cow up close. I think I'd be too scared to even touch it."*

"They're big, but they are nothing to be scared of. They are docile and are smarter than people think they are."

It was still too hard to imagine.

"What about your parents?"

"I would like to show you the Taurens... As for my parents... My mother is a gentle soul. She is very caring, and though she doesn't look it, is strong enough to work the farm. My father is a strong man, in body and in will. He wanted me to take on the farm when he was too old."

I tried to imagine what life on a farm would be like. *"What happened? Or isn't it time for you to take over yet?"*

"I didn't want to."

"Oh. The lure of the stars. I know it well. That's how I ended up in this situation." I hadn't meant for my words to come out

so negative, but it was too late. *"I wish I had parents. I've done some research into other cultures and I think cloning robs us of something important."* I'd never told anyone this. I'd always kept it to myself.

"I fear you may be right," he said thoughtfully.

I was actually a bit surprised that he agreed with me. And relieved. I was glad I wasn't the only one who felt this way.

Another question popped into my head. *"What is marriage like in your culture? "*

"Oh, the woman has to dress up in a costume made of feathers and dance on a tabletop, before confessing her undying love to the man in front of his whole family and all their friends."

CHAPTER 39:

Who is He?

"Really?" I felt mortified, as if he'd asked *me* to do that. Which is really stupid.

"No. I just wanted to freak you out."

I imagined him laughing. *"That was not nice. I thought you were serious."*

"I am."

What? *"But you just said—"*

"I know what I just said. It's okay. I am kidding."

"So, what is the real *answer to my question?"*

"Well, we have this tradition that the man and woman have to have their wrists tied together for a whole week so they can get to know each other really well. They have to do everything *together."*

I thought of all sorts of embarrassing situations. *"Oh, that would be... awkward..."*

"No. I am kidding again."

"What?"

"I am joking. They do tie their wrists together, but only during the ceremony. It is to symbolise the joining of bodies and souls."

I rolled my eyes, although the 'joining of bodies and souls' sounded so romantic. *"Can you ever be serious?"*

"Yes."

"When?"

"Now."

I doubted it very much.

Darion had a question of his own. *"Does anyone get married in New Aronia? Because without the need to reproduce, I wonder if people feel there is much of a point."*

I frowned. *"Umm, they form partnerships for companionship. And they can be with anyone, not just someone who is the opposite sex."*

"That sounds sort of... I don't know... unfulfilling."

My eyes drifted closed. *"It is. I guess that's why I was never interested in any partnership. My career became more important."*

"That is sad."

"Yeah." I sighed. *"I did have my friends, Oliana and Kaliya, but that's not a life partnership. Just a friendship."*

I felt a wave of exhaustion wash over me. I was so tired. I'd asked him to distract me, and it had worked, sort of. Maybe if I didn't fight the exhaustion and said goodnight now... But I didn't want him to go. I told myself to let him go so I could sleep.

"I'm so tired. I can feel myself drifting off to sleep, so I better say goodnight," I told him.

"Tamisan?"

"Yes?"

"What is wrong?" he asked.

I felt a little twist in my chest. I'd let my shield down. *"What do you mean?"*

"There is something wrong, but it is too hard to make sense of your thoughts."

"I just got sold—"

"No... It seems to be more than that," he said. *"I know you are shook up over being sold, but you seem to have come to terms with*

that to an extent. You know you are biding your time until you are rescued. There is something else — your emotions are high and there have been a lot of wild thoughts racing around in your head. Now, do not misunderstand me, I am not trying to pry into your mind — it is there in the front of your mind and it is really bothering you."

I realized I hadn't really been keeping my mental shield up properly. I was too tired. I closed my eyes. I wasn't really seeing what was in front of me anyway.

"Some of the images are... who is he?" Darion asked. His thoughts darkened.

There was no use keeping something like this from Darion. I wasn't *intentionally* keeping it from him — not really — it was just that I didn't know how I could even *begin* to tell him or explain. It wouldn't be easy telling someone something like that even when they *couldn't* read your mind. I didn't want Darion to see my wild thoughts and feel all of my fear from when that monster was kissing me. I shouldn't feel shame or embarrassment, but I did. I sighed.

"He was one of the buyers..." I started to tell him — and show him — what had happened with Turak, and then I blurted it all out. I tried to shield some of my thoughts, but besides being tired, I hadn't really mastered the skill yet, so he probably knew everything by the time I'd finished. It was awkward and embarrassing for me, and I didn't know how he would react. A small part of my mind wondered what he would think of me. I didn't do anything to stop Turak. Would Darion think that maybe I wanted him touching me and kissing me like that? But Darion listened, and comforted me. He didn't judge me. He told me it wasn't my fault. There was nothing I could've done

to stop him anyway. He was too strong. I could feel the relief spread through my whole body.

I could sense Darion's emotions as he thought about it. He was angry and frustrated. *"How could he...? Those bastards!"*

I could almost hear him snarl. *"I... couldn't stop him..."*

"I am sorry. I should have been there to stop him. And to stop them. I..." He trailed off. I could understand his frustration at being so far away when I needed help.

CHAPTER 40:

I'm Not the One You're Looking For

"It's not your fault," I told him.

"But, I... I need to get to you. This is taking too long."

I sighed. It *was* taking too long, and no one wanted him to be here more than I did, but the reality of the situation meant he couldn't transport himself here and get me. My frustration rose too.

"How could he treat you like that? How could they stand by? How could they sell humans?"

I'd been asking myself the same questions. There was nothing we could do about it now. And, of course, we weren't allowed to interfere with their culture. I wished I could change that rule. But what could I do anyway, even if I had permission?

After a while, he said, *"It just does not stop, does it?"*

"No." I wanted to cry. My emotions were raw and my nerves felt like they were on edge. Small tears welled up and ran from the outer corners of my eyes, wetting my hair. I started to tremble again.

"You should have told me," he said.

"But there was nothing you could have done," I told him, my hearts starting to race again.

"I could have given you support, like before."

Yes, I thought. *He could've, you idiot.* I got the impression he was hurt that I didn't call him when it was happening. Or afterwards. After an awkward silence, I told him I was sorry.

"Next time, please tell me. Please call me, and remember to use your Talent, okay? It is strong in you, and getting stronger, I can feel it." He paused for a few moments, sending thoughts of reassurance to me across the void that separated us. I started to calm down and feel a bit better. *"You better get some sleep now, okay?"* he said warmly. *"Sweet dreams. Hopefully, I will meet you tomorrow."*

That thought sent a small shiver through me. Tomorrow... Tomorrow couldn't come soon enough. I sent a mental 'nod' and wiped my wet face and hair.

I made a firm decision that I *would* call him, and that I would use my Talent if Anjou decided to try anything.

Darion stayed with me for a short while to see if I was going to be okay on my own, then he was gone. I smiled to myself. I would *meet* him tomorrow. Something stirred deep inside me at the thought. Something I couldn't identify. It was a warm feeling. A tiny spark of something that grew and spread through me and I wondered what it was. What it meant... Tomorrow...

I rolled over away from Anjou and hoped that that wasn't a big mistake. They say you shouldn't turn your back on the enemy. Then I thought that maybe it wouldn't be so bad if he tried anything from behind. Maybe I could get away from his roaming hands faster if I was facing away from him.

I had to force thoughts like that out of my head. I needed to get some sleep. Even if I didn't have to walk all day, I still needed my wits about me. I went through my relaxation routine. It took way too many attempts to get myself to relax, but I finally managed to drift off to sleep.

✦

I found myself walking through a mist. The mist was the purest white, and swirled around me slowly, obscuring my surroundings. A figure appeared in the mist ahead. The figure came closer. Closer. It was a man.

He seemed to glide, rather than walk, out of the mist and straight to me. I didn't move — just stood and stared. I could see his body and clothing fairly clearly, but couldn't see his face. He reached out both arms to me, and I stepped forward eagerly to him.

I found I was no longer in chains, and I held my arms out to him.

I knew this man was Darion. I didn't know how I knew — I still couldn't see his face — but I knew.

Just as he was about to wrap me up in his arms and take me away with him, he started to move back and fade away.

"No... don't go!" I begged, but he disappeared into the mist... I tried to run after him, but it was like trying to run in chest-deep water — I was getting nowhere fast...

No!

I woke to the sound of some kind of flying thing screeching across the sky somewhere above the forest's canopy, and to the soft, cold touch of rain landing on my face. It startled me so much that I sat bolt upright and looked around. Then I remembered where I was, and remembered to cover myself with my shackled arms. How could I have slept so soundly?

It's called exhaustion, I told myself.

I thought of the dream and wondered if I would ever meet Darion. It seemed I was getting further and further away from him and from Jannali, and now I was travelling by dinosaur while he was on foot, so how could he catch up? He seemed so close — close in my mind — but at the same time, he was so far away. Despair was knocking down my door, but I couldn't let it in. I tried to block it out.

I looked to my left, expecting to see Anjou in his bed next to me. He wasn't there — he was sitting on the log, watching me. He was always watching. I wished I was with Darion right now and not this barbaric animal. I didn't want to wait another second to see his face, to be in his arms...

In his arms? What was I thinking? I hardly knew him and I was dreaming about being in his arms? Was I that desperate to get out of the situation I was in?

I must be losing it, I thought to myself. *I've been in this insane jungle too long...*

The rain came down heavier and the water was dripping down Anjou's face. All his staring was making me feel uncomfortable and weirded out, so I pulled my ragged clothing in around me and held my arms up to my chest to try to keep it there. His eyes looking directly into mine reminded me of Turak... What did this man want from me anyway?

I sat staring back at him, and I dared to probe his thoughts. I was shocked by what I found. He and his partner had been travelling through the jungle when a large spotted sabre-toothed cat attacked them and his partner was killed. Her name was Kirana. She was carrying their unborn child. I could feel tears welling up in my eyes, thankful that the rain would hide them from him.

These visions I could see clearly in his mind. I could also see images of what he hoped — to befriend me and make me his partner. I guessed he thought buying a slave was the only way to find a partner out here. He couldn't go back home to his people because he was an outcast, and I doubted he would find a woman travelling alone out here in the jungle to be his bride. So he'd bought me to set me free and make me his mate. I guess he wasn't such an animal after all. It was almost romantic... Almost.

It was a bizarre way to find a mate, but then, this was a very bizarre planet.

I could feel more tears forming in my eyes. He kept staring. I tried to imagine what it would be like to have something so terrible happen to me. I didn't have to imagine the emotions. His were right there in my mind, and I could feel them in my hearts. After a while, I had to shut them out. It was too much.

No wonder he was upset when he realized we spoke different languages. It would be a huge hurdle for us to overcome if we were to be... whatever they called marriage in their culture. But that was something that could never happen. I could never stay here with him. I didn't belong in the jungle.

I thought I could see tears in his eyes despite the rain, and he finally looked away. For a fleeting moment I wished I could stay with him, to ease his pain. But I had my own agenda: to find Darion and get out of this miserable place!

I'm sorry, I thought, *I can't help you. I'm not the one you're looking for...*

A thought came to me — he should've bought the redhead. She'd shown me some compassion. She had a caring soul. They would make a good couple. Well, maybe... I was no expert.

There was also the fact that if he'd bought the redhead, I would've ended up being the property of Turak. I shuddered.

Dragging my gaze away, I looked around. The jungle looked different in the rain. All those bright colours seemed to disappear and all the leaves and branches hung down with the weight of the water.

I rubbed myself as best I could with the shackles on to try to clean off some of the dirt from the jungle, then sat watching the heavy rain until it stopped. Was that frogs I could hear? I'd never seen a real one.

My skin felt refreshed and alive with the much-needed moisture. Meanwhile, Anjou had waited till the rain eased and pulled some more food from the beast's saddle bags. He shared the food with me and again we ate in silence while I counted the spider webs covered in raindrops. How did they survive the downpours in this place? The webs must have been extremely strong.

Just when I'd had enough of the awkward silence and opened my mouth to speak, Darion called me. I quickly closed it again and answered him without hesitation — almost instinctively. His Mind-touch seemed so familiar to me now — as if we'd been doing this for years.

"How are you this morning?"

"Um, a lot better. Thanks."

"Are you having breakfast?" Without waiting for a reply, he continued, *"We had ours before that downpour. I will tell you one thing, when it rains here, it really rains! It is going to get so humid now, too. I mean, it's going to get so humid now."*

I chuckled. He was making an effort to not be so formal and stuffy. *"Yes. Definitely, but the humidity doesn't bother me like it used to. New alien skin and all."*

Darion's tone became more serious. *"What is he up to?"*

"Staring at me. He keeps staring at me." I told him about Kirana and why he'd bought me as a slave. *"I feel for him, but there is no way I can help him. I can't stay here in the jungle!"*

"That is sad. But don't worry — he is good looking. He looks strong and capable. He could look after you."

I sucked in a breath. *"What? Are you nuts?"*

CHAPTER 41:

Good News

"Yes. I am joking. We are coming to get you. We will not stop until we have found you."

The thought of them coming to rescue me was reassuring, and I felt like a little kid waiting for my Birthday party and all those presents. But waiting was harder than I could ever have imagined. I wanted it *now*. I wanted to get away right now. I didn't think I could stay here another day — or even another hour. But I had to.

"Good news," he continued. *"Starrick has been reprimanded for all the extra air and sea activity and is not allowed to send any scouts out until further notice. That means no more search parties for a while."*

I was pleased to hear about Starrick getting a rap on the knuckles and was relieved he wouldn't be sending any ships after me. For now. And at least ground patrols would be easier to spot if I did run into them.

I must've had a wild-eyed grin on my face; Anjou sat there with such a puzzled look. *He probably thinks I'm a little crazy,* I thought to myself. I wiped the silly grin off my face and tried to act natural. Darion was laughing at me. He knew exactly what was going through my mind. I didn't mind this time, but realized I should be more careful. There would be times when I wouldn't want him to hear my thoughts, although the previous night he'd probably heard and felt a lot more than I would ever want him to. I grimaced, but there was nothing I could do about that now.

I watched as Anjou pulled a number of large leaves off the top of the fire. There were still some glowing embers under there. He'd obviously been awake a lot longer than I thought. He grabbed a stick and started digging in amongst the coals. He pushed a couple of rough chunks out of the fire and onto a flat rock. They didn't look like wood. I stepped closer, curious to see what they were.

He used two short pieces of metal to pry the chunks open and I realized they were hollow and made of metal as well. Inside were several steaming, rounded objects that were a dark brown in colour. Were they eggs of some sort?

When he stabbed one of them with one of his pieces of metal, I decided that they couldn't be eggs. They had no shells and they were kind of lumpy.

Anjou brought it over to me and handed me the long piece of metal, then stabbed another one and took a tentative bite. It was still hot. I hoped they tasted better than they looked and took a small bite. To my surprise, it tasted like a potato. He smiled when he saw that I liked what he'd cooked for us. We ate in silence as I told Darion what we were eating. He was impressed.

I was so thankful for the potato things. I hadn't felt full after the other food we'd eaten, but the potatoes had done the trick.

After washing and packing away the things he'd used to cook the potatoes, Anjou pulled a bundle of animal hide from the side pocket of the beast's saddle and sat down on the log. When he unwrapped it and pulled out the contents, I could see that he held some clothing — clothing for a woman. There were two pieces. One was a garment that covered the breasts and part of the back, much like a crop-top, and the other looked like some underpants with a loincloth attached. He held them up so I could see them and then handed them to me. They were brown with an orange tinge, with numerous black spots of varying size and shape. And they looked like they might even fit me. I could only hope...

"*Anjou has given me some clothing made from animal hide,*" I said.

"*That's great. If they fit, you will not stand out as an outsider anymore.*"

He was so right. "*They've gotta be better than what I'm wearing!*"

I looked at Anjou with his hopeful expression, then looked back at the clothes. As I imagined putting them on, I could see that I was going to have a few problems trying to put them on with my shackles on. Would he trust me enough to take them off? Probably not. But he'd have to, otherwise, I wouldn't be able to do it. Then once he did take them off, he wouldn't turn his back on me in case I ran. But what he didn't know was, I had no intention of running right now.

I smiled at him and thanked him in Waikari, then held up my hands and asked him to remove the chains. I had nothing to lose in asking him. He thought about it a while, then stepped forward, pulling the key out of the pocket at his hip.

He removed the shackles and drew his dagger; just to be sure I wasn't going to run away. He stood there in a fighting stance, his eyes so intense. *If only he knew how easy it would be for me to get away!* I mused.

I didn't run because I could run right into old Allosaurus or worse. Or there could be someone worse than Turak out there.

For now, I would stick to someone with food, water, fire and the knowledge necessary to survive this hellish place.

Okay, so now I had to undress completely in front of him if I was to have some clothes that covered me properly. I would have to get it over with. He'd already seen much more of me than I'd wanted him to with the stupid wetsuit hanging open.

Rubbing my throbbing wrists carefully, I inspected them. They were worse than before, but I knew they probably wouldn't have had much skin left on them if Anjou hadn't given me the leaves.

I took my belt off first and let it drop to the ground. I couldn't help the shudder when I remembered the Beast-man trying to cut through it with the knife. Now this was going to be horrible and embarrassing. I turned my back to him, peeled the top half of the wetsuit off and slipped the spotted top on over my head. Besides wanting some privacy, I also didn't want him to see the gill slits at the bottom edge of my rib cage. Although they would probably look like weird scars to him, it was still something I didn't want to have to explain right now. He had been angry enough about the language problem, so I didn't know how he'd cope with me being an amphibian as well.

The top actually fit me quite well, and it surprised me that there was some support built into it somehow. It didn't completely cover my gill slits, but there was nothing I could do about it. After wearing rubber clothing that was falling apart for so long, this was bliss. I noticed some places where the wetsuit had been chafing too, mainly the crotch and under my left arm. No wonder it had felt so uncomfortable. It was definitely not meant to be worn for days on end, or while hiking through the jungle.

From the corner of my eye, I could see that Anjou was turned partly away from me so that he was looking at me through his peripheral vision. That made me feel a bit better, but only a bit.

Next, I pulled the rest of the wetsuit off my right leg and quickly pulled on the 'loincloth.' It also fitted me surprisingly well and felt very soft on my skin. I closed my eyes briefly and breathed a sigh of relief. The smell of the fur was a natural smell. It blended with the different smells of the jungle. These pieces of fur were so comfortable, especially after the rubber wetsuit. I looked down at the wetsuit and wanted to throw it in the fire.

Actually, I thought, *that would be a good place for it*. That way, there was no evidence left behind. 'No interference' and all that. I wouldn't be leaving behind anything that could influence their culture. I bent down and picked up the wetsuit and the belt and turned toward the fire, but the sudden movement had Anjou starting forward with the dagger in his hand.

I stopped and pointed from the wetsuit to the fire and he surprised me by letting me past so I could toss them in. Maybe he noticed how I'd thrown them down and somehow guessed how much I despised wearing them. To me, it was a constant reminder of what they had done to me, and what they were planning to do. I felt cleaner somehow, now that I'd taken it off. Tossing it and the belt onto the dying embers of the fire felt good.

The flames leapt up around them instantly. As they started to burn and melt, I instantly regretted it. The smell of rubber burning was awful and overwhelming and gave off black smoke. Anjou looked at me with a strange expression as he coughed and moved away from the fire. It really was a horrible smell. I was glad the potatoes weren't still in there.

I remembered Darion was still with me and let him know the clothes fit me. It was such a relief to be wearing something that wasn't falling apart down the front. I thanked Anjou again, and he gave me a crooked smile. I caught a thought that gave him great pain — these had belonged to Kirana.

CHAPTER 42:
He Was the One

"That's great!" Darion was saying, oblivious to Anjou's distress. *"Yes. They feel really soft."*

Anjou looked very apologetic when he came to me with the shackles in his hands. I could see the pain in his eyes when I held up my hands to let him put them on, and he could see how bad my wrists were.

I told Darion I'd burnt the wetsuit. He thought it was a good idea. I wondered if me being out in the jungle was doing any 'damage.' The natives had seen my wetsuit and the Bahadori saw how tough the material was, especially the belt. They couldn't even cut through it. I couldn't change what had happened or what they'd seen. I just needed to make sure I didn't mess anything else up. Somehow.

Darion interrupted my thoughts. *"I will have to go now. We don't want to wear ourselves out. You never know when you will need all your strength in this jungle!"*

"Yeah, you got that right," I agreed. I didn't really want him to go — big surprise there — but I knew he was right. We said goodbye and he left.

As I looked back at Anjou, he suddenly stooped down and grabbed one of my feet, lifting it off the ground and putting me off balance.

What the... "What are you doing?" I said. I had to grab his shoulders with both hands to keep from falling over and he flinched as the shackles dug into his back. I felt his strong muscles under my hands and quickly removed them as soon as I'd regained my balance. . He was pretty ripped, but I didn't want to be touching him. I didn't want anything to do with him or his plans for me. I definitely wasn't going to do anything to make him think he had any chance of it succeeding.

He wasn't deterred. He didn't seem to notice how quickly I'd pulled away from him. He looked at the sole of my foot, then dropped it, strode over to the beast and came back with a pair of boots made from the same sort of hide that I was wearing. My hearts soared. He was going to give me something to cover my poor feet!

I was glad he hadn't noticed the flap of skin tucked up on the side of my foot. That could have been a bit of a problem.

I gladly took the boots from him and put them on. They had some sort of strapping across the hide, maybe to stop them from falling down or falling off. The soles were also made of hide, but it was a lot thicker than the rest. What a great relief to have something on my feet after all the walking I'd done — even if they were a bit loose — and they were so soft that I felt like I was walking on velvet!

I looked up from my boots to see him gesturing for me to get up onto the beast, so I started to walk over to it while he picked up the water bags. I stumbled, so he put down the bags and adjusted the strapping on the outside of the boots so they were no longer loose. He seemed puzzled that I didn't know how to do this. Of course Sifayah had never worn shoes at all, so would never have seen boots like these.

It wasn't long before we were plodding along through the jungle again. We'd left the path and were still travelling away from the river, slowly weaving through the trees and vines. I looked down at my new boots. Anjou could not even *begin* to know how much I appreciated them.

It was starting to get hot as the sun climbed higher in the sky, but the clothing and boots didn't feel hot. Whatever animal the hide was from would have been perfectly adapted for these weather conditions. And of course the extra moisture in the air after the rain felt rather pleasant.

A sudden shriek from above made me jump and the hairs on the back of my neck stood up. Anjou pointed to a large colourful bird that had perched on a branch high above us. It gave another loud shriek. I looked at it for a few moments, then Anjou tapped me on the shoulder.

"Shakka," he informed me, still pointing at it like I was a child at the zoo. He repeated the word.

I nodded. "Shakka."

He smiled.

Somewhere off in the distance came a frightening roar that could only have come from a very large reptile, and we instinctively turned our heads in the direction of the awful sound. I shuddered as it roared a few more times, higher pitched and kind of frantic like it'd been hurt, and then it fell silent. I hoped whatever had attacked it would stay there and feast. I didn't want it to head in our direction. A shiver ran down my spine at the very thought.

I turned my attention back to Anjou. I knew I wasn't planning to stay with him, but thought it would be a good idea to learn the language as it seemed to be the main language spoken by the people of Althar 3. I pointed at a large leaf that was hanging down from a branch above us and asked if he could tell me what it was. I didn't worry about speaking Waikari anymore. There was no point.

Anjou happily told me the name, so I kept it going. He told me the names for almost everything we saw until we stopped again, presumably for some lunch. My enhanced memory helped me to catalogue most of what I'd learned. We dismounted and my rope was tied to a tree trunk. We kept our language lesson going all through the meal, and it was much better than eating in silence. It seemed to make Anjou happy too.

⊰•⊱

Once we'd started travelling again, I realized it had been a long time since I'd heard from Darion. I decided to call him and was surprised to find out they'd been busy fighting off a large dinosaur — among other things.

Darion was exhausted, but he let me read his thoughts to find out what had happened. As they trudged through the dense undergrowth, they stumbled upon the camp of the Bahadori. Going in there and making them release their captives was against the rules, no matter how much they wanted to do it. No interfering with the natives. Of course, this meant circling around the camp at a distance that would ensure they wouldn't be seen or heard. But as they were about to start out, a huge reptile burst through the jungle and grabbed one of the Bahadori by the shoulder and arm with its powerful jaws.

It looked like a larger version of the reptile I'd seen in the jungle before I was captured by the Bahadori. This one was

about four metres tall and looked even more like an Allosaurus than the smaller one.

The two slaves cried out and as they tried to run in chains,
the young male tripped over the female. Once they'd managed to get to their feet, they both managed to run in the same
direction. The other two Bahadori had drawn their swords
and spears. They tried to attack the beast, which had taken
a large bite out of the first Beast-man and had dropped his
lifeless body to deal with the two little pests that were poking
it with sharp objects. It roared loudly. I cringed at the sight in
my mind of the Bahadori with the missing arm and shoulder.

As the second Bahadori fell, Darion and his men were
already there with laser pistols firing. They didn't want to be
seen by the natives, but were not about to stand by while the
monster killed innocent people in chains. One of Darion's
men ran over so quickly that when the reptile turned on its
new attackers, its tail had sent him flying backwards into
the underbrush. A quick probe had told Darion he wasn't
seriously injured.

As they kept up their attack, the beast roared in pain and
it tried to grab another victim. I realized it was the roars that
Anjou and I had heard earlier. I'd thought it had sounded
hurt, but never imagined it was being shot by laser pistols.

The lasers ripped into its flesh and the men kept on firing
until it fell and eventually lay still on the soft earth. They looked
around to see the slaves huddled at the water's edge and the last
Bahadori sitting on a log, covered in blood and scratches from
the monster's claws. Not all of the blood was his. Darion strode
over to him. He recognized the scarred face from what I'd shown
him in my mind. He was the one that had cut me with the knife.
Darion was so angry that he struck him across the face with

the butt of his pistol, which knocked him to the ground. The Bahadori wouldn't know why he did it, but Darion didn't care.

CHAPTER 43:
My Secret Was Out

Darion searched the hides that the Bahadori wore and found a crude-looking key in a little pouch at his waist. He grabbed it and walked over to the slaves. They cringed at his advance, fearing he may give them the same treatment he'd given the Bahadori, but were relieved when he produced the key and unlocked each of their shackles and gestured for them to go. They wasted no time in running off into the jungle together, with smiles and warm words that I recognized as thanks from Anjou's language lessons as they went. I felt so happy for them and wondered how long they'd been in chains. I wondered if they would find their families and friends again.

The injured man in Darion's team had to have medical treatment as he'd broken his ankle when he'd landed, so Darion had ported him back to Jannali.

Darion was worn out because he'd used his mind to stop the dinosaur from charging and attacking them head-on. He hadn't been quick enough to stop the first man getting hurt; he'd run in unexpectedly.

"You have *been busy!"* I said. I could feel his fatigue, and thought I should drop the connection so he wouldn't be sapping what little remained of his strength. *"I can feel your exhaustion so I'd better go now and let you rest."*

"No. Stay with me a little longer," he insisted. *"I have eaten a couple of energy bars, so I will be feeling better soon."*

I did as he asked, though I wondered why he would want me to keep the link when he knew he could rest properly if we dropped it. Maybe he found comfort in me being there, just as I did when he was there for me. Whatever the reason, I wasn't going to ask. I was content to stay with him. We kept the link for a long time — not really sending any thoughts across — just being there in one another's minds was enough.

I thought about what Darion had shown me in his mind. He'd told me the team had to dress in skins in case they were seen by the natives, but it was hard to imagine until I could see the other men through Darion's eyes. They almost looked like they belonged in the jungle, but their hair was too short and well-kept. The laser pistols would kind of give them away too. I hoped they didn't get into too much trouble for letting the slaves and the Bahadori see them using modern weapons.

While Darion and his team were recovering, Anjou and I were travelling through the jungle. We came across another path, so the beast was able to pick up speed again. I gave a mental groan. I wanted us to slow down, not speed up. I wanted to be found. *Now!*

Oh, I'll never get out of here! They can never catch up! It's hopeless...

I made sure I shielded that little outburst from Darion. He had enough to worry about right now.

A few little four-legged furry creatures ran past us at an alarming rate, which startled us and caused the beast to step sideways. I thought I was going to fall off its back, but Anjou easily kept me steady with his arms on either side of me. As the beast recovered and continued on, I kept an eye on the place the creatures had emerged from, thinking it was very likely they were running from a predator. I was relieved when nothing came rampaging out of the scrub toward us.

I told Darion I'd heard the reptile's roars earlier. He barely answered.

"Shouldn't you be sleeping?" I asked him. I didn't want to sever the link, but I was concerned about him.

"No... Well, yes, probably, but I could not sleep right now — I may be low on energy, but I am too pumped up after what happened. Besides — this is nice..."

I couldn't disagree with him there. It was almost like we were sitting side-by-side in comfortable silence. So we kept it going until the beast came to a stop in a small clearing. Reality again. Couldn't we just stay where we were?

We dismounted the beast and I decided to ask Anjou what it was called. He told me it was a Rodon.

"I better let you rest properly now," I told him. *"We've stopped again and I need to be able to concentrate on what he is saying."*

"Okay," he reluctantly agreed, *"talk to you later."*

"Bye."

<hr>

We ate dinner and before Anjou prepared us some beds, it rained again. He'd quickly covered the area in the middle of the small clearing with some large leaves and I assumed he was planning on lighting a fire there. My skin felt refreshed, with the rain providing plenty of water to keep my skin from drying out too much.

I guessed the heavy rain would be good for keeping me and my clothing reasonably clean. I tried to imagine what I would smell like after a few weeks in the jungle without any rain. It would be unbearable. But even with regular rain, I was sure we would need to remove our clothing and wash it now and then — and even wash ourselves in the river.

Once the cleansing rain had stopped, Anjou gathered our water bags, which were nearly empty, and walked over to a nearby tree with broad leaves. Each leaf tapered down into wide cone shapes that collected the rainwater, and he carefully tipped one of them over until the water poured into the bag. Once it was full, he did the same to fill the other bag. So we didn't really need to rush back to the river once we ran out of water like I thought we would.

His method of collecting water was good to know for survival in the jungle, but at the same time, it was bad for me and my escape plan. If we didn't need to go to the river, how could I put my plan into action? I'd planned to 'fall' in and pretend to drown when I needed to get away from Anjou.

Anjou noticed the leaves under my shackles had fallen out. I wasn't really sure when I'd lost the leaves and was in a lot of pain. He pulled more leaves out of the pouch in the Rodon's saddle and brought them over to me, ready to put them on my wrists again. As he started to reach for my arm, his eyes widened and he grabbed my right hand with both his hands and pulled it to him. He spread my fingers out wide — the leaves forgotten as they fluttered to the ground. My secret was out.

CHAPTER 44:
Something Dangerous

Each time he'd come close to me — close enough to see my hands — I'd tried my best to keep my fingers close together so he couldn't see they were webbed, but I was busy thinking about how I was going to pretend to drown without a river to drown in, and my fingers were the furthest thing from my mind.

I tried to pull away, but it was too late. He stared open-mouthed at my hand, looked up at my face in disbelief, then seized my left hand to look at it too. I had no idea how to explain it to him. I didn't know enough words in his language to even try.

He asked lots of questions, holding up my hands and pointing to the webbing, but I could only understand a few words and couldn't give him an answer. I couldn't tell him my hands were webbed because I was an amphibian. I was sure from his reaction that his people didn't know about the Waikari and I was determined to keep it that way. I wasn't allowed to interfere and telling him about the Waikari would definitely count as interfering.

The Waikari wouldn't want the Jungle People knowing about them. They kept to themselves for a reason, and after discovering the slave trade, I was glad they'd stayed in the cove and out of sight.

Anjou became frustrated and paced up and down for a while. Then he motioned for me to sit down on a nearby rock and proceeded to pull one of my boots off. I gave a mental groan. He could see the webbing between my toes, but I kept the flap of skin on the side of my foot well tucked in and he didn't notice it. It wouldn't be something you would think to check for if you were looking to see if someone had webbed toes. I would never have thought of it.

He paced some more, thinking and muttering to himself. He kept looking at me with a strange expression on his face. Then he finally remembered the leaves. He picked them up and gave me the relief I badly needed. He then gestured for me to sit on a large rock as he started up the fire. I hoped he would think I had some sort of deformity and would leave it at that. Maybe he was worried about me passing on the deformity to our children.

My blood ran cold. Children. I didn't want to be with him at all, let alone have his children, but I guessed it would be something that would be inevitable in a society without any form of birth control. I shuddered. That was *not* going to happen. I wasn't sticking around, and if he tried anything now, I wouldn't let him near me.

We ate in silence, then Anjou found us some leaves to sleep on. I didn't try to contact Darion again that night. I thought it would be better to let him rest.

—◆—

In the morning it occurred to me that Darion and I had actually passed each other without knowing it. From what I saw of Darion's encounter with the dinosaur, and the direction the roars had come from, they were a lot further along the river. They'd travelled along the river bank and Anjou and I had gone away from the water and missed them completely. The thought made me so furious and so frustrated that I had to close my eyes and take a few deep breaths. How long would I have to stay in this awful place and play my role? I did *not* want to stay long enough for Anjou to think we had a chance at a life together. He should have picked the redhead... No! Then Turak would have been able to buy me! A cold shiver ran down my spine as I thought of that scenario again. It was a lose/lose situation for me either way.

I dragged my thoughts back to the problem at hand. Darion and his team would continue to the caves and wait for me there. I wished he could just come and get me. I felt a strong urge to contact him and tell him to turn back, but I'd lost my way. We'd been travelling on the back of the Rodon and I'd been in contact with Darion for a lot of that time, not paying any attention to where we were going. Besides, it was too hard to keep track of anything when all the trees, shrubs, vines and mushrooms all kind of looked the same. There was the odd tree that was taller than the rest, maybe the trunk of one of the taller trees that was much thicker than the others around it, and some scenery that stood out from the crowd, but only when they were right in front of you. Once you moved on, they sort of blended in with everything else again.

It was too difficult. They could wander all around the jungle for days and not find me. The caves would be the best place to meet. They were a noticeable landmark and they were close to the river. All I had to do was get back to the river.

I thought about my plan. Once we reached the river, I would wait till Anjou was taking the end of the rope over to tie it to a tree or something and yank it out of his grip. He was a bit more relaxed now than he was at first. I hadn't tried to run, so maybe he thought I'd be happy to stay with him. I'd have to gather up the chain and the rope so I could run, then I'd pretend to fall into the river and stay down. Anjou would think I'd drowned, and I could swim upriver to the caves and meet Darion there. Hopefully, they would have something I could use to get the shackles off my wrists. I'd have to ask Darion if he still had the key. I was hoping all the keys were the same.

I couldn't help thinking it would be cruel to let Anjou think I was dead, but I couldn't really think of any other way of escaping him without hurting him physically or having him still following or searching for me. It was the least-cruel option.

Now I just had to hope we would be heading back to the river soon...

I stood up and stretched as best I could with my hands bound together. I was so grateful that I didn't have to try to cover myself anymore. The clothing Anjou had given me was so much better than the wetsuit, even before it was cut. I was hungry, but I didn't want more of the same type of food.

Please, please, no more fruit or mushrooms! I need real *food. Something hot with plenty of flavour. A hearty soup or stew to line my stomach... Or maybe I would settle for some of that sweet meat...*

I knew I couldn't get 'something hot with plenty of flavour,' so the sweet meat would have to do. Or even those potato things.

Anjou was fossicking in his saddle bags for some breakfast and as he turned around, water bags in his hands, he froze and I could see a strange expression spread across his face. His eyes widened and his face drained of all colour.

He was looking past me and into the jungle. I felt a burst of adrenalin; there was something lurking behind me. Something dangerous. The hairs on the back of my neck stood up and I stared at Anjou, standing still as a statue. I couldn't hear anything behind me, and that scared me even more. It meant it was a predator, probably moving through the underbrush silently, ready to strike.

I could feel anger and sadness rolling off Anjou. I realized I could look into his mind and see what he could see. Another adrenalin burst hit me as I did — it was a large jungle cat like the one that had killed Kirana. I watched its movements through Anjou's eyes. It was creeping up and getting ready to pounce.

I could see what Anjou was thinking too. His spear was leaning on a rock to his left — for some reason, he'd taken it out of the long sheath on the Rodon's saddle. Maybe he was planning to kill something for breakfast... or lunch. His gaze flicked to it for a split second, judging the distance. He was thinking if he could get to it before the cat pounced, then he might be able to save me. I could feel all of the pain and guilt he felt because he wasn't able to save Kirana. He had a real fear that it would happen all over again.

The big cat was ready, and so was I. In the blink of an eye, it leapt out from the underbrush.

CHAPTER 45:
The Sweet Meat

I resisted the intense urge to run or scream or duck down into a ball and stayed still until it had taken two more leaps to get to where I stood, then I lunged forward and to my left. At the same time, Anjou had dropped our water bags and reached for his spear and rushed forward. I landed hard between a fallen tree and a large rock, and the jolt of pain to my wrists made me cry out. I turned to see that Anjou had dug the back end of the spear into the ground and held it in place so that the cat landed on it. It let out a deafening roar and fell to one side with the spear sticking out of its chest, writhing in pain and roaring again and again. Anjou was on him instantly, and he sliced its throat from ear to ear with his dagger. Blood burst from the cat's throat and splashed across the ground. My stomach churned and I turned away before throwing up everywhere.

I tried to think of something else, without much luck. I could hear the blood splashing on the ground as the cat's pulse pushed it out of its carotid arteries and it made disgusting, gurgling sounds in its throat as it tried to roar. I couldn't look. I threw up again.

The place I'd chosen to dive into was fairly soft. The leaves were large and still a bit green, so there weren't too many crispy brown ones. The rock was covered in such a velvety moss that it was like a short variety of grass, but I was still in a lot of pain from the unforgiving shackles. The leaves under the shackles were practically useless after the way I'd landed. I looked at my wrists. The shackles had dug into my skin on both wrists and blood was dripping along my arms. More blood. I didn't want to see any more blood. I'd seen enough on my thigh and all down my legs, and now the ground all around me was covered in it from the cat.

I felt like screaming at the top of my lungs. I wanted to get out of this jungle. This nightmare.

I have to get out of here. I need to run and I have to get to Darion. I don't want to hear — that — and see the blood. I don't want to know what Anjou's doing now. I closed my eyes tightly, as if that would make it stop somehow.

After all the things that had happened to me since I woke up at Maztec, I'd nearly been ripped to shreds by some prehistoric jungle cat. I couldn't stop the shudder that travelled down my spine. My body was trembling all over. I forced myself to take a few deep breaths. I needed to calm down and somehow stay sane.

After the cat's gurgling had stopped, I could hear some sounds I couldn't quite recognise. I dared to look up and instantly wished I hadn't. Anjou had dragged the dead cat into a position against a large tree root so its head was facing downwards to let the blood drain away. He had also removed his spear from its body and started to skin the beast. My stomach did a somersault and I turned quickly and threw up over the other side of the log again. Then I stayed there with my eyes closed, again trying to think about something else. It wasn't easy.

I thought about Oliana. She was always doing something to make me laugh. She had a good sense of humour and could always cheer me up when I was feeling down. But she would never be able to be my friend anymore. She was a part of my past now. Thinking about that didn't really help.

The sound effects I could hear didn't help either. My stomach lurched but there was nothing left to throw up.

I had to remind myself that this was the jungle. This was nature at its wildest. It was such a dangerous place and the law of nature was to kill or be killed. I was glad I'd stayed with Anjou and not escaped into the jungle alone. Without him, I wouldn't have seen or heard a predator like that. I would've easily been its next meal. Ice rolled down my spine.

I heard Anjou start a fire and after a while, I chanced another peek. Anjou had spread the different cuts of meat out on a large rock. I tried not to look at it. When I looked up at Anjou, he had an incredulous expression on his face. A quick probe told me he was puzzled at my reaction to him skinning and preparing the beast for food. But also, he was amazed I'd known exactly when to move. He'd been so sure I would be killed. The only thing Anjou had hoped for was to kill the cat this time. The last one had gotten away, taking Kirana with it. He'd tried so hard to stop it and had received some serious injuries for his efforts. The piece of animal skin that went across his chest and over his shoulder covered the scars from where the other cat had swiped its claws across his flesh.

I dared to look up and could see that he was starting to cook some of the meat for our breakfast. My stomach executed a backflip with a full twist, but I managed to stop myself from vomiting again. My stomach also growled. I was so hungry that I couldn't refuse the meat. I'd hoped for a hot meal and I was getting one, even if it was only meat on its own. I shouldn't complain. I should just toughen up and eat it. It's not like I was a vegetarian or anything. The meat would give me much-needed protein and give me the energy I needed to get through the nightmarish jungle alive.

It could even be the sweet meat I liked so much. If so, could I ever eat it again? I'd have to. I tried to think of how nice it had tasted. I knew that with all the meat I'd ever eaten, there had been a live animal that had been slaughtered, but it was very different to have it killed and butchered right in front of you.

I dragged myself up and sat at the other end of the fallen tree, away from my mess and closer to the fire. I watched him cook the meat and psyched myself up to eat it. When it was ready, he gave me some of it on a piece of flat wood that served as a plate. I was glad as it was still hot.

Okay, here goes...

I closed my eyes and opened my mouth and bit into it. The sweet meat! It was tender and sweet and tasted so much better when it was hot. I ate it all and made sure I didn't look over at the carcass of the big cat.

Anjou gave me some water and fruit he'd probably originally planned to have for breakfast. It was a fruit I hadn't tasted before. It actually tasted kind of like a pineapple and was just as juicy.

After I'd finished, I felt like I was full for the second time since I'd escaped into the jungle.

Escaped? Ha! That was a joke! Out of the frypan and into the fire!

I wondered if I'd done the right thing. I could've stayed at Maztec and contacted Darion from there. Then they could've sent people over to arrest Starrick and rescue me and any others. But I didn't know I *could* call Darion until *after* I'd escaped. I wouldn't have called out to him with my mind if I wasn't in trouble. My thoughts kind of lead me around in a big circle. It was maddening. I shrugged. There was nothing I could do about it now anyway. I was stuck in the jungle and would have to deal with it.

I thanked Anjou in his language and he smiled. Then he walked over to the cat and started hacking it up. I quickly turned away and watched a beautifully-coloured bird dance through the branches of a nearby tree. I didn't want to lose my nice breakfast, which really made no sense to me as he was over there slicing up more 'breakfast.'

CHAPTER 46:

A Spoilt Child

Later that afternoon, as I was leaning over to get the water bag from its place near the fallen tree, I heard a noise in the bushes behind me. Fear coursed through my veins. I whirled around, thinking it was another wild animal and I found that I wasn't that far off the mark — it was Turak!

My hearts stopped for a moment as the realization that he'd followed us sank in. He'd tracked us down. Somehow. I wanted to run, but I was chained up like an animal. My hearts raced.

Behind him was the redhead he'd purchased from the slave traders. She looked exhausted and dirty and she was having trouble standing. To track us on foot, he must've made her walk night and day. Maybe even carried her part of the way.

They may never have caught up if Anjou hadn't cut up the big cat for food. He'd put all the different cuts of meat into bags made of hide. Some he'd spread out to dry in the sun and some he'd hung over the fire to smoke. It had taken most of the day.

Anjou had seen them approach and was already taking a defensive stand. Turak smiled at Anjou, gave a warm greeting and they grasped each other's wrists in a kind of handshake. I couldn't help feeling uneasy — was he still after me? He must have been. Why else would he have tracked us?

I wished I wasn't tied to a tree. The urge to run was so strong that I had to clench my fists and take a deep breath. Maybe I could go over slowly and untie the rope while they were talking.

I remembered the water bag and grabbed it. My mouth had suddenly gone dry and my hearts pounded out a steady rhythm. As I sucked in the cool liquid, I watched the scene unfold.

While the two men continued to talk, they turned and looked directly at me and Anjou started to shake his head. Turak was looking me up and down like he approved of my new clothing. I didn't care what he thought. I sent a quick probe into Anjou's mind. From the images and a few words I recognized, my worst fears were confirmed — Turak wanted to buy me from him!

No!! The adrenalin was pumping through me now. How could I get away if Anjou sold me to him?

Anjou was telling him "naya." He was also refusing a swap between the two slaves, but Turak wasn't going to take no for an answer.

I looked across to the tree. Could I untie the rope before they noticed?

I wondered why Anjou would refuse so quickly and easily when he could have someone that spoke the same language. Someone who wouldn't be a wuss when it came to slaughtering an animal in the jungle and cutting it up for food. Maybe he didn't want to start again. I'd shown him I could learn the language quickly. And maybe he liked me... After all, he *did* just save my life...

But why did he like me? Why did he pick me? Why did Turak pick me? Was it the way I looked? Was it this body? Did that mean that that was all anybody would see from now on? Would they bother to look deeper? Would they see the real me?

I'd lost more than my body. I'd lost *me* somewhere along the way. Would everyone only see a pretty face? Would they see an alien? What about Darion? Would he be like the rest?

It was easy to work out why Turak wanted me, but why wasn't he satisfied with the redhead? Surely it didn't matter who turned out to be his sex slave.

And Anjou... Did he only want me for one thing too? Is that what men were really like, no matter where they were from? Maybe Darion was like that too, underneath everything. Maybe it was all just male instinct. It made me feel repulsed. I didn't want anything to do with any of them. I wanted to run...

I started inching my way closer to the tree.

The conversation between Anjou and Turak was turning ugly as they started to raise their voices. I was sure Turak always got his own way and that he would not accept Anjou's answer under any circumstances. Nothing Anjou could do or say was going to make any difference and I felt an impending sense of doom.

I kept moving slowly toward the tree. Maybe they wouldn't see me. Maybe they would be too busy arguing.

The redhead was cringing and stepping away from the conflict when, without warning, Turak raised a huge arm and struck Anjou across the face with the back of his hand. Anjou's head jerked violently to the side. He fell to the ground and didn't move.

"No!!!" I shrieked. I ran to where he was lying and crouched down to see if he was alright. A quick probe combined with my fingers on his neck told me he was unconscious, and Turak took the opportunity to grab my chain.

My blood boiled and my chest felt like ice as I stood to face him. I looked up at his cruel face and those defiant eyes. His smile quickly turned to a smirk. He'd gotten what he wanted like a spoilt child.

I squirmed under his gaze, hearts racing faster than ever. I desperately wanted to look away, but didn't want to give him the satisfaction of knowing how scared I felt.

To my surprise, he was the one to turn away first. Then he did something I *didn't* expect — he switched the rope so that it was tied to the redhead's chain — all the while keeping a good grip on mine. I tried to pull away when he was busy with her chain, with no success. The other end of the rope was, of course, still firmly attached to the tree, so when Anjou came to, he would find the other woman sitting there instead of me. She would be his new slave.

I was glad it was the woman who'd helped me. She was kind enough to help me, so I thought she'd make a good partner for Anjou. It was funny that I'd already come to this conclusion. It wasn't funny that I now belonged to a barbarian that had already shown how I would be treated as his property.

What am I going to do now? I thought desperately. *What will he do to me? I need to get away. I need to run. Even if it's not safe to be out here alone! I'll just have to take my chances!*

CHAPTER 47:

Alone With Him

I looked back down at Anjou, then across at the redhead, who slowly sat down on a tree root, totally worn out.

Anjou would be better off now with someone who spoke the same language, I thought, *and who wasn't planning to leave the first chance she got.*

It was a better outcome for him than the one I was planning, but not the best plan for me, because now I belonged to *him.* The *animal.*

Turak's upper lip curled into another smirk and my hearts rose up into my throat as I wondered what he would do next. He stood there and clenched his fists, which made me cringe, then beat one of them forcefully on his chest like a Neanderthal. He turned to our leftovers from earlier and shoved some of the cooked meat into his mouth, chewing loudly. Next, he collected up some of the meat that Anjou had dried out, as well as one of the water bags, and walked back over to where I stood.

You're nothing but a thief! I thought. *After all Anjou's hard work...*

He put a huge hand on my shoulder that made my hearts stop, spun me around, and gave me a shove to get me to start moving. I stumbled, but managed to stay on my feet. I started walking, slowly at first, but picked up the pace when he prodded me hard in the back with a finger. My chest tightened and my heartbeats quickened again until they were pounding in my ears.

What could I do? How could I get away from him *this* time? I did *not* want to be alone in the jungle with him... I needed a plan.

I was thinking hard while I walked. The shackles were already starting to cause a lot of pain. I lifted up my hands and could see that my wrists had started bleeding again. I grimaced. The jungle had brought me nothing but pain. I should've stayed and took my chances with the loony scientist.

My new body had started out with no scars and after only a few days, I had a huge knife wound in my leg, a grazed knee, a cut on my foot and I had lost skin from my wrists. It felt wrong to be damaging this body. I felt guilty for doing this to Sifayah, which was messed up. This body didn't belong to her anymore. It felt strangely like borrowing a friend's new Hovercar, and then driving it so carelessly that it ended up scratched and dented within a week. The friend would never trust you again.

Only, I wouldn't be giving this body back...

Soon we were away from the clearing and were trudging through the thick jungle. My mind was racing faster, trying to think of a way to escape... He was too strong for me. I couldn't try to fight him off and I doubted that I could outrun him, especially while carrying the long, heavy chain. There had to be another way. The first thing I needed was to get out of these chains... and the only way to do that was to get the key... I needed to get the key. Right now.

Turak didn't take Anjou's key from him, so I assumed his key must fit both sets of shackles. He probably kept it in a pocket similar to the one in Anjou's loincloth thing.

If only I could get my hands on the key. Then at least I'd be rid of this wretched chain, and maybe I'd have a chance of getting away.

My pounding hearts beat even louder. Without the chain, I might be able to outmanoeuvre him amongst all of the hanging vines and underbrush.

I sensed we were heading back toward the river, but I wasn't sure. We seemed to be going downhill. If we were, maybe I could somehow put the plan I had for ditching Anjou into action with Turak. I knew I couldn't just get the key, unlock the shackles and run. Even if I could outrun or outmanoeuvre him, he would hunt me down forever. I was positive of it now. He'd tracked me this far already — on foot. Who would do that? There was something not right about him. I had to make him think I was dead so he'd give up on me.

So getting the key from him before we reached the river was a big priority. I started to think hard about how I was going to manage it. I needed to use my Talent. My thoughts turned to the HoloMovies on telekinetic powers and how they were used to retrieve things the Talent couldn't see — teleporting them directly into the Talent's hands.

I went through it all in my mind. I recalled the explanations of how they did it. I needed to concentrate hard on the key. It would be difficult as I'd only seen the other key for a few moments. I knew what that one looked like and could only assume this one looked the same. Also, I had to assume it was in a pocket that was in a similar spot to the one in Anjou's clothing.

I groaned inwardly. I had some serious doubts about my ability to port the key into my hand. Even an expert would have trouble. But I had to try. I had to get away. There was no way I could stay with this maniac. His actions had shown me what was in store for me. That thought nearly made me trip over. I stumbled and he prodded me in the back again.

We'd only been walking for about ten minutes, ducking and weaving through the jungle while I tried hard to concentrate on finding the key, when I realized I should be contacting Darion. I'd forgotten again. He wouldn't be happy that I hadn't called him. I'd promised I would if I got into any sort of trouble again.

I reached out with my mind, but before I could call him, my foot got hooked on something and I came crashing down on a rock that was covered in a thick, grassy moss. It was the same kind of moss that had been covering the rock at the campsite. I cried out when I landed on my hands.

As I'd fallen, I'd seen that it was Turak's foot and not a tree root that had caused me to fall. But before I could even try to get to my feet, he was on top of me!

He landed with most of his weight being caught by his hands either side of me on the soft moss, but it still hurt. As he reached one large hand out and turned me over, I could feel something small and hard under his clothing at his hip. Maybe it was the key! It seemed to be located in about the same place as the key that Anjou had.

As I looked up into his dark eyes, I realized I was in real trouble. He was intent on doing more than kissing me. I couldn't look into his eyes any longer. I squeezed my eyes shut and he laughed.

He said something I couldn't understand, but I was *not* going to probe his mind to find out what it was.

As he grabbed one of my arms and pulled it up so my hands were above my head, I started to really panic. I felt exposed and vulnerable with my arms up, like I had no protection from him. I tried to bring my arms down, but he was too strong.

I opened my eyes to see what he was doing, just in time to see his face coming down toward mine and he began to kiss me again. I squeezed them shut again. *No no no no!*

All the emotions came flooding back, but with more intensity this time. This time I was alone with him — trapped by him... There was no one to help me... No one around to draw their daggers in protest *this* time...

He was kissing hard like before, and I was fighting the panic that gripped me. I felt helpless there with him on top of me. This could not be happening! It was painful and disgusting and terrifying and I tried to move my head to the side and I couldn't get away from him.

I wanted to scream, to cry out, to kick and punch and scratch his eyes out, but could hardly move. I was struggling to think about how I was going to escape, but I couldn't think with his tongue in my mouth.

Meanwhile, Turak was in no hurry. He could take all the time he wanted. He knew he was too strong for me. He knew he would get what he wanted. He knew I wouldn't be able to put up even the smallest fight — and there was nothing I could do about it.

But there was. I remembered the key. I *must* get it! I *must* focus. I needed to teleport it into my hand.

My mind kept screaming out "no" over and over again. *I have to stop him. I have to try. I...*

Suddenly, he stopped kissing me and got up off the ground, pulling me up with him till I was kneeling at his feet. He pulled my head back by pulling my hair again and stared down at me, gloating. I looked up at him and tried not to show my fear, but I knew it was written all over my face. My hearts were pounding so hard that I was sure he could hear them and he held my hair so tight it made my eyes water. So much for me trying not to show fear...

The key... I had to get it...

He spoke to me and the only word I could really understand was *brinza*, which meant *feet*.

His grin broadened as he started to push my head down toward his feet. I did *not* want to be forced to grovel, but couldn't escape his grasp. He kept pushing till my nose was touching his right foot, then he let go and stood back up.

You filthy pig!

CHAPTER 48:

The Key

I felt breathless. There was no way I was going to stay where I was. I started to get up and was pushed back down again, which hurt more than it did the first time he did it.

I tried to slow my laboured breathing. Tried to calm myself. *I need to focus and get the key...*

He made me stay there for a while longer, laughing cruelly, then pulled me all the way up to a standing position, and it felt like maybe he'd pulled out a large chunk of my hair in the process.

The key! I knew where the key was now. I had a much better chance of porting it this time. I needed to concentrate harder. But how could I? He wouldn't stop. He was out to prove he was the boss. He was my *master* and I had to obey him. He probably got a huge kick out of it. He was the Supreme Being — or so he thought. He started kissing me again.

No no no no no! Stop!

I couldn't do this. I couldn't stand it. I had to do something. I couldn't concentrate enough to get the key. I was going to fail. He was going to...

That was it. I realized I couldn't do this alone. I needed help. This time I would call Darion. I kept my eyes tightly closed and reached out for him. It was so hard to concentrate on just doing that one thing.

"Tamisan! What is happening?" Darion asked, but then he could *see* what Turak was doing. *"No no no! Push him away!"*

I was trying to turn my face away from Turak's, but his grip on my hair was too tight. I could barely hear or understand what Darion was saying.

I realized Turak was touching me. He was touching my backside and pulling me toward him. I tried to pull back, but I couldn't. His hand moved around to my stomach and up to my breast and I couldn't scream and couldn't stop him and my mind was going to explode.

I could hear Darion's voice in my head, but it was far away and all I could focus on was what Turak was doing to me and I felt like I was falling into a dark hole and it was swallowing me up and I couldn't breathe.

Darion was telling me to focus. I could hear him and it sounded like he was screaming at me and he was panicked. I couldn't help my panic and I had to try to listen to him or I'd go crazy. I told Darion I couldn't, and he told me I can and I have to and somehow I found the energy to focus on pushing him away.

I tried. I pushed him hard. It didn't work as well as it had with the Bahadori because Turak was holding me in place. He stepped back, puzzled. He couldn't understand what had happened.

"You did it! Do it again!" Darion exclaimed.

My legs were jelly. It was so hard to stand. Hard to breathe. If Turak wasn't supporting me, I would have sunk to my knees where I stood.

"Why did you not call me sooner?" Darion was saying.

I felt sick. I thought I would throw up all over Turak. It would serve him right, but I couldn't afford to make him angry. Things were bad enough as it was. Turak put his huge hand on my shoulder and pushed me slowly down to the ground again. My jelly legs gave no resistance.

"Do not *let him push you down!"* Darion almost screamed the words.

"I can't! My legs won't support me!" I wailed.

As soon as I was lying on my back, Turak sat on my groin with one large leg on either side of my hips while he pushed my arms up above my head again.

No!!!

He was playing with me like I was a toy. Leaning over me. He thought he could do whatever he wanted with his new possession.

"The key!" Darion yelled. *"Get it! Now!"*

"I can't!" I screamed back at him. *"I've been trying!"*

"I will help you!"

"Okay." I wasn't sure how I could do anything, but I'd try anything he suggested.

"I will help you concentrate. Be your anchor. Let us begin."

Why did I forget to call him? Why didn't I try harder to concentrate? I should have concentrated more and had the key in my hand already.

Panic. It made me lose all control.

I felt Darion's mind link with mine. *"Focus..."* His words steadied me. *"Think about the key. What it looks like. What it is made of. Picture it in your mind."*

Turak was staring down at me and I looked away. I looked at the spot where the key was. Just under the jungle cat skin. I'd felt it when it pressed against my skin. Turak was going to do more than press against my skin...

"Focus!"

He probably thought I was looking at his crotch. I closed my eyes. The animal started kissing me again and I felt like I was falling... spinning...

Need — to — concentrate... Need to... get... key...

Somewhere in the darkness I steadied my thoughts... Darion was there... My anchor...

"Focus..."

Key, key, key...

I couldn't feel my body anymore and it was scaring me...

Key...

Suddenly the key was in my hand!

"Yes!" Darion cried out. *"Now get free!"*

I tried to twist my hand around to unlock the shackles, but they cut into my skin. It hurt too much to put my wrists in that position.

"Hurry!"

I couldn't breathe. It was impossible to bend my wrist into position, so I decided to try kinetically. The key left my hand, went in and turned — the lock opened on one shackle, then the other. I had my hands free!

Feeling came rushing back to me and the weird numbness subsided — but wait — I had no loincloth on! And he was about to remove his!

CHAPTER 49:

Head for the River!

"NO!!!!"

I let out a mental scream with that "NO!!!!", and at the same time, pushed him away with both my arms *and* my mind, which sent him toppling backwards so hard that he landed with his back against a tree root about two metres away.

Darion let out a moan like he was in pain. *"Are you okay? Are you hurt?"* he asked eagerly. *"That was really loud! I probably would have heard that if I had been on the nearest moon."*

I couldn't answer — I felt so exhausted. So disgusted. And so dirty all over again.

"Tamisan! Can you hear me? Are you alright? Are you hurt?" I could hear the waver in his voice.

I rolled onto my side away from Turak and curled myself up into a tight ball. *"I'm... yeah..."* I managed to say. I didn't know which question I was answering.

"Are you hurt?" he asked again. *"Your scream nearly deafened me. I guess it was worse because of the Mind-link. I had to pull away from your mind."*

I couldn't answer a second time. The silence was awful. My emotions overwhelming. My hearts stuttered and my breathing was weird. It was hard to suck in air and push it back out. My body tingled all over and I felt so completely drained.

It wasn't just the shock of what he'd done to me that made me feel so terrible. I'd used up a lot of psychic energy.

"If you cannot answer, can you show me that you are okay?" The panic was still there, but he sounded a bit better.

I lay there on the ground, staring at the roots of a small bush nearby. I could hear Turak stirring behind me. I couldn't believe he was still conscious. I needed to focus, to open my mind when I felt I didn't have a mind left...

I finally managed to open up my shattered mind and could feel Darion's mind link with mine again, and I clung to it as if it was the only thing stopping me from slipping into insanity. He saw what had happened. Felt what I'd felt. I felt his sadness and his anger rising up — and something else. I wondered what it was, but couldn't form a coherent thought to ask him.

"Energy," he said, answering my unspoken question. *"You need it. Take it. Now get up and run!"*

I felt I couldn't even move, let alone run, but I could hear Turak stumbling to his feet and he was heading my way...

"Tamisan. You have *to get up. You* have *to get away from him.* Now! *I am not there. I cannot physically help you. You have to do this yourself. Now* move!*"*

I felt more of his energy flowing into my body as I got to my feet. I turned to see that Turak had managed to stand up, but then he fell to his knees again, with a dazed look on his face. I turned quickly and started to run through the jungle, realising as I did so that my loincloth was still on the ground behind me! I pulled my top back up over my shoulder to cover my right breast as I ran. Another thing I hadn't felt. What did he do while I was concentrating on getting the key? I couldn't worry about that now. I had to keep running. I used my Talent to pick up the loincloth and bring it to my hand. I imagined the soft fur and how it felt. Then I pictured the spot on the ground where it had been tossed. I couldn't believe it had worked!

I did that so instinctively, so why didn't I use my Talent when Turak was on top of me? What was wrong with me? Why didn't I stop him this time? He just seemed to make me lose my mind with fear. Made it so I couldn't even think straight.

The growth was so thick here that I had to duck and weave through vines and bushes and the trunks and roots of the larger trees. Everything seemed to pull at my hair and scratch my arms and legs. I could hear him running behind me, but didn't look back for fear of tripping on something — then I'd be back where I started.

I could still feel Darion's Mind-touch — we'd dropped the Mind-link he'd used to give me the energy I so desperately needed — but his touch was weak. How much energy did he give me?

"Do not worry about me," he told me. *"You need it, and I am eating some high-energy food bars, so I will be fine. Keep going."*

Ahead I could see a huge fallen tree that had actually made it to the ground despite all the vines holding it up, and there was no going around it. The trunk was wider than I was tall and I couldn't see either end of it as I approached it. When I reached it, I started to climb over, using the vines and branches to help me, but Turak caught up and grabbed my leg as I reached the top. I let out a scream and saw the smile on his face as he pulled me closer.

His tight grip hurt my leg as his fingers dug into my skin above my boot. With my mind, I started pulling his fingers off my leg — one by one, while I hung onto a branch to stop him dragging me off the trunk completely. His smile disappeared as he watched my leg slip out of his grip, and he looked up at me in disbelief. I swung my leg over the top of the trunk and jumped down the other side. As I started running again, I heard Turak jump down too.

"Head for the river!" Darion told me. As he said that, I thought I could hear the sound of running water somewhere up ahead and to the right, so I headed in that direction.

I went under a low branch, over a log, around a bush covered in vines that possessed lots of large wicked thorns and barely missed them, over a rock or three, around the root system of a fallen tree and into a ditch that looked like it had been dug by some huge creature I didn't even *want* to imagine. All the while, I could hear him following behind.

I looked around frantically. Where was the water?

The sound was getting louder and the smell was getting stronger, but the jungle was so thick that I couldn't see any sign of it or a break in the trees that would help me. The water seemed to roar now, like there were some rapids up ahead. It had to be close.

As I stepped on a log, it moved under my foot and I was somehow able to avoid sticking my right leg into a crevice between two rocks that would have broken my ankle with the speed I was running. It took some effort to plant my foot on one of the rocks instead and I kept on running, realising as I ran that that was no log — it was a large brown python! It must have been at least sixty centimetres in diameter!

I didn't look back to see how Turak got past it without being its next meal. The only thing I needed to worry about was that he was still chasing me. He was close behind, and was gaining on me.

I could hear his footsteps getting closer. I kept going. It sounded like he was gaining on me. He was getting closer with each step. The back of my neck tingled at the thought of him being right there. I needed to know how close he was. I *had* to know. I imagined him right behind me, reaching out his hand to grab my long hair... to touch my shoulder... I *had* to look.

CHAPTER 50:

Stay Down!

I turned back for a quick glance. He wasn't as close as I'd imagined, but he was only a few metres away.

My head was pounding now. Exhaustion was slowing me down, dragging at me like my limbs were made of lead, but I had to keep going. I had to get to the river and 'drown.' Then I could rest under the cool refreshing water. I would float away down the river.

It occurred to me that if I couldn't breathe underwater, I'd probably drown for real. I was too weak to swim.

I felt so worn out that I started to think I wouldn't make it. And I could feel how weary Darion was feeling too...

After running and ducking and weaving for what seemed like forever, I was amazed he wasn't giving up, even though I'd thrown him through the air. Maybe he was just *that* stubborn. Maybe his pride was hurt. I couldn't let him catch up with me again. His wounded pride could be enough for him to kill me... after he was finished with me.

"He is not *going to catch you again!"* Darion told me. He sounded determined, but so faint in my mind.

I could easily smell the water and hear it roaring even louder now. Why was it so loud? The rapids must have been right where I was planning on 'falling' in. I would have to be careful. The last thing I needed was to hit my head on a rock or something for real. Now if I could just find it...

He was getting closer. I could hear him. So as I ran, I picked up rocks and small branches with my mind and threw them behind me, hoping to stop him or at least slow him down. Ducking under a branch and around the trunk of a smaller tree, I started running again, but the ground suddenly fell away beneath my feet. I had so much forward momentum I was able to clear the ledge without hitting any tree roots or rocks, but it was a long way down — about five metres to the water below. I had found the river, but wasn't ready for the drop.

There was a second or three of sheer panic as I sailed through the air, arms and legs flailing. On the way down, I saw a waterfall to my left, and I curled into a ball, hoping if I made myself as small as possible, I might avoid hitting anything under the surface. I plunged into the water right next to the base of the waterfall where the water was the deepest. I was sure my hearts had stopped beating till I hit the water.

"*Stay down!*" Darion called. I could hardly hear him.

I sank straight down like a stone till my feet lightly touched the rocks on the bottom, pushing all the air out of my lungs. I made no attempt to swim to the surface — I let my body relax, as if I was unconscious. My body slowly uncurled itself and I made sure I was face down. My arms floated outwards and I opened my eyes so I could see what was happening around me. I didn't want to get too close to the bottom as the strong current from the falls would pummel my body against the rocks.

I realized I'd forgotten to breathe, so I sucked in some water and felt it being expelled through my gills.

I quickly slipped my loincloth up onto my wrist and let it float there. I couldn't be seen holding onto something while I was supposed to be unconscious.

I chanced a peek up toward the shore and I could make out the distorted image of the rocky ledge that I'd fallen from through the turbulent water. I saw Turak's foot slip over the edge, causing some dirt and rocks to splash down into the river, but he didn't fall in. He stood on the bank looking down, waiting for me to come up for air. I faced the bottom of the river again — just in case he spotted me. The water started to push me downriver. I willed him to see me floating face-down and unmoving. I needed him to think I was dead. I wanted him to give up the chase.

What would I have done if he'd fallen in too? What *could* I do? He was too strong. But I had the advantage. He couldn't breathe underwater. I could try to keep him down under the surface, but he could really hurt me — even kill me — before he drowned. I couldn't do it anyway. I couldn't kill anyone.

I could outswim him. Take off so fast his head would spin. The down side would be that he would know I was still alive. But I would be free. The only other thing I could think of was to still pretend I was dead, but I wasn't sure if that would work. He would grab me and drag me to the shore, and I didn't think I could convince him I was dead then. He would see and hear me breathing.

I tried to relax, letting the current take me away. When I came close to any plants or rocks on the bottom, I used a hand to carefully push myself away from them. If he'd somehow followed me downriver and was looking into the water, he wouldn't be able to see me clearly, so a little movement of my hand would not be noticed.

I was hoping he would think I'd hit my head or something when I fell in. The fact that it was such a long way to fall would help with that scenario. I could only hope that now I'd be rid of him for good.

I could hear Turak calling after me. I shuddered. He roared in frustration — probably because he didn't see me come up to the surface, and the sound made me shudder again.

I realized I was shaking uncontrollably. I had to try to calm down. I could imagine him trying to make his way downriver to find me, but I had to stay still and drift with the current.

"It is alright now," Darion reassured me. He sounded a little better now. *"Try to relax and let the cool water refresh you. Drift far enough away so he cannot see you and I do not think he will follow. From what we know of the tribes on Althar, they seem to avoid the water. My guess is that they cannot swim."*

His voice seemed so far away. I knew he needed to rest now too, but I didn't say anything.

Soon I felt I was far enough away that Turak wouldn't be able to see me, and I relaxed a little more, but didn't try to swim to the surface. I didn't try to swim at all. As I drifted in the current, it felt so clean and peaceful in the water. And I felt so dirty, so disgusted, after what Turak had done. I knew the water couldn't wash away what I felt, but it helped. It was strange to feel that way. I shouldn't feel dirty. I didn't do anything wrong. But I couldn't help it. It wasn't that my skin felt dirty. It was something deep inside. It was hard to describe, even to myself, but it was horrible. I hoped that the feeling would fade away. And soon.

I felt the tears come and let it all out. I needed to release all the stress and fear. It was like I was purging it out into the water. It was very strange, crying underwater. My tears mixed with the river water, instead of running down my cheeks.

I remembered my loincloth was still hooked on my arm, so I dressed myself shakily as I drifted. I'd drifted all that way while I was half naked, and was too shocked to even realise it or think to do something about it...

I floated... All I could hear was the water rushing and bubbling all around me... It was so, so peaceful...

Then it occurred to me that Darion was gone. He must have been so exhausted after giving me all his energy and had let go once he knew I was safe so he could recover — and that's exactly what I needed to do. I was completely and utterly drained. I was surprised I even had the energy to put the loincloth on. Maybe Darion had said goodbye to me and I hadn't even heard him...

I closed my eyes and rested. Floated along with the current, face down below the surface of the water. To passersby, I might have looked like a dead body floating downriver. I didn't know for sure and didn't care.

CHAPTER 51:
Relief Was Bliss

I wasn't sure how long I'd drifted for, letting my mind and body recuperate. I think I dozed for a while. At some point, a branch from a sunken tree had gently caught me up and stopped me from drifting too far downriver and I'd had enough sense to put my arms and legs around it to make sure I stayed there until I was ready to start swimming again. I didn't want to drift all the way out to sea. I had to swim back up to the caves to meet up with Darion if I was going to get out of this dreadful place in one piece.

Once I'd recovered enough, my senses came alive and I wondered how far downriver I was. I should have found something to cling to a lot sooner. I could have been any-where.

My body ached all over. I looked down at my wrists. They looked terrible. They were starting to show their bruises too, but the broken skin didn't look as bad now they'd been soaking in the water for a while. I looked down at the cut on my thigh. It wasn't too bad either, considering how deep it was. I was healing fast.

I'd rested long enough. It was time to get moving, so I pushed off from the branch and headed for the surface to take a look around. I came up slowly and kept my nose under the surface so

I wouldn't be easily seen. Turning slowly, I surveyed the banks. No people or wildlife. Good.

The river was wider here, but the jungle was still very thick. I looked a bit further downriver and noticed I was actually near the fork in the river. I had drifted a long way. From there, if I went to the right, I'd be heading toward Jannali like I'd originally planned. Of course, there was no use going there now; besides the possibility of getting lost, I still had no idea where the entrance was. All I had to do was go back the way I'd come, get past the falls and up to the caves to meet up with Darion. He could port us all back to Jannali from there.

The thought of meeting Darion made me feel warm inside, even in the cool water. My heartbeats sped up a bit. He would take me away from here. He'd make everything alright.

That sounded kind of fairytale-ish, but it wasn't that I was helpless. I wasn't some damsel in distress waiting to be rescued. I was actively doing something to get myself out of this nightmare. It was just that Darion would provide the last part of the journey.

I slipped under the water again and started to swim up-river. I had a lot of catching up to do.

Swimming was difficult with the fur boots on. They were waterlogged and I couldn't push through the water like I could when I was barefoot. I knew I would be able to travel a lot faster if I took them off. My hands were basically for steering and manoeuvrability, and my feet and legs were for speed. Pulling the boots off my feet and holding them in my hands, I started off again. It made steering harder, but I was able to swim much faster. It was a fair compromise. I would definitely get there a lot faster this way.

My thoughts turned to Darion. I needed him. I needed to hear his voice. I had to reach out to him. I didn't want to be alone any longer.

"Darion?"

I was concerned for him. I needed to make sure he was okay. He'd given me so much of his energy. Another part of me was insisting he'd be fine. He'd even told me he would be.

"Yes, Tamisan. I am here. Are you feeling better?"

I felt a strong wave of relief flood through my veins. *"Yes, I am now, but I've drifted pretty far downriver. All the way to the main fork. Almost to the ocean."*

"That will not be too much of a problem for you. If you swim back up-river, we can still meet at the caves as planned."

Yes. I could do it. Relief was bliss. I soaked it up. It spurred me on and made me swim faster.

Having Darion there in my mind made me feel so much better — made me feel calm. He was my anchor. My rock. He made it easier to cope with being in this horrible jungle with all its barbaric inhabitants and terrifying creatures. I wasn't sure which of the two was worse.

He told me they'd been walking for a while and he'd been waiting for my call. He'd been trying to decide whether to call me or wait a little longer, but I'd beaten him to it.

"Well, now you will *have to hurry up because we have arrived at the caves,"* he informed me. That was some good news. Now all I had to do was find the caves, too.

Darion sounded a lot better now, but I *had* to ask. He'd seemed so weak. *"Are* you *alright now?"*

"Yes, I am okay. I am feeling refreshed after some high-energy food and a sleep — just as I told you I would. You need not worry about me. We will set up camp at the mouth of the caves and wait

for you." He paused. *"Now Tamisan, you have been through hell today and I am still worried about you — are you sure you are okay?"*

"Yes," I replied. *"My wrists are kind of burning and I'm very hungry, but I'm okay. I'll be a lot better though when I get to the caves and we can all get out of here."*

"How fast can you swim?" he asked.

"Pretty damn fast!" I answered, and let him *see* how fast I was going.

"Whoah! That is amazing!" he said. *"At that pace, you should not take very long. You may even make it by nightfall — in which case, we will leave a light on outside the caves for you."*

"Please do!" I didn't want to spend another night in the jungle. I didn't want to be *alone* at night in the jungle, either.

"The Waikari are a pretty amazing race!" he exclaimed, and I knew exactly what he meant. Besides the psychic abilities, I found it so exhilarating to be swimming under the water, ducking and weaving in and out through all the weeds, rocks and fallen trees in my path.

I told him about how the Waikari played in the sea and jumped up out of the water like dolphins do back on Earth, and how they loved to dive off the rocks into the thundering surf for hours. I felt a pang deep in my chest. Thinking about that brought back memories of Sifayah's times with Jarleth at The Dive, staring into each other's eyes and melting into each other's arms...

"They really loved each other..." Darion said ruefully.

"Yes..." I agreed.

There was something special about sharing your thoughts and feelings with someone. Sifayah and Jarleth needed no words to communicate their feelings for one another, just as Darion and I needed no words now to share Sifayah's past together.

I hadn't realized it, but I'd slowed down considerably while I was getting lost in all the emotions Sifayah's memories brought on. I apologized and picked up the pace again.

"No need to be sorry," Darion told me. *"You need to pace yourself. You do not want to wear yourself out or you will not make it here by dark."*

"I know."

"Is this wearing you out too much? Should we stop talking like this?" he asked me.

"No." Although I couldn't see him, I knew he'd chuckled.

"What's so funny?" I asked.

"Oh, I was just amused that I knew you were going to say that."

"How did you know?"

"I don't really know. Maybe our minds are in sync. Maybe we can just connect easily."

Something stirred inside me. I'd had some similar feelings about a sort of connection between us, but had dismissed them. Maybe there was something more to this. Maybe he felt the same... No... I was being silly again...

CHAPTER 52:
Living Vine

Trying to keep a mental shield up while these thoughts were running through my mind was hard work, so I tried to change the subject.

"How well can you swim?" I asked, with a cheeky kind of smile in my voice.

"Oh, I thought I was a fairly good swimmer, but you put me to shame!" he informed me.

"We'll have to go swimming together when this is all over."

"I'm glad to hear you thinking past getting out of here." He sent me a warm smile.

"I have to make it now," I said, *"I'm nearly there."*

"Yes," he agreed, *"And if — when — you make it, I will take you swimming with me."*

I felt a warmth rush through me. *"It's a date!"*

I'd been swimming for a while before I reached the waterfall again. I was amazed at how quickly I'd made it so far upriver. I'd been alone for only a short time. We'd stopped talking to each other before we became too tired. Again.

The water was rushing past me at a great rate and it'd been increasingly difficult to keep up my pace as I'd approached the falls, but I was determined to get to the caves.

There were lots of fish here. I hadn't seen them last time. I wasn't exactly paying attention. I was too busy pretending to be dead. I'd passed many on my journey back up the river, swimming past me. Watching me. These ones kept to the edges as the rushing water from the falls was creating a strong current. One of the bigger fish was rainbow coloured. I thought it looked beautiful.

There was a wide variety of creatures in the river, but I didn't have time to stop and admire them.

The only way I was going to get past the falls was to get out of the water altogether and walk around it. I surfaced and carefully looked around. I couldn't see anyone on either bank, so I headed to the bank on the right as it seemed to be the easier route. Also, it was the opposite side from where Turak was the last time I'd seen him. He was probably on his way back to steal the redhead back from Anjou, but I wanted to be as far from him as possible. I started to shake at the thought of him and what had happened, but I needed to pull myself together. I needed to do this.

I put my boots on and crept out of the water, keeping an eye on the far bank. My body felt so heavy because I'd been weightless for so long. My hair clung to my back as the water poured from it and down the backs of my legs. My boots felt like they were lead-lined and the fur was squishy, but taking them off wasn't an option.

I found a place to start climbing to get around the waterfall.

I stopped and squeezed water out of my hair first. I tried to squeeze some out of my clothing and boots too, to try to make walking easier. It helped a bit.

I kept looking around me, especially at the far bank, expecting to see Turak any second. I needed to slow down my breathing. My hearts were pounding and I was shaking so much just thinking about the possibility of seeing him that I could hardly climb. I stopped half-way and tried to calm my nerves. I closed my eyes and took some deep breaths, trying to relax my tight muscles, but my mind conjured up a picture of Turak creeping up on me and I quickly opened them again. After taking in some more deep breaths, I was finally able to make it to the top.

Despite the rest I'd had, I felt exhausted again as I made my way around the base of a fallen tree. I also realized my stomach was feeling very empty. Anjou and I hadn't eaten lunch. He'd been so busy preparing the meat. He'd almost finished when Turak arrived, so I assumed we would have sat down to another delicious meal of the sweet meat if the Neanderthal hadn't turned up and taken me away. I felt a cold shiver run through me at the thought. I forced myself to think of something else.

As I was looking around the jungle to make sure there were no people or creatures or Turak about, I spied what looked like the kind of tree that bore the Chumana fruit. I was so hungry I *had* to go and see if that's what it was. I started walking toward the tree. I had to make my way over a log or two, under a low hanging vine and over some rocks to get a better view. I was right — it was a Chumana tree. I didn't think I'd ever forget what those flowers looked like.

I went over and carefully picked some fruit, keeping my face well away from the flowers. There was no way I was going through that again.

As I filled my stomach, I started to relax a bit more. The large boulder I'd been sitting on while I ate wasn't the least bit comfortable, so I stood up to rub my backside, and almost came face to face with a large python hanging from the tree above me. Its large head was just above level with my face. I stifled a scream and fell backwards over the rock in my haste to get away, my hearts racing. I scrambled away as fast as I could.

The snake responded by lazily sliding down so its head rested on the top of the rock and its body followed behind, slithering down out of the tree. Then it started to slink down the side of the rock toward me.

Instinct took over. I rolled to one side and got to my feet faster than I'd ever done before and backed away from the monstrous thing that looked like a huge living vine, keeping it in my sights. I'd dropped the fruit, but there was no way I was going back for it.

I moved back further. I was concentrating on keeping my eye on the snake and trying to look around at my surroundings to see which way to go when my foot plunged into a hole in the ground. Pain shot through my left ankle.

Looking down as I fell onto my backside, I could see that it looked like a kind of burrow. As I pulled my foot out, the owner of the burrow lunged out and wrapped its jaws around my foot.

CHAPTER 53:

The Roar Had Actually Come from Behind Me

I screamed, but the thought of Turak or someone else hearing me had me biting my lip to stop myself from making any more noise.

The thing was a mammal of some sort with strong jaws, sharp teeth and brown fur, about the size of a medium breed of dog. I could feel the intense pressure of the bite on my foot and it was so painful, but its teeth didn't puncture the hide boots and I found myself thanking Anjou again for giving them to me.

I pulled my leg away from the creature. It held fast. I pounded desperately on its head with my fists, but that only made it bite harder. It wasn't going to let go. My foot was really starting to hurt from the massive pressure, but nothing I did made any difference.

Thankful it hadn't bitten me on the bare foot, but still in a panic, I tried to think fast as to what I could do or what I could use to get it to open its jaws. My breaths were coming in short gasps. I had to think. It started to growl at me as it looked up at me with cold, wicked yellow eyes.

I screamed at it and pulled its ears. Then it shook its head from side to side and nearly knocked me over onto my back, but I managed to grab onto the trunk of a small tree. I needed to stay upright. The thought of being mauled by the ferocious little creature made me shudder. My hearts were pounding and my mind racing and the pain in my foot was almost unbearable.

Breathe, I told myself. I needed to remember to breathe and try to think more clearly.

Then I felt something sharp and I gasped — one of the teeth had broken through the boot and sank deep into my heel. I just managed to stop myself from crying out again, but instinctively pulled my leg back. It only made the tooth sink in deeper. I bit my lip to stop myself from making more noise. I really didn't want to attract any attention to myself. The thought that Turak could still be somewhere in the area was something I couldn't shake. And I'd already cried out once.

I stared down at the animal and tried not to move my foot. As it prepared to shake its head again, there was a split second where it loosened its grip and I took advantage of that and pulled my foot quickly. I managed to get my foot out, but not the boot, and it slipped off.

I turned and ran toward the river and the beast started after me. I was amazed at the quick reaction I'd had when it was adjusting its hold on me. I wasn't sure what I would've done if it hadn't loosened its jaws when it did.

I'd only run a few paces when I heard a loud, high-pitched squeal and turned to see the animal had been grabbed by the python. The python had already started to coil its body around the creature. I turned and started running again, my hearts pumping. I'd forgotten about the python once I'd been bitten and cringed to think that I could've been its victim instead.

I had to jump over fallen logs and weave around some smaller bushes to get to the water and I could hear the creature give one last squeal. When I reached the edge, I dived straight in.

I was lucky there were no rocks or logs in the water below me — or any creatures like the one I'd seen along the way, hiding in a dark corner. It looked like a crocodile from what I could see. It didn't seem to notice me as I swam past and it was a huge relief.

As soon as I was under the water, I ripped off my boot and started swimming as fast as I could. I didn't slow down for a long time. My heartbeats slowed and I allowed myself to relax a little, but did not reduce my speed for another five minutes or so.

I could still feel a sharp pain in my foot and swimming only made it worse, but I had to keep going. I willed the boot back into my possession and considered putting it on to protect my bruised and bleeding foot, then decided against it.

I finally looked at my foot. There was a small red ribbon swirling around it in the water. It was still bleeding. I concentrated on it until it stopped oozing blood. I hoped something wouldn't pick up my blood trail in the water and come after me.

Before I started swimming again, I thought I'd better have a peep above the surface to see where I was. Looking out cautiously, I could see a small tree near the edge of the river that looked like it might have some of the other fruit on it that Anjou had given me — the long red ones. I was still really hungry, so I thought I should chance going ashore to have something more to eat. I knew I needed to keep my strength up. I made my way closer to the shore. It *was* the same type of fruit.

I put my boots on and squelched my way over to the tree. They were as delicious as I remembered and I wished I had some sort of bag to put some in for later. This time I was sitting on a fallen tree and I'd checked the area thoroughly for holes in the ground and any logs that weren't really logs.

I looked up through the canopy. The sun was disappearing over the horizon. I couldn't stay here any longer. Maybe I could use the boots as bags. Or maybe that would be too awkward to carry through the water.

Once I'd finished eating, I pulled off my boot to inspect the wound on my heel again. It was a small puncture about half the size of a pea and was deep and painful. I was worried it would get infected out here in the jungle, but I'd have to wait until I made it to the caves and Jannali. The wound was still closed. I'd done a good job.

Thank you, Darion — again! I thought.

Just as I put the boot back on, the peaceful jungle sounds were shattered by a deafening roar, and I saw a large croco-dile-like reptile raise its head above the water right in front of me. It was much bigger than the one I'd seen earlier. Maybe it had been following the scent of the blood from my foot. I instinctively jumped up away from it, but at the same time realized the roar had actually come from behind me!

I turned to see an Allosaurus look-alike like the one that had attacked the Bahadori come charging toward me out of the trees.

CHAPTER 54:

I'll Be Here for Hours

I tried to scream, but nothing came out of my mouth. I looked around wildly. I had nowhere to go with one monster on the shore and one in the water. Then I saw a small crevice in between two large boulders that looked big enough for me to fit into. That seemed like my only option, so I ran and ducked down into the hole. Tucking my legs up and wrapping my arms around them so that there was no part of me sticking out, I could see the Allosaurus staring in after me. It looked like it was trying to work out if it could fit its muzzle into the crevice when it was distracted by the roar of the water lizard. I couldn't see anything from my hidey-hole, but judging by the other's reaction, it had probably climbed up out of the river and was headed his way.

He turned his full attention to the crocodile thing and side-stepped to avoid the huge jaws that were attempting to bite off his leg. He immediately lashed out with his own set of deadly, razor-edged teeth and sank them deep into the other's neck. It roared in pain and thrashed its whole body around, hitting the fruit tree and the log I'd been sitting on, then I couldn't see it again.

The noises were terrifying as they both struggled and roared, and I could see the croc's tail come into view every now and then. The larger reptile had not let go, and I could see it moving around violently as the other one still struggled, until finally the croc stopped moving.

I was glad I couldn't actually see more than the croc's tail as the Allosaurus look-alike started to feed on him. I wished I couldn't hear it either, but I couldn't sit there all day with my fingers in my ears. I needed to do something, but what?

My stomach churned, knowing what was happening right outside my little hole. Now I'd have to wait — wait for him to finish, and for any other critter that may happen by to finish their pickings.

I'm not going to make it by nightfall, I thought bitterly, *I'll be here for hours! I won't meet Darion and I'll have to spend another night in the jungle — probably right here in this hole!*

I sat brooding, wishing the beast would just go away so I could get on with my journey, so I get out of the jungle at last. Without realising it, I was putting all my thoughts and energy into that one thing — to be back in the river and on my way. I kept saying it over and over in my mind until suddenly I felt cold and wet!

The cold took my breath away and when I breathed in, I got a mouth full of water. For an instant I didn't know what had happened, but the only explanation for me to suddenly be in the river was that I'd actually teleported myself there!

I looked around. I was back where I'd stopped to look above the surface. Nothing could've made me look above the surface *this* time. I took off my boots and sped off before something *else* tried to eat me.

I didn't get to take any fruit with me like I'd planned, but I was grateful to be alive.

Porting must use a lot of energy because I felt like I weighed a ton, even in the water, but I kept going. I still couldn't believe I'd teleported myself without even knowing what I was doing. Well, that wasn't entirely true. Right before it happened, there was something familiar about the way I felt. I sort of knew what I was doing. Part of me knew. The part of me that was Sifayah. Sifayah had done it before.

It was just that the part of me that was Zhenna didn't really believe I could do it. Maybe that part of me was holding me back. Maybe I shouldn't listen to that voice in my head that planted the seeds of doubt and told me things like that weren't possible.

As I thought about it all, I weaved my way up the river to Darion. To freedom.

⸎

I surfaced. It was dark. The sun had set a short time after I'd escaped from the two reptiles. Darion had informed me about half an hour before that they'd finished setting up camp and had 'turned the light on' for me in the form of an electric lamp placed outside the entrance.

I'd surfaced every now and then to check for the light. I didn't want to go past it.

The darkness didn't really bother me — I could easily see my surroundings above and below the water. I kept on swimming quietly on the surface of the water, scanning the banks for a sign of Darion's light. Nothing yet — but wait — what was that up there through the trees? Could it be the light?

I looked closer. It was definitely a light, but was it the right one? I kept swimming on the surface, keeping an eye on the light, watching it grow bigger. It didn't seem to flicker like firelight, but I wanted to be sure. Once I reached a point where staying in the river meant I would be travelling away from the light, I started heading toward the shore.

Looking around the jungle as I climbed up out of the water and over some tree roots to reach the shore, I could see no signs of any natives. Just a few birds darting about in the darkness.

Good.

I didn't want to see any*one* or any*thing* between the shore and the caves.

But then I caught a glimpse of some movement to my left. I froze and strained to see. It was a small dinosaur, possibly a young Rodon, ambling along through the underbrush further downriver. It saw me, but continued on.

I sat on a tree root to put my boots back on. There were a number of crawly things wriggling around amongst the leaf litter, but I did my best to ignore them. I would never get used to them, but I had to face the fact that they would always be there, no matter where I went on the planet. I gave my soggy boots a squeeze and pulled them on.

Now I had to get close enough to determine if it was Darion's light and not some barbarian's campfire. I started walking in a half-crouch to keep from being seen. My hair and clothes were heavy with water again and my foot was throbbing, so I squeezed some of the water out and pushed on. Sometimes the trees blocked my view, but I kept going. Nothing would stop me now. I came around a large tree trunk and could see the light more clearly. It was no flickering fire — it was a light the inhabitants of this planet had never seen before — an electric lamp on a post about a metre high. I could see the cave's entrance behind it.

Then it hit me. Darion was right there, a few metres up the hill from where I stood. I would finally get to meet him. I was suddenly nervous. Up till now, I'd only talked to him within my mind, but seeing him face to face would be totally different.

What would I say? What should I do? What would he think when he saw me, dripping with water and limping up the hill? I felt like I knew him. Like he was a good friend, an old friend, but I'd never met him. It was a strange feeling. And I felt anxious. Was I actually scared of meeting him?

My heartbeats picked up and I started to feel kind of shaky. I was going to see him at last. I picked up the pace and walked more upright now, trying to ignore the pain in my foot. I wanted to get there quickly.

Then as I stepped over a tree root, my left foot slipped right down into the leaf litter and jammed itself in between two of the roots. Pain shot through my ankle, but I managed to stop myself from crying out.

CHAPTER 55:

Hi

I groaned. *Oh, it just never ends!*

I took some deep breaths to try to calm down as the pain receded a little. I tried several times to pull my foot out. I could see I wasn't going to get anywhere by pulling, so I sat down carefully on one of the roots and tried to wriggle it free. It didn't help. It only caused more pain. It wouldn't budge. *Why did it have to be the left foot again?*

I moved my toes and my foot slipped a little in the boot. Maybe I could get somewhere if I slipped it out of the boot. I tried again and my foot came out, minus the boot. *Yes!*

I pulled the empty boot free and put it back on.

When I stood up, pain shot up the side of my leg from my ankle, which made me cry out, but I headed up the hill to the caves, looking to see if there was any movement. They probably heard me cry out. Then something moved in the glow from the light.

"Darion?" I called, *"I'm outside."*

I could see the cave entrance more clearly as I got closer. My heartbeats quickened. I was finally going to meet him.

I made my way up the hill, ducking under a low branch, and as I straightened, there were three men waiting at the entrance. I recognized Darion immediately from what I'd seen in his mind.

I kept walking up, limping a lot more than I would've liked, but I couldn't help it. I stopped when I was about a metre away from them. It seemed to take forever to walk the last few metres.

"Hi..." was all I managed to say. I was looking directly at Darion, looking straight into his blue eyes, and it was making me come undone. To finally see him after everything I'd been through was unbelievable. I'd been waiting for what seemed like forever and I'd started to think it would never happen.

He was smiling. The glow from the lamp cast shadows across his face and I could see that it was a genuine smile, like he was happy to see me too.

He was taller than the men that stood either side of him. Spotted fur covered half of his muscular chest. His short brown hair was kind of messy on top and he had some stubble on his face, with there being no razors in the jungle and all. It was almost comical seeing them wearing spotted skins like the locals.

"Hi yourself!" he laughed, and he stepped forward.

I didn't know what to do — should I shake his hand or just stand there? I felt nervous, and... shy. What should I do? What was he expecting me to do? I felt silly. I wanted to fall into his arms, but maybe I should give him a quick hug or a handshake or should I give him a nod or a wave?

"What took you so long?" he asked.

I opened my mouth to answer him, realized he was joking, and then my body decided — without consulting my brain — to step forward and wrap my arms around his torso. He hesitated for a second before putting his arms around me.

My hearts pounded and my breathing was kind of ragged. I could feel the tears welling in my eyes. It was so good to be holding him at last and it was comforting to be in his strong embrace after all that had happened. I was a sponge, just soaking him in.

Doubt wriggled its way into my brain. I had never been so forward with a guy before, and I didn't even really know Darion. But he didn't pull away from me.

Tears rolled down my cheeks as I laid my head on his chest, the fur soft on my face. I kept my eyes closed, shutting out the jungle. I needed the comfort and the feeling of safety that he was giving me. I thought about everything that had happened and soon I was sobbing on his shoulder — I couldn't help it.

Darion seemed to understand, and he kept holding me and stroking my hair.

"It's okay," he whispered.

I tried to answer, but no words came out.

"It is so good to see you at last," he added, still holding me close while I cried.

My sobs finally stopped and I felt like a heavy burden had been released from my mind and body. I was exhausted, but felt lighter.

I realized I was making him wet, but I felt him shake his head at that thought. *"Do not worry about it,"* he told me.

While my right hand rested on fur, my left hand was touching his bare back. His skin was warm and soft and the muscles underneath were flexing with the movement of his arm. His muscles were hard, but moved fluidly under my fingers. Something about him stroking my hair so gently put me at ease. I could forget where I was for a while. I couldn't help the small smile that spread across my face.

I didn't want this to end. I could've stayed there forever.

But... Was he holding me so close just to comfort me? Or was there more to it than that? Him stroking my hair like that didn't seem like something that a guy would do if he was only holding someone to comfort them. At least, I didn't think so. It seemed more intimate than that.

After a while, I felt almost like I was sinking into the ground. The exhaustion was pulling me down and I could hardly stand.

"What's wrong with me?" I asked. I opened my eyes and could hardly see anything. The blackness was creeping in at the edges of my vision. Was I going to faint?

CHAPTER 56:
You Should Not Try it Again

"It's okay. It is just the shock of everything that has happened to you. The adrenalin has run down and you're feeling drained. Let yourself relax and I will support you."

As Darion was talking, he put his arm under my legs and picked me up and started walking back into the cave. I felt like a rag doll in his arms. My cheek was resting against his bare chest and I felt safe and warm. I could hear his heartbeat. One single heartbeat... I focused on it, on its rhythm.

"What happened to her? Is she alright?" someone asked.

"She is exhausted. She needs to rest," Darion informed them.

He put me down on a blanket in a sitting position so my back was resting against some furs spread out on a rock.

"You have managed to keep it together up till now because you *had* to keep going," he told me. "Your survival instincts took over. Now that you have let go of that, your body is saying 'enough.' Let yourself rest..."

I did as he said. Just let myself go. Closed my eyes. It was a great relief to relax and feel safe for the first time in a long time. My brain felt fuzzy as the tension left me.

I heard Darion sit down opposite me and my eyes flew open. Once our eyes met, I couldn't look away. After a few moments, he broke eye contact to grab some food.

He smiled. "Are you hungry?"

"Starving."

"Then let's give you some *real* food!"

I nodded. My stomach gurgled and Darion chuckled.

Darion handed me a shallow container of food and a water bottle. I still felt drained, but I opened the food container and ate slowly. Real food at last! Cooked meat and vegetables. My stomach felt warm and my tastebuds were alive again. After the diet of jungle food and so much fruit making my insides so queasy, this was heaven. It wasn't that I didn't like the fruit, it was just that my body wasn't used to the fruit-only diet and I was always left hungry — well, most of the time. The only things that had come close to a nice hot meal were the potatoes and the freshly cooked sweet meat from the jungle cat. I pushed those thoughts out of my head and savoured every mouthful like I hadn't eaten in a week.

Darion introduced me to the men in his team. There were five of them and I promptly forgot all of their names once I'd heard them. My brain must have been really fried because I would normally remember things like that. My mind was kind of buzzing. It seemed like I had earplugs in. Sounds were sort of muted. I hoped I would feel better after eating something and resting.

The other men grabbed food containers for themselves and settled down to a meal too, so we weren't the only ones eating. We may as well have been alone, though. We barely noticed the movement and conversation around us. We had so much to talk about — mostly about the trip here.

At one point, I realized that someone was saying something to Darion. "I am sorry," he said, "I wasn't paying attention. Could you repeat that?"

The other man frowned. "I asked when we'd be returning to base."

"It will have to be in the morning," Darion informed him, "I am still too exhausted right now. We should be safe in these caves until then."

He gave a curt nod and returned to his meal.

Once I'd eaten the last mouthful of food, I shifted to get more comfortable and pain sliced through my ankle, making me wince. I put my meal container aside and pulled off my boot. My ankle was swollen and was starting to turn purple. The bite wound had started oozing blood again — no doubt from getting jammed between the tree roots. I hadn't looked at it, just shoved the boot on so I could hurry up the hill to Darion.

"That needs to have a support bandage," Darion told me, and he reached over behind the rock he was leaning on and pulled a first aid kit out of one of their bags. I told him what had happened to it.

"I would have come down and helped you get your foot out," he said.

"But you've helped me so much already," I replied. Maybe I'd been too proud and too stubborn to ask for help. I was an idiot.

Once the first aid kit was open, Darion motioned for me to bring my foot closer to him. When I did, he gently pulled it up onto his lap. He started with an antiseptic spray, then followed with some SkinGro to promote the growth of new skin and the tissues underneath. I felt the sting of the antiseptic and the cool relief of the SkinGro. I was so thankful. I'd been so worried about it getting infected. Then he sprayed on some BruiseGo to stop the bruising. It wouldn't take long to heal now.

"You should have been a doctor," I told him.

"Nah. I'm no Healer." He smiled while he bandaged my ankle. "Where else are you hurt?"

"Oh, just my wrists, thigh, and knee. Oh, and scratches all over. So, not much at all."

He treated all of my injuries, and then handed me two pills to take. "One is to promote healing and the other is a one-dose antibiotic treatment."

I wasted no time and swallowed them with some water. "Thank you."

"Do you need a painkiller?" he asked.

"No, I don't think so." The pain had already started to subside, but wasn't gone completely. "Actually, yes."

His eyebrows drew together. "So, yes or no?"

I giggled. "Yes."

He handed it over with a smile.

He was quiet for a while, then he told me he was impressed that I'd ported myself into the river. "You are getting better each day," he told me.

It felt good to hear him say that. I felt warm inside. My confidence was growing with each achievement. There would be no stopping me once I'd had some more training. It would change my life. I could change my career.

I wondered how I could get a position in a company with a botched up ID. Maybe the people at Jannali could sort that mess out for me, and maybe with my chosen name on it instead of Rajendra Shea.

I tried not to dwell on those thoughts too much and took another sip from the water bottle Darion had given me. Although there was plenty of water to drink from the river on my way there, somehow it was still better to be drinking it out of a bottle.

"You should not try it again, though," Darion continued, "not until you have been properly trained. It is very dangerous and you could be killed if you get it wrong."

CHAPTER 57:

I Would Do it All Again in a Heartbeat

A chill ran down my spine at the thought. "You did tell me before, but I didn't do it intentionally. And I did it without any problems; Sifayah had done it before."

"Yes, I know, but it is still dangerous without expert training. Please understand this. I am not trying to denigrate what you did. I need you to know there is a significant risk. There have been cases of people porting themselves into space, into the path of oncoming traffic, and, as I told you before, even inside walls. I do not want anything like that to happen to you."

"Oh, um, no." Thinking about that made me cringe inside. "I understand... Thank you."

"No problem." His smile seemed to light up his face in the dim light.

After thanking him again for the meal and telling him how wonderful it tasted after the diet I'd been on, I looked at him and smiled. *"I still can't believe I'm finally here with you,"* I sighed. At least I was starting to feel more at ease. There was really no reason for me to feel shy in front of him.

"Well, it's me. In the flesh," he reported. I looked at him. There was a lot of his flesh right there for me to see. I couldn't help looking at the bare side of his chest and remembering how the muscles in his back had felt under my hand. I pushed those

thoughts away for later. I didn't want him to see them in my mind.

I tried to think of something to say to fill the silence, but he beat me to it.

"So, did you say you were studying at the Interplanetary Academy of New Aronia on Earth?"

"Yes."

He finished off his drink and shifted closer to me.

"I haven't been to New Aronia. I did go to Earth once, for a holiday. Somewhere near the equator. We only stayed a few weeks. It is cooler than Moftar in a lot of places, but the place I stayed was fairly warm. I like the warmer weather."

I laughed. "You should like it here then!"

He laughed too. "Yes, I do, but it is a bit too humid. On our farm, I spent a lot of time out under the sun. I decided a long time ago that I would not be a farmer, but I still wanted to be somewhere where I could enjoy the sun, not be hidden away from it. I like the outdoors too much."

I chuckled. "So you landed a job with Voyager Division and spend your days underground."

"Yes, well, they did promise that I'd be outdoors a lot more than this."

"In other words, they lied."

"Yes."

"My job didn't match the description either."

I stopped fiddling with the lid on my drink bottle and looked up at him. He kept on smiling and I felt a rush of warmth all over. What was he thinking? I knew I wanted to spend more time with him. I wanted to get to know him better after this was all over. I wanted to be close to him. I wanted to feel his strong arms around me again, making me feel safe and... wanted. I needed to feel wanted. To feel loved...

I wanted to feel the hard muscles of his chest against my cheek and hear his heartbeat again...

His smile grew wider and he raised an eyebrow at me. I wondered what he meant by it, but then realized I wasn't shielding my thoughts. My face flushed red and he chuckled softly. I had to get a handle on this mind shield thing. It was embarrassing.

"I am sorry," he said, *"I should not have laughed."*

"No, you shouldn't have. It's not fair. I'm new to this." I tried to sound like I was upset about it, but couldn't stop a smile from forming on my lips.

He smiled apologetically.

We'd finished eating, so Darion placed both our containers in a bag, making sure he sealed it so the smell wouldn't attract any wild animals while we slept. The others must have done the same with their rubbish, but I hadn't even noticed that they'd already finished eating and were getting ready to go to sleep.

I felt a rush of exhaustion. My body was telling me it desperately needed to rest.

"We should get some sleep now," he said.

"Yes, okay," I yawned.

Darion explained to me that he really did need to rest before teleporting us all back to Jannali. I opened my mouth, but he cut me off. *"No. It is not your fault."* He set about getting things ready for us to go to sleep. *"It is a combination of everything. Besides, I would do it all again in a heartbeat."*

He smiled as he said it. His face looked handsome when he smiled, and the smile reached his eyes. It wasn't anything like Starrick's fake smiles. Every one of *his* smiles was cold and empty.

I stood up and looked around while Darion organised our sleeping bags on the floor of the cave. The sleeping bags were made of a synthetic material that looked like hide. The natives didn't seem to use beds of hide, but at least it would seem to them that we were using something familiar to them if any did show up.

The mouth of the cave was wide and tall, with a few boulders near the entrance that looked like they'd fallen from somewhere above the cave a long time ago. There was a small clearing in front of the opening, which allowed us enough room to make a fire. We were all sleeping just inside the entrance so we wouldn't get wet if it rained.

"Aren't we going to build a fire?" I asked. The fact they hadn't lit one had me worried.

"We don't need one," one of the men told me. "It's not cold and we don't need to cook anything."

I looked up into his brown eyes. I couldn't remember his name. "Umm, all the natives do it. I think it keeps the wildlife away at night."

His face went a bit pale. He was probably imagining the Allosaurus look-alike barging into camp. "Uh, Captain? Permission to light a fire, Sir?"

Another man turned around to face the first one. I re-membered Darion telling me he was the leader of the team. The captain glanced at me and said, "Permission granted."

He'd probably heard what I'd said.

I sat down on a sleeping bag and Darion sat next to me. My body felt like lead. I slowly slid down into the sleeping bag and Darion pulled his closer and sprawled across it, facing me. My eyelids were heavy and it was hard to keep them open, but I

didn't want to close them. I wanted to lie there looking at him...
forever...

CHAPTER 58:

Well, This is Cosy

Yeah, silly, I know. But I couldn't help it. I was a goner. I'd give myself a mental slap tomorrow and try to treat this as a professional relationship. I couldn't get carried away.

Tomorrow we were going to Jannali. I couldn't believe I was finally going to get out of this nightmarish jungle and back to civilization. I wished we could go now. I didn't want to wait till morning. It was my fault Darion didn't have the energy to port us there now. He'd given me so much of his energy so I could use it against Turak. If I'd been able to get the key by myself, I could have gotten away sooner. Darion wouldn't have needed to give me so much energy... I was so stupid.

"Now, stop that," he told me. *"You can't blame yourself for what happened."*

"But I should have been able to do it."

"Under those circumstances? You are only learning how to do these things. How could you concentrate?"

"But Sifayah was an expert."

"Yes, but you are not there yet. Do not worry about that now. You can't change things by beating yourself up about it." He pushed some hair behind my ear. *"Let's get some sleep so we can get out of here in the morning."*

"Okay." I smiled at him. I couldn't help noticing him using contractions more and more. It made him seem less stuffy and more like someone his own age, which I assumed was only a year or two older than me.

I tried hard to look at his gorgeous face... My eyelids were closing... I fought to keep them open... I laid there looking into his eyes... but my eyelids were so heavy...

As the remnants of sleep left me, I noticed I wasn't lying on a bed. It was hard and lumpy and felt like fur. My eyes shot open and I sucked in a breath. I wasn't alone. Panic seized me and it took a few seconds to recognise Darion lying on his side sleeping next to me. I felt relief wash over me and I had to force myself to breathe slowly and calm my pounding hearts.

It was kind of weird waking up next to a man, especially one I hardly knew... but then, I *did* know him. We'd been talking to each other for days. Our minds had been joined in a Mind-link more than once — and there wasn't any way I could think of to get much closer to another person than that.

I lay there facing him, wondering how all of that had affected the way I felt about him. It made me feel close to him, but the fact that it had been such a short time made me doubt what I was feeling. I needed time to sort my head out.

I could see his sleeping face more clearly in the morning light. I could see well in the dark, but it wasn't the same as seeing things in daylight. Things weren't quite as clear in the darkness, and the colours were muted.

He *was* as handsome as the image of him I'd briefly seen in his mind. I looked up at his short hair. I liked the way it was sticking up on top. My eyes followed down his strong nose, to his sensual lips. His jaw wasn't too square and he looked scruffy with all the stubble on his face. He looked so peaceful when he was asleep and as I looked at him, I felt a strange feeling — a warmth in my chest. A flame had ignited in my soul. It was like no other feeling I'd ever felt before...

I closed my eyes again, hanging on to that feeling, and soon fell back to sleep.

❦

The next time I woke, I managed to keep myself from panicking. Then I felt Darion stir.

"Are you awake?" he whispered in my mind, though no one else was going to hear him.

"Yes." I opened my eyes and saw that he was lying there with his eyes still closed, so I did the same.

"I hope you do not mind me sleeping this close. Once you fell asleep I couldn't help it — I felt like I needed to be near you, like I had to protect you while you slept. Does that sound silly?" He sent a grin with that thought.

"No, I don't mind, and no, it doesn't sound silly at all," I answered, and let him *see* how good it made me feel to be there beside him.

"I was not sure how you would react to me lying here with you after all that has happened to you..."

I wasn't sure what to say, but he could still *see* how I was feeling, so he'd know that it was okay. I didn't feel in the least bit afraid here with him, though I wished he hadn't reminded me of those things. Of Turak. I wanted to forget them forever.

"I'm sorry for making you remember that…"

I sighed and tried to forget it all. *"It's okay. I can't push it out of my mind and not deal with it. I will get past this."*

"You will," he said with confidence. After a while, he said, *"I think we have had a strong connection to one another from the moment we first spoke to each other. I hope you feel it too. You opened your mind to me and we were one."*

I felt my hearts swell up in my chest and tears formed in my eyes. I didn't know what to say. And the way he'd said that we were one. It was strange to hear Darion describe it like that. But… that's what it had felt like. Maybe that's why I'd felt so alone after he'd withdrawn from inside my mind. And afterwards, when we had to do it again, it'd been the same feeling of oneness.

The area between us and around us felt like a private, shielded cocoon, protected from the savage world around us. I wanted to stay there forever. I could feel his comforting thoughts and emotions, reaching out and enveloping me, and I welcomed them, sucked them up. I couldn't get enough.

Is this what you call a natural high? I pondered.

"Yes. But this is only the tip of the iceberg. There are so many things Talents can share together that the Non-Talented can never achieve."

I'd forgotten — again — that he knew everything I was thinking. I smiled to myself. I said nothing, continuing to take everything in. We were letting our minds relax, letting our thoughts and feelings flow.

I could feel warmth flowing through every vein, every cell, in every fibre of my being. Was this what it felt like to be in love?

I could also feel something else... Something encroaching on paradise... There was someone standing over us, watching us...

My eyes flew open and I gave a start. Dr Starrick was standing at our feet, looking down at us with a malicious smile on his face. We both sat bolt upright and I saw there were laser pistols pointed at us from three directions, and four more pointed at the other members of Darion's crew.

We'd been too engrossed in each other to hear the men sneak up on us. Darion cursed under his breath.

"Well, this is cosy..." Starrick's smile turned to a smirk.

CHAPTER 59:

It Was All for Nothing

My stomach sank. What did he want? There was no way I was going back to Maztec. I opened my mouth to tell him but nothing came out.

Starrick started to laugh loudly, almost hysterically. "So you thought you could get away from me, did you?" He was looking directly at me.

"What do you want?" Darion demanded.

I noticed they hadn't bothered wearing skins to try to pass for natives. Typical. He didn't care about anything.

"I want Zhenna Rhodarma," he replied. It was strange hearing my former name, probably because I was not Zhenna anymore. "She still needs to be under medical observation at Station Maztec due to recent injuries."

"And what *are* these 'recent injuries'?" Darion demanded. "I do not see any injuries! Are you worried about her wellbeing, or that someone will find out what you have done to her?"

All but one of the laser pistols had trained on Darion, but Starrick waved them back. "What nonsense has she been telling you? She is simply recovering from injuries suffered in an attack by the Varekai in which all other passengers on her shuttle perished, and she almost joined them."

Darion rose to his feet, despite the weapons following him. "That is a lie and you know it!" he shouted. "I know what you did to her — not only did you perform the Eibhlin Process on an unwilling victim, but the donor body is not even human! What did you hope to achieve by doing this? She will never be the same — will not be able to return to her life! Anyone can see she is *not* human!" *"No offence,"* he added privately to me.

I'd slowly risen to my feet as Darion was blasting Starrick.

Starrick changed tack. "It was either that or let her die," was his defence. "She was badly burned and when we found her there in the jungle — the only survivor — we had to do something!"

"So now you admit it..."

I stopped listening. I was reading Starrick's patchy thoughts as he was talking about me being badly burned. It didn't add up. I could follow what had happened in his mind — but it wasn't remotely the same as what he'd told me. I was unconscious from a stunner blast when they'd brought me in, but *not* fatally injured and *not* at death's door! He'd just wanted an excuse to perform his experiment.

There would be no other survivors to tell the tale — well, none that could speak coherently, anyway.

Then I picked up on the fact that there were no Varekai... it had been Starrick's men who had attacked us!

No! It couldn't be the truth! It was all for nothing. All of the things I'd been through. It was all his fault!

I can't believe it! I didn't need the transfer. I could've stayed in my own body. The others would be safe. Sifayah would be... she'd be in his lab, but still alive. It's not fair! He needs to be stopped and we need to see if there are any others still alive!

My mind seemed ready to explode and my hands clenched into fists. "You bastard!" I yelled at him. "You lied! I didn't need saving! You only did this to me to see if your new *'procedure'* would work!"

Starrick stammered some incoherent babble, amazed at how I could know. Darion stared at me, but he understood where I'd gotten that information.

"She — she lies..." Starrick mumbled.

"No! *You* lie!" Without even thinking, I pushed with my mind and Starrick fell backwards onto the floor of the cave. Not a wise move with all the laser pistols pointing at us, but it was too late. Luckily, the men holding them didn't seem to know what to do.

As Starrick picked himself up — slightly dazed — he laughed and shouted, "I knew it! I knew it! She was telepathic *and* telekinetic, and you have inherited it! I suspected it — especially when you requested all those HoloMovies about the psychic and the paranormal — but I wasn't a hundred percent sure — till now. You have mastered it well."

This only made me more furious. My hearts were trying to beat their way out of my chest and my face flushed with heat. I had to fight hard to control my temper. How could he have done this to me just to try it out? What right did he have to play God with peoples' lives? What about the people who had suffered because of him? How could he do this? All for his own personal satisfaction. My breathing was shallow and my fingernails were digging into my palms. I needed to calm down, but I couldn't.

"It does not make what you did right!" Darion countered. "We will report you to the authorities. Besides the legal aspect, Tamisan's life was not in danger at all! And you lied about the

Varekai as well!" He'd picked up that last bit of information from my mind.

Starrick looked confused. "Tamisan?"

"I've changed my name," I said proudly, though I was shaking with rage. I tried taking some slow, deep breaths, but it didn't help much. "One that *I* chose."

"Well, Zhenna, Sifayah, Rajendra or Tamisan, it doesn't matter what you call yourself; you are coming back to Maztec with me — *now!*"

I could feel Darion ready himself; he knew what I planned to do. He sent a warning to his men to get down.

As I started to push Starrick and his men backwards, I realized Darion was trying to tell me to disarm them instead, so it didn't go as smoothly as I'd hoped. It felt kind of awkward and everything seemed to happen at once. As Starrick and the others fell onto their backs, one of them fired his weapon and it hit the roof of the cave before Darion could teleport it out of his hand. It sent pieces of rock showering down on top of us all. Darion and I managed to duck down behind a rock for cover, and one of the rocks hit me in the shoulder, sending pain slicing through my arm. I didn't think it was too serious, but it made my arm feel like I couldn't move it properly.

"Quick, down that passage!" Darion urged, and he pushed me through an opening in the rock at the side of the cave with both his mind and hands, just as more lasers were fired. Someone had found a weapon pretty quickly.

Behind me someone yelled out "Nobody move!" but I was out of the firing line now and kept going.

When I looked back, expecting to see Darion stumbling along behind me in the dark, he wasn't there. *"Darion?"*

"Keep going!" he told me.

I wanted to turn back, to go and see if he was okay, but his voice was clear inside my head, *"Keep going! I am okay."*

I really had to push myself, fighting the urge to go back. Just put one foot in front of the other and ignore the pain in my foot. The tunnel I was in opened out a bit and I was able to stand fully upright. I kept going forward. *"Darion?"*

No answer.

Panic.

"Darion? Can you hear me? Are you okay?"

Still no answer. I looked back. Nothing.

My breathing was fast and erratic. My face felt cold. What had happened to him? Did he get shot? Was he...? My blood ran cold.

"Tamisan?" Relief flooded through me.

"Darion? What's happening?" I asked quickly. *"Are you okay? Why didn't you answer me?"*

"Was busy... Starrick has me."

CHAPTER 60:

Show Me Where You're Hurt

I felt the adrenalin shoot through me. My stomach clenched. I should have stayed.

"No — you would just be caught too, and you're the one he wants. Stay where you are — no, keep going further into the caves. Your advantage is that you can see in the dark and they can't."

I sensed something was wrong. Something was wrong with Darion. I could feel it. I could feel pain — pain in my shoulder — and it wasn't the one that had been hit by the falling rock. I realized that that was where Darion could feel pain. *"Darion, you're hurt!"*

"It is only a nick on my shoulder — I will be fine. Keep moving." He paused. *"How did you know?"*

"I could feel it... in my shoulder."

"That is unusual," he told me. *"Your empathic ability and your strong link to me must have made it possible."*

Did that make me a freak? Would I ever be able to blend in and be normal again — even amongst Talents? Or would I spend the rest of my life being the centre of attention in some lab somewhere?

I kept wandering through the dark caves, feeling helpless. It seemed like I'd finally found Darion, only to have him taken away from me. After all the time I'd spent struggling through the jungle and waiting for the chance to meet him. It wasn't fair.

I'd been so close to getting out of this nightmarish place.

Darion had stuck by me from the moment I'd called out for help. But now he was wounded and held at gunpoint by the madman that had turned me into an alien for the fun of it.

It was too much. The despair turned to anger. I was determined that Starrick wasn't going to win this time. He'd caused me so much pain already.

But what could I do about it? How could I help Darion?

I turned back toward the entrance of the cave with no idea of what I was going to do once I got there. I only knew I couldn't leave him. My anger boiled and my mind raced. I could come out of the cave with one great big push that would send them all flying, but that could hurt Darion and his men as well. I could come out with my hands up and make out like I surrendered, so I could assess the situation before making my move, but what *was* my 'move'? I had no idea.

It was hopeless. I wanted Darion to be back with me and to be safe. I *needed* to make him safe. I had to have him with me and away from danger. The thought of him getting hurt or killed was too much. That image flashed into my mind. Of him lying motionless on the ground. A surge of emotions swept over me and I squeezed my eyes shut as my knees turned to jelly. My legs gave way and I fell down onto my knees with a wave of exhaustion. I stayed there a moment to try to steady myself.

"*What?*"

It was Darion's voice, but it wasn't in my head. It took a few seconds for my brain to process what had happened and I opened my eyes to find him standing right in front of me!

When he didn't react, I realized he couldn't see that I was kneeling at his feet in the darkness. I leapt to my feet and wrapped my arms around him, tears in my eyes. He gave a start, but quickly realized what had happened.

His arms were instantly around me and he held me tight. *"Tamisan! You teleported me?"*

I didn't want to let go. Tears ran down my cheeks. The thought of losing him was something I couldn't think about right now. I pushed it from my mind. He was here with me and that was all that mattered. He held me close.

I felt drained of energy again, like I did when I ported myself into the river. Then I remembered how dangerous it was to be teleporting someone without enough training. *Oh no! I could've hurt him or killed him!*

"You were coming back. I told you not to. I was telling you to turn back when you ported me — did you not hear me?"

"N-no," I whispered. My tears were wetting his shoulder. I'd been so wrapped up in my thoughts that he had no chance of getting through.

"We must move," he told me. I reluctantly released him and we started walking.

We trudged along holding hands, with Darion stumbling every now and then. As we walked, I kept thinking about the injury to his upper arm. I wanted to see it — to see how bad it was. My imagination kept trying to fill in the blanks. It conjured up pictures of anything from a small singe to a gaping hole in his upper arm. I fought back tears.

"Do not worry about me," he said.

"I can't help it."

"And I'm glad to be away from Starrick, but you need to be more careful."

"Yeah. I know. I didn't do it on purpose. I just wanted you out of danger." I couldn't help the feeling of disappointment. He'd praised me for doing it and the warning stung. Again. I told myself to get over it. He was right.

When Darion felt we were far enough away, he switched on a small torch. Once we had the torch to guide him, we kept up a faster pace until the sounds behind us had long since died away. It was only then that we dared to rest. We knelt down on a patch of soft soil on the cave floor.

It was wider here than the passageway we'd been travelling along, but not by much. The ceiling was a little higher too, about three metres tall at the highest point.

"Show me where you're hurt," I said at last. I couldn't wait a minute longer to see if he was alright. He shone the torch at his left shoulder and I could see the blackened fur, which made me gasp. *"Let me look at it,"* I urged.

He tried to lift the fur up away from it, but it was too difficult and painful, so he opted to take the whole strip of fur off instead. I helped him unhook it from where it was attached to the loincloth at the front, which caused a little flutter in my chest as the back of my hand grazed his stomach, then I carefully lifted it over the wound. He winced.

I couldn't help staring at his bare torso. His muscles were firm and taut, but not bulging excessively, and his chest had hardly any hair. I quickly looked away before he could see me ogling him. Back to the task at hand...

CHAPTER 61:
You Look So Beautiful

The laser had burned a thick line across his upper arm, below the shoulder, so it was only a scratch, so to speak. So, he hadn't downplayed it to stop me from turning back.

The wound had also cauterised itself, so there was no bleeding to contend with. I felt some of the tension leave me and I cursed my overactive imagination.

"I have a small Medikit in my belt," Darion told me as he pulled it out and held it up. *"There should be something in there for burns."*

I took it from him and pulled out the burn cream, then gently applied it to his arm. He winced as I touched him, but remained still and silent otherwise. I noticed he was looking at me intently while I busied myself. If I'd have looked at him then, I wouldn't have been able to concentrate on treating his wound, so I didn't look up into his eyes until I'd finished and applied an adhesive bandage.

When I finally did look, I found I couldn't look away. The warm feeling I'd experienced when I was looking at his sleeping face started to grow again.

We sat there in the torchlight, not saying anything with our mouths *or* our minds and Darion smiled. Not a full smile, it just tugged at the corners of his mouth, barely visible. I smiled back.

It reminded me of Sifayah and Jarleth. How they didn't need words... they knew what the other was feeling... I felt a pang in my chest at the thought of Jarleth never seeing her again.

"You look so beautiful..." he breathed. It was barely audible.

I didn't move. I was content to get lost in his eyes.

The silence was shattered by an ear-splitting screech that made both of us jump. I let out a yelp and turned to see a huge bat-like creature flying away above us and into a wider area of the caves up ahead. Darion instantly shone the torch on it and we both watched it weave its way through the largest of the stalactites and disappear from sight.

"That thing is huge," he said.

My hearts were pounding and I took some deep breaths to try to calm myself. I was shaking all over. *"Yeah."* I guess it was silly of me to think we were alone in here.

Darion put his arms around me and drew me close. I could hear and feel his heart pounding as I rested my ear on his bare chest. I closed my eyes and enjoyed the sensations.

After a while, as our heartbeats returned to normal, he gave me a little squeeze and said, *"We should keep moving."*

We stood and dusted ourselves off and he said, "We missed breakfast."

I'd forgotten all about my stomach, which suddenly started to complain loudly. *"Where are we going to find food in here?"*

"I have some energy bars in my belt. They are not very filling I'm afraid, but they're good revivers."

With that, he reached into the other pouch on his belt and produced two energy bars, chocolate flavour. I couldn't re-member the last time I'd eaten chocolate. I ate slowly, savour-ing every mouthful, and I think I might have made a little moaning noise.

The exhaustion from porting Darion into the cave started to subside. The energy bars worked really well.

"How is your arm?" I asked.

"It feels much better now, thank you nurse," he reported.

I was suddenly reminded of how he'd helped me with the wound on my leg. I instinctively looked down to see how it was healing and moved the skins of my loincloth out of the way — it was almost completely gone — although the disinfectant and SkinGro must have accelerated the process.

"I'm a fast healer!" I exclaimed.

He looked down at my leg, shining the torch on it so he could see it better. *"Yes, you are. I had a shipsuit for you, but it is back at the entrance to the caves. I was going to ask you if you wanted to put it on before I ported you back to Jannali, but Starrick ruined that."*

"He has ruined a lot of things... but it doesn't matter. I don't need a shipsuit."

He paused and had a look of concentration on his face.

"The others are okay," he informed me. *"I have made contact with each one's mind. Two of them have been captured by Starrick. The others are in the caves. No serious injuries."*

"That's good. I mean about no serious injuries..." I couldn't say anymore. He was still looking at me. I desperately wanted him to kiss me. I didn't know where that thought had come from, but it was true.

He raised an eyebrow. I'm sure my face turned red.

"We should not stay here too long," he told me. *"It could be dangerous with Starrick on our tails."*

He was right. That was how we'd been caught in the first place. We'd let our guard down. *"Yes, okay."*

Darion put the strip of fur back around his shoulder. I gave him the Medikit and he put it back in his belt. We made sure we took the wrappers for the energy bars with us. We didn't want to pollute the area and we didn't want any natives finding something that shouldn't be here either.

We walked further into the labyrinth of caverns, stopping every now and then to listen for any signs that we were being pursued, hearing nothing each time. Darion told me he'd made contact with his superiors telepathically and they were sending some soldiers — six of them. He would port them to the front of the caves when they were ready to go. He also informed me that he had two more energy bars, so we ate them while we walked.

I savoured the taste of the chocolate again.

My foot was giving me pain and I walked with a slight limp, but it felt a lot better than it did before. As we continued to walk, I noticed we seemed to be going downhill. Under different circumstances, I would've been really intrigued by the caverns and tunnels under the mountainside. But I'd had enough. I couldn't wait to get out and get to Jannali.

"How is your foot?" Darion asked.

"A bit painful, but it feels better with the bandage for support," I replied. *"If it weren't for the boots, it would've been a lot worse. That oversized rat would've ripped half my foot off. I'd be in a real mess."*

The soft soles made walking on my injured heel a lot more bearable too.

"That thing was a mean piece of work," he said. *"I hope there are no little horrors like that in these caves."*

The thought made me uneasy. *"If there is, we'll be ready for 'em,"* I told him as I looked around me. I was determined to get out of these caves and to Jannali in one piece.

We kept going through the darkness. I thought about what we did to Starrick and his men outside the caves. Being telekinetic meant wielding incredible power for those who had enough Talent. The things I could do! Actually, the things I could do were beginning to get a bit scary. I imagined that kind of power in the wrong hands. Now *that* was scary!

No wonder there were people who were against those with Talent. People who feared and hated them. People like Kami. They could also imagine — or maybe some of them had seen — the scary things that could be done with the mind. *What's the limit?* I wondered.

Was there a limit to the weight I could lift? Was there a limit to the distance I could push it?

Now another thought came to me. Could someone lift *themselves* up into the air using telekinesis? That *would* be something truly amazing.

Darion stopped and told me it was time to port the soldiers. I forgot all my thoughts of floating on air as I tried to focus on him instead. He sat on a rock and readied himself. As he sat with his eyes closed, I stood watching him. I liked looking at his face, drinking it up.

Porting six people must have been very draining on his mental abilities, but he kept his composure, and soon he opened his eyes and told me he was finished. There were only two of Starrick's men at the mouth of the caves, and they'd been taken by surprise and arrested immediately.

Darion told me one of the soldiers had some Talent — he was a Finder — but was only rated at a T6. He would be a great help in locating the rest of the men.

I couldn't help wondering why they hadn't used this Finder to locate me and teleport me out of the jungle days ago.

"He has been ill and was actually in the infirmary until this morning. The illness prevented him from being able to locate you," Darion told me. *"Even now, he is not completely well."*

"Oh..." Now I felt guilty.

"Don't worry about it."

Darion looked deep into my eyes in the torchlight. *"We will be safely at Jannali soon."*

"Good." I stood there looking back at him and a familiar scent reached my nostrils. *"Hey! I can smell water!"*

We hadn't had any water since the previous night, and I was feeling very dry.

Darion sniffed. *"Your nose is better than mine — I cannot smell anything but dirt. Lead the way!"*

I led him in the direction of the water. As we went, the torch started to blink intermittently, making it hard for Darion to see where he was going. It was frustrating. If it gave out now, we'd be reduced to him stumbling through the total blackness again.

We headed down a narrow passage as the smell became stronger and we could hear the sound of running water. We walked as fast as we could with the unreliable torchlight until the passage opened out and we were standing in front of a small rock pool with a mini waterfall, surrounded by stalagmites of different sizes. I looked up to see that the stalactites were very long in this area. From all the extra moisture, I assumed.

My mouth felt even drier looking at the water and we both moved forward to get a drink. As we approached the water's edge, loud screeching cut through the silence. About a dozen bat-like creatures flew down from the roof and swooped at us before flying out of the cavern and down a large passageway.

One had gotten its claws caught in Darion's hair and as he tried to pull the creature free without getting bitten, he fell into

the water, with the bat thing breaking free and flying away at
the last minute.

CHAPTER 62:

You're the One They Want

I instinctively lunged forward to try to stop him from falling in, but failed. He fell in with the torch in his hand, but dropped it as he plunged under the surface. The water wasn't deep, so it was easy for him to push his head back up out of the water.

"Darion? Are you okay?" I said aloud.

He stood up in the waist-high water. "Yes, but it is extremely cold!"

The torch flickered and died as the water leaked into the casing. I let out a moan. Darion was basically blind again.

"Take my hands," I told him.

I guided him out of the pool without too much trouble and tried to console myself with the fact that we wouldn't have to wait too much longer. Then we'd be out of here.

We both knelt down to drink. Then I scooped up some water to wet my face. That felt better, even though it was icy cold. We moved away from the water and rocks, and sat down on the soft cave floor.

Without the warmth of the jungle, Darion started to shiver. I wrapped my arms around him, trying to use some of my body heat to warm him.

"*Now this is nice,*" he said. He put his cold, wet arms around my shoulders and I sucked in a breath. "*Feeling better now you've had a drink?*"

I nodded against his chest, although my skin was still so dry. Diving into the pool would solve that problem, but it would be impossible to help Darion warm up if I was wet and cold too.

My mind wandered. I thought about what Starrick had done.

"*You know, I'm glad I have these abilities now,*" I told him, "*but I get so mad when I think that Starrick did this to me because he* could, *and because he wanted to learn more about the Waikari. Who does he think he is anyway?*"

"*I think he thinks he is some kind of god,*" Darion mused. "*But he doesn't have the right to play God, and we need to make sure he pays for what he has done to you and Sifayah and the others.*"

Sifayah.

I hadn't thought about her for a while. My life had been changed forever, but Sifayah's had been extinguished. Jarleth and her family and everyone in the cove would never know what had happened to her. A tear ran down my cheek.

A thought struck me. "*How did Starrick find us?*"

"*I'm not entirely sure,*" he answered. "*I've thought about it and I think he may have implanted a tracking device of some sort somewhere on your body — possibly under the skin.*"

I was shocked. I thought things like that only happened in HoloMovies. Surely no one would actually do that... Yes they would. *Starrick* would.

Maybe he'd implanted a tracker when this body still belonged to Sifayah, or maybe he'd done it after the Eibhlin Process. Either way, it meant Starrick could still find us in the labyrinth of caves, even in the complete darkness. The thought was un-nerving.

I felt the back of my neck and quickly ran my hands down my arms and legs, but couldn't feel any lumps. Then I realized it was most likely well hidden, so we would have to listen out for the sound of anyone approaching.

It was possible there may not have been a tracker, of course, but Starrick had a large area of jungle to search, had been basically grounded by the authorities at Jannali, and the jungle was so dense that it would've been near impossible to find me without one. We'd have to assume he could track me and be fully prepared for it.

It was nice being close to Darion again. He'd stopped shivering and I hoped he didn't pull away from me now that he was warmer. I couldn't help wanting to stay in his arms. Nothing in my former life compared to the way Darion made me feel. I didn't want to go back to that meaningless existence.

I knew I shouldn't be letting myself feel this way when we'd only known each other for such a short period of time, but I couldn't help it.

A little voice drifted into my mind, telling me that I only felt this strongly because I'd never had feelings for a guy before. I wanted to swat that thought away, but what if it was true? I would have to deal with that, but not now. I needed to keep my sanity while we were still in danger. I promised the voice that I would explore all of that stuff later, when I was at Jannali and safe.

I felt Darion's muscles tense beneath my hands. *What is it?*

"The Finder has located the others and they have been captured. They are on their way back to the entrance. We can meet them there."

It sounded like a good plan. *"Couldn't you have ported us there sooner?"*

"Yes, but I wanted to make sure there was no chance of being ambushed by any of Starrick's men. Don't forget, you're the one they want."

I shuddered. *"I know."*

I looked up at Darion. He stared straight ahead as he smiled at me. I giggled. It was weird being the only one that could see.

"What's funny?"

"Oh, it's just weird that I can see you, but you can't see me."

He went cross-eyed and poked his tongue out, which made me laugh out loud.

He made a move to get up. *"Let's get another drink, and we will be on our way."*

The disappointment I felt when he let go of me was eclipsed by the thought of getting out of here. I only had to hang a little longer.

We stood and I led him over to the rock pool so we could drink. He let the soldiers know we'd be appearing next to the big rock at the entrance.

I was nervous. I'd never had someone else teleport me any-where before.

"Don't worry, I will be doing all the work — unless, of course, you want to join with me and we will do it together. It will be safe."

"Well, I don't know..." The thought of being that close to him again in a Mind-link caused my heartbeats to quicken and made the decision easy. *"Okay. For practice."*

He smiled and took my hands in his. They were warmer now. *"Close your eyes and open your mind to me."*

I did as he asked. Joining together *as one* with Darion was incredible. I wished we could keep the link forever.

Feeling his energy level rise, I added mine to it. His thoughts were on the cave entrance. He pictured it clearly in his mind, every detail, and I could see it clearly too. Now he gave a push toward that thought, then dropped the Mind-link. *"Open your eyes."*

I opened them to find we were standing at the mouth of the cave, next to the rock, just as Darion had planned. I gasped. Two of the soldiers were facing our direction, expecting us to appear, and gave a greeting. They didn't seem unnerved by the sudden appearance of two people from out of nowhere, so I guessed they were used to things like that.

The sun was setting in the jungle and I could hear the sounds of lots of different birds as they settled down for the night.

Darion talked with the men and they gave him an update on what was happening. All teams were on their way back to the cave's entrance. There was a brief pause as Darion checked in with all the members of his team. They weren't sure how long it would take them to get back.

Darion introduced me to the two soldiers. Commander Totino Kozienko and the Finder, Corporal Lazuli Idrial. Darion immediately turned to Lazuli and worked with him to locate each team and teleport them to us.

I watched them arrive in groups of two or three. Starrick looked startled when they appeared and all of them squinted in the sunlight, switching off their torches as an afterthought.

Darion, Lazuli and I were offered some food and drink, which we gladly accepted. The soldiers understood that teleporting used a lot of energy and that Darion and Lazuli needed to eat before we could get back to Jannali.

We sat down together on our bedding from the night before to eat. It had been folded up and made good comfortable cushions.

"The jungle doesn't look so threatening now," I comment-ed. *"It must be because we're getting out of here."*

"Yes," Darion agreed. *"Maybe now you can sit and admire its beauty again, instead of looking for the next thing that is going to stop you getting away or try to eat you for dinner."*

It seemed he was right. The colours of nearby flowers stood out amongst all the greens, and I was reminded of that first glimpse of Althar's beauty when I'd stepped out of the Outrider not long before the attack. Those thoughts brought back mixed feelings. It seemed like such a long time ago, like something that happened in a dream.

I looked down at my tanned body and the spotted hide and knew it wasn't a dream. It was all real. I was in Sifayah's body. There was no turning back and no second chances. I spread my fingers wide to show my webbed hands. I didn't even *want* to hazard a guess as to what they'd done with my real body. Since I wasn't actually dying before Starrick had started the procedure, my body may have been kept alive and been a part of another of his maniacal experiments.

Starrick ranted while we ate. Funnily enough, he wasn't happy to see us this time.

"We will see that justice is done," Darion told him as we finished our food and stood to face him.

Starrick stood with both hands bound in front of him. He spat at Darion, and it landed on the dirt at our feet.

"The research I am conducting is very important," he said. "It can save lives. It can *change* lives. Improving the quality of life for a lot of people throughout the Known universe..."

He could see we weren't listening, which made his face turn red and his eyes bulge out.

Darion crossed his arms. "It does not matter what you say," he told him. "You are being transported to Station Jannali where the authorities will deal with you."

"Not in your lifetime!" Starrick yelled, and he reached out suddenly with his bound hands, grabbed a pistol from one of the soldiers and fired it directly at Darion!

CHAPTER 63:

I'll Be There with You

Darion instinctively ducked while we both *pushed* upward on Starrick's hand so that he missed his target. The first two shots went up into some nearby trees and the third hit the roof of the cave. Rocks showered down on all of us again, some of the larger ones hitting Starrick in the head and knocking him to his knees.

Darion ported the gun out of Starrick's hands and two of the soldiers pulled Starrick back to his feet. One of the soldiers uncuffed one of Starrick's wrists, pulled both hands around and secured the cuffs behind him. They stood either side of him, holding his arms firmly. He wasn't going anywhere.

Everyone had been hit by debris or dust and we stood brushing it off.

"Jannali can deal with this little outburst too. They can add attempted murder to the long list of crimes," Darion told him. There was a waver in his voice. He was clearly shaken and was struggling to keep his emotions under control. A trickle of blood ran down Starrick's forehead and down his cheek.

Good, I thought angrily.

My heart rate was erratic and I stood glaring at him and trying to catch my breath. Darion could've been killed if we hadn't used our Talent so quickly. I could have lost him before we were able to get to know each other. Three shots. He'd fired three shots. He wasn't messing around. He intended to kill Dari on... I imagined the scene, with Darion's lifeless body lying on the ground and me falling to my knees beside him. Tears welled up in my eyes and I had to wrench my thoughts away and try to think about something else. I thought about our time in the caves. How he'd made me feel. That was a good distraction.

I looked up at Darion. He took some deep breaths — trying to calm his nerves so he could concentrate on porting everyone. Watching him had a calming effect on me. Maybe because I could feel the peacefulness he was projecting with his mind. I went with it.

After a few minutes, he was ready.

"We will have to do this in groups of four," Darion explained to us. "Starrick and three of the soldiers first."

The two holding Starrick readied themselves and a third stepped in behind him.

Do you want to help me again? Darion asked me.

When I nodded, he immediately took up the Mind-link and we shipped Starrick off to 'face the music,' as they used to say back on Earth. We kept going until we were the only ones left.

"Wait!" he exclaimed when I readied myself for our turn.

"What is it?" I asked, wondering why he wanted to stop. Was he as worn out as I was?

"I just wanted to be sure that you're ready for this. There will be questions, briefings, and medical checks when we get to Jannali."

I thought about that and cringed. I hoped it wasn't like Maztec. "I'm ready."

"I'll be there with you."

I smiled. I felt safe with him.

He put his arms around me. *"Good girl."* Then he kissed me on the forehead and ported us to Jannali.

I opened my eyes to find myself in a room similar to the large foyer area near the lab with the water tank at Maztec. The room was full of people — some I recognized as members of Darion's team — the loincloths kind of gave it away — and some were the soldiers that had been sent to help us. There were many others. I couldn't see Starrick and I was glad they'd already taken him away. I didn't want to see him right now. Or ever.

I assumed they would be taking him to a secure location. I didn't know if the underground bases had a brig or holding cells or whatever, but I imagined there would be somewhere suitable to lock him up.

I heaved a deep sigh as I kept looking around. So this was Station Jannali. I felt the relief wash over me. We'd made it! We were finally back in civilization. We no longer had to look over our shoulders wondering whether we were going to be the next meal of some wild cat or dinosaur or other nasty creature that just happened along. I closed my eyes and let that soak in.

The relief was making me feel weak. The exhaustion from helping with the teleporting was there, but this was different. And it added to the way I was already feeling. My knees were weak.

I let out a long breath. No more Bahadori. No more Turak. No more dirt and leaves and crawly things. I couldn't wait to have a hot shower. I thought of Anjou. I hoped he and the redhead were okay. I wanted to picture them riding away on the Rodon to somewhere far away from Turak. I needed to hope they were long gone when he'd headed back that way. I was sure he would seek them out if he thought I was dead. It wouldn't be hard for him to take the redhead back.

A wave of exhaustion hit me. I started to regret helping Darion port so many people.

Darion tensed next to me. *"Hey, are you okay?"*

I looked up at him and I didn't need to answer. He could see it there on my face. He put an arm around me. *"We both need some rest. Don't worry. We'll be able to sleep soon."*

Sleep. Yes. That would be good. On a bed. A nice, soft bed that was *not* made out of leaves...

"What took you so long, Darion? We were beginning to worry you'd been attacked by a wild animal or something."

I opened my eyes. A large man with a greying beard and temples stood in front of us with a puzzled look on his face.

CHAPTER 64:

Always

"Sorry, Dr Aimery," Darion said. "We had to catch our breaths before porting here after we had done all the others."

Dr Aimery looked as if he were about to say something, then he looked at me, smiled and decided against it. After a pause, he shook Darion's hand and said, "So this is the girl, huh? The one you risked life and limb for?"

"Yes, Dr Aimery, this is Tamisan. Tamisan, this is Dr Zoran Aimery. He is in charge here at Jannali."

I couldn't help the little flinch I felt. Dr Starrick was in charge at Maztec and he was clearly insane. I hoped Dr Aimery was nothing like Starrick.

"I'm very pleased to meet you," he said as he extended a hand out to me.

I put a smile on my face and shook his hand. "It's nice to meet you, too," I told him.

Dr Aimery fired off a lot of questions about what had happened, and Darion answered them for a while, but then he reminded the doctor that we both needed a wash, some food and some sleep.

"Yes. Very well," he replied, rubbing his beard. "I'm sorry. That's right. Down to the Infirmary with you to get checked out first. Briefing will be tomorrow morning at oh nine hundred. I have organised quarters for Tamisan to stay in—"

"That will not be necessary," Darion told him. "With your permission, she will be staying with me."

The doctor opened his mouth, closed it again, then nodded once. He didn't ask any questions about it.

I could hardly believe what I'd heard. He wanted us to stay together? I looked up into Darion's eyes, and he gave me a warm smile. *Is that okay with you? I didn't think you would want to be alone.*

"Yes," I replied, *"I just didn't expect it — I don't know what I was expecting..."*

What *was* I expecting? To be alone in a small poky room like I was at Maztec? To have them run tests and experiments on me? I didn't know. Probably. Maybe. I'd put all of my thoughts and energy into finally getting out of the jungle and getting here to Jannali and just hoped it would be better than what I'd been through at Maztec.

The fact that I'd be staying with Darion made me feel a lot better about it all. I didn't want to be alone. I didn't want to leave his side. His arm around me felt safe. It was a barrier to the outside world, even now that we were no longer in the jungle.

We said our farewells to Dr Aimery and were given an energy bar each before heading straight to the Medical Facility. The medical staff were quite intrigued with my gills, and Darion told them they would have plenty of opportunities to study me at a later time, which made me cringe. It reminded me of Maztec.

They apologized and stuck to the routine check-up. I couldn't help feeling anxious. I didn't want more tests. I felt like telling them to go get the data from Maztec and leave me the hell alone. It was bad enough that they'd told us they needed to do blood tests on both of us as a precaution.

Darion told them what he'd done to treat our wounds and the nurses cleaned and dressed them all again. They told us I didn't need any antibiotics because of the dose I'd already taken. They gave Darion a dose because he'd been shot. I cringed just thinking of the word 'shot.'

Once they'd finished with our wounds, the blood samples were taken, as well as full Bio-scans. The nurse informed us that according to Starrick's files, the Waikari didn't seem to carry any known diseases that affect humans and the interaction between the staff and the *specimens* they had 'acquired' hadn't resulted in any illnesses. Of course they had to be sure, and there was also the chance we could've picked something up while running around in the jungle.

So they *did* have access to the files at Maztec. I hoped that that would mean fewer tests for me.

We had to stay there for about half an hour until the initial blood results came back — which were negative. I thought I was going to fall asleep while we were waiting.

As we walked down a long corridor leading to Darion's quarters, I couldn't help wondering what the future now held for me. I hadn't even dared to think about it while I was still in the jungle. I'd kept blocking it out and focusing on surviving.

We finally reached Darion's place. He pressed his thumb on the lock and the door swished open. As we entered, I looked around the room. It was fairly spacious, with comfortable furniture and bright pastel colours. It was a big improvement on the tiny, boring little room I'd been forced to stay in at Maztec. He welcomed me to his home and pointed out some clothes that had been laid out on an Easi chair for me.

He gave me the Grand Tour. There were two bedrooms, a bathroom, separate toilet, and the lounge and dining room were open plan. The small kitchen was nestled in a corner off the dining area and they had a bench separating them. Darion ordered us some food from a dispenser in the kitchen wall and offered me a drink. As I accepted it, he suggested we wash ourselves straight after we'd finished our meal. I nodded. The drink was made from fresh fruit similar to an orange, and was cool and refreshing. The food was delicious, but I didn't even stop to think about what it was — I was too hungry to care. Meat of some description and some vegetables, in a red sauce.

We sat opposite one another at Darion's dining table and enjoyed the time together. His eyes were something I couldn't easily look away from. So blue. So perfect. Something drew me to them like a magnet. I could stare into his eyes forever.

When we were finally finished, Darion rose and walked around to me and held out his hand. I was still looking into his eyes as I put my hand in his. I stood and he led me into the bathroom. *"We need a wash,"* he whispered into my mind.

I looked around. It was rather large for a bathroom, especially considering we were in an underground base, and I mused that it was big enough to dance in.

"Okay then, let's dance!" Darion grasped both my hands and started to dance, so I immediately joined in. He was quite a good dancer. He hummed a tune and we moved to the rhythm. I felt myself smiling. I loved dancing.

As we danced, I looked around. The blues and whites on the tiled walls reminded me of the ocean. The colours seemed to swirl around, chasing each other across the room as we passed them by. There was a large shower cubicle in one corner and a spa in the other. The spa was a pale aqua colour and was a fair size.

As we came to a stop in the middle of the room, Darion let me go and opened a cupboard built into the wall. "Here you go," he said, handing me a white bathrobe. "I'll have a shower once you've finished."

My smile was wide. "Thank you."

"Any time."

He bowed deeply and turned with a flourish. Once I was alone, I set the robe on the side of the vanity and stripped off my dirty skins and boots.

The shower was refreshing and made me feel like a new person. I wanted to stay in there forever, but I was tired and I knew Darion was waiting for his turn. I sighed and switched it over to drying mode.

I emerged wearing the bath robe and Darion smiled. "Won't be long. Make yourself at home."

I wandered into one of the bedrooms and curled up on the bed. I was barely aware of Darion curling up behind me a while later and I slipped into sleep.

—◆—

Somewhere in a thick fog, I found myself looking for Darion. I searched near the river and in the jungle, but couldn't find him. Suddenly Turak appeared, towering over me. He wanted me. He held a pair of shackles in his hand. I couldn't run. I couldn't move. He came closer and I tried to run and I couldn't get away from him...

He grabbed me by the hair and pulled me to him. He started touching me and kissing me, pressing hard against my mouth and hurting me. Suddenly, he pushed me down onto the ground and I landed in the leaf litter. He moved closer... closer... No no no! I tried to scream...

I screamed out loud as I woke up.

Darion was awake at once. "What is it? What happened?" he asked, his arms instantly around me. I was shaking all over. I simply let him read my thoughts and he held me closer, stroking my hair. "The dreams will pass."

I could feel the anger and the frustration he felt. I knew he felt guilty because he wasn't there to protect me or take me away to safety before Turak had caught me out there in the jungle. I looked up at him. "It's not your fault," I said. "You got there as fast as you could. It's my fault. If I hadn't gone into the jungle by myself in the first place—"

"Hey, do not start blaming yourself. You had good reason to want to escape from Maztec. Besides, as crazy as it seems, if you didn't end up in the predicament you were in with the Bahadori that made you call out telepathically, we may never have met."

Darion was right. I wouldn't have screamed out for help — wouldn't have reached out with my Talent — if those hideous beasts weren't cutting my clothes off. And although I was utterly terrified at the time, I was glad we'd found each other.

Darion had helped me, guided me and risked his life to save me, and now I was in his arms. It made me feel warm inside. My shaking eventually subsided.

If I had've worked at Jannali like I was supposed to, I would've met Darion here, but nothing would be the same. I wouldn't have any psychic abilities and we wouldn't have lived through all those experiences together. And he wouldn't have had to save my life... It would just be an ordinary job for both of us. Nothing could have drawn us so close together.

"*Yes,*" he agreed, "*it would not be the same.*"

I looked up at him and our eyes met. It felt good to be warm and clean and in a comfortable bed.

"*I am here for you and I will help you through this,*" he told me as he held me close. "*Always.*"

The tension leached out of my body and seeped its way into the mattress. As I stared into his eyes, I wanted to get closer to him. I had the urge to lean forward and kiss him. Now where had that come from? I kept my shield up, not wanting him to hear that. I closed my eyes again and enjoyed the warmth of his body.

I opened my eyes. I'd fallen asleep again. I felt warm and completely relaxed, like I'd had a really good night's sleep. I didn't want to move from the bed. I wanted to soak up the softness, the warmth, the fact that there was a roof over my head and I was clean and dry and there were no little crawly things moving through the leaf mulch toward me. Nothing crawling in my hair. No one waiting to put chains on me. No mushrooms or weird and dangerous plants or dinosaurs or jungle cats or little furry things with sharp teeth. I sighed. This was heavenly.

I turned my head and saw that Darion wasn't beside me this time. But before I could wonder where he was, noises coming from the other room caught my attention. It sounded like he was in the kitchen. Just the thought of the kitchen made me feel hungry, so I forgot that I didn't want to move from the bed and dragged myself out from under the covers. I needed some clothes. I was still wearing the bath robe.

I looked around Darion's room. The bed I was sitting on was covered in blues and whites and was on the opposite wall from the door. There were doors built into the wall on my left and a dresser on the right and a chair in the corner near the door. The room was painted in several shades of blue.

I noticed the clothes that had been on the Easi chair the night before were laid out on the chair in the corner for me. I smiled as I walked over to see what was there. There were two outfits, one was a blue one-piece, long-sleeve/long-leg suit similar to a shipsuit and the other was a long aqua-coloured dress. I thought the shipsuit thing would be the most appropriate for now. I noticed an open drawer in the dresser and when I peeked in, I found some underwear. I wasn't sure who'd organised them or how they'd know what size I was. I tried them on. They were comfortable and they fit me fairly well.

I dressed quickly, used the bathroom, and followed the sounds till I reached the kitchen. It felt strange to me. I'd never been in a relationship before, and now I was heading to the kitchen to see what Darion was organising for our breakfast. It was exciting.

Were we in a relationship? Now that was something I would think about later. We had a big day ahead of us.

"Good morning!" Darion said aloud as he picked up some plates of food ready to bring to the table. He was grinning broadly.

"Hi," I said, and I couldn't help staring at him as he walked to the dining area. He wore brown trousers and a pale blue shirt that had the top two buttons undone, showing off part of his chest.

I grabbed the two mugs he'd left on the bench top and joined him at the table. Hot chocolate. My favourite drink. The smell was heavenly. The taste was even better.

As we ate our toast, he explained that we'd have to speak out loud in front of other people, even to each other, so that we weren't being rude to the others.

That made perfect sense to me. "Okay," I said.

Oops. If that was the case, I'd been more than a little rude to Darion's men when we were in the jungle.

Then he added: "We will be meeting with Dr Aimery as soon as we've finished our meal."

My hearts sank a little. I'd forgotten all about the 'briefing' while we ate. I didn't want to go and talk to Dr Aimery and a whole bunch of other people I didn't know about my horrible experiences in the jungle and at Maztec. Not right now. I wanted to stay with Darion and get to know him better.

"I know you don't want to go. I don't want to go just yet either, but we agreed to meet him at oh nine hundred, so we need to be there. There will be lots of questions to answer, but take your time and answer them as best you can. I will be there with you, so do not worry."

"Okay," I replied.

I didn't want to say that I wanted to stay here forever with him... That I didn't want to be a lab rat again... That I wanted to be selfish and hold him close to me and kiss him and feel the rush of sensations I felt whenever he was close to me...

I really needed to get a grip. I kept thinking about kissing him and I needed to stop.

I hoped he couldn't hear what I was thinking. I was trying to practice keeping my mental shield up. I didn't want him to hear my whining.

It occurred to me that I didn't know how many other Talents there were on the base that were telepathic. I didn't want them reading my every thought. I needed to practice more than I'd thought.

We finished eating and left as soon as I'd brushed my hair. It was a tangled mess. Darion took my hand and led the way. The corridors looked the same as the ones at Maztec. It was more than a bit creepy.

Dr Aimery was waiting at the door to the conference room for us and greeted us with a warm smile. A real smile. That was a good start and a huge relief.

He stepped back and motioned for us to go in. The room was large and had a huge oval table in the middle with chairs all around it, and only three out of the twelve were empty. I started to feel like the butterflies in my stomach were taking flight. We were offered two of the seats and Dr Aimery sat in the third. All eyes were on me as the butterflies played joyfully.

There were cameras facing me and Dr Aimery explained that they were recording it all on video for their records, and also for the courts. This made me even more nervous, but I was determined to tell them all what Starrick had done.

Dr Aimery started by asking me to tell them what had happened since we were all attacked in the jungle.

When I'd finished telling my unbelievable story and had answered a few of their questions, Dr Aimery told me that Starrick was in deep trouble. He also said they'd been over to Maztec to sort out the mess and had made a few discoveries.

I felt my body tense. What kind of discoveries could he be talking about? I was suddenly eager to hear what he had to say.

CHAPTER 65:

Do You Want to See Him?

Firstly, Starrick's records showed that after my consciousness had been transferred to Sifayah's body, my original body had been the subject of another experiment. A failed experiment. It had been used as a donor and the procedure went wrong. According to the records, my body was terminated.

I felt kind of numb and strange and sad. It was like I was now a ghost. My consciousness was all that was left of Zhenna Rhodarma. And it was even weirder because I'd already been told that my original self was long dead. But then I'd started to think maybe there was a chance that I'd — she'd — survived, but now...

Did I have to mourn my death twice? Now that was one of the weirdest thoughts that had ever passed through my brain.

Dr Aimery said he would get back to that subject later and I was left wondering what he'd meant.

Then he told me the pilot of the shuttle had been shot and killed at the landing site. My stomach twisted. I didn't know the man. I didn't even know his name.

"We assume they killed the pilot because he was the only one who would recognise the uniforms that Starrick's men were wearing."

I bowed my head. "What was his name? I didn't even know his name."

"Vorago Amras," he said. "He was a good man and an excellent pilot."

I closed my eyes.

He told me that the man I'd seen in the corridor that had Mosuti's brain waves all scrambled up in his head had been terminated. That made me feel kind of hollow inside. And to think, those two guards were taunting him. Laughing at him because he couldn't string two words together. They didn't care at all. My jaw clenched. Tears threatened to flow. Those *bastards*. How could they be so cruel?

What was his name? Karlen? No. Kaylan.

Then Starrick tried to transfer brain waves from Larissa to Bazeelia, but they were just as scrambled and Bazeelia went crazy and trashed her room. Another termination. Most of the other experiments were disastrous as well.

I wanted to leave so I couldn't hear any more. I wanted to cover my ears. I wanted to hit something. I wanted to scream. Did they get anything right besides *my* transfer? What was wrong with them?

It was probably because they were trying too many new things. When the equipment was used the way it was supposed to be used — for the original procedure — it was a success nearly every time. I remembered reading that information somewhere.

They found two more of the Waikari people — both males — with the minds of other crew members in their heads. They couldn't remember who they were, but they were definitely not Waikari minds. And they couldn't really talk properly. That part of the brain was scrambled. Sifayah probably knew both of the Waikari that were now 'dead.' I hoped it wasn't Jarleth or Sifayah's brothers. That thought made me shiver.

I couldn't help but wonder if they could've tried again and made it work. That would wipe out the scrambled minds... Maybe they hadn't gotten around to it yet... or something...

Kami and Lanu had also been failures and had been terminated. I didn't know them very well, and Kami was a jerk, but it was still horrible hearing that they'd been murdered. Maybe it was their minds that had been transferred into the two Waikari men's heads.

I thought about Mosuti. I needed to know. What had happened to him? A feeling of cold dread welled up inside me.

But there was more news: Janssen Malakua was missing. My stomach twisted. *Missing? How could he be missing?*

They'd searched everywhere and suspected that the tall blonde from Shakira had somehow escaped into the jungle. Records indicated that he wasn't captured at the campsite with the others. There was no mention of him, which meant he was alone out there in the jungle, like I had been. If he was still alive... Dr Aimery assured me they were doing all they could to find him.

I liked Janssen and hoped they found him soon. I'd suspected Larissa liked him a whole lot more. She should have admitted it and got to know him. Now it was too late.

Larissa. They'd mentioned failed transfers from her mind to Bazeelia's, but hadn't mentioned her.

"What about Larissa?" I ventured.

Dr Aimery's eyes snapped to my face. "One thing at a time. Please," he said gently.

I wasn't sure what to make of that. There must have been more news he wanted to tell me first. I fidgeted and waited and tried to be patient. And waited some more.

Please be okay. Please be okay...

"First, we need to tell you about the Linguist, Mosuti Kyah," he said.

My insides froze. I prepared myself for the bad news. The tears were ready to flow. I could feel them. There was a pause and I was sure it meant the news was bad. It could only be bad. My mind was screaming *no no no!* I felt shaky. I was glad I was sitting down. I needed to take slower breaths—

"He somehow managed to come out of this unharmed," Dr Aimery told me.

My breath caught. "What?" How? After the failed experiment with Kaylan, I'd feared the worst. I'd pictured his brain as scrambled as that other guy's. Then I remembered the process doesn't harm the donor. Why hadn't I remembered that before? All this time I was imagining all sorts of horrible things.

"He is here if you would like to see him," Darion told me.

My jaw dropped. *Here? Now?*

Then, it hit me that Darion knew about this. I looked at him. "You knew?"

"Yes," he told me, "but we needed to tackle one thing at a time. We needed to get you out of there. You were not ready for all this back then."

Tears formed in the corners of my eyes. "You knew how I felt about him and the others. You should've told me!"

I couldn't believe he'd kept this information from me. I felt like he'd betrayed me somehow. I clenched my jaw. I thought he'd shared everything with me, but he'd held back on something really important to me. Mosuti was a good friend.

"I had good reason not to tell you sooner," he assured me, "and there is more to come. Much more."

That stopped me. *More?*

"*Yes,*" he told me, "*Let us tell you everything, but one thing at a time, okay?*"

"*Okay,*" I agreed.

"Mosuti is here now," Dr Aimery interrupted. "Do you want to see him?"

"Yes!" I said without hesitation.

Dr Aimery pressed a button on a console in front of him on the table and told the person on the other end to bring Mosuti in. The door to the room swished open and in walked Mosuti, large as life!

CHAPTER 66:

Who is We?

Adrenalin flooded through me and I felt the sting of tears. My jaw must have hit the floor. I couldn't believe it. He didn't look any different. His eyes were still so alert and clear; his dark hair a mess of curls.

I was so happy to see him again and I jumped up and wrapped my arms around him. He only hesitated for a second before his arms encircled me. He was here and he was alright and his brain wasn't messed up and the relief was so intense. The tears came easily and I started to cry on his shoulder. I couldn't help it.

Then I remembered that to him, I wasn't even the same person. He would be weirded out by this strange woman who'd rushed out and crushed him in a bear hug. I started to pull away, but he held me close.

"It's okay," he whispered. "It's good to see you." *"And I hear you've gained some extra abilities, too,"* he added.

"Yes!" I replied eagerly. My hearts were pounding. I remembered how much I'd wished I was telepathic back aboard the Acronis when I was talking to Mosuti about it.

"I'm so glad you're safe," he said. *"There is so much you will be able to do with your mind — it's amazing. We'll talk about it later though."*

My mind was racing. I had a million questions. I pulled away from him and looked up into his rugged face, still unable to believe it was really him. It was almost like seeing a ghost.

"Amazing..." he sighed. He was looking at me as if he was trying to see the real me in the new face.

"I thought you were dead!" I said, my voice cracking a little. "So... how...?"

"I guess we would have been used as body donors soon enough," he told me, "but I think Starrick hadn't gotten round to it yet. We weren't told anything, so we didn't know about you or that you'd escaped, but he was obviously angry about it. I noticed a dramatic change in mood at about the time they tell me you'd managed to get free. Eventually, the soldiers from Jannali freed us."

I felt strange. The whole time I'd been at Maztec and half the time I was in the jungle, Mosuti had been there, close by, probably in a little room like mine, alive and well. If I hadn't escaped and let people know about what had happened to me, I shuddered to think what would have happened to him... So, in a roundabout sort of way, I'd saved him. Maybe even saved his life. That was weird.

Starrick was crazy. He must have really thought he could get away with all of this.

I looked into his dark eyes. "Starrick is so manipulative. He told so many lies. He told me everyone was dead, including me — my body. According to him, I was the only one they managed to save by using one of the natives as a donor.

"I found out later that my life wasn't in any danger at all. They just wanted to experiment on me. There was a guy named Kaylan that had scrambled bits of your memories in his head when I read his mind, and I worried you'd ended up the same way… I thought it was too much to hope for to see you alive and unharmed…" I trailed off. The tears were welling up again.

He gave me a wide smile. "Well, I'm okay now, thanks to you and the people here at Jannali."

My mind was still running at top speed, trying to take everything in, still refusing to believe he was okay and was standing in front of me and I had to keep telling it I didn't have to worry about him anymore. I kept going over everything in my head. But then one of the things Mosuti said stuck out in my mind — he said 'we.'

"Wait a minute," I said, "you said *we*. Who is *we*? Who else is there?"

Mosuti looked to Dr Aimery and the doctor nodded for him to tell me.

"Larissa."

I froze. I think my hearts stopped. I had to remember to breathe. I realized I was wringing my hands and tried to stop myself. I'd been hoping and at the same time I was thinking it was too much to hope for. I couldn't believe it! *Two* survivors! After everything I'd been through, all the while thinking they were all dead, that I was the only one left, I'd found out there were two others. I wasn't the only lab rat. Wasn't the only one brought to Maztec for Starrick's sick experiments.

They kept the others hidden from me, and by the sounds of it, they kept me hidden from them too.

I felt a tingle of anticipation. "Where is she?" I asked. "Is she here too?"

Dr Aimery gave a nod and spoke into the device on the console again.

I felt a strange sensation sweep through me. What would she do? Would things be awkward between us? I hadn't known her for long enough for us to have a rock-solid friendship. Maybe she wouldn't want to be friends now. I didn't know what to expect from her. I didn't know what I'd say to her. I didn't know what I'd do if she kept her distance or didn't want to see me. That would be hard to deal with.

I wouldn't blame her if she did. It would be weird for her because I didn't look the same. But, either way, I'd have to deal with it.

The door swished open. Tears filled my eyes and I couldn't breathe. Larissa rushed in and as soon as her eyes found mine, she stepped forward and gave me a big hug. It must have been weird for her, but it didn't stop her from hugging me anyway. I loved her for that.

We both shed some tears and Larissa stood back to look me up and down. It seemed like she'd grown taller, but it was me that was shorter now.

"Zhenna? Is it really you?" she asked. My former name sounded odd to me now. Wrong somehow. How did that happen?

"Yes, it's me. I'm only different on the outside." I told her, which wasn't entirely true. I'd changed so much on the inside that I hardly recognized myself anymore.

"You're even shorter now," she said.

She looked the same as I remembered her. Her long white-blonde hair still reminded me of a beautiful waterfall and her green eyes shone with tears. On the trip out here, we'd found out we had some things in common, like our interest in art. She loved to draw too, unlike my friends back on Earth. I'd been looking forward to working with her and Mosuti and the others once we'd gotten settled into our jobs at the base. It was horrible how things had turned out. This was nothing like what any of us were expecting.

I couldn't help wondering what would happen when Mosuti and Larissa went back home to their friends and relatives that had been told they were dead. Thinking that and then finding out they were alive would really mess them up, but I guessed they would be beyond happy to have them back alive.

I still didn't know what was going to happen with me. Whether Kaliya and Oliana would find out about what had happened to me and whether I'd be going home or... I didn't know.

"I have something to tell you..." Larissa said.

CHAPTER 67:

The Jungle is a Dangerous Place to Be

She told me Starrick had experimented on her and given her psychic abilities. I gasped. How could he have done that? Starrick didn't tell her anything about how they'd done it. She found out after she'd arrived at Jannali.

The records told the story. One of the times that Starrick had hooked me up to the EEG, they'd recorded some extra activity that was outside the normal areas of the brain and had mapped it. My breath caught. That was the time I'd used my Talent without realising I was doing it. I cursed myself for letting it slip, although I had no way of controlling it.

Once they'd isolated the right areas, they managed to only transfer those areas of the brain across to Larissa's mind. It was a success, and they managed to keep every part of her consciousness intact, although she had no idea how to use the Talent. They said that with some training, she'd be able to master it. A Talent at Maztec had given her some rudimentary lessons and Mosuti had been training her since they'd arrived at Jannali.

I wondered if she was telekinetic too.

I realized Starrick had known back then that I'd inherited Sifayah's Talent. He'd pretended not to know, and kept asking me questions about any memories that might not be my own. Then he'd managed to give the abilities to Larissa without throwing her into the body of an alien to do it. I wished it had been the other way around, that they'd put Larissa's mind into Sifayah's body and given *me* the Talent afterwards.

I immediately regretted my selfish thoughts and scolded myself for even thinking it. But I couldn't help it after all I'd been through.

When I thought about it, I could see that if it had happened that way instead, I wouldn't have met Darion and I wouldn't be able to breathe underwater. I sighed to myself. And Larissa might have been the one in love with Darion...

No. This is the way I'd rather have it... With me the way I am now... And with Darion in my life...

Wait. In love? Had I really thought that? Did I love him? I'd never been in love, so how could I know?

Both Larissa and Mosuti told me that once the people from Jannali arrived at Maztec, all hell had broken loose. One of Starrick's men had later told Dr Aimery that Starrick was actually out in the jungle looking for me when the raid started. They had informed him straight away and he'd given the order to 'terminate all specimens' in a vain attempt to cover things up. His men started going through each of the rooms, killing everyone they could. A chill ran down my spine thinking about it.

Both of them managed to use their Talent to save their own lives.

"I knew their intentions before they even opened my door," Mosuti said. I'd never seen him look so serious. "I exerted some pressure on their minds as soon as they barged in so they couldn't move. I slipped out of the room and locked the door. Then I released them and heard them fall to the floor."

"I'd only just managed to lift a cup in my last lesson," Larissa added, "so I didn't know what to do. I could hear the commotion and could hear screaming. Could hear them getting closer. I picked up the little table in my room, ready to charge at whoever came in through the door. I didn't know what to expect and just hoped for the best.

"As soon as I heard the sound of the door, I ran forward and barged into something. I hoped to knock any weapons away from me with the table. I doubted the table would stop a laser pistol.

"I fell on top of the man at the door with the table between us. As he hit the floor, his pistol fired and hit the man behind him. I couldn't look. There was a big blackened hole in his chest and I felt sick. The man under the table was unconscious, so I ran.

"I didn't know where I was or which way to go, but then I found Mosuti. I couldn't believe he was alive."

They managed to keep out of sight till the soldiers from Jannali found them. Then they were taken back to Jannali.

I stared at them. They'd had their fair share of danger too. And Starrick was willing to kill them all without even batting an eyelid. He really was cold and inhuman. "Starrick is crazy. He thought he could do this to us and get away with it," I told the others.

They both nodded. Their lives wouldn't be the same again after this. Maybe he really *wasn't* sane. But how do you excuse the men and women that worked under him? They didn't seem to have a problem with it either.

Larissa gave me a small smile. "I'm going to start formal training for my Talent once I get back home to Shakira."

"That's great."

Then she frowned. "I'm hoping they will find Janssen soon."

"I hope he's alright." I said. "The jungle is a dangerous place to be." Then I added, "But I think he will have a better chance of avoiding trouble than I did. It's definitely not a good place for a female on her own!"

Larissa agreed. "I wish... I should have told him I liked him..."

CHAPTER 68:
I Warned You to Sit Down

"Don't beat yourself up about it. You didn't know."

"I thought we'd have a chance to get to know each other while we worked."

I offered her a smile. "Me too."

She smiled back. "I would like to catch up with you later on — after I finished my first semester of training maybe," she said.

"I'd like that very much," I said, "I'd like to catch up with you too, Mosuti."

"Yes, of course," he replied eagerly, gesturing to both of us.

"Maybe you can teach us more about how to use our Talent," I suggested.

"Oh, yes. There is much for you both to learn…" he said, his smile kind of turning into a smirk.

Larissa and I nodded in agreement.

"So, did they tell you everyone was dead, like they did to me?" I asked, looking at both of them.

"Yes," Larissa told me, and Mosuti nodded.

"They fed me some garbage about contacting relatives and sending bodies back home to Earth and the others' home planets," I said. "They must have sent back ashes or something. Told them all that we were burned to death, or some other rubbish." I felt kind of sick in the pit of my stomach at the thought. All the people that were told their loved ones were torched and reduced to ashes — or whatever lame story Starrick had come up with. I felt for them.

Oliana and Kaliya would have held a funeral or memorial service for me. They would still be grieving. Oliana probably hadn't finished the paper she was behind on based on the Rings of Saturn and might not have been granted a second extension for it.

Tears started to well up in the corners of my eyes again. This was an emotional rollercoaster. One that I would like to get off of right now.

Then I thought, *They will have to tell everyone the truth. Tell them they were the victims of terrible experiments first, then they were killed.*

Of course, some people will be welcoming Larissa and Mosuti back home. I started wondering about myself again. What could they do in my case? Would they tell Kaliya and Oliana the truth?

"What happens with me?" I asked Dr Aimery. "Will you tell my friends what happened? I mean, I'm not even me anymore, so I don't know how that would work."

"Well," he said, and he paused as if he was trying to create a good effect, "that is one thing we must decide on. But first, there is something else we need to tell you."

What? There's more? I stared at him. Just when I was starting to calm down and get used to the fact that at least two of my friends weren't dead, he was going to hit me with something else? I felt the tension in my jaw and tried to relax. My body had gone rigid and I couldn't help feeling uneasy.

What other news could he have to tell me? I wasn't sure I wanted to know, but I had to know. I had to know all of the details, no matter how bad they were. I had to know what else he did to us. To the Waikari.

"You might want to sit down," Darion told me.

I sucked in a breath. *"No, I'm good,"* I replied. It couldn't be that bad that I would need a seat... Could it?

He looked like he was going to say something more, but changed his mind.

"What is it?" I asked Dr Aimery, remembering to say it out loud.

He took a deep breath, "You might want to sit down."

"No, I'm good," I told him. I frowned. What were they going to tell me? What was so bad that they were insisting I sit down?

Dr Aimery cleared his throat. "Okay. You — ah, Zhenna — was not terminated like the records show. We found her at Maztec. She was rescued too."

I sucked in my breath. *"What...?"* I suddenly needed to sit down. My legs were refusing to hold my weight.

She's alive! She's alive and I'm alive and this can't be happening. But it's happening. There's two of me... How can there be two of me?

"She is here," he continued, "waiting for my signal like the others. Just say the word and I will send her in."

I felt strange. My face felt cold. I felt the hairs on the back of my neck stand up. But in my mind, it was impossible. My mind was telling me it wasn't true. Could *not* be true.

Oh. She's waiting. Like the others. I can see her. I'm not ready to see her. What will I do? What will I say to her? This can't be happening. But it is. But I do want to see her. I need to see her. I need to make sure she's — I'm — alright.

I felt frozen. My mind ticking over like a computer that's trying desperately to add mismatched data together. It basically meant there was one person split into two different bodies. It was too much.

I looked at Darion. His brows were drawn together. I must have looked pale. He was looking at me like he thought I needed to be taken straight to the Medical Facility. "Are you okay?" he asked.

I couldn't answer. I was feeling light-headed. I felt terrible. Someone told me to breathe. It was then that I realized I hadn't taken a breath since Dr Aimery had made his announcement. I let my breath out, sucked in another big breath, but then forced myself to breathe normally. It wasn't easy. As I started to sway, Darion jumped up and grabbed my arm to steady me, then guided me to my seat.

"I warned you to sit down," he said.

I still couldn't answer. There were two of us. Two Zhennas — kind of. But I'd changed. Changed the way I thought and acted. The way I reacted to situations was different. And I'd even changed my name. I'd come a long way since that day in the jungle. But what about my old self? What had she been through? Had she changed too? I realized how much I really wanted to see her.

I looked up at Dr Aimery. "Can I see her?"

"Are you sure?" Darion asked me, "I thought you were going to faint..."

I was. I still might. "I'm okay," I assured him. "I have to see her."

Dr Aimery made the call. It seemed to take forever for the door to open, then in walked Zhenna Rhodarma, dressed in a red shipsuit with a smile on her face. Almost as if nothing had happened.

CHAPTER 69:

It's Good to See You

I sucked in a breath. I stood up and took a few shaky steps forward. Zhenna stopped in her tracks, hesitated, then said, "Hello."

I couldn't believe my eyes. There I - she was; still her old self even after the Eibhlin Process. My brain refused to deal with it. I was struggling to process it all. There simply could *not* be two of me.

But she's here and I'm looking at her and she'd be freaking out looking at me and wondering if it's really her in this body.

It would be strange for her to see me and imagine that it's her in my head, but to me, I was looking in a mirror. Only the reflection wasn't mimicking my every move. It was *way* beyond weird.

I still can't believe it.

My hearts were pounding too fast. "Hello," I said. "This is going to sound kinda strange, but it's good to see you!"

"It's really good to see you, too. Are you really me? I know they told me what happened, but I still can't believe it!" Zhenna exclaimed.

I had an overwhelming urge to cry. "Yes. I'm you, but I'm me. I'm kind of different now. It's hard to explain."

She opened her mouth to speak, but nothing came out. Closed it. Ran a hand through her hair. It must have been just as hard for her.

I wasn't sure what to say, but I thought one of us needed to break the silence.

"I can't believe you're still alive!" I told her. "Starrick told me my body was badly burned and I was clinically dead, and that's why they transferred my — your — our — consciousness into this body."

I was aware of all the eyes on us while we stood there staring at each other, but forced myself to ignore them.

"Yes, well, as you can see, I'm still here and very much alive. My life — your life — wasn't in any danger. I had a splitting headache when I woke up, and all my muscles were stiff and sore from the stunner blast."

She grimaced when she mentioned it. It must have been painful.

"He didn't tell me about you or any of the others," Zhenna continued. "The 'everybody is dead except you' story seems to be the one he told to every single one of us. I don't know how he pulled it off, though. I didn't see anyone else the whole time I was there. When I was taken to the lab or Medical Facility, there was never anyone else in sight."

"Yeah. Same here. I managed to zap the lock on my room with static electricity and went for a walk around. I found a man with Mosuti's mind scrambled up in his head. That was scary. I even found a Vid, but couldn't access anything. I was caught on camera doing it and Starrick gave me a bit of a roasting over it." I cringed at the memory of my failed attempt at trying to call someone. "Starrick wasn't happy."

Zhenna was nodding and I glanced around the room. Everyone was watching us. I wanted to curl up in a corner and hide from them. Or ask them to leave.

"Starrick wasn't happy when you ran away," Zhenna told me.

"Yeah. Mosuti told me. I managed to get away, but got myself into some worse trouble. The jungle was so horrible..."

She nodded. "Yes, they told me."

It was so strange talking to and thinking of Zhenna as a separate person. Well, we *were* separate people now. It was like there'd been a fork in the road. Our lives up until Starrick decided to play God were the same. After that, everything was so different. It was like I was split in two. Each part taking a new path. Zhenna had stayed at the station, probably bored to tears, enduring some tests every now and then or something, until she was rescued by Jannali's soldiers. While I'd gone through so much pain and so many things kept going wrong. I shuddered just thinking about it. Would I ever be able to think about Turak and the Bahadori without feeling this way? Would the nightmares ever go away?

A lot had happened, but I'd grown stronger because of it. Even changed my name because I didn't feel like me anymore.

A thought struck me. When this mess was sorted out, Zhenna would be going home — back to Earth. Back to my life and my friends. To Kaliya and Oliana. My/her friends would be so happy that she was still alive after being told I/she was dead. But I wouldn't be able to go back. I felt a pain in my chest. In my hearts. I felt as if someone was about to steal my life. It was like identity fraud.

When Zhenna returned, it would be like she was moving in and posing as the real Zhenna (even though she *was* the real Zhenna) and stealing my life, living in my apartment with my

best friend. Meanwhile, the real Zhenna, the *other* real Zhenna
— me — would be staying at Jannali. I could never return to
that life. Tears welled up in my eyes and streamed down my face.

CHAPTER 70:

The Locket

Darion rushed forward. "What is it?"

"I'm sorry," I said, turning away from Zhenna. "It's just that I realized that... Z-Zhenna will be going home to my... her frie nds... and..." I couldn't finish.

I turned to him as he wrapped his arms around me. "Shhh... It will be alright."

He stroked my hair and it made me feel better. All the sadness was eating at me and he was keeping it at bay, blocking it out with his strong arms around me. It was hard to stay standing when I felt like the world was pressing down on me. My world was slipping away. I had to let it go and console myself with the fact that Oliana and Kaliya won't be living their lives thinking I'm dead. They would still have me in their lives, only it won't be me...

Zhenna put an arm around me and told me she was sorry. "I feel bad that I'll get to see Oliana and Kaliya again and you can't."

It felt so strange to have my arm around me... Her arm around me... This might just drive me crazy.

I didn't want to be rude to her, but I kept my eyes closed. I needed to block everything out for a while. I needed to hold Darion. He was my anchor when I was in the jungle and he was keeping me sane right now. *"I can't even tell her to tell them I said hello..."* I told him.

He held me tighter. Despite his best efforts, I found myself sobbing on his shoulder.

Zhenna kept talking. Maybe to make me feel better. Maybe to change the subject. She told me that when she regained consciousness, Starrick was there to reassure her and tell her his lies, but then he wouldn't let her out of her room. She knew something was wrong, but couldn't do anything about it.

She'd heard the commotion when the men were going from room to room, killing people at Maztec, but when her door opened, it was soldiers from Jannali and she was taken out of there.

"I was amazed when I found out all the things that have happened to you," she told me. Zhenna was clearly struggling with all of this as well.

My sobs slowed, then stopped. I turned to look at Zhenna. She had tears running down her face.

"It isn't all bad," I told her, "I have these abilities now, and they are amazing. Do you remember when Mosuti showed you — me — us how to have a conversation using telepathy and we wondered what it would be like to be able to send thoughts back to him?" She nodded. "Well, it's even more incredible than we imagined!"

Talking to Zhenna about that was weird. When it happened, we were the same person. Thinking about this was seriously messing with my mind. I could see the smile on Zhenna's face. She was trying to imagine it.

"It's really amazing!" I sent to her, and the look on her face was priceless.

I had a thought. Zhenna might have some Talent. I'd suspected it. I told her telepathically and let Darion hear me tell her she should get herself tested. *"It will change your life,"* I said, *"for the better..."*

We talked for a while, out loud, and Larissa and Mosuti joined in. They'd been at Jannali together since they'd been rescued and had spent some time together while Darion was out looking for me and another team had been trying to track Janssen.

While we were talking, Larissa turned to me. "Hey, Zhenna," she said.

"Yes?" Zhenna and I said together, then stared at each other. I couldn't help a giggle that escaped me and neither could she.

A couple of the others chuckled. It was kind of funny and kind of strange.

I ended the awkward moment. "Call me Tamisan. That will avoid confusion."

Larissa smiled. "Uh, yeah. Okay." Then she seemed to remember her question. "So, what are you going to do now?"

"Umm. I don't really know," I told her. "I'm still trying to get my head around everything."

There was still something that kept eating at my thoughts. Something I needed to know. Who was the *real* Zhenna?

It was obvious that the woman that still looked like Zhenna would be the one going home, but we were both the same person. We started life as the same person. I guessed that legally, Zhenna would retain her identity, qualifications and belongings, but where did that leave me? I had nothing. Nothing but memories.

But things were different now. Things had changed for me. I had a new life now. I had Darion and my Talent opened up a whole new world for me. When I thought about it, my old life would be kind of boring in comparison. But I would miss Oliana and Kaliya so much... I turned to Zhenna.

"Could you do me a favour? When you go home, could you organise to send me copies of all of our photos, please?"

"Yes, of course!" Zhenna said at once. It looked like she was trying not to cry again.

I smiled. I was so grateful to her. "Thank you."

"They recovered our stuff from the Outrider and I thought you might like to have this..." She reached up and unhooked a silver chain from around her neck. I stopped breathing. As she lifted it out from under her clothing, I saw that it was my locket. I choked back a sob and the tears came flooding back. The locket that I thought was lost forever. The one Kaliya had given me for my birthday.

Then it hit me. "Wait. They gave you stuff from the Outrider?"

She frowned. "Yes, but only about half—"

"They gave me half too. The *other* half."

"To keep the lies going, I guess..."

I tried to push down the anger. I looked at the locket and more tears ran down my cheeks. "Thank you..." I whispered. I didn't have to tell her how much it meant to me.

"It won't replace all that you've lost," Zhenna told me, "but I know how much it means for you to have it back..." And she put it around my neck.

Words couldn't express what I was feeling, so I didn't even try, I just wrapped my arms around her.

CHAPTER 71:

You Look So Cute When You Blush

I woke up wondering where I was. Feeling warmth and soft blankets filled me with relief. I opened my eyes. I could hear Darion's steady breathing behind me and feel his arm draped over my waist. The weight of his arm gave me comfort. It was nice not to wake up alone. I could feel his body pressed up against mine and I didn't want to move. I still had a hard time believing I was here with him. In his bed.

We'd had some lunch and gone to sleep not long after getting back from the briefing. I'd been so exhausted and my brain was still tangled up with my heart somehow. My mind was still reeling from it all. It would take a long while for it to sink in. I wondered if I'd ever be able to come to terms with there being two of me. Probably not.

My stomach made a loud growling sound, so I reluctantly made a move to get up. I sat up slowly and swung my legs over the edge of the bed and stretched out my arms. Darion stirred and his eyes fluttered open.

I smiled apologetically. *"Sorry. I didn't mean to wake you. I'm hungry. What time is it?"*

He simply pointed lazily over at a digital display on his bedside. 18:04. My stomach was starting to feel like I hadn't eaten for a few days, even though we'd only slept for a few hours.

Darion got up and walked around the bed so he could sit next to me. After stretching his arms, he put both of them around me and kissed me on the top of my head. I closed my eyes and breathed deeply and it warmed my soul. *I could* so *get used to this.*

"How are you feeling?" he asked me.

"Good. I'm still a bit weirded out, but once it all sinks in, I think I'll be okay."

He pulled me closer and leaned down next to my ear. "It is a lot to take in all at once, but I think you're right. You will be alright."

His breath tickled my ear and sent a shiver down my spine. I buried my face in his chest. "Yes. And I'm so glad they're alive. I can't believe they're still alive. After thinking they were dead for so long, it's hard to convince my brain they're okay now."

He started drawing little circles on my arm with his fingers. I was sure he wasn't aware that he was doing it. And I didn't mind one bit. "Yes. And I'm glad we were able to save them. Now we just have to find Janssen alive."

I felt my body tense as I thought about Janssen. I knew first-hand how dangerous the jungle was and I hoped he survived long enough to be found. *"Yeah."*

Darion's stomach growled loudly and I giggled. *"I think you are not the only one that is hungry,"* he said. He loosened his hold on me, visited the bathroom, then headed out to the kitchen. As soon as he started making noise in the kitchen, I rose to my feet, went to the bathroom too, then followed my stomach to the kitchen.

As soon as I got there, Darion passed me a piece of chocolate. *"For energy,"* he told me.

I smiled and took it from him eagerly. I didn't care what it was for, it was *chocolate*. I didn't need a reason to eat it.

While Darion organised some food for us, I wandered back down to the bathroom to take a shower. *"When you get out of there, can you try the dress on?"* he asked me.

"Yes, okay." That wouldn't be a problem. I was dying to see what it looked like.

When I was finished, I put the dress on. I liked the aqua colour. It looked nice with my tanned skin and black hair. It had thin shoulder straps and it clung to my torso and showed off my curves. The hem along the bottom of the skirt was uneven and kind of wavy and hung down past my knees. Darion nodded his approval as I entered the kitchen again. His eyes travelled the length of my body and he smiled. "You are so beautiful," he said.

My breath caught. I wasn't used to compliments like that. I felt the heat creep up my face as I grabbed our food and headed to the table. "You're not so bad yourself."

I was feeling almost light-headed and my hearts felt too big for my chest. I couldn't keep my eyes off Darion all through dinner. I wondered how I could feel so much for him after knowing him for such a short time.

We talked about what sort of jobs I could do if I decided to stay on at Jannali. I could do the job I originally applied for, or maybe I could make use of my Talent somehow. I wasn't sure what I could contribute. I would have to speak to Dr Aimery.

After eating a delicious meal, we stood up and he stepped toward me. "I meant what I said before. You are beautiful."

I could feel a blush creeping up my cheeks again.

"And you look so cute when you blush like that."

The heat in my face intensified. I didn't know what to say.

Darion moved closer and lifted my chin with his finger. He looked into my eyes, as if he was waiting for something. He must have found what he was looking for, because he dipped his head and gently pressed his lips to mine.

My eyes fluttered closed and my hearts pounded. He pulled back and kissed me again.

I felt his arms around me and slid my hands up to his back. He stopped. I opened my eyes and his face was centimetres from mine. He was searching again. Maybe he wanted my permission to continue. I tipped my head up and kissed him back.

He sucked in a breath and the kiss became more heated and less gentle. I melted into him and felt the raw sensations running through me.

Then from out of nowhere, Turak's face flashed in my mind. Panic struck me and I jerked away. My hearts felt like they were trying to escape my rib cage.

CHAPTER 72:

We Will Take it Slow

Darion pulled back immediately. "Are you okay?"

"Sorry! Uh, sorry. It's not you! I... I saw..." I just let him see what was in my mind. I needed to slow down my erratic breathing.

He held me closer. "I am sorry. I shouldn't have—"

"No. It's not your fault," I said. "I... It was... good until... It just popped into my mind." I ran a trembling hand through my hair. "Ugh! Is this going to ruin things for the rest of my life?"

"No. We can get through this. We just need to take it slow."

I looked up at him. He was willing to help me through this. I smiled. "Okay."

I reached up and boldly brushed my lips against his.

"Are you sure?" he asked against my lips.

I nodded.

He kissed me gently. Kissed my bottom lip, then the top. My hearts still pounded, but my trembling had stopped. He stopped and just held me close. *"We will take it slow."*

A musical tone sounded, making me jump. There was a call from Dr Aimery on the Vid. His face appeared on the screen and he was all business. He told Darion there'd been some new developments concerning Dr Starrick, and he wanted him to come to see him right away.

I wondered what could be so urgent that it couldn't wait till morning, but Darion had terminated the call and was already organising to go.

"Don't worry," he told me. *"I would say he wants to tell me the latest news — probably about what the charges are and whatnot. Or they could have found some new evidence. I should not be too long."*

"Can't it wait till morning...?"

"No. If Dr Aimery wants me there now, I must go now, but I will be back later and I will tell you all the details."

He gave me a big hug and a long kiss that made me forget for a few moments that he was leaving. Then he headed out the door, telling me to make myself at home.

I felt disappointed that Darion had been taken away from me. I'd been planning to spend the evening with him. I told myself he wouldn't be long and I would have him all to myself again. Then I told myself to stop being so selfish. I was acting like a child. Darion had responsibilities. Dr Aimery was his boss and Darion had to do what he was asked.

Then I thought maybe there was more to it than what Darion thought — otherwise Dr Aimery *would* wait till morning. Something must have happened. I thought about calling out to him, but decided to let it go. I would wait till he got back to find out whatever it was.

Maybe Starrick had tried to hurt someone again and they'd had to subdue him. The image of him with a black eye formed in my mind. It would serve him right if they roughed him up a bit.

After Darion had gone, I looked around his quarters again. It was so nice to be back in civilization after spending so long in the jungle. The carpet was soft under my bare feet and it felt so good to not be covered in dirt and leaves.

I had to keep reminding myself I was safe. There were no crawlies or animals trying to eat me. Also, there were no savage natives trying to capture me, chase me, kill me or rape me. I shuddered. It seemed that in a barbaric world, that was the only sort of fate awaiting a female. I didn't really find out much about the cultures of the Bahadori or the Charan or any of the slaves' races, but it seemed that part of it was to treat women as animals, or a lower caste. They were definitely not treated as equals. Only Anjou seemed to really care about me and about Kirana.

Sifayah's people weren't like that. The women were treated with respect, as it was recognized they were the bearers of the children of the tribe. They were an essential part of the continuing existence of their race.

As I thought about this, I looked for something I could do to amuse myself. The open plan for the kitchen, lounge and dining areas made for fairly spacious living quarters. I walked over past the Easi chairs and across to the cabinet that held Darion's collection of HoloMovies. Browsing through them, I found one on Moftar's history that I thought might be interesting and sat down on the nearest Easi chair to watch it. I thought I might as well find out about Darion's home planet.

Although it was fascinating, I was still tired and I dozed. I woke to the sound of the door opening and my hearts picked up their pace. Rising quickly to my feet, I padded softly around the Easi chairs to greet Darion, but when I got there, the smile quickly faded from my face as Dr Starrick was standing before me with torn clothing and blood running from his forehead and down the side of his face.

Ice rushed through my veins at the sight of him. How did he get here?

He stepped in and before I could speak or react in any way, grabbed me by the throat with one hand and thrust something sharp into the side of my neck with the other.

CHAPTER 73:
The Next Five Minutes

I cried out as the pain sliced into me. I staggered back and covered my neck with my hand as the pain spread instantly, followed by a strange feeling. A feeling I couldn't describe. Warmth and... something else. Alarm bells were ringing in my mind. I heard the door slide shut behind him. I saw the glee in his eyes. I saw the blood trickle further down the side of his face.

I instinctively pulled my hand away to look at it and there was a small amount of blood on my palm. I looked up at him, dumbfounded. Did he stab me? Was I going to bleed to death right here in front of him? Then everything kind of went in slow motion.

A sneer crept across his lips as the feeling spread all over my body and down to my toes. My jaw worked, but no words came out. All I could do was stand and stare.

"You may have gotten away last time, but you'll not be so lucky again," he told me.

He waved a hand in front of my face as he spoke, and I could make out that he was holding a needle and a small syringe. I hadn't seen a real one before — they hadn't been used for such a long time as injector guns were a lot less painful, but Starrick had somehow gotten hold of one and probably used it to escape. I guessed he might have had it hidden on him somewhere and they'd missed it when they searched him. Maybe in a small compartment in his belt or a concealed pocket or something.

The pain and the strange feeling were becoming more intense by the second, and I knew I was in trouble. I was struggling to keep standing. The HoloMovie still played behind me and he started to laugh.

I looked at the syringe. There was still some liquid in it. I didn't want him to inject any more of that stuff into me, so I concentrated on it to try to take it from him kinetically. I managed to rip it from his hand and push it across the room. It clattered to the floor in the kitchen somewhere. He looked surprised, but had a look of determination on his face.

"Okay. I'm going to stop the charade. No more bending the truth for you. You know what you've done? What you've done to *me* by escaping and calling on the people here at Jannali?" Starrick snarled. "You have ruined my career — *and* my life! All those years of research. Gone. My life's work. You have made it so I'll never work again! You hear me? I *know* you still can."

What did he mean by "I know you still can"? What was in that syringe? Was it going to make me go deaf?

"W-what have you d-done t-to me?" I stammered. I wasn't sure whether I was having trouble speaking because of the shock or from whatever was in the syringe. I couldn't help panicking. I had no idea what the drug was going to do to me or what he planned to do. Would it kill me?

What could I do? I was alone with a madman. I didn't know when Darion was coming back, or *if* he was coming back. Starrick might have gotten to him first. I quickly pushed that thought from my mind. I couldn't start thinking about that or I'd fall to pieces. I needed to keep it together. I needed to think.

My brain was kind of hazy. It was becoming harder to think clearly.

I needed to call Darion. I had to try. I reached out with my mind, but it was like looking into mist. I couldn't find him. I tried to push the panic away. It didn't mean that he was hurt or... No. He was fine. I just couldn't reach him.

I had to get out. I had to get out of this room and away from Starrick before I collapsed. I tried to push past him, but it was like trying to move a wall. He was too strong. Too strong physically, but not mentally. I tried pushing against him with my mind, but it didn't work. As the drug worked its way through me, my mind and body were giving out on me. I could hardly hold myself up. I couldn't read his mind either. I felt a sinking feeling in my stomach. I was in more trouble than I'd first thought.

He laughed.

What was I going to do? I looked around wildly. I could try to call Darion on the Vid, but I knew Starrick would stop me before I got the call to connect.

"You were *my* project," he continued, "no one else's. They aren't going to take all the credit for something *I* developed! You're *mine!* I created you and I can end you. Now everything is ruined and they won't let me continue my work — all because of you! They've closed me down and taken everything away from me. All my research..."

I tried to call Darion again, with no luck. I kept looking around the room, desperately trying to think of something I could use, some way to get out.

"That drug will soon leave you fully paralysed," he informed me as his eye twitched. My stomach sank. Paralysed? I had to do something. "In the next five minutes, you will not be able to move. You will be able to breathe, you will be able to see, and nothing more. And you won't be able to use your kinetic or telepathic abilities either... and it will serve you right. You have ruined years of research. Years of my work. And now you will be at my mercy..."

Starrick had a wild look in his eyes. They were kind of glazed over — like he wasn't seeing what was in front of him — and he was ranting on and on. I doubted he was still in touch with reality.

"... No one is going to use *my* experiment to transfer Talent and make money out of it!" he was saying, "No one — you hear me? You belong to me. I created you, and they can't have you! I won't let them!"

I was sure now that Starrick intended to kill me. I had to do something, and fast. I concentrated on a heavy-looking ornament on a small table near the wall and threw it at him with my mind and hit him square in the chest. I was surprised it worked. He grunted and fell down hard, but as I stumbled toward the door, he grabbed me by the ankle, bringing me down to the floor with him. I was reminded of when Turak had tripped me in the jungle.

Starrick kept talking. "This is what I'm going to do: Once I've explained to you what my plans were before you ruined them and made you understand what you've done, I am going to enjoy killing you slowly." My blood ran cold. "Then, I'm going to sit here and wait for Lover Boy to return so I can kill him, too, but not before he gets a good look at your dead body and feels the pain of losing you."

CHAPTER 74:

It Was Time to Fight

My hearts were hammering in my chest and I had to blink the tears away. What kind of a man was he? How could he sit there so casually and talk about killing us like he was discussing whether to add a new painting to the dining room wall?

"I had so many plans," he told me, as if he didn't just tell me I was about to die. "So many plans. I need to make you understand what you ruined. The people that wanted a better looking or younger body would pay top credits for it. Then we could use *their* bodies for the people that had a terminal illness or whatever. *Those* people would not be worried if the body wasn't perfect, and we would charge them less. It would solve a lot of problems with where to get the donors from..."

I struggled to free my ankle, but it was no good. My mind was fading away. Like when I was poisoned and hallucinating in the jungle. Starrick's iron grip on my leg caused the memory of Turak to rush into my head again and I cringed. He had hold of me and I was so afraid of him and what he would do to me if I didn't get free. The panic was swallowing me. I had to focus. This was *not* Turak. I had to get my head straight. I had to get him to let me go. I started *pulling* Starrick's fingers off one by one, glad my Talent wasn't failing me this time, and was soon free.

Relief hit me. I could do it. I could get away from him. I could do *anything* with my Talent. Then there was a feeling, a rush, a buzz in my mind. Yes. I *could* do anything! And he couldn't stop me!

I managed to get to my feet, but Starrick was already standing up in front of me, blocking the door. This puzzled me for a moment. How did he get there so quickly? I didn't think I was moving slowly. It didn't matter. I could still win.

He rubbed his chest. "Then I had this brilliant idea," he continued, as if nothing had happened. "A long-term deal with the client to organise to clone them when they are young, so that when they grew old and wanted a younger body, we could give them a replica of themselves, many years younger!" He looked so proud of himself. He paused briefly for extra effect. "They wouldn't have any moral issues with the donor because they *are* the donor!"

Why was I standing here listening to him? The door was right there — all I had to do was lunge towards it while he was raving.

I thought I'd try it — but as I lunged, so did he. He managed to grab me by the left arm and knocked me off balance, but I didn't fall this time. From the corner of my eye, I saw the ornament on the floor, so I heaved it at him again. He must have seen it and was ready this time. It only glanced off his upper arm and didn't seem to have hurt him. I thought of throwing more things at him, but was reluctant to damage any of Darion's belongings.

Then I realized how stupid that was. He could *kill* me and I was worried about breaking some household items?

With that resolved, I started *throwing* other things at him, including the little table that had held the ornament. He soon let go of my arm. Ironically, it was Starrick that fled the apartment.

I charged after him. I should have called Darion or Dr Aimery on the Vid or tried again with my mind, but all I could think of was hurting Starrick. He'd done so many horrible things to me and the others. He was going to pay for what he'd put us through.

An overwhelming sense of power swept over me. I had telepathic and telekinetic power and I was going to use it. There was no doubt in my mind that I was the most powerful Talent in the universe and that I could do anything and everything. I could feel the power coursing through my veins. It was time to fight. And he deserved it.

I will get him, I told myself. *He deserves to suffer. I will make sure he feels pain and knows that his experiment turned on him. I will make him regret it all. He hurt us and killed the others and he needs to be stopped and when I'm through with him, he will beg them to lock him up to get away from me. He is nothing. He is a small, insignificant bug, and I am going to squash him!*

The drug wasn't performing the way he said it would. In fact, it was having the opposite effect. Maybe because I wasn't human. My mind was racing. My actions faster than normal. My heartbeats thundering. And my sanity seemed to be slipping away from me.

Starrick was walking quickly down the corridors at first, but as I started hurling any and all nearby objects at him, hitting him in the back, head and legs, he started to run. Pictures flew off the wall and hit him, then smashed on the floor. The hunter had become the hunted.

A loud screeching sound started up and small lights in the ceiling that I hadn't noticed before started flashing red. An alarm had been triggered. Probably because Starrick was on the loose. That didn't worry me. It simply meant that I'd have to get to him before they did.

As he turned a corner, a man came out of one of the doorways that Starrick had just passed and turned to look at him. He turned back to see me, started to say something, but I *pushed* him so hard that he fell and slid along the polished floor of the hallway, hitting the wall with a thud. I didn't care if I hurt him or not, although somewhere, in a small part of my brain, I felt sorry that I'd done it. But I didn't slow my pace. The man was not important. My only concern was chasing Starrick. I couldn't let anyone get in my way.

A flash, a glimpse of what was in his mind. He was frightened of me, but puzzled as to why the drug wasn't working, why I wasn't paralysed like the guard outside Darion's quarters.

The guard? There was a guard? I hadn't even noticed him.

That was the first time I'd been able to read his mind since all this started. But the fact that my Talent didn't seem to be working properly didn't deter me. I felt invincible. I *was* invincible. Maybe I could be like a superhero and fight crime. The bad guys wouldn't stand a chance. I could do anything a superhero could do. Even fly if I wanted to. Why not? Size and weight didn't matter. I could lift anything, so why not myself?

As I turned the next corner, another man had stopped Starrick as he'd tried to enter what looked like a restricted section. I didn't care what the man was trying to do or what he was saying. He was in my way. He needed to get out of my way. He needed to back off. He got the same treatment as the other man in the corridor. Another little insignificant insect that I could shove aside like a useless toy. He shouldn't have interfered. I needed to get Starrick and make him pay.

As the man slid across the room, Starrick smiled at me and pulled open the door. I couldn't let him slip away. I raced after him. As I entered, I wondered what the room was. There was a short hallway, then the room opened out into a huge area with a ceiling that was about three storeys tall.

My brain was working hard to provide me with the information I needed to work out what all the machinery was that was humming away in the huge room all around me. But before I could do that, Starrick told me.

"The Generator Room," he sneered, "Careful what you throw around in here. If you damage any of these motors, the whole base could be without power, and we *need* power to provide us with air — among other things."

CHAPTER 75:
OVERLOAD IMMINENT

I stopped in my tracks. I may have had superpowers, but he was right. I would have to rethink my strategy.

Starrick wasn't standing still, however, he was rushing from one generator's console to another, playing with the controls.

"What... " I started to say, then I realized I couldn't feel my legs from the knees down, or my hands. I looked down at them in disbelief, my question forgotten. They felt like they weren't even there anymore, but they didn't look any different.

I thought of calling out to Darion, but I didn't need him. I could handle this on my own. *I* was the superhero, not him. What was that little worm going to do? Nothing I couldn't do myself. I didn't need him. I didn't need anyone. I was going to fix this problem and I could do it, even if I couldn't feel my hands or feet. I would make do. I would find a way. I could do this.

Starrick was still playing around with the controls. It was annoying me. I wanted him to stop. *I* was in control now, not him. Control. Yes... But no... I was losing control. I couldn't feel my legs and hands. They didn't respond very well when I tried to move them. It was like trying to move in a dream and something was holding you back. It was all slow motion.

I tried to walk, but fell forward onto the hard floor. Somewhere above me, Starrick laughed. I tried to get up. My legs wouldn't obey me.

No! I can't lose control now. I have to do this. I am the one to bring him down. And I will not tolerate him laughing at me!

I had to regain control. *Think. How am I going to regain control? My mind. I could use my mind. I could do anything.*

I concentrated. My right arm moved, then my left. Now for the legs. Yes. I couldn't feel them, but with my mind, I could move them using kinetic energy. I stood up. I could see the disbelief on Starrick's face.

"It should be working. It should have worked long before now." He was talking more to himself. "Ah, but of course! The Waikari physiology must not be as close to our own as I first thought. No matter. I will fix things. You won't have to suffer long..."

What was he talking about? Won't have to suffer long? What was he planning now? It didn't matter. I would stop him...

At least he'd answered one of my earlier questions. He'd counted on me having a human reaction to the drug. Then I would've been helpless and at his mercy. I almost laughed. It was so ironic. Now I was after *him*. He would be at *my* mercy.

I had to concentrate to keep myself upright and started walking slowly toward him. I thought about what he'd said back at the apartment about all his plans. He *was* insane.

He called it a 'brilliant idea.' It was an *insane* idea. For one thing, if he *did* clone someone and raised the clone to adulthood, wouldn't that clone *be* a *person?* Wouldn't they have their own thoughts and feelings, just like anyone else? Wouldn't he still be killing a human being? Wouldn't they also have a soul? I knew the answers, but he didn't seem to know or care.

"Can't you see the full picture?" he started saying, as if he hadn't even been interrupted by me chasing him through the base. "You need to see the big picture. Step back. Look outside the square... And now — now that I can see that Talent can be transferred too! Oh! The possibilities! People would be knocking down my door for a chance to become a Talent! I will be the first person to do it. The first to have these services available. And there is a whole planet full of donors here! And a whole race of Talents to choose from!"

He was so ecstatic thinking about all the happy, satisfied customers and all the credits he would make, and all the glory for being the first. All the while, he was fiddling with controls and rushing from one generator to another. Like a bird building several nests at once. It made me feel sick to even think about all the plans he had. How many people he would be wiping out. I wavered and nearly lost my balance.

I had to concentrate, but the alarm was blaring and my mind was still fuzzy. What was he doing? Why was he rushing from one console to the other?

He suddenly remembered he was angry with me. "*You*," he said, pointing at me, his finger waving threateningly in the air. I couldn't see it clearly. It looked like my vision was starting to fail me too. "You have ruined it all. You have taken away my glory. Robbed me of the recognition I deserve..."

He looked around the room wildly when another alarm started to sound, grinning like a madman. The alarm was a lot louder than the first one. I'd managed to walk over to one of the consoles and squinted at the screen. There were red letters flashing a warning and I could make out the words OVER-LOAD IMMINENT. Looking from the screen to the face of the maniac in the corner, I realized what he was trying to do.

If he overloaded the generators, the explosion would be huge. It could possibly blow the whole base apart. The expression on his face as he saw that I'd worked it out was indescribable. He looked so delighted and almost like he was proud of me for solving the puzzle.

Why was he happy about this? He'd be killed too. There was no way he could rig this up and escape the blast. This didn't make sense to me. Maybe he didn't care about that. So what, I'd ruined his life, so now he was going to kill himself and take all of us with him?

There was one thing I did know. I didn't want to die.

If I didn't stop him, he would kill everyone in the base. He had no right... He couldn't be allowed to do this. He had to be stopped and I was the one to do it. I would squash him like a bug. And I would teach him a lesson he'd never forget...

CHAPTER 76:
I Would End This

There was another noise, but this one was in my head. Something trying to be heard over the alarms. It was an annoying kind of sound. I tried to block it out, with no success. Then I realized it was a voice. Someone was calling me.

I looked around, but there was no one in the room but me and the lunatic at the controls. He was grinning broadly at the screens with their warnings of impending doom.

The voice kept calling me. It was definitely in my head.

How can I think with all this noise? I thought, *There's too much noise. Need to block out all the noise. I need to be able to think. How can I stop him? What can I do?*

"Tamisan! Can you hear me?" It was Darion. I'd forgotten him in my anger and my state of mind. But I didn't need him. I needed to think.

"Tamisan! Can you hear me?" Darion was *screaming* at me in my mind. Trying desperately to get my attention.

"What do you want?" I hissed back at him. I was really annoyed now, but maybe if I answered, he would go away.

He asked so many questions about where I was and what was happening that I almost didn't answer him. Why should I explain anything to someone who was beneath me? An ant that I could squash under my shoe.

"Tamisan, please, tell me what is happening! Are you okay?"

"Of course I'm okay!" I snapped. "I. Am. Perfect! I am better *than perfect!*"

"What? *Are you feeling okay? They are telling me you are in the Generator Room. Is that correct?*"

"Yes, that would be correct," I spat. He was interrupting my thoughts. "Go away. I'm trying to think. I need to stop the overload."

"*What?*" his voice exploded in my head. "Overload?"

There was a pause, then he said, "*The engineer is telling me the generators are going to blow up if we do not stop them from overloading. Starrick has somehow re-routed the power to flow from one generator to the next instead of out into the rest of the base. If we do not route it back out again, this place will become a big hole in the ground.*"

"Okay, okay, I get it, but how can I do that?" I was still angry with him for annoying me, but maybe he could tell me a bit more about what was going on. It couldn't hurt to find out more so I could be the hero and save the day.

"*Try to get to a console and I can give you the codes to get into the system and maybe we can help you counteract his commands. We cannot gain access from outside, but we think you will be able to do it from one of the consoles in there.*"

I looked across at Starrick. He was hard at work in the corner again. Good. I could do this while he was distracted.

It was harder to move my legs now. The drug was starting to do the job it was designed for. Concentrating on each step, I edged closer to the nearest console. I kept a watchful eye on Starrick and tried not to make any sudden moves. I didn't want to attract his attention.

I made it to the console and started to type in the login details Darion told me — though it was even harder to do than walking. Trying to manipulate numb fingers was nearly impossible, so I curled all my fingers except one and tapped the keys one at a time to try to avoid mistakes.

The logins seemed to be getting me into all the right places, but then a message appeared on the screen that read: "ADMIN CONTROL OVERRIDDEN." I gasped.

"He has overridden all security protocols and has total control," Darion said. *"How did he do that?"*

I looked up from the screen. Starrick wasn't in the corner. I looked around and found that he was standing right behind me. *Uh oh...*

"Get away from the console!" he yelled as he stepped forward and pushed me toward the wall.

I was already unsteady on my feet, so I fell easily, hit my head on the wall and slid down to the floor. Pain exploded in the back of my head and white light danced in front of my eyes for a second.

As soon as my body hit the floor, I pushed myself up again with my mind and this time I was *really* mad. How *dare* he? *I* was the one that would be doing all the pushing. *I* was the superhero.

I will pick him up and squash him and rip his head off and pull his arms off and...

As I *picked* Starrick up off the floor and *threw* him against the wall, I heard part of what Darion was saying to me. It was something about changing the connections manually, but the cables were up about ten metres from the floor.

Starrick looked like a rag doll lying on the floor.

Darion told me they usually used hover drones to do the maintenance on them, so there wasn't any way for me to climb up to get to them. He also said he was outside the door to the Generator Room waiting for the team of workers to cut their way in as the doors were all sealed by Starrick. They had drones waiting to be let in.

Starrick came up behind me and put an arm around my neck while I was busy listening to Darion. I felt the panic rise up inside me, followed by such a strong hatred that I gasped. He was such a bastard! He killed and tortured people and called it science. I needed to end it — right now. I would teach him a lesson he'd never forget.

I peeled his arm from my throat with my hands and my mind and shoved him backwards into the nearest wall. He hit hard and slid down to the floor again.

I was on him instantly with my hands around his throat. I would end this. He would pay for his crimes. He made some garbled sounds in his throat and I squeezed harder.

CHAPTER 77:
Which Ones?

"Tamisan! Stop! Do not do this!"

I could hear the voice in my head, but could barely make out what it was saying... *Stop? Stop what? Oh — stop choking Starrick? Why? He deserves to die!*

"No! He doesn't deserve to die! We can work it out! He needs to go to trial! Otherwise, no one will know what really happened. Please, Tamisan! You need to let go. You need to let the authorities sort it out. If you kill him now, no one will know."

"But... he... I need to... I can't..." A cold feeling washed over me. It felt like the cloud in my brain had lifted a bit and I could think more clearly.

I faltered. I looked down at Starrick's red face and bulging eyes and my hands fell away from his neck.

"I... ah... I don't..." I couldn't think. What was going on? What was I thinking? I'd been ranting and raving and sounding like Starrick and I was... I was going to *kill* him? *I'm losing it... I was going to do what he has done to the others and that would make me as bad as him and I don't want to be like him. How could I even do this?*

"Tamisan. It wasn't you. It was the drug. Don't worry about it. We will be through the door soon. We will be there to deal with him. We will fix the generators. Hang tight."

I sat there on the floor looking at my hands. The hands I just used to try to kill someone. I couldn't believe it. How could I? Where did all that anger come from? I must be crazy. Like him.

"No! You are not crazy!"

Tears were streaming down my face. *"I-I'm just as bad as him!"*

"No! You are not! It's the drug! This is not you!"

I realized Starrick was no longer lying on the floor in front of me. I looked up and saw that he had returned to the consoles, checking the progress of his plan.

Darion was telling me things would be alright as soon as they got in there. They were nearly through.

"Wait," Darion said suddenly. *"They are now telling me the power level has risen to a dangerous level. To simply re-route the power back to the rest of the base will actually overload those circuits. We need to divert the power to the base's shields instead. They can handle the extra surge."*

"Okay, which cables?" I was in no condition to comprehend what he needed to tell me, but I had to pull myself together to stop this from happening. To stop everyone from dying.

"Do not worry. We will do it."

"Just tell me! Which ones?" I needed to know *now*. He must have sensed how urgent it was for me to know.

I looked up. I spotted the cables that needed to be moved as Darion described them. Two of them had to be changed over to another junction so the power would be able to get out and away. But how could I get up there? I looked around to try to find something I could use. Maybe a rope or cable of some kind that I could throw and climb up.

Nothing. There was nothing. Panic was starting to take over. I needed to think.

There were plenty of cables everywhere, but they were all plugged into something. If I knew how everything worked and what they were all for, I would know if any of them could be unplugged and used like a rope without causing any problems. I knew I couldn't disconnect anything. Okay — plan B. Only, I didn't *have* a plan B.

"Do not worry about which ones," he said again. *"We are coming through the door. We are almost through."*

What I did next, I didn't really stop to think about. If I had, I might not have pulled it off. I *lifted* my own body off the ground and literally flew straight up to the cables. I could lift all sorts of objects, and size and weight didn't matter, so lifting my body was easy.

"Which ones do I have to change again?" I asked as I pushed my body over to the cabling.

Darion sighed. He probably thought he was helping with my anxiety to tell me something I didn't really need to know. So he told me again anyway. *"The one on the right, near the big cylindrical tube, marked with a huge symbol with a lightning bolt that is surrounded by two cloud-looking things. And the one on the left, with the same symbols. They need to be plugged into the other junction right next to where they are. But do not worry about that, we have a drone waiting and will send it in as soon as we get through."*

Another alarm started sounding. Darion and his team would be too late. Starrick called up from below, "You're too late! That alarm means the death of us all!" He started to laugh hysterically.

The sound of his laughter creeped me out, but I had to concentrate. I unplugged the cable. *I can do this. I can do this. I will fix it. I will stop him. We're not going to get blown up. I will stop it all.*

As I hooked up the second cable, I felt an incredible weakness flood my mind and body. I was losing my energy and my concentration. I was almost completely numb and I felt like I was detached from everything that was happening around me. Like I wasn't really there anymore. It was all in slow motion. I heard the click as it locked into place. I heard sounds below me. Maybe they'd made it through the door.

I couldn't move. My body wouldn't obey me and the cabling started moving slowly away from me... I realized I was falling... Then everything was fading into blackness...I heard a loud boom and something flashed so brightly that it hurt my eyes and I could see nothing else...

CHAPTER 78:

The Blackness

The bright light faded and was replaced by blackness. There was a short period of blackness, and then I felt like I was floating on a cloud. Floating away... floating in the blackness... I wanted to float away and stay there. It felt good to float and have nothing to worry about and no body and no pain and no problems and no jungle and no monsters...

What was happening? Where was I? Where was Starrick? Where was Darion? I'd fixed the cables, hadn't I? And I'd been flying! Or floating... But then I'd started to fall... And now I floated in the blackness... Maybe that wasn't such a good thing after all. I could feel panic start to invade my nice world of blackness. Then I thought, what did the blackness mean?

I wondered if maybe I was dead. Maybe the drug had slowly worked its way into my brain. That would explain why I was here floating instead of feeling the pain of landing on the cold steel flooring and maybe breaking some bones. I was still pretty high up in the air when the bright light flashed.

I'd heard stories of people who had died and had been re-vived. They said there was no pain, but their stories almost al-ways told of a bright light before them that they started to move toward. And they all said they felt really good. Really happy. Then for some reason they came back. Some said it was because they realized they weren't ready to go, that there were still things they wanted to do in their lives, and they moved away from the light. Others said they'd started moving away for no real reason. Then they found themselves back in their own bodies.

Only, for me, there was no light, and no really good feeling. Just darkness and the floating sensation. And the terrible numbness. They say it's different for everyone. Maybe I wasn't meant to see a bright light. Maybe it depended on what you believed in. Back when humans were all about religion, some people said they'd seen Jesus Christ standing in the light, waiting for them. Others saw the light and all their loved ones that had died, waiting for them, welcoming them. There was nothing like that for me. Did that mean there was no one waiting for me when I died? I had no parents, siblings or grandparents that had gone before me. Cloning made sure of that. Was I destined to be alone in the blackness forever?

I waited. Time was hard to judge. It felt like I was floating for about five or ten minutes, then I could sense Darion's mind. It was faint and far away, but it was definitely him. He was calling me. There was an urgency in his tone. He wanted me to follow his voice, to come back to him. I tried to reach out to him, started to follow him, but he faded away. Then he was gone completely. I felt distraught and alone and I wanted to cry.

If I was dead, what would Darion do? How would he deal with it? We'd wanted to spend more time together to get to know each other. I couldn't leave him. I couldn't cause him that much pain. I needed to follow his voice because I didn't want to die and leave him. But how could I follow him now he was gone? There was no light to move away from, so I had no way of knowing which way I should go. Or if, in fact, I could 'go' anywhere.

I continued to float for a while longer, then I started to come down from wherever I was floating. The first thing I heard was some beeping sounds. What was beeping? A sense of dread worked its way into my mind. Those beeps sounded like medical equipment.

I opened my eyes slowly to find it didn't matter whether they were open or closed, it was just as dark either way. That was odd. I could see in the dark in the caves, but this was pure blackness. Where was I? What was going on?

As I lay there trying to process everything, I could sense some of the feeling had started to return to my body, but I could only feel my eyes and my face, sort of. Then I realized there was something in my mouth. I gagged. It felt like something hard was in my mouth and right down my throat. A tube. I gagged again and couldn't stop the panic rising. The beeps increased in speed. What had happened to me for them to put a tube down my throat to help me breathe?

"It's okay," a gruff voice said from out of the darkness, startling me. "Looks like yer breathin' on yer own now. Just 'ang on and I'll check things out an' I should be able ta remove the tube."

I tried to calm down. Tried to take some deep breaths and stop gagging, with only limited success.

"Alright, the readouts 're good. We're good ta go... 'ere we go." The voice was deep and raspy. I could hear the clicking sound of him turning switches off somewhere to my left. "I'll just remove the tube that runs from yer mouth to the machine first..."

I felt a slight tug that made me gag as he detached the section of tubing, then I could hear him remove the tape that was holding the tubing in place. I couldn't really feel the tape being removed from my face — only a slight pull, but I could feel something in the back of my throat.

"This'll feel real uncomfortable, maybe even painful," he informed me. "Ready? Go." Then he withdrew the long tube as I gagged uncontrollably. He was right. It did hurt. A lot. I was relieved when I didn't throw up once he'd finished.

He used a cloth to wipe my mouth. "Sorry. Nothin' I could do ta make that a more pleasant experience."

I wished my throat was numb like the rest of me, although I should be pleased that I was feeling anything at all. I swallowed a few times, still wondering what was going on and why I was here. I tried to speak, to ask him what happened, but couldn't move my mouth. In fact, I couldn't move at all besides being able to open and close my eyes and swallow.

My breathing quickened and my hearts pounded harder. I couldn't feel them pounding, but I could hear the beeps from the monitors increasing in speed. Why couldn't I move? Where was I? Why was I in a dark room?

I thought about that last question. The man that had removed the tube wouldn't have done it in a pitch black room. He would have switched on a light. The only logical explanation was that I couldn't see anything. I started to panic even more.

CHAPTER 79:

Just Breathe

"Are you okay?" he asked, "Can you 'ear me? Don't panic. Just try 'n' relax. Yer gonna be jus' fine."

I blinked a few times. How could I relax?

"Anyway, I'm Korizan. Good ta see ya awake." There was a pause. "Hey. I'm over 'ere."

I couldn't see anything and couldn't respond to him. The beeps got faster.

"Can you see me?" His voice sounded closer, like he was leaning over me. I desperately wanted to answer him, but could only blink again. *Somebody help me... Why am I like this? What's going on? What happened to me?* The same questions kept going around in my head.

"She's awake. No response to visual stimulation," he said, as if he was talking to someone else in the room, "But she blinked a couple times. Yeah. Right away. Yes." I heard a beep. He must've called someone. "Tamisan, if ya can 'ear me, blink yer eyes."

I blinked and heard a small sigh of relief. "Okay, that's good. We can communicate. Blink twice fer yes an' once fer no. 'Kay?"

I blinked twice slowly. It was all I could manage. I could hear the beeps slow down a bit, but they were still too fast.

"That's great," he told me. "The doctors 're on their way. Now, can ya move any part of yer body?"

I blinked once.

"Oh, not at all?"

I blinked once again. I didn't think my throat counted as a part of my body that I could move. I could sort of feel it, but couldn't really move it.

"Okay. I'll tell the docs. Can ya feel yer arms or legs?"

One blink.

"Oh. Can ya feel anythin'?"

One blink.

"Okay, yes, we'll let them know and they can reassess ya now that yer back in the land of the livin'."

That was a creepy choice of words, considering I thought I'd died.

Too many questions were buzzing in my head. My body felt almost as numb as it had while I was floating. Before I'd woken up. All I could do was lie there, staring at nothing. I felt my eyes fill with tears. At least I could feel *that*.

What if I stay like this? What if it's permanent? I thought. *How can I do anything? How could I live like this? With everyone having to look after me and feed me and dress me and wash me and...*

A thought popped into my head. Maybe I was back at Maztec.

No! Not again! I thought with another surge of panic. The beeps sped up again. *What has Starrick done to me? Is that drug making it so I can't move? He told me that's what it would do.*

The beeps kept increasing in speed, so I took some deep breaths and willed myself to calm down. I needed to think rationally. People were talking somewhere above me, but I was too preoccupied to listen to what they were saying. If I was still alive and lying in a bed in a Medical Facility, then I must have stopped the base from blowing up. I had to be in the Medical Facility at Jannali. That made a lot more sense. Maybe I was injured after I fell and they'd taken me here to treat me. That would explain the tube in my mouth and the monitors.

I started to think my situation must be more serious than I realized. All the possibilities flashed before me. Spinal injuries, broken bones, internal injuries, head injuries, paraplegic, quadriplegic— *Stop it!* I told myself.

I needed to find out more facts and stop my mind from overthinking things. I also told myself I would have to wait and see what happens. The drug may take some time to wear off and I might be fine. I decided to wait. There was no need for all the negative thoughts. It was making me crazy.

Just breathe...

I lay there in the darkness trying to keep calm. Even though I'd just resigned myself to waiting, my mind wouldn't let things lie. All the possibilities... No. I had to block them out. I reminded myself to keep breathing slowly.

I tried to feel for any pain in my body — anything that would suggest I didn't escape uninjured, but could feel nothing. Maybe I had head injuries. Or neck injuries. I could be in a full neck brace and not even know it.

I realized someone was calling me, so I blinked twice.

I heard a deep voice, but it wasn't the man that had taken the tube out. What was his name again? Korizan?

"Tamisan, I am Dr Nambiri. I would like to ask you some questions. Is that okay?"

I blinked twice.

"Okay. You can move your eyelids, so can you feel them?"
Two blinks.

Sigh. "Good. Can you feel the rest of your face?"

One blink.

"Okay. Can you feel any other part of your head?"

I guessed my throat could be included in that so I blinked twice.

"Great. So, which part? Your ears?"

One blink.

"Okay, your scalp?"

One blink.

"Your neck?"

That was close, so I blinked three times, hoping he would somehow understand.

"Three blinks? What does that mean? Does it mean maybe or that I'm close? Does it mean maybe?" he amended.

One blink.

"Alright. Does it mean I am close?"

Two blinks.

"Okay... so, not your neck... your throat?"

Two blinks.

"Okay, great. We're making progress. Maybe you could do three for when I'm close and four for maybe?"

I gave two blinks. It felt better to have some alternative answers besides yes and no. Although, with each no I was feeling more and more lost and anxious. *I can't stay like this. I can't...*

I heard a commotion and I heard Darion's breathless voice as he entered the room. He sounded like he'd been running.

"Tamisan! It is me! I'm here! Are you okay?" I could hear the waver in his voice and it sounded like he was close to tears.

All I could do was blink twice. I could feel the tears in my own eyes welling up again. Could hear him but could not feel or see him. I felt alone and kind of cold, even though I couldn't feel anything.

I tried to call him, tried to reach out to his mind, but felt nothing and was met with silence. It was like I was in a dark void.

No no no no no! I can't stay like this! I need to get out of here! What if I can never move my body again? What if I've lost my Talent? What will I do? And what if I can never see again?

How could I go through life without being able to see? That would be worse than almost anything I could imagine. I tried to picture it. Always in darkness, not able to see even where I was walking — if I could ever walk again. I would need a proximity sensor to get around. I cringed at the thought. And the thought of never being able to draw or paint again made me feel like my heart was shrivelling up inside my chest. It would shrivel and die if I couldn't express myself through my art.

"Mr... Andiyar, is it?" the doctor asked.

"Yes. Tell me — how is she? I was told she was conscious, but she cannot move?"

"Yes, Mr Andiyar, that is correct. She is aware of her surroundings and can hear and understand us, but can only blink her eyes at this stage."

CHAPTER 80:

Déjà Vu

I heard a gasp and assumed it was Darion.

"Tamisan—"

Dr Nambiri cut him off. "Before you talk to her, I want to let you know we have been communicating with her by asking questions and she responds by blinking twice for yes and once for no. This may be of some help to you. Also, she cannot see anything."

Another gasp. "What?"

"We think it's temporary. From the flash. There is some mild retina damage, but it should heal."

My hearts sank. What if it doesn't heal? I needed to calm down and try to slow those beeps down somehow.

Darion's voice sounded closer as he thanked the doctor. "Tamisan. I am so glad you are awake. Can you hear me?"

As I blinked twice, my tears spilled from my eyes. "Do not cry, my love. I am here now and everything will be okay. I am sure this is only temporary. We think it's the drug he gave you. It needs time to get out of your system, like the poison that was in your body when you first found me, remember?"

I remembered. It came flooding back to me. Lying on the floor of the jungle with the Bahadori leering at me. Blood dripping from the knife in his hand. My blood. The panic. The hallucinations threatening to take me over again. The screams in my mind that wouldn't come out of my mouth. I heard the beeps speeding up again. It seemed so long ago that I'd been in the jungle feeling so helpless and out of control. Kind of like I was feeling lying in a bed hooked up to machines and not being able to feel or move. It was a weird kind of déjà vu.

Then I realized Darion had asked me a question and blinked twice.

I could hear the doctor and the guy that had removed the tube — I assumed he was a nurse — talking quietly somewhere nearby. Then there was the beeping from the heart monitors as well. I focused my attention on Darion and tried to block out all the other sounds. I was so grateful he was here and I could still hear him, even if I couldn't see or feel him. He would help me through this. Just knowing he was here was a comfort. He would rescue me again. Somehow...

I sighed — then gagged again — even though the tube was gone.

Darion's voice was panicked. "Are you okay? Doctor, she was gagging. Is that normal? Is she okay?"

I could hear the doctor's footsteps approaching. "Yes, she is alright. We have only just removed the tube from her throat and she has told me she can actually feel her throat and her eyes. The gagging is a normal reaction after having the tube in for so long."

I heard Darion sigh and I imagined him running a hand through his hair. "Okay. Thank you, Doctor."

The doctor explained to Darion about the other blink codes for 'close' and 'maybe,' and Darion thanked him again.

What did the doctor mean by me having the tube in for so long? How long had I been unconscious?

I took some deep breaths. I couldn't keep freaking out all the time. There was nothing I could do about how long I'd been lying here, so worrying about it wouldn't help me.

As I was trying to breathe normally again, I smelled something. I tried to sniff the air. I could smell Darion. My hearts beat faster. It felt like such a victory, just to be able to smell anything again. I was glad that the first thing I could smell was him. That earthy scent. It was a comfort to me.

I heard Darion ask about the increase in my heartbeats. Dr Nambiri assured him it was fine. He explained that they had to hook up two heart monitors for me so they could monitor both of my hearts separately. The machines weren't designed to monitor more than one heartbeat and would only give false readings if they only hooked up one of them.

While they were talking, I wondered how I could tell them I could smell. It would be impossible. The only thing I could do was wait for them to ask.

"They said you cannot see," Darion said slowly. "Can you see anything at all? Anything like shadows and light?"

I blinked once.

"Is it just black?"

I blinked twice. It sounded like he was choking back tears. Tears spilled from my eyes and I wished I could comfort him somehow.

I thought about what had happened with Starrick and the generators and couldn't help wondering what had happened after the big flash of light. I'd obviously blacked out for longer than I thought — longer than a few minutes. But it had only seemed like such a short time. Half an hour at the most. But it had to have been long enough for them to bring me to the Medical Facility and put a tube down my throat to help me breathe and hook up the machines. The only explanation I could think of was that I must have been in some sort of coma...

Where was Starrick? How did I escape being killed by him or the fall? I *must* have fallen. I felt it. Saw it happening. Saw the cables and connectors moving further away as I fell away from them. But where did I land? I had so many questions. And I couldn't ask any of them. It was so frustrating to not be able to say anything. I wished they would assume I wanted to know and simply tell me.

My thoughts were still kind of cloudy, like there was a fog hanging over me. I tried to move my body to see if anything would respond. I still couldn't move at all. I tried my right hand. Nothing. My index finger. Nothing. My toes. Nothing. I couldn't help the devastating feeling that was creeping through me. I tried to fight it and push it back down deep inside me. I couldn't let it out. I couldn't let it take over. I would get through this. I would recover.

"Do you remember what happened?" Darion asked.

Instinctively, I tried to answer, but nothing came out, so I blinked my answer. I could remember a lot of stuff.

"Do not try to talk yet," he told me.

I wished I could talk. I desperately needed to know what happened to me. If I was badly injured. If I was going to get better.

I tried to call telepathically, with no luck. What was wrong? Why couldn't I use my Talent? What if I'd lost it for good? I didn't think I could cope with that.

CHAPTER 81:
The Thought of Losing You...

I felt numbness. How long would I feel like this? How long had I been unconscious?

The questions were eating at me. I lay there wondering what I would do if I lost the wonderful gift I'd only recently been given. To go back to the way I was before with no telepathy and no kinetic ability... I would have shuddered at the thought — if I could.

Wait. Darion had told me not to try to talk. Did that mean my mouth had moved? Something must have given it away and let him know I'd tried. Maybe I was starting to get control back. Although I did gag, so maybe that was all it was.

A spark of hope started to burn inside me anyway. I couldn't stop it. I didn't want it to grow, only to find out I was going to stay like this. That would be too much. The beeps picked up again. A humming sound told me a Bio-scan was running down the length of my body.

The doctor started talking to Darion again before he could say any more. I listened to their voices. I wanted to know if they were pleased with my progress, or whether they were thinking there was no hope for me. They seemed pleased, but also a little worried. This didn't help me feel any better.

I tried again to move. My hearts sank. My body would not obey.

The doctors assured Darion that this was good progress. They examined the data from the Bio-scan and said it would take time for me to recover. The DV-2000 was still in my system. Then they told him to rest and let me rest too, and left. They would return soon to check in on me.

When they were gone, Darion told me he wasn't going anywhere and that he was sure I would make a full recovery. He started to tell me some of what had happened. "Starrick escaped from custody while we were sleeping — that's why I was called out to see Dr Aimery."

I heard him shift in his seat. It sounded like he was sitting in a chair near me. He might have been sitting on the bed next to me, but I had no way of knowing.

"Aimery sent a guard to stand watch outside our door to keep an eye on you, to keep you safe, but while Dr Aimery was briefing me, Starrick shot the guard in the shoulder with the same drug he gave you and had used the guard's thumbprint to open the door."

I listened, amazed. How did Starrick find me? Jannali was a big place. Was he still able to track me?

"I felt something really strange while I was with Dr Aimery," he went on. "A feeling I've never felt before. I felt like something was wrong — really wrong. I cannot describe it, but I reached out for your mind and got nothing. Then I *knew* you were in danger."

The tears in my eyes fell and must have rolled down either side of my face. I couldn't feel them once they were no longer flooding my eyes.

"I reached for your mind again and could feel nothing at all." He shifted again. "I ported myself and Dr Aimery to my quarters, but we found it empty and the guard unconscious outside. As we ran out of there and down the corridors, I tried to reach for your mind again and found some very mixed up thoughts. Then I couldn't get through to you for a while. The next time I got through, you did not seem to be yourself."

He sniffed and asked me to close my eyes. He wiped my tears away with a soft cloth. I wondered if he'd have to do that for me for the rest of my life. Just thinking about it brought more tears.

Darion continued after wiping my eyes again. "Then I could not reach you again. There were reports of you using your Talent to hurt people and they thought you were working with Starrick. The guard at the door to the Generator Room said you had thrown him into a wall so Starrick could get in."

I started blinking wildly. I needed to tell Darion it wasn't true.

"It's okay. I don't believe you would do that. It was the drug he used. It made you do some awful things."

I blinked rapidly again. The drug had made me crazy.

"When we couldn't find you, I felt so lost. The thought of losing you..." He had to stop and I could tell he was choking back the tears. "They managed to locate you and confirmed on the Com that you were in the Generator Room with *him*," and he said the word 'him' with such disgust. "And then we were told that he was working with the computers to cause all the generators to overload. He had overridden the security system and we couldn't get into the room. That is when Aimery ordered the door be cut through."

His voice changed to something between puzzlement and a sort of sadness. "You were not yourself. You said some horrible things... I could not understand what was going on at first."

His voice trailed away. I could vaguely remember something about that, about thinking he was beneath me, but my mind was fuzzy. I'd been angry with him and I said some nasty things. Tears flowed from my eyes and he wiped them again.

"Don't cry, Tamisan. I know it was the drug…"

I tried to open my mouth. I wanted so much to say I was sorry, but of course, nothing came out. I wanted to scream. I needed to scream. Was I going to be trapped inside my own mind for the rest of my life? *No. It can't be. I can't stay like this. I won't be able to do this. I can't handle this. They have to fix this…*

"Do not try to talk," he told me. "Take it easy. It will take time before you can move or talk."

There was a small spark of hope. I must've been moving some part of my mouth or something. Enough for him to know that I was trying to talk to him.

He continued his story. "I was shocked when we finally made it into the room and found Starrick standing there alone. But when I saw what he was looking up at — wow! It was amazing! You were flying!"

I remembered that part, too. I was amazed that I'd managed to do it. Just using my mind to push myself from below and then move my body around so I could reach the cables. It was easy really. I should've tried it earlier.

But what about me falling? I desperately wanted to know, but I didn't want to know. How badly was I hurt?

CHAPTER 82:

The Blood on You Was Not Your Own

I heard a sound like he'd run a hand through his hair or over his face. "But then you started to fall. I ran to catch you and Starrick ran to attack me with a knife. It all happened so fast. They shot him as you landed in my arms and he fell against us... We all kind of fell together in a heap on the floor.

At first, I thought he had stabbed you in the chest, and could not see what had happened until they removed his body. The blood on you was not your own... I... I'd failed you again. I was not there when you needed me the most. I am sorry..."

He couldn't continue. I tried to call him both mentally and physically. I needed to tell him it wasn't his fault. He didn't fail me. He was there for me at the end. The beeps raced faster.

"Shhh. Do not try to talk," he half whispered, "and do not try to use your Talent yet."

Did he know I'd tried to call him? Or had he assumed I would try and hadn't felt my mind touch his?

"The doctors said this would probably happen when you woke up. It is the drug he gave you — DV-2000. It contains some kind of agent that blocks the neural pathways in the brain, and it is particularly effective — and dangerous — to Talents because it blocks their psychic abilities as well."

I heard the rustle of clothing and a heavy sigh. "You were in a coma and after a day and a half of the doctors telling me things were not improving, I decided to take matters into my own hands."

A coma? A day and a half? How could it have been so long? This was crazy — it seemed to be only a few minutes, but I knew I was wrong.

Darion lowered his voice. "They do not know it, but last night, I placed my fingers on your temples and *called* to you. I reached deep into your mind to try to pull you out of yourself. I had only ever seen it done once before, but I *had* to try. It is very successful in bringing people back from near death or from a coma. I guess it worked."

So that was why I'd heard him calling to me as I was floating! He'd used his Talent to reach into my mind. I desperately wanted to tell him it had worked — that I'd heard him — but I couldn't. I blinked rapidly, hoping he would understand that I'd heard him. How could I get my message across?

"Rest now," he told me. "I will try to rest too." My hearts sank. He didn't get it.

Then Darion kissed me on the lips and I actually felt it. Not properly — I was still too numb — but I felt something press against my mouth. I blinked rapidly again to try to tell him. Maybe if he started asking questions, I could answer yes or no and tell him that way. My hearts sped up again.

"It is okay. I know you want me to stay and talk to you, but we both need to rest."

No! You don't understand! I need to make you understand! I felt it! I wish I could just tell you! This is so hard. I can't do this! I thought helplessly as I blinked some more.

"I must go — they will not let me stay with you — but I will return in the morning. Please try to rest. I will see you then."

I heard his footsteps fade as he left the room. I cried — if you could call it crying. I wanted him to come back. I wanted him to kiss me or touch me again to see how much I could feel. Maybe I might be able to feel him touching other parts of my body. But it would all have to wait for the morning. He was already gone.

As I lay there trying to calm down and control my breathing and stop crying, Dr Nambiri came into the room.

"Don't worry. Darion will be back in the morning. Try to rest now. There is every chance you will make a full recovery. It's just going to take some time."

He wiped my tears away. "I need to ask some more questions and check the data on the machines and then I will leave you to sleep."

⸻ ◆ ⸻

Dr Nambiri asked me if I could feel any of the rest of my body, but all I could tell him was no. He didn't ask me if I could smell. He finally asked me if I could feel any part of my face that I couldn't before. I needed to tell him that I felt Darion's kiss. I blinked twice.

Twenty questions later, he finally understood that I could feel my lips. I couldn't communicate that they were kind of half numb still, but maybe that wouldn't be the case by morning, so I wouldn't have to worry about it.

His tone didn't suggest that he was disappointed or shocked at my answers, which was probably a good thing. But I was disappointed enough for both of us.

"Now, Tamisan, these are good results, so try not to be too upset. You have no other physical injuries, so it is the drug that you were given that has caused this to happen." He paused, and when he spoke again, he was closer to me. "Can you see anything at all?"

One blink.

"Can you see any light or shadows at all?"

One blink.

"Okay. What about when I shine a light into your eyes?"

I waited, but didn't see anything. One blink, followed by a twinge of panic. That couldn't be good. It had to be really bad if he'd shone a light in my eyes and it didn't make any difference. I started to breathe faster and the beeps picked up speed.

"Your pupils reacted, so that's a good sign. We'll have to wait a bit longer then. Now don't you worry about it. We just need to wait it out. Your eyes were exposed to a very bright flash and need time to recover. We have dimmed the lights in the room for you. I am confident that your blindness is only temporary."

Hearing him actually say the word 'blindness' made it seem more real. I couldn't stop the pain it caused or the tears that spilled from my eyes.

He kept on reassuring me as he wiped them away. Kept on telling me it was all temporary. Things would be better in the morning.

After telling me to try to rest, he said goodnight and headed out the door.

I was left alone with my thoughts. That wasn't a good thing. It was really hard to relax and rest, but after trying for about an hour or more and telling myself I would be better tomorrow, I eventually dozed.

⸺⊷◈⊶⸺

The next time I woke up, I forgot I couldn't move. It was a shock when I tried to roll over and my body refused to obey. Then I remembered what had happened and my eyes sprang open to darkness. It was like a stab to the heart. I was trapped in a body that no longer worked. The darkness was still so complete. There were no shadows, no hint of light. Of course, I was in an underground base so there would be no light coming in from a window or anything. I could be in a pitch dark room if they'd left me to sleep.

But the heart monitors would have lights on them, I was sure. There should be a small amount of light coming from them.

I sucked in a deep breath. I would have to deal with this. The smell of antiseptic hit me, stirring up a memory from somewhere. I searched my mind, trying to pinpoint when and where it was from. There was something I couldn't quite catch. I could remember hearing voices from far away as I was being wheeled through a corridor... Something in my brain was telling me it was straight after the attack in the jungle... Could it have been from before they did the Eibhlin Process? Back when I was still me?

The more I tried to dig up the memory, the further it slipped away. I finally gave up and sighed.

I thought about what happened in the Generator Room. I'd definitely fallen and Darion had caught me. I still could be badly injured.

Maybe I had a spinal injury. Maybe that was why I was numb. Maybe they didn't want to tell me yet and were letting me think

it was the drug's effect instead. Despair was creeping in on me,
but I didn't want to give in to it. There was no clear evidence
that I was going to stay this way. I had to focus on that. I had to
believe it.

CHAPTER 83:
Veggie Soup

I can feel my eyes. I can feel my lips a bit, and I couldn't do that at first, I told myself, *And if it was a spinal injury, I would be able to feel my head and anything above the break. Wouldn't I?*

Then I remembered what Dr Nambiri had told me before he left. No physical injuries. I mentally kicked myself for getting all worked up again.

I guessed it was morning, but had no way of knowing for sure.

My toe twitched. I tried to move it. It moved! So did the others! And the toes on my other foot! More progress! Maybe I was going to recover after all! Maybe it wasn't that bad. Maybe I just had to be patient. I could do that, couldn't I? The beeps on the monitor were going crazy and I was breathing fast and hard.

I had to calm down. They would think I was having a heart attack or something. But I didn't *want* to calm down. I wanted to get up and jump around the room and the fact that I couldn't just added to my frustration.

Wait. Just wait, I told myself. *It will get better. I will walk again. I will recover. I just have to be patient.*

That was easier said than done.

I tried to move other parts of my body, with no success. I'd have to be content with my toes.

Where was everyone? What time was it? Maybe it was the middle of the night. Maybe I'd only slept for an hour or two. I'd have to lie here until someone came into the room. I couldn't even press a buzzer to call the nurse. And if I could, I couldn't ask the time anyway.

I lay there waiting impatiently for Darion to return or for someone to come in…

When I finally heard the door open, I breathed a sigh of relief and waited to hear who it was.

Footsteps approached and I could smell a fresh minty flavour in the air. "Hey, you're awake." It was Korizan's deep voice. "How ya goin' today? Feelin' betta this mornin'?"

I blinked twice.

"That's good. Can ya tell me if ya can feel any part of yer body that ya couldn't feel yestaday?" he asked hopefully.

Two blinks.

"That's great!" Then he went through the process of asking a heap of questions so I could tell him what part of my body I could now feel. It was long and frustrating.

He eventually left the room, promising he'd be back with Dr Nambiri. I had to tell myself again to have patience. It was going to be a long process, but I was going to get past this. I heard the hum of the Bio-scan as it passed.

Not long after Korizan left, the door clicked open again, startling me. I didn't expect him back so soon. As I listened to the footsteps, a familiar scent filled my nostrils. Darion. Warmth spread through me.

"Hey," he said softly. "How are you this morning?"

I blinked twice. What else could I do? There was no code for how I was feeling.

His voice sounded closer. "The nurse told me you can feel your toes?"

Two blinks.

I could practically hear him smiling. "I *told* you you would recover fully."

⁂

Two days later, I could move my mouth enough to talk. I could also move enough of my body to clumsily push myself up into a sitting position, but I wasn't able to walk yet. Getting to this point was a long and hard process. Regaining movement a little at a time was frustrating.

My speech was incoherent at first, which was embarrassing.

They'd finally said I was ready to eat real food. And if I succeeded without bringing it back up again, they would remove the tube from my nose.

Korizan brought in a tray of food. I wanted to eat a feast, but he'd already told me I had to start on liquids before I could eat anything heavier. I heard him lift the lid off the tray.

"Veggie soup!" he exclaimed excitedly, knowing I still couldn't see. "Pureed veggie soup, that is." It smelled so good that I wasn't worried about the fact that it wasn't something solid that I could get my teeth into. Darion helped me find the spoon and bowl and as I started to eat, they both warned me to go slow or I'd make myself sick. I made sure I did what I was told. The last thing I wanted was to bring this back up and have an empty stomach again. And I wanted to lose the feed tube.

"It's good," I told them between mouthfuls. It was hard to find the bowl with the spoon and I was making a mess, but Darion kept guiding my hand.

I was itching to remove the eye patch they'd given me, but I had strict orders to leave it on until my eyes recovered. Too much light too soon wouldn't be good for them. They'd started putting it on between the check-ups and Darion's visits after that first day and it was frustrating when I couldn't blink to communicate.

Also, they said I would probably regain my sight slowly, which would mean everything would be blurry and I would be straining my eyes all the time trying to focus on things. So I'd have to be patient if I didn't want any permanent problems.

"Do you want me to do it for you?" Darion asked.

"No. I want to do something for myself for a change." I knew I was being stubborn, but I couldn't help it. I needed this, even this tiny bit of independence. Darion didn't argue. He kept guiding my hand.

Once I'd finished, Darion took my spoon and replaced it with a cloth to wipe myself. I'd made a mess. It was embarrassing, but I didn't care. I'd done it myself and my stomach felt so good to have something in it after so long. When I'd finished, he cleaned off the bits I'd missed.

Korizan told us they'd tried to order a Personal Proximity Sensor for me to be able to walk around the base without running into anything once I was on my feet again. I had mixed feelings about that. I wanted to be able to move around without someone holding my hand, but the fact that they'd ordered one sort of solidified the fact that it could be permanent, and that scared me too much. What would I do if it was?

CHAPTER 84:
You Have Love

"We didn' get a good answer, though," he told us. He cleared his throat. "This is the official message from the company: 'Voyager Division will provide the patient with a Personal Proximity Sensor if the blindness proves to be permanent. The company will not order such a device unless it is deemed necessary by the treating physician. Once ordered, it will take four weeks to arrive on the planet, Althar 3.'"

My stomach sank to my knees. It sounded so horrible worded like that. How long would it take to work out if this was permanent? Then after that, it would still be four weeks before I could even use it to get around. Tears stung my eyes.

"That is so typical," Darion spat.

I could hear the shuffle of feet. "Yep," Korizan added. "Well, I should go now. I'll leave ya both alone now. Bye."

We both said goodbye and I heard his shoes shuffling across the floor again, followed by the click of the door. We were alone.

Darion put a hand on my arm. "Hey. Don't worry about it. You will not need it."

"Yeah." I wasn't convinced.

"I mean it," he told me. "You will not need it. You will recover."

I tried to smile, but my lips trembled. Before I could answer, Darion pulled me into his arms and I leaned my head on his shoulder. I tried to draw strength from him and pull it into myself. I needed to believe that I would not be like this for the rest of my life. But I couldn't. There was always that nagging doubt.

There was another thing nagging at me. It wouldn't go away. I kept thinking about what I did when I went after Starrick. I was crazed. I wanted to really hurt him. I wanted to make him pay for what he'd done to me. At one point, I don't think anyone could have stopped me. If I had've caught him before the drug made me lose the use of my legs... I shuddered.

"What is it?" Darion asked.

"It's... um..." How could I tell him?

"It is okay, Tamisan. You can tell me anything."

"I was thinking about, uh, when I chased after Starrick. I mean, I was crazy, you know. I was really after him. I was going to kill him. I almost killed him. I wouldn't have stopped for anyone. That's not normal."

I felt Darion's arms around me tighten a little. "You stopped for me. You weren't yourself, my love."

The words, *my love* seeped into me and melted some of the anxiety I was feeling. "But... there's something wrong with me. What's wrong with me? I turned into a monster when I went after him. I thought I was the most powerful being in the universe."

He started playing with my hair and it was soothing to my soul. "You were under the influence of that drug he gave you."

I pushed myself away from him a bit. "But I wanted to *kill* him! I tried to kill him!"

Darion kissed my forehead, then leaned his forehead against mine. "You were not thinking clearly. You were pumped up on that stuff. I know. I tried to talk to you and I could see it in your mind. It wasn't you. You could never do any of those things that you were thinking. You didn't do any of those things. You stopped when I asked you to. Do you remember?"

He was right, of course, but I couldn't help being scared of what I could have done. Then I remembered the men in the hallway. "What about those men that I... that I hurt. In the corridors. Are they okay?"

"Yes. As I told you the other day, one had a nasty bruise on his elbow from hitting the wall and the other had a concussion from hitting a doorway. They are both back on duty."

I winced. I felt so guilty. "I'm... I'm sorry. Are you sure they're alright? Can you tell them I'm sorry?"

"Yes. They are fine. You were not yourself. I will tell them, but no one blames you. It is Starrick's fault."

I felt like I had all this hate and anger built up inside me. Not just for Starrick, but for the Bahadori and Turak as well. "I... I feel... I just want to... I don't know, hit something when I think of him... and the... the Bahadori and T-turak," I stumbled.

Darion kissed my forehead again, but this time, he kept his lips there for a few seconds. "Listen to me very carefully. It is perfectly normal to feel this way."

"It eats me up inside. What they did. What do I have left but anger toward them all?" And that feeling like I was dirty was kind of still there, though not as strong as before.

Darion's arms were around me again. "What do you have left?"

I nodded against his chest.

"The answer to that is simple."

I frowned.

"You have love."

The frown faded. He was right. I did have love. I had Darion's love. And I had my love for him. I felt warmer inside, as if the coldness in my hearts had melted. It wasn't an instant cure, but it went a long way to make me feel better.

I pulled away from his embrace, cupped his face with both my hands — mainly so that I could find his mouth — and kissed him. I wanted to thank him. To thank him and to show him how much I did love him.

The kiss started off slow and sweet, but then it changed into something more. Like he was the air that I breathed. I pulled him closer and deepened the kiss, our hands roaming over each other, and I couldn't get enough of him. His tongue entered my mouth and I thought I would fall off the bed.

It seemed like we'd been kissing forever when we finally broke apart, mainly for air. It seemed I did need real air after all. Then we sat and held each other close. I realized the bottom half of my eye patch was wet. I didn't know I'd been crying. I didn't know I could feel like this. It seemed like there'd been a lot more missing in my life than I'd realized. Not just the love of parents and a family, but the love of the one that you would want to give your life and your heart to.

I held him close. I didn't want to let him go ever again. I wanted this moment to last forever. But, of course, there was no pause button. Time just marches on.

I felt Darion's muscles tense up under my hands. He tightened his hold on me. What was it? What was wrong? Maybe he didn't feel the same way I did.

"Are you okay?" I asked.

He stopped moving. He stopped breathing. "I — uh — it's nothing. Do not worry about me."

I pulled away a bit, as if I was looking him in the eye. "Hey, you can tell me. It's okay."

He leaned his forehead against mine again and sighed. "You look at me like I am a hero. I am no hero. I feel like I failed you. Every time you needed me, I was not there. I took too long to find you. Then when you were locked in the Generator Room with that madman…"

CHAPTER 85:

Me Too

I sucked in a breath. I didn't realise he felt this bad — this guilty. "No. Don't say that. It was *not* your fault. The jungle is a dangerous place. You didn't put me there. You were there in my mind when I needed you. You can never know how much that meant to me. I couldn't have escaped from Turak without you and without your energy.

"And then there's the fact that you were locked out of the Generator Room. It wasn't like you couldn't be bothered trying to get in or whatever." I wrapped my arms around his neck. "You were there in the end, when I needed you the most. I'm sure I would have broken some bones if you hadn't caught me, or worse."

"But, if I had reached you before that... or before Turak could... do those things..."

I pulled him closer so my mouth was next to his ear. "You can't do this to yourself, Darion. He didn't do the horrible things I knew he was planning. I'm okay. I'm dealing with it. You've been helping me deal with it. You can't change the past. It's all over now, and I'm still alive. And you're here now. We're finally together. That is what you want, isn't it?"

As soon as those words were out of my mouth, I started to wonder if he did want us to be together...

"Yes," he answered without hesitation. "Yes. I want us to be together. Forever."

Hearing that did strange things to my chest. It felt all fluttery inside. "So. I don't want to hear any more stuff about you being a failure. You are *not* a failure. You *are* a hero to me."

I kissed him again and held him until we were interrupted by my next liquid meal being brought in.

⬥

I had the sensation of almost weightlessness as Darion wheeled me through the corridors toward his quarters. It was so good to get out of the Medical Facility. I still couldn't walk or see, but Darion had assured them he could look after me. I'd been eating solid foods for a day and had regained almost all feeling all over. Just not enough to coordinate my legs yet. And I no longer had the annoying tube in my nose.

I still felt anxious about it all. I was so afraid I would be stuck like this, or maybe stuck without my sight, and that Darion would be stuck with me forever, always looking after me and being my eyes. I didn't want that. I hated feeling like this, but I couldn't help it.

Or maybe he'd get sick of it all and leave me... I couldn't bear to think about that.

The wheelchair twisted and turned down a few more corridors until we reached his door.

I felt apprehensive. This would be the first time I'd been here since everything had happened. I was kind of glad that I wouldn't be seeing it. That would only make it worse. The memories started coming back to me. This was the door that

Starrick had barged in through and stuck that needle into my neck.

I shuddered as the door swished open. Darion wheeled me forward. "This is it. We are home. Would you like something to eat or drink?"

"No. Thanks."

"Are you okay?"

"Yes, I think so."

"What would you like to do?"

Kiss you until we both can't breathe. "I'd like to sit on the Easi chair with you for a while."

The wheelchair turned and he pushed me over to the chairs and helped me sit down. The cushion dipped down as he settled himself next to me, and he put an arm around my shoulders.

We were finally alone. Sure, we'd had times in the Medical Facility where we were alone together, but there were too many times when we'd been disturbed by Korizan or Dr Nambiri or someone else.

My hearts beat faster. No one would barge in on us here. This was perfect.

I want to sit here forever and hold you and kiss you and not let go. I thought. I wished he could hear my thoughts the way he used to.

"Me too," he said, and I gasped.

My fingers curled together in my lap. "What?"

He squeezed my shoulder. "I heard part of what you were thinking," he said. "It was like a cloud in your mind, but I heard you. Just as I thought I would try to see if I could reach your mind, I actually could."

I choked out a sob.

"Do not cry," he said.

"But..." *I'm so happy...*

He squeezed my shoulder again. "This is good progress. Not long now, and you will be fully recovered."

He pulled me to him and our lips met. I felt warm tingles rush through me as he kept kissing me and I wanted to melt into him. My arms wrapped themselves around him automatically and I enjoyed the feel of his warm body through his shirt.

I liked being alone with him like this. Now we could relax and do whatever we wanted to. My hearts pounded faster thinking about it.

I needed to get closer to him. I wanted to pull him closer until our bodies melted into one, knowing that it wasn't possible, but wanting it just the same. His kisses became more intense, more urgent, and I wanted more.

I wished I could see him. See his face. I pushed that away, I didn't want to ruin this moment.

As his hands moved upward, his fingers caught on my shirt and pulled it up and exposed my skin. I jumped as his fingers grazed my back. Darion immediately apologized and I grabbed his hand and put it back where it was. "I'm okay. I jumped because it tickled."

I knew he thought I'd gotten scared or maybe had a flashback, but I needed to let him know I was okay.

Slowly, he pushed his hand up under my shirt and made circles on my skin. He left a trail of fire where he touched my skin, making me feel alive. My hearts hammered in my chest as he slid the other hand up beside the first. His kisses left my lips and trailed across my jaw and down my neck, making me come undone.

My hands roamed across his shoulders and up his neck and into his hair. *Can you hear me right now?*

He nodded against my neck.

I'm so happy, I told him. *I want to be with you like this forever.*

"*Me too.*"

I heard you! I couldn't wipe the smile from my face. I wished I could see if he was smiling. I missed his smile.

CHAPTER 86:

Deep Down, You Know it Too

My smile faded and I couldn't help the dark thoughts running through my head. What if I didn't get my sight back? I didn't want him to feel like he had to stay and look after me. I didn't want to be a burden to anyone, least of all him.

"You would not be a burden. I will stay by your side, no matter what the outcome is. Even if it takes a year for you to see again. Even if it's never. I will not abandon you. I promise."

My eyes stung. I didn't want to burden him, but I needed to hear those words. I wanted to rip the patch off and look at him. My fingers twitched with the urge to throw it across the room, but I couldn't go against what they'd told me. I needed to do the right thing or risk being blind for life.

Darion held me close and stroked my hair. I loved it when he did that. It gave me a comfort I'd never felt before. Not even when Oliana or Kaliya had given me hugs.

Thinking of my friends made me feel sad. I already missed them so much, and now I had to spend the rest of my life knowing I couldn't see them again and that they weren't even missing me. My hearts twisted in my chest.

The other Zhenna had gone home. Back to my/her friends and life. What do I do now? Who am I now? I didn't know where to begin.

Darion stopped stroking my hair. "Don't be upset. You know who you are. You are strong and beautiful and honest and caring."

"I don't feel like any of those things," I told him. "I don't know who I am anymore."

He pulled me back a bit so he could look at my face, even though I couldn't see his. "Do you feel like you are still Zhenna Rhodarma?"

I thought about it for a moment. "No."

"Do you feel like you are Sifayah?"

I shifted a little in his arms. "No. Definitely not, but I already told you this."

He cupped my cheek with his hand. "I know you have changed and grown into someone else since you were changed. Do you agree?"

I took a deep breath. "Yes."

"As you've said, you are a mixture of those two people, but also something more. I don't see someone without a personality. And I *don't* see someone without a soul."

"But—"

"I am telling you the truth. Nature has somehow found a way to make you and Zhenna two different people. Two different souls. I believe that a body cannot exist without a soul. You have one. I know it. And deep down, you know it too."

I opened my mouth to argue, but what was I going to say? How could I deny it when he was probably right? I didn't really think that a body could exist without a soul. It seemed impossible to me.

Our bodies were a vessel for the soul to inhabit while we lived these lives and after our deaths, it would pass back over into the place where the spirits existed, waiting for their turn to return to this universe of ours. Somehow, I must still have a soul... somehow.

Darion held me a little tighter. "You cannot keep grieving for your lost life. I am not saying you shouldn't grieve. I think that it is a normal reaction to what has happened, but you need to move on and decide what you want to do with your new life."

That made sense. I couldn't change things, so I should move forward.

Darion put a finger under my chin and lifted it slightly. "Could you really see yourself going back to your old life now?"

"No. Not really. It would be dull. I wouldn't be happy doing what I did before... I don't want that again. I miss my friends, but there are a lot of things there that would not make me happy."

His other hand moved to cup my other cheek. "What do you see yourself doing? What do you *really* want to do?"

"I want to be with you," I told him without hesitation.

I was sure I could feel his smile. "What else?"

"I would love to be able to paint and draw in my spare time. I want to work here at Jannali. I want a new life here... But... I can only have that if I... if my eyes recover..."

"And they *will*," he said.

⸻◆⸻

The next day, before Darion went to do half a day's work, I managed to walk. I was relieved about that fact, of course, but not being able to see was scaring me more than I wanted to admit, even to myself.

Was there something wrong with me when I couldn't be happy about being able to walk and talk again? I should've been grateful for what I *did* have. But all I could think about was what I'd lost.

I quickly worked out how to get around Darion's quarters, counting the steps from one place to another. I had it all worked out in my head, but it was still difficult for me. I spent my time hoping it wouldn't be like this for the rest of my life.

I sat on the Easi chair, thinking hard. The closer it got to the time when I could get the patch off of my face, the more anxious I became.

What if this is permanent? What if they take it off and I still can't see? What am I going to do? What if I could never paint or draw again? What if— I had to stop myself. I couldn't go there again. That kind of thinking didn't help. It just drove me crazy. I had to try really hard to keep my spirits up. It wasn't easy to keep trying, but I did.

I'd also tried every day to contact Darion's mind and was always disappointed. I was so worried that that was permanent, too.

The door swished open and I froze. A flash in my mind of Starrick stepping into the doorway and sticking the needle into my neck made me gasp.

"Tamisan?" Darion called to me. "It's me." I wondered if he'd seen my reaction.

"Hey," I answered, trying to make my voice sound normal. "How was your day?"

I heard his shoes against the carpeted floor, then the Easi chair dipped down as he sat down next to me. "Good." I turned toward him and he leaned in and kissed me lightly on the lips.

"Not very eventful, but still a good day. I spent most of it moving stock."

He meant moving them with his mind, of course. "Sounds real interesting," I said, the sarcasm obvious in my voice. "I missed you. Did you miss me?"

He responded by giving me a soft kiss on my shoulder and trailing small kisses from there all the way up my neck until he found my lips. Then his kisses were fire.

I let him kiss me like that for a while — a long while — then I said, "I'll take that as a yes."

As we held each other close, I tried, as usual, to touch Darion's mind, and it worked! I could feel the presence there in my mind. I felt an adrenalin rush, like I'd gone for a ride in my first Hovercar. Tears welled up in my eyes and started wetting my eye patch.

He started to ask me what was wrong, but stopped halfway. He knew the answer. *"This is great!"* he exclaimed. *"It is incredible! I told you. We just had to wait. We needed to be patient."*

I choked back a sob. He brushed some hair out of my face and kissed me.

"We'll tell the doctors later," he told me.

He'd been working with me each day, trying to use telekinesis to remove the last remnants of the drug and to see if I could regain my psychic abilities, but he didn't have any help from my Talent like he'd had before with the poison. And now all our hard work had paid off. Up till that point we'd only been able to have one-way telepathic communication, like I'd originally had with Mosuti.

"I missed this!" I told him excitedly. *"I was starting to think I would never be able to send to you again!"*

We hugged each other and relief flooded through me. I reached out and could touch his mind again without any problems. It was almost like the first time I'd encountered Darion's strong mind. It was intoxicating. I hugged him tighter.

Then I thought, *What about telekinesis?*

Could I do it?

He sensed my tense body and read my thoughts. *"Try it,"* he urged.

"But I can't see."

He stood and pulled me to my feet. *"I will help you."*

He led me into the kitchen and left me standing in the middle of the floor. I heard a cupboard door open and close and Darion grabbed my right hand and placed a cup into it.

"Try lifting this cup," he said.

A chill ran through me and I took a deep breath. *I can do this.*

I concentrated. I wasn't sure how to do it if I couldn't see the cup. I hadn't done this before. A flash of memory told me Sifayah had done some exercises with Tasha that involved lifting objects while blindfolded. That was a relief, but it didn't guarantee that I would be able to do it too. *Alright. I can do this. Just concentrate. Breathe. But what if it doesn't work?*

"Don't think like that," Darion told me. *"Concentrate. You can do this..."*

I tried to concentrate again. I pictured the cup in my hand. Focused on moving it. Lifting it... It started to move, slowly at first, but then I made it rise up from my hands! Yes! I'd done it!

"I knew you could do it!" Darion exclaimed as I lost my control over it and it fell to the floor.

"I can't do this!" I felt like stomping my foot like a child.

"Yes, you can!" he told me. "Don't let this stop you."

CHAPTER 87:

I Had Never Felt So Afraid

I heard him pick up the cup. I was glad it was made of plastic. I felt him put it back into my hands.

"Try again," he urged.

I was feeling like a total failure, but tried again. It rose up and hovered there for a while, then fell to the floor again.

He placed it back in my hands.

"Again. Try to reach out and feel the cup. I move things at work that I cannot see. It takes practice."

My face was flushed. I didn't want to feel like this anymore. I wanted to stop. It was no use. *"No, I can't do it."*

"Yes you can," he told me. *"You need to try until you do."*

"I can't!" I wailed. I knew I was being childish, but thinking I wouldn't be able to control my Talent because I couldn't see was too much to deal with.

"Just give it another try," he said quietly. *"Don't give up so easily."*

Tears streamed from my eyes. The patch was soaked. "Easy for you to say..." I mumbled.

I was frustrated, but why was I getting so upset? Darion was right, but I couldn't bring myself to do it.

Darion didn't get angry or impatient with me, he simply held me close.

"Will I ever get it right? Will I ever see so I can get it to happen?" I sobbed.

"Yes," he assured me. "Look how much you have regained already, since... since it all happened. You can do this."

After holding me for a while, he urged me to try again and I reluctantly agreed. I took a deep breath. I held out the cup and concentrated hard. *What if I can't do it?*

I pushed that thought away and started again. There were more doubts creeping in, so I shoved them all aside. And this time, I did it without dropping it.

"I knew it!" Darion exclaimed. *"You just had to keep trying."* He wrapped me up in one of his big warm embraces and kissed me on the top of my head. *"There is no stopping you now! You are almost completely cured. Starrick did not 'claim his project' and he did not take your Gift from you. You are almost your full self again. I will call Dr Nambiri and let them all know about this."*

Almost completely cured. Almost. The only thing that still wasn't right, that still hadn't returned to me, was the one thing I wanted the most. Anything else would be bearable, but for me to not be able to see for the rest of my life — I didn't even want to *think* about it.

Darion gave me an extra-tight hug, picked me up and swung me around in a semi-circle and set me down on the floor so gently and with so little effort that I could have sworn he used his Talent to do it.

He pulled back slightly and his body tensed. "When Starrick was shot, and I saw all that blood, I — I thought I had lost you," he said, his voice wavering. "I had never felt so afraid... I don't know what I would do without you. I love you so much."

I felt overwhelmed, but there was a warmth spreading inside me. Like my hearts were swelling up inside my ribcage. I could feel something similar pouring out from him too and I sent my *"I love you, too"* back to him, loud and strong.

———◆———

While we waited for my appointment to have the eye patch removed, we linked our minds to make sure the last of the DV-2000 had left my body. We also tried to speed up the body's natural healing process with my eyes. Neither of us were healers, so I didn't know if we'd succeeded.

When it was time to go to the Medical Facility, I prepared myself. I didn't want to get my hopes up, but Darion was very confident.

As we walked to the Medical Facility, I tried to be positive, but it was hard. *I could never get used to this — walking in the dark,* I thought as we slowly made our way along the corridors. *Please let it be alright... Let me see again...*

When we went in, they sat me on something soft. It felt like a bed. A woman greeted us in a cheerful voice. She pressed a button to raise the bed up a bit. I assumed it was so that she didn't have to bend over to remove the patch.

"Now, you have been applying the gel each day?" she asked me.

"Yes." There was no way I would've gone against the doctor's orders when I so desperately wanted to see again.

I heard the sound of wheels against the floor. She'd probably pulled a trolley over, filled with whatever she would need to clean my eyes.

"Now, Tamisan, I'm going to remove the patch, but I don't want you to open your eyes just yet. I need to wash off every bit of the gel first."

I nodded.

"It's not that the gel can't go in your eyes. It's perfectly safe. It's just that it can make your vision blurry. If that happens, we won't know if it's your eyes, or the gel."

I nodded again. I didn't want to talk. I just wanted the patch off. I wanted to know if I was going to be able to see or not.

"Okay. Here we go." She removed the patch, and I had this overwhelming urge to open my eyes and see if I could see anything. I had to wait. I had to control myself. I didn't want the gel in my eyes. I wanted to know if I could see clearly. I... just wanted it to be alright.

"Wait right there. Don't open your eyes. Oh. Hang on. I will only be a sec."

I waited. And waited. What was taking so long? Surely they had the solution right there so that they could bathe my eyes straight away. I fidgeted and felt I had to get up and pace the room. I flinched as something touched my arm, until I realized that it was Darion's warm hand. *"Sorry, my love."*

His reassuring touch made me feel a bit better.

I sat still. I needed to see. Even with my eyes closed, it didn't seem as dark... Maybe... Or was it just wishful thinking?

Come on! I thought, my hearts beating out a rampant beat. I opened my mouth to ask what the hold-up was, but then felt a warm cloth on my face.

Finally!

The woman took her time cleaning off every little smidgen of gel while I twitched and seethed. *Hurry up! Come on, come on, come on...*

Finally, she stopped wiping. "Okay, you can open your eyes now."

I took a deep breath as I opened them. I had to squint so my eyes could adjust and everything was blurry. My hearts sank.

"What do you see?" Darion asked eagerly.

"How is it?" the woman asked, "Can you see anything at all?"

My hearts were still sinking. "Yes, but it's so blurry…"

"Great!"

"That's really good news, Tamisan! Now remember, you haven't used your eyes for a long time, so they need to adjust. Keep blinking…"

I kept blinking and concentrated on a spot on the floor. Closing my eyes for about five seconds seemed to help, so I did it again, then as Darion asked me if there was any improvement, I looked up at his smiling face and I could see him! It was still a bit blurry, but after a few minutes, my vision cleared. I could see! I wasn't blind! The relief made me feel like I was floating on air, and the tears made everything blurry again.

CHAPTER 88:

You Are All Mine

Stepping into the apartment again now I could see was not a good experience. My anxiety rose and I had to take slow, deep breaths. Darion had an arm around me. There were flashes of memories and I had to get a grip on reality and tell myself it was in the past and Starrick was dead and gone.

As I looked around and the familiar floral scents of the room hit me, I managed to calm down again. I sighed and let the tension leave me.

"How are you doing?" Darion asked me.

I smiled up at him, admiring his gorgeous blue eyes. I'd missed them so much. "I'm good. Better than I thought I'd be. I'll be okay."

He smiled and swept me up into his arms as the door closed behind us.

Dr Aimery had told us we could move to another apartment if we wanted to, so I wouldn't have to deal with the memories, but I'd politely refused. I'd thought about it, and I didn't want to do it. I didn't want to force him out of his home.

I'd also had a couple of conversations with Dr Aimery about employment prospects at Jannali. Of course, a lot of things hinged on whether my sight returned, but I really wanted to take Mosuti's job as Linguist. It would have been difficult if I couldn't see, but I didn't have to worry about that anymore.

"I will need to talk to Dr Aimery about that job," I announced. I still couldn't believe I could see.

"Yes, but right now, you are all mine…" He raised an eyebrow and I burst out laughing. I couldn't help it. Tears sprung to my eyes as I thought about how I wouldn't have been able to see that brow lift if today didn't go well. "Come here," he said, and pulled me down onto the Easi chair with him.

I was so glad I'd recovered after everything that had happened. I'd been so worried about it that I'd had trouble sleeping. Now I could relax and let all the tension and worries leave me. I imagined it all pouring out of my body and seeping into the chair.

I lay my head back against the chair and closed my eyes. I jumped as I felt Darion's lips on my shoulder. He trailed little kisses of fire all the way up the side of my neck, across my jaw, and finally reached my lips. By the time he got there, I was breathless. He kissed me and gently nipped at my bottom lip with his teeth, which drove me crazy.

I stopped kissing him and looked up into his eyes. I'd missed seeing his handsome face. "I'm so glad I can see you again," I told him.

"I missed looking into those big brown eyes of yours, too." Then he kissed me till I could hardly breathe.

⎯⎯⎯◦⎯⎯⎯

The day before I was due to start my new job, a delivery arrived at the door. The delivery guy pushed a large box on wheels in through the doorway. Darion thanked him and put his thumbprint to the tablet he held out.

As the door swished closed, I walked slowly toward the box, excitement brewing inside me. "What is it?"

Darion's smile widened. "It's yours," he told me.

I felt the sting of tears and my heart rates picked up speed. By the size of it, I assumed that it must be something expensive. No one had ever given me a really expensive present before. "What is? What's in there?" My voice was almost a whisper.

He took a step closer. "You'll have to see for yourself."

I tried to stay calm as I looked at the box and tried to imagine what was inside. Actually, it wasn't a box, it was a small shipping container. It was sealed and the digital display had the word *locked* written across it. "How do I open it? Do I need a key, or just a thumbprint?"

Darion reached out and pressed his thumb to the right of the display and I heard a swoosh as the air-tight seal broke. Of course it would be keyed to his thumbprint if he was the one that purchased it. The container split down the middle and opened up to show a large multitouch screen mounted on a stand that held it at a comfortable angle that would be ideal for... drawing. My hearts felt like they'd swapped places in my chest. "Is that... ?" I couldn't finish.

"Yes. An Artmedia machine. It has all the software you will need for drawing, painting and 3D modelling."

My hearts skipped a beat. "Really?"

Darion's smile melted my insides. "Yes, really."

I never dreamed he would buy this for me. I didn't think anyone would. I'd given up long ago on ever being able to seriously pursue art of any kind back home. But this wasn't Earth. Maybe on other planets, art was allowed to flourish and not decline in favour of more intellectual pursuits like it was back home.

I couldn't look at it anymore. Mostly because of the tears making everything blurry. I turned to Darion and practically crash-tackled him as I hugged him as hard as I could. "Thank you so much!"

"Hey — ouch! Ease up."

I loosened my hold on him. "Sorry," I whispered into his ear. *"Thank you! I love you, Darion Andiyar. You have no idea how much this means to me. Or, I guess, maybe you do!"*

He *could* read my mind after all.

⸻ ◆ ⸻

This is the end of this story, but not the end of this book. Keep reading for some extra goodies:
An excerpt from the second and final book in the *Tamisan Series*, **ENIGMA**
An offer of a free book
A list of other books by Susan McKenzie
About the author

⸻ ◆ ⸻

Did you enjoy this book?
Help the next reader to enjoy it too.
Reviews are such a fantastic way for people to express the way a book made them feel. A way to share it with the world.

Indie authors don't have the huge budgets that the big New York publishers have, but we have something more powerful. We have loyal readers like you.
It would be so awesome if you could share what you thought of this book by leaving a review on the site where you purchased it.
Thank you so much.
Sue

Keep reading for an excerpt from the second and final book in the *Tamisan Series*, **ENIGMA**

Excerpt: Enigma (Tamisan Book 2)

Chapter 1: Why did I think I could do this?

Stepping out into the sunlight was like stepping into one of my nightmares. The jungle with its vines intertwining around the trunks and branches of trees, the flowers and fungi dotted amongst the green, the smell of earth and damp wood, the humidity crowding in on me. The memories it evoked were choking me.

I took a few deep breaths and tried to push my fears aside.

We'd touched down in a clearing in the jungle made by fallen trees and as I stood at the door of the shuttle battling my demons, I was struck by the sheer beauty of the trees and flowers that were growing beyond the immediate area and by the height of the tallest trees. They had to be at least sixty metres tall.

Despite the magnificence of my surroundings, my breathing became shallow. I had to fight to keep control of my emotions.

Moss grew on rocks and tree roots, vines hung from branches, and flowers of many different colours bloomed in amongst the greens and browns.

The sense of deja vu made both my hearts hammer wildly in my chest. The last time I did this — landing in the jungle — it had ended in tragedy.

The humidity pressed in on me, but, unlike the first time, it didn't bother me. My skin drank in the moisture without causing the least bit of discomfort.

The other members of my team stepped down onto the ground but I hesitated. I forced myself to slow my breathing and calm my thoughts. I could do this if I concentrated on the present.

I forced myself to move and took the three steps to the soft earth and stood behind everyone in the clearing — if you could call it a clearing. It looked like a war zone. Trees strewn about the floor of the jungle, some of them caught by the branches of surrounding trees, which stopped them from reaching the ground. I gasped when I saw blood on one of the nearby tree trunks.

"Looks like a couple of dinos had a wrestling match," Darion said with a chuckle.

That got a few laughs from some of the other men on our search team, but it had the opposite effect on me. It made me think of the two dinosaurs that fought right in front of me while I hid in a crevice between two rocks only a few weeks ago. One had resembled an Allosaurus from Earth's distant past and the other looked like a giant crocodile.

My hearts picked up speed again just thinking about it. I could almost hear the horrific sounds of them fighting.

Darion turned to me. "Are you alright, Tamisan? You look a little pale."

His voice brought me back to the present. "Uh... Yeah. I'm fine."

I took a deep breath to try to relieve the tightness in my chest. I didn't want any of them to know how much being back in the jungle again was affecting me. I needed to be strong. I'd spent a lot of time convincing Darion and our boss, Dr Aimery, that I was up to the task. I wanted to help in any way I could. After all, the man we were searching for was part of my original shuttle crew when I'd first arrived on the planet about six or seven weeks ago.

I closed my eyes for a few seconds and collected myself again. *I can do this.*

Boots crunched in the leaf litter and I opened my eyes to Darion's open arms. I melted into them, needing to feel his arms around me. It grounded me. My heartbeats levelled out and my breathing slowed.

After a while, I reluctantly pulled away from him and gave him a warm smile. I used telepathy to send him a thank you.

He returned the smile and I melted a little. *"Anytime, my love. Shall we get moving?"*

I nodded and we turned our attention back to our mission.

Commander Totino Kozienko gave our team final instructions before heading out. I could see his bulging muscles on his bare arms and half a bare chest, but he didn't look very 'commanding' dressed in a loincloth made of spotted hide. In fact, we all looked strange in skins. But blending in with the natives was key.

He turned to us. "You two, stay in the middle of the group." When we both nodded, he turned back to the group. "Alright. Move out."

As we moved further away from the ship, the fresh musty smell of earth and the refreshing scent of the nearby river filled my senses. Fragrances from the nearest flowers soon followed.

It was such a nice change from the air conditioning in the underground base. I breathed in deeply and was hit with a wave of memories from the last time I was in the jungle.

So many things had happened to me after I escaped from the crazy scientist who thought he could play God and transfer my consciousness into the body of one of the natives of this planet, a young woman named Sifayah.

Sifayah was from a race of people known as the Waikari, who possessed psychic abilities. They could speak to each other using telepathy, which came in handy because they lived half their lives underwater. Certain members of the Waikari tribe also had the power of telekinesis. Sifayah was one of the strongest in the tribe with this Gift and had been trained well.

My consciousness had been transferred into her mind and I'd only had her left-over memories to guide me in how to use her Talent. I was still amazed at the things I could do now.

There were also physical differences. I still looked human, but I now had webbed hands and feet, and two hearts.

I'd gained a lot: power and gills and abilities. But I'd lost so much at the same time. My life. My friends. My identity. I didn't really know who I was for a long time.

Things were better now, though. I had a new life and new friends, and my life had purpose again. I could use my abilities to help the Voyager Division study the people on this planet, and help find Janssen too.

I needed to stop thinking about it all and focus, though I was finding it difficult to do.

What was I thinking? I was so naive to think I could just come back here and carry on like nothing was wrong, like nothing bad had happened to me out here.

Memories of being chased through the jungle and attacked by a man who thought he owned me came rushing up into my mind. My hearts were pounding again.

I can't do this. Why did I think I could do this?

Chapter 2: Is this gonna be an issue?

I had to calm down. I couldn't let anyone know how the memories were eating at me.

Darion turned back and realised I'd stopped walking. "Hey. It's okay." He turned back and put an arm around me, steering me over to the nearest fallen tree. "Sit down. Take some slow, deep breaths. You'll be okay."

I did as he said, leaning against his side once he'd settled next to me. I closed my eyes and centred my thoughts.

It's okay. I'm okay. Turak isn't here. He can't hurt me.

I pushed thoughts of what Turak almost did to me aside and concentrated on my breathing while Darion whispered that I'd be alright and rubbed my back. Once my heartbeats slowed, my thoughts turned back to our mission. We had no time for this. We needed to find Janssen.

Darion looked down at me. "Feeling better now?"

"Kind of."

He leaned down and softly pressed his lips to mine, making my body come alive and leaving me wanting more. "How about now?"

I nodded, feeling a little flushed, with a helping of guilt. We were holding up the team. I needed to be strong right now.

"Then why the frown?"

"I... I just don't want to be like this. I don't want to be weak. I want to help find Janssen and be a productive member of the team and not a burden."

"You are not weak. This is the first time that you've been back out here. We knew it would be difficult."

I nodded again. "You're right."

I took a calming breath. *I can do this.*

"Yes, you can!" He'd picked up my thoughts easily as I wasn't shielding my mind from him. It was reassuring to hear him say it and to hear his voice in my mind.

I smiled at him. I just needed to think rationally.

I sighed. "Okay. I'm good. Let's get on with this."

Darion looked into my eyes and smiled.

"Andiyar," Commander Kozienko barked. "Is this gonna be an issue?"

"No, sir," Darion assured him. "It is her first time back in the jungle, but she's okay now."

The commander grunted in reply. "Alright, let's get moving."

We stood up and started off into the jungle again, moving along the river's edge. I looked back and saw the shuttle disappear as its cloaking device was activated. The pilot would stay with the ship until we returned, unseen by any natives or animals that might happen to pass by. As long as they didn't bump into it...

We had a couple of trackers in the group — Commander Kozienko, who used the old-fashioned method of tracking footprints and looking for clues, and Corporal Lazuli Idrial, who used his psychic ability to 'find' people and objects. His rating was only a T6, but he was good at his job. He'd been sick recently, which had slowed down our search for Janssen, and we were hopeful that this mission would be successful now that he was back on the team.

We were also hoping that if Janssen was still alive, he would still be wearing his boots. That would separate his footprints from any others. The natives were usually barefoot or wore boots made of animal hide.

The natives were unaware that there were people in their midst from the other side of the universe studying them from an underground base. We were wearing clothing that looked like it was made from animal hide to try to blend in. Well, except for mine. Mine were genuine jungle cat. They were given to me by one of the natives to replace my damaged wetsuit. It had been cut through from top to bottom by a being who was half-man, half-beast. I shuddered at the memory.

As we meandered along next to the river, I tried to push any negative thoughts aside and enjoy the scenery. Plants were tangled around each other while the larger trees stretched high up into the canopy and blocked out most of the sun's rays. It was slow-going as we had to duck under low-hanging branches and vines and climb over roots, rocks, and fallen trees. Just about everything was covered in a bright green moss and the leaf mulch was thick on the ground.

I tried to ignore the creepy crawlies we passed, but it was difficult. Spiders and beetles and large ants and some seriously weird-looking hairy caterpillars with spikes and a colour pattern on their backs that looked like a big eye.

The humidity was extreme. I watched Kozienko pull out a handkerchief and mop his forehead and noticed that Nykolar was panting and I sympathised with them. Nykolar was the only other person besides Darion and I that wasn't a soldier and he clearly wasn't as fit as the rest of us. He worked with electronics in Security. I wondered what he was doing out here. I thought it was odd that he would volunteer to be on the search team.

After about five minutes, my breathing and heart rates were back to normal. The sights and sounds of the jungle stopped making me jumpy and I started to feel more confident. I could do this.

I was able to think about the job at hand. It wasn't going to be easy to find Janssen; the jungle was so huge and so dense that it was probably like the proverbial needle in a haystack. But we were hopeful. I'd survived, even though I'd been poisoned by a plant that made me hallucinate and had been captured and sold by slave traders. I was hoping that Janssen, being a tall, well-muscled male — who had some experience with hiking and camping according to his files — would be able to do a better job than I had. A *lot* of people could've done a better job than me. I was born and raised in a city back on Earth and was totally clueless. Which was why I'd been doing some self-defence classes since I'd recovered from being attacked by Dr Starrick, the scientist who had captured my crew and I in the jungle and experimented on us.

The thought that he'd only grabbed us because he needed some test subjects to play with still sickened me and I was glad he was dead.

Movement caught my eye. One of the men was trying to squeeze past a small tree covered in flowers and fruit and my stomach dropped to my feet. "No! Don't!"

He turned to me with a questioning look.

"Keep away from the flowers!" I yelled. "They're dangerous!"

He rolled his eyes and continued on.

I was running towards him before I realised it. "No! Stop! It will—"

Chapter 3: Incoming!

It was too late. The plant had a self-defence mechanism. The bulb on the base of the flower popped and the pollen went straight into his face. I quickly pulled him away from the tree.

"Water!" I cried out to no one in particular. "We need to wash his face!"

I was already pulling out my water bottle and as he slowly sunk to the ground, coughing and wheezing, I rolled him onto his side and poured water on his face. I had to get the pollen off. The others helped me and poured some of their water on him as well.

Memories of the horrific hallucinations I'd experienced from this plant raced through my mind. My hands shook as I tried to move faster. It was already too late. The pollen had started to affect him. He was disoriented and looked at us with a dazed expression. This guy was in for a rough time.

Darion knelt down next to me, looking me over. "Are you okay? You didn't get any on you?"

"No. I'm fine. Don't worry."

His eyes were intense. "Are you sure?"

"Yes. I'd tell you if I did. There's no way I want to go through that again."

I couldn't blame him for worrying. He saw what I'd gone through last time. And helped me use my telekinetic ability to expel the poison from my body.

I gave him a reassuring smile and looked up at the commander. "He needs to go back to Jannali, right now." Station

Jannali was the underground base we were working from. "The hallucinations will hit him hard and fast."

Some of the men just looked at each other. Darion stepped forward. "I'll take him and be back in a few minutes."

Everyone looked to Kozienko. "Do it," he said.

As Darion approached the guy, he started to scream and lash out with his arms and legs. "No! Keep away from me!"

Darion moved back. "We need to take you to Jannali," he told him.

"No! How could you— What— No, no, no, no, no!" He batted his arms at an invisible foe and screamed again.

Darion turned to us and said, "I'll be back," and before anyone could say anything more, they both disappeared.

The rest of the group looked dumbfounded.

Kozienko finally spoke. "You all need to listen up," he barked. "You were briefed on this. There is a good reason that Tamisan is on this mission with us. She's been in the jungle before and has experienced this shit first-hand. Some of you have been out here too, but others haven't. Anyone else who refuses to listen to her warnings from now on, gets teleported back to base immediately and will have to answer to me! Is that clear?"

"Yes, sir!" was the hasty reply.

He looked at each person in the group. "Good! Now we wait for Andiyar to get back. Be alert."

I couldn't help wondering how I was supposed to give these men guidance if they wouldn't listen to me. I had to hope that they'd listen now that the commander had spoken to them.

Once Darion reappeared, we travelled through the jungle along a wide animal track. I shuddered to think of what might be able to easily walk through here, but pushed it aside. We were armed and alert. We understood what could come trudging along on its way to the river for a drink.

When I was in the jungle by myself, I narrowly escaped being the next meal of a smallish Allosaurus look-alike. I say smallish, but it was at least two metres tall.

I looked up as it seemed to be getting darker down here on the floor of the jungle. It was hard to see through the canopy but it looked like it might rain.

At the sound of crashing footfalls through the underbrush, I turned and jumped back a couple of steps as a large dinosaur that resembled an Anatosaurus stumbled out onto the track and veered away from our group. Relief flooded through me once my mind registered that it wasn't a predator.

Everyone raised their weapons and I shouted, "Don't shoot!" They didn't lower them, but they didn't shoot either. "It's not dangerous! It is a herbivore. A Rhodon."

Everyone visibly relaxed and watched the Rhodon as it tried to decide what to do. I was so glad they'd listened to me as I didn't want to see it hurt.

We stood still and watched it pass. It had four solid legs similar to an elephant's, and a long tail protruding from its large body. Its neck was thicker and shorter than the tail, with an oval-shaped head. It finally chose to avoid us and trudged off into the foliage.

Once it was gone, I added, "I told you about them in the briefing. The natives have domesticated them and use them like horses, although that one looked wild."

They all lowered their weapons and we started moving again as the sounds of its footsteps died away. It took a while for my heartbeats to return to normal. Having two hearts was good for swimming long distances, and I assumed that to be one of the reasons why the Waikari had more than one, but having both pounding against my ribcage the first time I woke up in this body had made me think there was something wrong with me.

As we walked, I looked at the trees that seemed to go on forever. I hoped that Kozienko knew the way back to the shuttle, because I hadn't been paying attention while trying to wrestle with my fears. All I knew was that we were still near the river.

In a pinch, I could teleport back to where we'd landed. I could easily picture the fallen trees in my mind.

There was an order from the commander to halt and we gathered around where he crouched in the middle of what looked like a smaller animal path heading off through the bushes.

When we reached him, he pointed at the ground. "There," he said, as if we could all see what he was seeing.

I looked closely, but couldn't see anything unusual.

He looked at us, then clenched his jaw in frustration. "Can't you see it? Look. A boot-shaped print."

He pointed at an area to the right and I leaned closer. There was an indentation in the soft black soil, but whether it was boot-shaped was up for debate in my mind. But then again, what would I know?

Just as I was straightening up again, someone screamed, "Incoming!" and all hell broke loose.

⁕

ENIGMA *(Tamisan Book 2)* is available right now. Use the QR Code to grab your copy!

Or type this into your browser: https://books2read.com/enig
ma-tamisan2

⸻ ◆ ⸻

Keep reading for a chance to sign up for a free novelette, ***THE ALIEN***

⸻ ◆ ⸻

BOOKS BY SUSAN MCKENZIE

THE JADORI SERIES (ONGOING SERIES):
Fire and Magic is being released in a serialized format (1 chapter per week) on reamstories.com right now!

THE TAMISAN SERIES (COMPLETED SERIES):
Tamisan
Enigma

A Tamisan Novella – Shakiran: Larissa's Story

THE LIGHTNING TOUCH SERIES (COMPLETED SERIES):
Touch of Lightning
Power of Lightning

*Just remember, a completed series means you can binge read the whole series now — no waiting for the next book to release.

About the Author

Susan McKenzie is an Australian author who loves creating worlds of fantasy and science fiction with fascinating characters and slow-burn low-spice romance.

Her books are full of interesting and relatable characters who use their psychic abilities or magical powers to fight their way out of trouble.

She loves stories that hit you in the feels.

She's not a typical author coffee addict - but chocolate? Now that's a different story. When she's not writing, she loves to paint, draw, sing, and play the guitar.

Get in touch with Sue.

Follow Sue on her Ream site for early access and bonus/deleted scenes:

https://reamstories.com/susanmckenzie

Follow Sue on her Amazon author page:

amazon.com/author/susancarter

Visit Sue's website:

http://susanmckenzieauthor.com

Follow Sue on Facebook:
https://www.facebook.com/SueMcKenzieAuthor